THE PESTILENCE

M.V. BLACK

ISBN 978-1-959182-55-9 (paperback)
ISBN 978-1-959182-56-6 (hardcover)
ISBN 978-1-959182-57-3 (digital)

PART I

In early morning, on the First.
Or, on whose first, or First.
Because, of.
Or, whose early, or.
Course, where, or when.
"Or when, or where?"
Else to start, or.
Where else?
To be.
Gin.
"Or, on the Second, or."
On the Third, Fifth, Sixth, Eighth, Fourth, Seventh, Tenth, Twelfth,
Thirteenth, Eleventh, Thirtieth, Three Hundredth, or.
On what.
"Or?"
On whose.
"Or, on?"
Which, or on.
What First.
Because, of course?
"What, or which, or whose First."
Is, also, or can, also, be?
"A bit like the last, or."
For, or to, an.
Can the, or a, last one, two, or more, also, be?
Other, or.
"A bit like the first one, because."
Because?
"What one day."
Or, because.
Which Day One.

Or, because.
"What day one."
Or, because.
Which day one, or.
Because which last day, or.
What Day One.
"Or, because."
Whose day one, or.
Because whose last day, or.
"Whose Day One."
Is quite like whose.
Or, is.
"Quite like what's?"
Day Two, or.
Because, of course, were we not.
Second Day.
All born at once, and.
"Because what, which, or whose Day One, is, or might be?"
Or reborn, or.
Quite like, if not exactly.
"Or, if not precisely."
The same as the next, or like.
Or, the same as.
The previous one, or.
The same as, or like.
The last one, or.
Like, or the same as.
Another, and.
"Or?"
Because, what day is but one more day, or but one more number, or
yet one more measure.
"Of the."
Or, of my?
Or, of our.
"Passing of time, or."
The passing of time, or.
The passing of the time, or.

Of the year, or of?
"Whose year, or."
Of?
"Which, or of."
What, or whose.
Whose, or what.
"Time, or year," and.
Or?
"Of course."
Whose, or what's?
"Or what's, or whose."
If not mine, *or your.*
Measure of time, measure of the passing of it, or measure of the year,
or?
"And, so."
Did the man, or.
Merely.
Just, or un.
Just, or only.
"Or mirror-ly?"
Or un.
Justly.
A man?
Or.
"On the flip side?"
Or.
"On the other hand."
Or.
"In the other hand?"
Or.
"On this hand."
Or?
In this one?
Or?
"On that hand."
Or.
In that hand.

"Or?"
Both: a bit of a man, and a bit of the man, or.
Both a bit of the, and of a.
Boy, or?
If not a, and if not the.
Wo.
Man, *or girl,* or.
Does this mean.
"Or?"
Does that mean.
"Or?"
And, if so.
Does it?
And, but if?
Or, if rather.
Does this mean.
"This?"
Of course.
And, or.
And, if so.
So as?
"To be."
Most certain.
"And, most sure?"
And, so as.
"So?"
To be.
"Most thorough, and so as."
To be?
"Most rigorous, and."
Though, too.
"Of course."
Which I can.
Not be.
"Without, also?"
At least.
A bit of.

"Healthy doubt, even if."
The point of doubt, is.
"And, even if."
The point of doubting is to end up.
With, or in.
Or.
"In, or with."
Or with, or in.
"Even more certainty, and."
So.
"And, so?"
And, if so.
Or, if so?
But, of course, does.
"This mean."
This.
Then, does that mean?
"That."
But, of course.
And, if so.
And, if but.
And, but if?
Or, if so.
"Rather."
Because, of course, it does.
What?
"Because if it did not, what?"
Else would.
Or.
"And, what else might?"
It mean.
Now, and.
Then, now.
Or, rat.
Her?
"And now?"
What if.

Rather.
"That means this."
Or, if rather?
This means that.
"Or, rather."
What happens, when.
"Or what happens, where."
That becomes this.
"Or, where."
Or, when.
This becomes that, and.
Or when, and where.
"Or."
This becomes that, and that becomes, this, or.
When.
Where, and when.
"And, or."
The hunted become the hunters, or.
Where.
When, and where.
"Meanings do change, and."
The prey do become the predators, and, the predators, the prey, or.
Or?
Where, and when.
And, if so.
The guilty become the innocent, and the innocent, guilt, or.
Or when they flip, or.
When, and where.
Where they are flipped.
Those on the top become those on the bottom, and.
"And, but if."
Those on bottom get back on top, or.
If so.
When they are flipped, or where.
"They flip, or."
Flop, or.
And, if not.

Are flop.
But, of course.
Ped, or.
"Not, as if."
They, *or we?*
"Or you."
Are all pan.
Or you.
Cakes, or.
On the left hand.
Or, if not.
"In the left hand."
Or, if not.
On, or in, yours, or.
On the hand, or.
If not in, or on, yours, or.
If not.
"On the left side."
Or if not on, or.
If not in.
Your hand, or hands.
Or, if rather.
On, or in.
In, or on.
Your hand, or if.
Not on.
Your, or if.
Not on his.
Left side, or if.
Not on, or if.
Not in yours.
Or, if.
Not on the hands, or.
If not on, or if not in, yours.
Then, or now?
Now, and then.
On the right?

Side, or hand, though.
Or.
And, if not.
In the right?
Or.
"And, if not."
Or, if not?
On a hand.
Or.
"If not in a hand."
Or.
"If not on the hand."
Or.
"If not in the hand."
Or, if.
"And, if."
And, if.
"Or, if."
Not in a hand.
"And."
If not on a hand.
Or.
If not a hand.
Either, right.
Or, left.
And, too.
"If not in, or on."
Both.
Because.
"Of course."
What right hand should, and ought.
Or ou.
"Not know."
Ght it? Should it, or mu.
What the left is doing, and.
St it, as we.
Because should, and ought.

Ll as qui.
"The left not know."
Te so mo.
What the right is doing, and.
St re.
So, must one.
Cip.
"Choose, or."
Ro.
So, must?
Call.
"One be chosen, and, or."
Y, and fair.
Chosen by whom, or by what, and.
Ly, ou.
So for what, and.
Ght, and s.
"If not on."
Ho.
And, or.
Uld, the r.
If not in.
Ig.
"A, or."
Ht k.
Both hands.
Now w.
"Then, per?"
Hat the left is do.
Haps?
In.
Not on.
G, to.
"Or, not in."
O, be?
A hand, or hands.
Ca.

At all.
Use, of co.
"Or?"
Ur.
But, rather.
Se, as all, every.
"What might."
One, and as every.
Or, what does.
Bod.
"Being, on."
You.
Or being, in.
Ght, and s.
"Either, both, or neither, have to do with."
Ho.
Knowing what the other is doing, or.
Uld k.
"Have to do with knowing, at all."
Now, do se.
Or with not knowing, and.
Cret.
If not.
S on.
"In, or."
Ly ma.
If not on.
Ke one, and all, every.
A hand.
One, and, or, e.
"Then, rather?"
Very.
Then, rather.
Body, si.
"Or, now, rather?"
Ck, so.
Too, in.

Or, on?
"On, or in?"
Or, if rather.
"In, or on."
A palm.
"Or."
And, if.
Or, if.
In, or on.
"My palm?"
Or, if.
"Rather, on, or in."
My palm, and.
Or?
"If not?"
In.
Or, on.
"Or, if not."
On, or in.
Mine.
Then, if.
"Or, if not?"
In whose, or.
"On what's, or."
And, so.
If not in, or.
"On mine, then."
Or now, or.
"Here, or."
Now.
Or, then.
"On, or in."
Whose, and.
Then, now.
"And, now, if."
And, if now.
Then, now.

Or, now, then?
And, then, now.
On, and in.
A hand.
Then, also.
In, and on.
"A palm, too."
Of course.
"And?"
Or, rather.
If on, or if in, the hand?
"Or, if."
In, and.
Or, on the hand?
Or in, and, or on, your hand?
"Or, if in mine."
Or, if in his, or if on his.
Or, on His.
And, if so, not on, or not in, mine.
Or, in mine.
Or, so he does think, or know, or.
Or, in Hers, or.
And, if the hand.
Rather, than.
"A hand."
Or?
"If either, rather than my hand."
Then, or now.
"Or, now."
Or, then.
"On, or in, whose?"
Or, rather.
"In, or on, what's, or?"
And, if.
"Not in."
Or, if?
"Not on mine."

Or, if.
Then, or now?
On, or in, whose?
And.
And, so.
"And, so?"
And, so.
If, but.
What, which, or whose, hand.
"And?"
Or, hands.
As then.
Or.
"As now?"
Or, if.
As if?
So, what.
As what?
Did he raise.
"Or."
Or?
"Which I did raise."
Or.
Rather than?
"What was raised."
Or, what were raised.
As if.
By another, or.
As if.
"By what is."
Or, by one who, *or Who,* is.
Or.
"By who is."
Or, by what is.
Anyone, or anything?
"Other than."
What, or who is.

Not me.
"And, so."
And, so?
"Or, so."
What is.
"Of course."
My choice.
And, or.
"What is my decision."
Or, yours.
"To raise?"
Or, not to raise.
For, and by.
And by, and for.
"Myself."
Or?
For your.
"What is."
Self, or.
My choice.
"Or."
What should.
"And."
Or?
"At least."
What ought to be.
My choice.
"My option."
And, my decision.
"Because."
If not my choice.
And, if not yours.
And, if not my decision, whose.
"Whose?"
Or what's, and.
Or, What's?
And, if not my option, to.

"Raise, or not to."
Raise what is to be raised.
For, and by, me.
Or by, and for, you.
Then.
Or, now.
Or, now?
"And, now."
And, now.
Or, then.
Or, now?
"Whose choice."
And whose decision, and.
"Whose option."
Is it, or.
"Will it, or."
Must it be, for me.
If I will not choose, or de.
Cide for my.
Self, or.
By, or for.
If I am not per.
Your.
Mit.
Self.
Ted to, or let.
Decide, or choose.
And.
Or choose, or decide.
"But, and."
And, if so.
And, so if?
"Or, if so?"
And, if so.
Not my hand.
"Then, whose."
Or, now, whose.

"Because."
Or what's, and.
"Because?"
If not raised.
Or risen, by you.
By what, or by whom, and.
Of course.
As yet.
Because.
As yet.
And, yet.
"Because."
He was.
"And, because."
You are.
And, because.
Of course.
"And, I am."
Just only.
And, only, just.
Beginning to wake.
Though, not.
"Of course."
Was he?
"Or, am I?"
Just being born, or.
"Because."
Of course, also.
"Because?"
He was not born yesterday, either.
"And, too?"
Because, also.
"I was not, and."
Because.
You were not, what?
"If not my left."
Or, if rather.

"Not in it."
Or, if rather.
"Not on it."
Or.
"If not."
On, or in.
"What, or."
Whose left.
Then in, or on, whose.
"And, if."
Not my right.
"Then, whose."
Too, and.
"Or?"
And, if.
Because.
Of course.
And.
"But."
"But?"
And, if so.
"And, if so."
Not on.
This one.
Hand, right.
Or, if.
Rather?
Not in.
This one.
Left one?
Then, or now.
Now, or then.
"Or, now?"
Or, then.
"Or, both?"
Then, and now.
"And now, and then."

In the right one?
"Or, in my right one?"
Or, in your right one.
Or, on my left one.
Or, on my left one.
"Or, in my left one?"
Or, in your left one.
Or, on my right one?
Or, on your right one.
"Or."
If not about hands at all, then.
"Or, now?"
Perhaps, now.
"Or, perhaps, then?"
About palms.
"Or, about?"
A palm.
"Or?"
About the palms.
"Or?"
"About the palm."
Or?
"About my palm."
Again?
"Or."
And, if so.
Because.
About my palms, again.
"Then, about?"
Or, now, about?
My left one.
"Or, about?"
My right one.
Or a.
Bout your right one, or.
"About my right one, or."
Or?

"About the one that is."
Left to me.
Or, right to me.
Whoever he is, and.
Or, about the one.
"That is right to her?"
Or to me, or about.
"The one?"
That is correct to me, or.
About.
The one that is right to them.
Or, for them.
"Or?"
Or, the one that is right for, or right to, you, or.
About the one that is my right one.
Or, about the one that is your right one.
Or, about the one that is my right one.
Or?
"About the one that is my left one."
Or, about the one that is my left one, or.
About the one that is your left one.
Or?
About the one.
"That is left to them, to him, to her, or to it, and."
Whoever they are, and.
Or whatever it is, and.
Or?
"About the one that is wrong to me."
Or, wrong to, or wrong for, you, or.
Wrong for, or to me, and.
Or, about?
"The one that is wrong to it, to him, or to them, or?"
Her, or for.
"Why might I care."
Or, how might you care.
"Or, how might I care?"
"Or, how might I care."

About what is left.
Or, about who is.
About what is right.
Or, about who is.
To, or for, them.
Him, or it?
"Or, about?"
Me, or.
About.
"What is right to, or."
For her.
"Or?"
About, or for.
What is wrong.
"To, or for."
Her, or for.
"Or, to?"
It, or to.
"Or, for them, or."
For, or to.
"It, too?"
Or.
If not.
"Necessarily, always."
For all?
"Or for all, for."
All times?
"Or for all, in."
All places, or.
"Not necessarily?"
Or, just.
"Or, only?"
Or me.
Rely a.
Bout.
Or, about
"Right, or left."

Left, or right.
"Wrong, or left."
Left, or wrong.
"Or, about?"
What is right, and wrong, or.
"About?"
What is wrong, or right, and.
"Or?"
If not, necessarily.
About who is.
Or?
About palms.
At all, or a.
"Or, hands?"
Bout.
Or, even if it is.
Now, here.
"Just, only, or merely, so?"
For me?
Who cares?
"Which, or."
If left, or.
If right.
Or if whose, or what's.
Or What's.
Right, or left.
Or, Whose.
Left, or right.
Or.
"Or, if right, or left."
Left, or Right.
Or if right, or wrong.
Wrong, or Right.
"Or, if."
Wrong, or right.
To, or for, whom.
"But, because."

Of course.
Is not?
"The issue, or."
Is not.
If he.
At issue?
Re, or if the.
"What I decide, is."
Re, were an is.
Or what I say to be, is?
Sue, at all, or?
"And, so."
In your own house, and in.
Your own room, if is it yours, or.
If it is yours, or.
If either, or if both.
Are, or.
If it is ours, or.
Except that now, and except that here.
They are mine, and, so.
They are mine, and, so.
Here, and now.
"And, so?"
Now, and here.
"In my house."
And, in this house?
And, in your house.
And, in my room.
And, in your room.
And, in this room.
And, in my room.
"And, in my bed."
And, in my bed.
And, in this room.
"And, in this bed."
And, at this time?
"The issue, is."

Or, whose issue, is?
"About this palm."
Which is mine.
And, not about that one.
Which one?
And, not about the one that is not yours.
Or mine, or.
"Which is not mine."
Whether this, or.
Whether that.
Or both, or.
And, so.
Not about.
"What is not mine, but."
About?
What is whose.
"If not mine."
Or yours.
Or, rather?
Or mine.
How might I care.
"Or, why might I?"
Care about what is not mine.
Or, about?
What is not yours.
That, or.
Your hand?
"About this."
Which is.
"This to me, of course."
But what is that.
To, or for.
Me, and for, and to.
Another, or.
For, or to.
If not, also, or necessarily, the same, or.
All others.

The Same, to, or for, you of.
Of course.
Course.
Or, about?
"What might be, that."
To them, to another, to her, to him, or to it, while.
"Or, whereas?"
Might, or more than might, that, to, or for, me, be.
"Also, what is, or, also."
What might be, *or what is*, this, to, or for them, or.
For, and to me, and.
For, or to, another, or.
"To, or for, her, him, or it, and."
Or, rather.
"And, too?"
Too?
"Or, about?"
Whatsoever.
Or, about whosoever.
"But, because."
Of course.
"Do I not care?"
And, too.
"Of course, be?"
Cause.
Because.
And, be.
I do not care.
Cause you do not care.
Now, about.
This one, here.
Which is.
"Right here."
And, which is.
"Right now."
Be.
Before me, and.

Fore you, and.
This hand.
Or, about?
Which is?
In front of me, and.
Which is in front of you, and.
Which is in front of him, and.
Which is.
A palm, and which is.
A hand.
But, which.
"And, of course."
Is not the hand.
But, which is.
Just, only, or merely.
"Or, unjustly?"
My hand.
"And."
And?
Or?
And, which.
Is the one.
"Which is up."
And.
Which is the one.
"That is here."
And.
Which is the one.
That is open.
"And?"
Which is the one.
That is.
"Turned up, and?"
Which is the one.
"That is?"
Up.
Turned, and.

Which is the up-turn.
Ed hand, which does.
Want everything, everyone, and all, and.
Though, of course.
"So?"
And, which is.
The hand that does not fil.
Ter, dis.
Crim.
In.
Ate, *dis?*
Might it be left.
Tin.
"To, and."
Gui.
"And?"
Sh, or dif.
Though, and even if.
Fer.
Might it be?
Ti.
Left.
Ate, be.
"For, and to, me."
Tween.
Who cares?
Things, and peo.
Except, that.
Ple, or?
Or, except this, or.
Between objects and per.
"How might I forget?"
Sons, or.
Or, rather.
"How might I remember."
Or, how might you.
Or, why might I.

Or, why might you.
Even if might I like to.
Be able?
"To remember, or to forget."
And.
Or?
"Even if I might like to."
Be able to.
"Forget."
What might be?
"Or, what is."
Right to, and.
If not, also, or ne.
Right for them.
Ces.
Or, what is.
Sari.
Or who, or what.
Ly for you, too.
Or what is.
Or who, or what.
Is good, or bad.
Bad, or Good.
"Bad, or good, or."
Or?
"Right, for."
Whom, or for what.
Universally, or other?
Wise, or.
"Or, to him?"
Or to, or for, her.
Or, to.
"Or, for it?"
Or, for.
"Or, to her."
And, even if I more than might like to be able to forget.
"All about them."

And, or.
All about her.
Or, and.
"All about her."
Or, and.
All about this, and.
Or, all about that, or.
"This is?"
Or, that is.
"Of course."
And.
"Whosoever she might be."
And.
"Whosoever she is."
Or, was.
And.
Who.
So.
Ever he is.
Or was.
And.
"Whosoever he might be."
And.
Is, or was.
"Whosoever they might be."
And.
"Whosoever they are."
And.
"Who."
Or what?
"So-ever it might be."
And?
"What."
Or, who.
"So-ever it is."
And.
"But, as much as might I like."

Wish, or.
Want, or need?
To be able to.
"Forget, can I do so."
Only if.
And, if so, only.
"If?"
Or, only.
"In so far, as."
They might let me.
Who, or what.
Soever they are, or.
"Only?"
Or just, or unjustly.
"Or, merely?"
In so far as.
"Or?"
Merely, just.
"Or, only?"
As long as.
Might they let me.
Be.
"Or?"
If so only, if.
Might she let me.
Be.
"Or?"
And, if so only, if.
I do stop asking for permission to be able to.
"And, if?"
Or.
So, only if.
Might it let me.
"Forget all about it."
Or, forget all about her.
Or, forget all about him?
Or, all about you.

"Or, forget all about them."
Or, about?
"All that did happen, or."
About all that did not.
Happen, or.
"About all that should have happened, but did not?"
Or, about.
"All that I might have hoped did, or would happen, or."
About?
Or.
So as?
To be.
Or?
So as to be able.
To be.
"As selfish."
Or.
So as?
"To be able to be."
As.
"Self-."
Indulgent, or?
As self-cent.
E.
Red, as.
I would like.
To be.
"And, as?"
Hedonistic, as.
You do want to be.
Selfish, and.
"As self-indulgent, and."
As self-centered, as.
I do want, and as.
"I do, or as I would."
If let, or if per?
Mit.

Ted to be, or.
As I, or as you?
Do choose to be.
"And, as?"
I do need to be.
"And, as?"
Self-indulgent, and.
"As selfish, and as self-?"
Cente.
Red, as?
They are, and as.
Everyone is.
Regard.
Less of the con.
Se.
Que.
N.
Ces, and re.
Gard.
Less of the rest of them, and.
"And, as?"
Every.
Body, is.
I more than might?
Like, need, wish, hope, or.
"Want to be."
But?
"But, of course."
Why ask for their.
His, her, or its.
Permission to for.
Get, or to re.
Member, or.
To be?
"And, too?"
Because.
Who does not know?

"What they should."
Or, what they ought.
"Is not me?"
Not you?
Or.
"Am I not?"
And, because.
"I am not."
Because you are not?
One who.
"Does not know."
What I should.
Or, what you should.
"Or what I ought."
Or, what you ought.
So, as?
"To be played as some."
One's, some.
Body's, or as?
Everyone's, or as.
Everybody's, or.
"As someone's, fool."
Or?
One so dumb, idiotic, or mo.
Ron.
Ic, so as.
To be played, as.
No one's, or as.
Nobody's, or.
A fool, or as.
"One?"
One?
"To be played?"
As somebody's, or.
"As anyone's?"
Or, as anybody's, or.
"As nobody's, or."

As no one's fool.
"And, because."
Of course.
"And, too?"
Also, is.
Nobody, and, also.
"Is no one."
Also, someone, or.
"Also."
Is no one.
A some.
Body, too.
And, so.
"Or?"
And, so.
Or, as?
But, because.
"Of course."
I do know.
As does he?
Or, as do I.
Or, as does she?
Or, as do you.
Know, too.
All, or everything?
"Everything, or all."
About everyone, or.
Do you, or.
"About everything, or?"
"Do I, but."
Know?
Or can you.
"That, but."
Or ought.
Of course.
Or should.
To for.

Your, or.
Get is to be for.
Except forgotten by what, or by whom.
Gotten.
"And, that?"
Also, and, too.
"Is."
To be forgotten is to forget.
And, or.
As much as, of course?
To forget, or.
I do, also, know.
To be forgotten.
What each, and what every.
By whom, or by what, or by What, or.
Idiot, fool, or moron.
For what reason, or rea.
Too good?
Sons, or for ab.
"For his."
So.
For her.
Lutely, for.
"For its?"
No rea.
Or, for their own good.
Son, or reas.
"Does not know."
Ons, at all, re.
Is that, and.
Son.
"That is all knowing."
Able, un.
And, that is all know.
Rea.
Ledge remembering, then.
Son.

"Or, now?"
Able, or ot.
And, now.
Her.
"And then, too."
Wise, and.
So?
"If to remember is to know."
And, if.
"To know is to remember, then."
And, now.
"And, now."
And, then.
"Is to forget not to know?"
And, not to know.
"Is not to remember."
So that?
Of course, and, too?
"Do not the dead forget, or."
At le.
If, also.
As.
"And, too?"
T in so.
Is to be forgotten to be dead, so.
Me way, or way.
"Or must the dead rely on being remembered, in or."
S.
Der not to stay, or re.
Main de.
Ad, *of course.*
Is to forget to be for.
Gotten, and, if.
Per.
To be for.
Haps, or mo.
Gotten is to for.

Re, is it bet.
Get, so, also.
Ter to be for.
Not to for.
Got.
Get is not to be for.
Ten by so.
Gotten, and.
Me, an.
If to be dead is to be for.
D.
Gotten, or.
If, rather, is?
To forget to be dead.
"Is, or must be?"
To remember.
And, to be remembered.
"To live, or."
To be alive?
"Or."
And, if so, too.
Must knowing be living, and?
"Must the living know, and."
Or?
Must to live, be.
"To know, and?"
Must those who know, live, and?
Must to know be.
To live, and?
"So, must."
To live, be.
"To know?"
Even if.
"Or, rather."
Remembering, what.
"To forget."
What, or whom.

Or, though.
Or to be for.
"For."
Gotten by what, by What.
"Get."
By Whom, or by Whom.
"Ting whom, or for."
Is the gift, or.
"Getting what."
Or, too.
So as, or.
"Forgetting what, or forgetting whom."
In or.
Might be?
Der, to.
Or remembering, who.
Re.
"Or?"
Me.
Remembering what.
Mbe.
Might be.
R, ma.
"Or, who might be?"
Ke ro.
"Good, on."
Om, or s.
"Oc."
Pace, f.
Cas.
Or ot.
"Ion."
Her thin.
Or, for some.
Gs, peo.
"Or, at?"
Ple, or per.

Times, ex.
Son.
Cept, of.
S, or.
Course.
Good, or.
Good for what.
And, except.
"Good for whom?"
And, or.
"Too?"
Good, according to.
"What, or?"
Good, according.
To whom, or.
"Good, according?"
To which, or to what, or.
"To whose measures."
Or, good.
"According, to?"
Whose standards.
Or, good.
Or, Good.
Or, bad?
Or, Bad.
"According to what."
Standards, and measures.
Mores, and means.
"Determinations, or evaluations, and."
Or, rather.
Or, rather.
"And, too?"
According to which, what.
"Or, according to whose?"
Quantifications, qualifications, appraisals, evaluations, determinations, assessments, mores.
Stand.

Ards, and me.
As.
Ures, and.
Measures, or standards, and.
Standards, and measures.
"Mores, and means?"
Or.
"Or, also?"
And, too.
Because, of course.
"Cannot all re."
Member all, or ever.
Thing, and.
Too, be.
Cause.
"Of course."
Cannot everyone remember everyone, everything, or all, and.
"Too, because."
Of course.
Must some memories.
And, some people?
Take precedence over others, and.
"Too, because."
Because.
Of course.
Some are more important that others?
Is not living in memories, or in the past.
And, too, because.
"Dwelling on."
Of course?
Or, dwelling in.
While some are less.
"What has been, and."
So.
In what is no longer, and.
So.
In what is not, and.

So.
What is a failure, to.
Live in the present, or.
What is failing, to.
Think, or to dream.
Of the future, and.
"So, what is?"
To be trapped, in.
"The return."
Of the eternal, but?
Is that, or.
Is this?
Necessarily, so bad, or.
"Too, of course."
Because.
Is too much thinking, too much thinking.
Memories can weigh you.
"Or one?"
Down, too.
"Also."
And, so.
"Might to forget to be relieved."
Of the pres.
Sure.
S, and of the we.
Ights, and.
Of, and from.
"And from, and of?"
The chains, and.
Weights.
"Of me."
Mory, and, of.
Memories, and?
So, in.
Deed, might.
"Or, is?"
The pre.

Sent bet.
Ter, or pre.
Fer.
Able, of course?
Of, and from.
But, only.
"Of course."
And, as long as.
One is able, let, or per.
Mit.
Ted, to?
"Own the present, and."
Or, only?
As long as.
One can.
Seize, or take.
"The moment?"
As one's own, and.
As long as one can take it.
Back from?
"The weights, chains, and memories, of."
The past.
The fu.
"And, of?"
Tur.
And, from.
E, too.
"What, and from whom, was."
And?
"Of whom, and of what, has been."
And, so, to forget.
"Might, also."
Or, necessarily?
"Be?"
To.
"Free oneself?"
For what could?

"From what, and from whom."
Was, and has been, and from.
"What could have been, for what."
Could, and.
"For what can."
Or, for what will.
Be, and.
"But?"
Whether, or not, determined, or destined, already.
By another, or by me, and.
Or by something, or by someone else, or.
"And."
Of course.
And, if so?
"What fool?"
Determined, or destined.
Idiot, or moron.
Destined, or de.
Moron, idiot, or fool.
Ter.
Who, of course?
Mined, by whom, Whom, What, or what, or.
"I am not?"
Or, you are.
"Does not know."
That, but.
Of course.
"To forget?"
Might, in.
Deed, be bet.
Ter than for.
Giving what, or than.
Forgiving?
Whom, or what.
"Or both what, and whom."
Does not de.
Or Whom, or What.

Serve to be for.
Or What, or Whom.
Given, and.
"Is to be forgotten."
And, that.
"Of course."
To be forgotten, is, also.
But.
"To forget, and."
To be forgotten by Whom, or.
Which might, also, be good.
By What, by what, or.
For some.
By whom.
In some places.
"And, at times."
To forget, or to be for.
Got.
Ten, or.
"To be forgotten, or to forget?"
By whom, or.
"By what, or."
By what, or.
"By whom, or."
By both, or.
By everyone, everybody, and or.
So that?
By all.
"One can be free."
Not to have to be.
"All for her?"
Or, Her.
Or, all for them.
"Or, all for it."
Or, all for her.
Or, all for me, or.
Did he not quite.

"Like to have to ad?"
Mit, *or did you,* not quite like to have to, so grum.
Bling, low.
But not necessarily, not.
Forgetting you?
All for me, and?
So as.
Because.
To be all for you, a.
"Of course."
Gain, or for.
Who does not know.
The first time, or.
"That, too?"
Do only ele.
Phants remember, all.
Everything, or everyone, and.
"Because, of course?"
Who does want to.
"Or, who can afford to be?"
So gray, or.
"So grey, all of the time, and."
Or?
And, be.
Cause, of course.
Who does want to be re.
Who does want to be for.
Membered by the De.
Ced to be?
Vil, or by.
Or, to have?
His de.
The heart of an elephant, with.
Mons, and.
Out get.
Who does want to be for.
Ting care back, or in re.

Gotten by Go.
Turn, so.
D, G-d, the gods, or god.
Is not caring im.
Des
Possible, and?
Ses, and.
In such cases, or.
"In such sit?"
U.
At.
Ions, at le.
As.
T, is it, and would it be?
Most irrational, most illogical, and most unreasonable, and?
If not necessarily, also?
Most impractical, or.
"Most?"
Inexpedient, and.
So, trying, to?
Forget, and.
"So as."
Not to have to please?
Or, so as?
"Not to have to."
Appease.
Whom, or what?
What, or Whom.
Or what, or whom.
Or Whom, or What.
"And, too."
Or, if?
"So as."
Not to have to con.
"So as?"
Form to any.
To any?

One's, to any.
To any?
Body's, to every.
To every?
Body's, or.
To everyone's.
Standards, measures, mores, qualifications, quantifications, appraisals, assessments, or expectations, of.
"Or, for me."
And?
If not hers, though.
For him, and?
"Or, so as."
Not to have to be.
Nd over back.
Wards, or.
At least.
Not more than any others would, or have.
Because, of course, you are.
Not a martyr, saint, slave, or servant, and.
Because I will not be made to be one either, and.
Because.
I will not be made to do, or bear, have, or handle, more than I can afford to, or.
More than you will, or decide to, or.
More than I should.
"Or, more than I ought to."
Or, more than they would.
Or, more than you would.
"Or, more than I should."
Or, more than I can.
Or, more than I ought to.
Or, more than I can afford to.
Or, more than is fair.
To, and for, me.
"And?"
Or?

Though, but.
"Of course?"
Fair for.
"Or, fair to whom, or."
Fair to, or.
Fair for what, and.
"Or."
Fair according to what, or fair according to whom, and.
"So?"
And, even if.
"To forget, might."
But, only if not must.
"Be to for."
Give.
And, even if?
"To for."
Give might, or.
Might not be.
To forget.
"And, even if."
Of course.
"Is to for."
Give, divine.
And, even if?
Of course.
Is not, necessarily, to for.
Give to for.
Get, but?
"Like much else."
Of course, is not the beast, or the de?
Vil, him.
Self, di.
Vine, as well as, of course?
"Does the Goddess."
Choose what, and choose whom?
Ever divine, and ever un-erring.
To forget, if to forget, or to forgive, and.

If to for.
Get, or if to for.
Give forgive, or forget?
Whom, or what, *or What, or Whom,* and, so?
Or, for what rea.
Forgiveness will not be true.
Sons, or re.
"Real, or actual?"
As.
If, and when, and where.
Ons, if for any at all, or.
Or where, and when, and if.
"It is forced, and."
Be.
Cause, of cour.
Se.
"And, too."
Might one.
"And, too."
Because.
One might for.
Give without for.
Getting.
"And, even if."
One might for.
Get with.
Out for.
Giving.
"And, even if."
Ought some things.
"And, even if."
Ought some people.
"Be forgiven."
And, even if.
"Ought some."
And, ought others.
"Be for."

Gotten.
For one's own good, and.
In spite of all their needs, wants, wishes, hopes, dre.
Am.
S, and de.
Sires.
"To be remembered, which?"
Of course.
"Is not either."
A right, or.
An entitlement, and.
Even if.
Of course?
"Ought some other people."
And, even if.
Ought some other things.
"Not be."
Either, for.
Given.
"Or for."
Gotten.
Or, either.
Forgot.
Ten, or for.
Given, while?
And, where.
"Might some others."
Only, be?
"For."
Gotten for a bit.
Only, so as?
Or, only.
"In or."
Der, to?
"Be re."
Mem.
Be.

Red, later.
Or?
So as.
If so, only, so as.
To remember other people, persons, and things, and, or.
Might I be.
Reminded of them, of it, of him, or of her.
Later, when, and where.
"Or where, and when."
I would prefer not.
To have to remember.
Or, you would not prefer to have to remember, or.
"I would prefer not to have to remember."
Or, one would not have to, or.
And when, and where.
"And where, and when."
I would prefer not to have to for.
Give, or.
Where, and when.
I do choo.
When, and where.
Se, or de?
Cide not to, or.
"When, and where."
Or where, and when.
One would not pre.
Fer not to have to re.
Member, because.
Of course, because.
"As well as am I not one."
Of course?
Or, one.
"To de."
Mand that one remember, and.
Or, that one know?
Or, one.
"To force an."

Ot.
Her to re.
Mem.
Ber, and?
Or any, or all?
Others to re.
Member, and?
"To remember."
Or?
"To demand to be re."
Mem.
Be.
Red, is.
But more force, and.
"Which are?"
Or, which is.
But more de.
Man.
Ds, and.
Or, quite so of.
Ten, can be?
But, because.
"Of course?"
All knowing is remembering, and.
"Because?"
All remembering, is?
Or, is all knowing, re.
Knowing, so.
Me.
"To be forced to remember?"
M.
Is to be forced to know, but.
Be.
"Know whom, or know what?"
Ring, so.
And how, and in.
Which way, or ways, be.

Cause.
"Quite so very self."
Ish, is?
To demand such time.
"Or, such space?"
In the life.
"Or, in the mind."
Of another.
Is, of.
Course.
"So demanding, and quite so."
Devilish, and qui.
Te so.
Demonic, and.
Quite so very needy, and.
Too, be.
Cause.
"Of course."
Do not all.
"And, too."
Does not every.
Thing, and, too.
"Does not ever."
Yone.
"De."
Serve to be forgiven.
Espe.
Ci.
Ally those who are not sorry, as well as.
Those, too.
"Of course."
Who do.
Only say they are sorry, so as.
To keep repeating.
Or, those who do only apologize in or.
The same wrongs, damages, trespasses, or harms, and.
Der to get you to let you.

Or, those who do only apologize.
R gu.
Because he, she, it, or they.
Ard dow.
Do think, assume, or presume, that.
N, so as to use, or.
They ought to, or should, and.
So as.
So, too.
To ab.
Does not everyone.
Use you ag.
"And, too?"
Ai.
Do not all.
N, or so as.
"And?"
To use you, or me, against you, or against me, and, or.
Too, does not every.
So as to gain so.
Body de.
Me ad.
Serve to be for.
Van.
Gotten, or re.
Tag.
Mem.
E, over me, or over you, ag.
Be.
Ai.
Red.
N, or for the first ti.
Me, or.
"Re."
Member.
Ed, or for.
Gotten.

How, or.
If at all.
"And, too?"
Because, of course, I am not one.
Dumb, or stupid.
Or, one.
"Ignorant, or arrogant."
Or, one.
Arrogant, or ignorant?
Enough, not to know.
"Or, one lucky enough to get away with pretending not to know?"
That, but.
Of course.
I am supposed to care.
But, of course.
I do, also, know.
"As I should?"
And, as you should.
"And, as I ought."
And, as I ought.
And, as I should, and.
"As I should."
That to care.
Because one, or.
Because you.
Or, because, I am.
Supposed to, or.
Because.
One should, or, because.
"One ought to, or be."
Cause one is forced to?
Though, of course.
"Forced by whom?"
Or, forced by what, and.
Or, because.
One does hope, or, because.
"What does want, or, because."

One does plan.
To be cared about, or for, in return.
Which is only most fair?
Reasonable, or rational, or.
"Be."
Cause one does just, or un.
Justly.
Expect to be cared for, or about, or.
Though, of course.
What does real, true, au.
Then.
Tic, or gen.
Ui.
Ne, caring.
Stop to care for, or stop to care about, justice, or.
Stop to care if caring is just, right, correct, or proper, or.
Justly, merely, or only.
Does real, genuine, au.
"Care to be cared for, in return."
Then.
"Far different."
Tic, real, act.
Than caring because one actually.
U.
"Or, because?"
Al, or true caring.
One truly does.
"Or, because?"
One really does.
Or, because one does not care, need, want, desire, or plan.
To be cared for in re.
Turn.
But, because.
So as.
"To be?"
Most true.
"And?"

So as.
"To be."
Most real.
Is.
Tic, or?
"And?"
So as.
"To be."
Most realistic, or?
"So as."
Of course.
"To be?"
As one.
"And as every wise man."
Would, or should, be, to.
"Be most."
Practical, and.
"So as?"
To be.
Most honest, that or.
"This is, if?"
Being most honest is, or.
"Can be?"
Also, being.
"Most real."
Or, also?
"Most true, and."
Also, and, too.
"That, or."
This is.
If being true, or True?
Is, also.
"Being most real, or being."
Most Real, or?
Most honest, or.
"This, or."
That, also.

Is, if.
"Being most real is, also, being."
Most true, and.
"Of course."
That, or.
"This, is."
If.
"Is to be?"
Most real, also.
"To be."
Most real.
Is.
Tic, or if.
"To be?"
Most realistic, or.
"Most real?"
Is, also.
To be?
"Most prac."
Tic.
Al, also.
Or, if.
"To be."
Most realistic, or most real.
"Is, also?"
To be.
Most ho.
Nest, ever.
"Or, always?"
Or, also.
Always, if not.
All ways, or.
If is.
"To be?"
Most hon.
Est, also.
"Or, al."

Ways, or.
Ever, most.
Practical, most wise, or most poss.
Ib.
Le?
Or, too.
"Of course."
Without assuming, or.
"Without presuming."
Is to be most true, ever, and, al.
Ways?
Or, always.
And, always.
"Or, always, and, ever?"
Most realistic, or most practical.
Though, of course.
Because, I am.
As yet.
As yet?
"One who does care."
Most wisely, most practically, most realistically, or most peacefully,
or most serenely?
If, so, only.
"As I should?"
Or, if.
So, only.
As I ought to.
And, if, so, only.
"So as?"
Not to be hated.
Or, if, so, only.
So as.
Not to be?
Stoned to death.
Even if.
"They do all hate me."
For what.

So.
Ever reason, reasons, or non-reasons, or.
"Quite so unreasonably, because."
They do really, truly, and actually.
Hate them.
Selves, be.
Or, do they?
Cause.
"Of course?"
How can one.
Two, or more?
The most, the many, or the all, or.
"Another, one."
Two, or more.
Actually, truly, or really.
"Love another?"
If one does not love oneself, though, too.
"Of course?"
How can.
"Or, how might."
One love oneself, if.
"One has never been loved either, or before, and."
Or if when, and where, one is not.
So, if I do, only, care.
Loved in return, or.
"Most reasonably, most rationally, most reliably?"
Of course, which.
Most certainly.
Does only make sense, but.
"Or, most surely."
When, or where, or ever has.
Most wisely.
Love made sense, or.
"Or, most practically?"
Or, most realistically.
So, do I, and, so.
"And, because?"

You do.
Of course.
"I am one."
Wise enough.
Not to try to blame myself?
"For it."
Or, myself?
"For the way I am, which is."
The way I must be, and.
Which is the way you are, who you are, and the only.
"Which, also, is?"
Way you can be, and.
The way they have made me, and.
They?
"Also, of course."
I am not one.
"Not to try."
To care about.
"Or, to care for."
Everyone.
Or, for.
"Everybody, or."
About all?
Or.
About anyone.
"Au."
Then.
Tic.
Ally?
Truly, or really.
"Real."
Ly, or truly?
More than I should.
Or, more than I ought to.
"Or, more than everyone."
Or, more than everybody.
"Or, more than all."

Do care.
About, or for, me, or.
"More than anyone, or."
More than any.
Body does.
"Care for, or care a."
Bout.
Me, or.
More than she does care for me, or.
More than he does care about, or for me, or.
"More than it does care for, or about me, or."
Because, of course.
"And that, or."
This is?
"Of course."
Whatsoever it is, and.
"Too, of course?"
Whosoever she is, and.
"Too, of course?"
Whosoever he is, and.
"Too, of course?"
Who, or what.
"So ever."
Everybody, everyone.
"Anyone, and anybody, are."
If not just, or only.
"A word, a name, or an idea, and?"
Or.
If a word, a name, an idea, or a concept that I do not believe in, then
who?
Or, Who.
"And, or."
Or?
"Of course?"
Because.
I do care enough.
For me to care.

To be fair to me, and be.
Cause.
Of course?
If you do not care for you, who can, or who will, and.
"If you are not fair to you, who can."
Or, who will be, and.
If?
"I do care enough for, and a."
Bout, about, and for.
"Me not to try to care about, or for."
Any, every, or all.
Who do not care back, or for.
"All, every, or any."
Who do re.
Fuse to care back, or.
"For any, all, or for every."
One, two, or more.
"Body, or one."
One, or body.
Who do only care to use me, and be.
Cause.
"Of course."
To give a care.
Must one get one, and.
"Too, because."
Of course?
To get a care.
"Or a heart?"
Must one give one, too.
"And, because."
I, also, am.
"And, too."
Because, of course?
I am, also.
And, too.
"Because."
I, also, am.

"Not one."
So hopefully foolish.
Or, one.
"So foolishly."
Hopeful, enough.
To think.
"To try?"
To pretend.
That, necessarily?
"To care a."
Bout is to be cared about.
Or, to be cared for.
Or, necessarily.
"That to be cared about."
Is, necessarily.
"To care for."
Or a.
Bout, or for.
What, or whom, or.
And, too?
"Because, of course."
Also, am I.
And, too?
"Because, of course."
"I am, also."
Not one?
"To try to pretend."
That should.
"That ought?"
Or, that.
Can all.
Be cared about, *or for,* equally.
Oh?
Or in the same way, or.
Ways, or.
That all.
Or more.

"Or that."
To make up for the past.
Everyone.
"Or that."
Everybody does deserve to be so cared about, or so cared for.
"Because, too."
Of course.
Why waste one's time caring about, or caring for.
"One who does refuse to be cared for, or about."
One, or more.
"Who do refuse."
To reciprocate, or.
About, or.
"For any."
The most, the many, or.
"For the all?"
Or, about.
"Anyone, or about."
Or, for.
"Everyone."
For, or about.
"Everybody?"
Who is not anyone.
Someone, or somebody.
"Anybody?"
Or someone, or somebody?
"Or, anybody."
Really.
At all.
"Truly, actually?"
Or.
"Anyway, and."
Or anyways, even if.
Of course, not every way, and.
Who, or.
"What, are merely."
Only, or?

"Just, or un."
Justly.
But an idea, and.
"Or, though?"
Of course.
"If, but."
An idea.
Whose idea.
And?
"Or, if."
Not the Idea, but a mere idea.
"Or, if rat?"
Her.
Quite so far more actually, or.
"If, rather?"
Quite so far more truly, and.
"Or, if rather?"
Quite so real.
Ly, but.
"Of course?"
How can the Idea.
Or an idea.
"Be Real, or?"
Be made so, or.
Be real, or.
"Rather, how can an idea."
Be Real, by.
"Definition, and?"
If but an idea, or.
"Even if."
The Idea, which.
"Of course."
Cannot be owned, or which.
"Of course."
Cannot be had, and.
"Too, which."
Of course.

"Cannot be pos."
Ses.
Sed, and.
Or possessed by whom, or by what.
If not by myself, and.
Which, of course.
"Is not anyone's, but."
Which, of course.
"Is everyone's, or?"
Is everybody's, but.
Of course?
Or.
What, rat.
What is in the air, as if.
Her, also, per?
To be taken, had, or grasped.
Haps, might be.
Though, of course, not as if.
"And, if?"
A thing.
Rather than, if whose.
Or an object, or.
Not whose.
"Idea, is but."
An idea, or.
"Even if?"
It, also, is.
"May, or might, be?"
The Idea, if the Idea is not Real, of course.
And cannot be.
Any less, or any more.
Than can the ide.
Than the ide.
Or can, or is, the Ide.
A is re.
Al is, or.
Al, or.

Than the real is ideal, or.
Than the Ideal is real, or Re.
Than the ideal is, or can ever be, real.
Al, or.
Or, made real, or made Real.
Or, if it could be.
"Or, real?"
Or.
How to care about.
"Or, for."
All, or?
"For, or."
About all others, or.
"For ever."
Yo.
Ne, or.
For every.
Body, or for the ever.
Bodies, or for the every.
Ones, who.
"Are, but."
An idea, or.
Why, or how.
"Or how, or why."
Care about.
"Or, for?"
Or, for.
"Or, about."
Another, or for any, or for all others, if.
One has never been cared for, or about, really, actually, or truly.
"Or."
How to care for oneself.
"If one has never been cared for, either, or."
How to expect to be cared for.
"Without caring, first, or back, or, too, and?"
Because.
"Who so ever said caring, was."

Or, is.
"A right or an entitlement, or."
That it is an ob.
Li.
Gat.
I.
On, because.
"Of course."
True, real, or actual.
Caring can never be forced, dic.
Ta.
Ted, or man.
Dated, and?
"Because, of course."
To get a damn.
"Or a heart?"
Must one give one.
"Too, and."

*   *   *   *   *

But, so.
"Who cares, or."
How, and.
"Or, if so?"
Quite so.
Far more simply.
Or simple?
Back to those hands.
Or, to those.
"Or, back to these?"
Whether bad, or Ba.
Hands, and.
D, go.
"So, and?"
Od, Go.
To one, right.

Od, all, or me.
"And one left."
Rely parti
Of course.
All.
"To one, left."
Y so.
And, to one, right.
"And, too?"
Of course.
"Which are?"
Or which, then, were?
Or which, now are.
Or which were, then.
And, there.
"Palms up?"
And, then.
And, face up.
"And, up?"
And, to.
"And, to the sky."
Or?
Which were.
"At least?"
And, which are.
"Up to."
Something, but.
"If not quite exactly, to."
The sky, because.
We are.
"Or, because."
I am.
"In."
Side, but.
These four walls, which, of?
Course do make.
"And which do make a room, and."

And, or?
"Or, this."
Is, and.
"Because?"
Sky is not.
Exactly, or pre?
Cise.
Ly.
"What is."
Inside, but.
Rather, what is?
Here, in.
This house, or.
Side, is.
In that one?
"More like air."
Though, if, in.
Deed, we we.
We?
Re out.
Side, of co.
Ur.
Se, it would be sky, and.
But, if rat.
Her, in?
Deed, we were out.
Side.
"What would be."
Sky, though.
But, too.
"Of course?"
Whosoever we are.
"And, be."
Cause?
Of course.
"I am only one person."
And be.

Cause?
"I am now in."
Side these four walls, and be.
Cause, now.
"I am in this room, and, so."
All things, all hap.
In here.
Pen.
What is.
Nin.
More like air.
Gs, do have.
Than like sky.
A cause, or ca.
Though, both.
Uses, at le.
Though, both?
As.
"Or, what I do know."
T, as long, as one do.
Is that.
Es see.
"Air is."
K, or sea.
What.
Rch for one, or for on.
"I cannot see."
Es, and.
Though, of course.
"Do I not need to see."
Someone, or something?
In order to know.
"That, what is."
Is, and.
If not who, *or Who?*
Is, too.
"And, is?"

Or, though.
And, but.
"And, but?"
Or, though.
"Or, though?"
Or, but.
"Because."
Because?
Not what.
"Sky, but."
Sky, but?
And, so.
What, so?
What, really.
"Is really?"
Is really.
"Or?"
Or?
"What is."
What is?
"More accurately."
More accurately?
Or, most so.
But what.
Is not, not.
Necessarily.
"Because?"
Of course.
I said, think, or, be.
Cause.
"I have thought, or, because."
I have said.
Or, because.
"I have de."
Cided, that.
It was not, *or is not,* or.
"But, rather."

Of course?
"What is."
"Is not what?"
Is not.
And, of.
Course.
By definition?
"What is."
In spite, de.
Spite, with, or with.
Out me, what is, what has be.
En, and what, or who?
Ever will be.
Not sky.
And, what.
"Here, in this room."
Is more like air, than like sky, and, so.
Or, because?
What very well cannot be both.
And, so?
"What is clear, and, so."
And, so?
What is not colored, and.
And?
"So, what."
Is neit.
Her.
"A light blue."
Nor.
"A dark, mid."
Night kin.
D of type of blue, eit.
Her, and.
And?
What is not clou.
Ded, and.
So, what is clear?

Too?
What is not cloud.
Y, or grey.
Or gray.
Or sil.
Very, or.
"And?"
So.
"What is more like air."
Like air?
But, as I have said, or.
Or?
"But, with no one hear."
Ing, and.
And?
With no.
Body listening, rather.
Rather?
"What have I me."
Rely thought.
To my.
Or, to your.
Self.
Self.
Because, of.
"Course, and."
Too, is.
To speak, to speak, rather than.
"To think, and."
So.
"Or, if rather."
I did.
And, if do I, or.
If do you, or.
If do I?
"Think, rather than say, or."
"If, rat."

Her?
I do say a.
Loud, what did I me.
Or, what do you, merely?
Rely.
Think?
Or, mirror-ly?
"Or, if so, what I did on?"
Ly.
Or, what you did, only?
And, even if.
"Or, if?"
What I did just.
"Or, what I did quite so un."
Justly, think?
"To my."
Self, or to your.
Self, of course.
But?
"Who is but one."
As I am.
And, not another, as am I.
And, as you are.
"And, as am I?"
And, as you are.
Who I am.
"But one."
Of course.
Of course?
"And, not who I am not, and?"
Because, here.
"And, because now."
In the eternal.
Present, and.
In your, and in mine, and.
"Because here."
So?

"So?"
In ours, and.
In my eternal.
Present, if not in the eternal.
Present, am I.
And, you are, and.
"I am."
Not who I was.
"And not who I will be, and."
And, so.
Of course?
Because I am here.
Here?
In this room, and.
Because I am here, in.
Side this house, and.
"So, that which."
And, not nec.
Ess.
Ari.
Ly, who.
Does sur.
Round me.
"Quite so invisibly, is."
More like air than like sky, and, too.
What is air, and.
"What is clean."
And, too.
"What is clear."
Here, in.
"In this house, that is."
And in this house, which is.
"Just, and only."
Only, or just?
"And, on."
Ly, and just.
Or, un.

Just, and only.
Or, on.
Ly, and un.
Just.
Or, which is.
Fair, or un.
Fairly?
Un.
Fair, or fair, and which is.
"Merely a house.
And.
And not the, or the, on.
Which is not the on.
Ly, hou.
Ly one.
Se, or.
What is?
"Of course."
My house.
Or, ours.
Or some.
Thing like it.
And, so.
"In."
Side, which.
Now are.
"Or, in."
Side, which?
I am, now.
And, here?
Of course.
"And, in which?"
Are now.
And, here.
My raised hands.
And, there.
Or?

"In which."
Now, pre.
Sent.
Ly, are.
My hands raised, or.
In which, now.
Are mine.
And, in which are yours.
"Presently, or currently, or."
In which.
Currently, and presently, are.
"In which."
My hands are, now, raised, that.
"Or this?"
Is, if.
Does the or.
Der, or.
Does.
The Or.
Der?
Mat.
Ter, and.
"Or?"
Or, does the order in.
If does the or.
Di.
Der.
Cat.
The order?
E the im.
"Of the words."
Port.
Change the me.
An.
An.
Ce.
Ing.

Of them, or?
Is the first most important, or.
If does the order change my.
Does who comes second, or last.
Or, change the?
Have all the power, by.
Meaning, and.
Forcing all others to come, or be, first, or?
If is not your meaning, the me.
Ever, and al.
An.
Way.
In.
S, do?
G, the me.
Es the best come last, or.
An.
As all do, ought, or should know, will.
Ing, and.
The last come first, or.
"If is not the me."
An.
In.
G, your meaning.
"Or, if so."
Is not their meaning, also, yours, and?
Rather, if is it.
If is not yours, also, theirs, and?
But, what is it.
And if is not theirs, yours, and.
"About more than the meaning?"
If is not yours, theirs.
Or, if is it.
Whose is right, or.
But, what is it.
Whose is correct, if.
"Or, if is what?"

Right it not, necessarily.
Or, if is this, or if is that.
Correct, and if correct is not, ne
"Or, if is life."
Ce.
About more than the me.
S.
An.
Sari.
Ing of it, or.
Ly what, What, who, or Who, al.
What is, or.
So, is right, or.
What could be.
More than, be?
Yond, or past, meaning, or.
If is it.
"Or, if might it be."
More than about my me.
An.
Ing of it—found, created, discovered, de.
Rived, projected, or.
Original, or con?
Not.
At.
Ive, or?
"By, and for, me."
Of course.
"Or?"
If is it.
Or, if it is.
About more than my finding, or about more than my making.
Meaning in it, or of it, or.
If me.
Ani.
Ng is no longer a given, or what is, and, or.
"If, rat."

Can meaning be, as is it, with.
Her, is it.
Out wor.
"More than about my words finding, or about their making, meaning."
Ds, as.
"In it, or of it, but."
Ever, and as al.
Of course.
Ways, has it be.
But, who are they?
"If not more."
En, or?
Or, less.
"Than you are, and?"
Or.
"If is it about me."
Or be.
Cause it is me.
An.
Ing, will.
And must it be, a.
Bout.
"My finding my own me."
An.
Ing in it, and finding, it.
"For me, and by me, and."
Rather than.
"Letting, or."
Rather than.
"Permitting?"
Him, it, or them.
Or, her.
"To find?"
Or, to tell me.
"What the meaning, is."
Or?

"What it might be, and."
Or, what.
"It might be."
Universally, or.
"Gen."
Er.
Ally, or?
Generically, or.
If can the meaning be any.
Thing at all, might it be no.
Thing, too.
Or.
Rather.
If the me.
To, or for.
An.
All, or rat.
Ing can be any.
Her.
Thing, at all, it the me.
"Spec."
An.
If.
Ing no.
Ic.
Thing, at all.
Ally, and.
Or, rather.
"What particularly, and."
Or, rather.
And, what.
"Is far more important, which is."
What is.
"What it does mean."
To, and for, me, and.
Because, of course.
"Because?"

What is life.
"Without death, and."
Or, without what, and.
Without whom.
One is not, and.
Because, of course?
Or, what does life, or who is.
Or, Who is?
Need, want, or care for what, or for whom.
It is, or is not, or.
"How to consider, one."
One?
Without the other, and.
"Because?"
How to think of one, without?
"The other, and."
Or without the Ot.
Because?
Her, and.
"What would life, or what could life?"
Be, without death, or.
Too, of course.
"And, quite so, likewise?"
What would, or what could?
Death be, without.
"Life, and?"
Because, though.
Would not death be without life, and.
"Of course."
What could, or.
Cannot life be, and is not, with death, of.
What would, up be.
Course.
Without down, and.
"But, of course."
What would, or.
Though are such.

And.
Such are.
What could down, be.
Very important things.
Without up, and.
"To think about."
What would light be, with.
To consider.
Out dark, and.
"And, to con."
What would dark, be.
Temp.
Without light, and.
Late, and.
Or, what does light need dark, and.
Too, what are.
Would, and can, not light be with dark, and
Too, what are.
Can, and would, not dark be with light, and.
Such big questions for the morning, and for.
"When."
And, for where.
"Here, and."
For now.
"When I am."
Just, and only.
"And where, and when."
And when, and where?
"I am, but."
So, on.
Ly, just now.
"And, just here?"
Waking, and, or.
Awakening, and.
Only?
And?
Though might man.

Y ot.
Hers, and though.
"Might all?"
And, too.
"Or?"
Though, also.
Might many think, though.
"Of course?"
About what might not others, and.
Or, about what.
"Might not others, and."
As well as which, also?
"Might, or."
Might not.
"Have ans."
Wers, and?
Or.
"While ot."
Hers do stay, or do re.
Main, un.
Answerable, or?
While others are not meant to be.
Answered at all, or?
And, so, are.
Rhetorical, or.
Which, also.
Might all have.
Different answers.
"At, or in."
Different times, and.
For different people, in.
"Different places, and."
For different people, *or for dif.*
Fe.
Rent per.
Sons, or.
Others, which, also?

"Might, or do."
Not.
Have answers, at all.
"And, so?"
What might, also, be.
"Rhetorical, too."
Which does mean.
They are not meant to be answered, of.
Course.
And.
"But?"
All, or.
"At least?"
Some of which.
"All might."
Or, more than might, be?
"A bit too much for me to hand."
Le no.
W, and, so?
Rather, might I go back, to.
"Quite so far more ea."
Sily, and.
Back to.
"Quite so far more sim."
Ply, *if not, necessarily.*
Simplistically, to.
Contemplating, and.
"To looking at."
And, to staring at these palms.
"And, at."
My palms.
And, at your palms.
Which, now.
"Are right here, and."
Which now.
I can see, just, or not just?
But only, if not necessarily, unjustly.

Now, and here.
"Before me, and."
Which are.
"Now, and."
Here raised.
To, and towards.
"And, towards."
And, to?
My roof.
Or, to your ceiling.
Palms, up?
If not, also, ne.
And, if so.
Ces.
"Because, again."
Sar.
Though, why re.
Il.
Peat.
Ly, the ce.
Of course.
Il.
What, or who.
Ing.
"Or Who?"
Or What, is the same, or.
The Same, or.
What can.
Not be, be.
Cause when, in time.
Time does change things, if.
Not necessarily ever, or always.
Does, or can?
It change people, persons, ideas.
Or the Idea, or the idea, which.
Can only change.
If when, or if where.

It, or they, are let, or permitted, to.
"Or?"
Which life does change.
Or is that, or is this.
Life, or?
God, or which.
"The Goddess, her."
Self, does.
Change, without?
Asking for per.
Mission, or for.
The, or any.
"Help she does not need, and."
Or.
"If not my hands."
Or, because.
"Not in them."
And, if not my roof.
But mine.
And, if not under it.
Then, or now?
In, or on.
Whose, and.
"Because."
Because?
"And, too, because?"
Or, if, rather.
Far more accurately.
If not necessarily.
"What, which, or whose palms."
All ideas, or.
Are now raised.
And, if not necessarily.
"To, and."
The i.
Dea, or the I.
Or does, or does not, the ide.

Dea, do all ide.
Al, or the Ide.
As, peo.
Al, or.
Even if they ought to, and.
Even if they should.
"Towards, and."
But, according to whose, or what's.
"Should," or "ought," and.
To my ceiling.
Or, to yours.
Which, of course, is more like.
Or, to ours.
"Or, too."
Or, to mine.
Which is?
Quite so far more accurately.
"More like."
A ceiling than a roof, because?
Of course.
"Once again?"
I am in this room, and.
"Because, once."
Again?
"I am lying on."
Or, in?
"This bed, and."
Because, once again.
I am inside, looking up.
"At that, which."
Does make that which is a.
Bove me, a ceiling.
Or so-called.
Rather, than.
"Ou."
Though as birds, bat.
T.

S, or pl.
Side, fly.
Ane.
Ing over.
S, or.
Or, rather than.
"Looking down."
At this, or.
"At my house, which."
Is?
"From the outside, more like."
A roof, than a ceiling, and.
"So."
Which, of course.
"Is not the only ceiling."
As well as, also, like.
Wise, if only a bit.
"Also."
Like these hands?
"Which, of course."
Are my hands.
"And, which are not."
Anyone else's, and.
Which, also.
Are not everyone's, or eve.
Ry.
Body's, or.
And which, of course, are not.
The only hands.
"In the world?"
Of course.
But, which.
Even if?
"They are."
Are the only ones that I can see, now.
Or here, or there.
Or there, or here.

"Or now, and."
Which, of course.
Does not, necessarily, mean.
That they are.
Or, that are they?
"Or, that they are?"
The only hands, that.
This, or that, is.
Or that, or this, is.
The only ceiling, or the only roof?
In this town, in this world, or in this uni.
Verse, of course.
"Or?"
Which, also, does not mean.
"That those?"
Or, that these, which.
I cannot see.
Are, also, not.
"Or, that they are not?"
Or.
"Or?"
"And, if."
And, if?
"But, if?"
But, if?
"And, even if."
And, even if?
"So, and?"
So, and.
And, even if.
And, even if?
"And, if."
And, if.
"And, but if."
And, but if.
"Or, if but?"
Or, if but?

"And, if but."
And, but if.
What are.
These, here.
"To, and for, me?"
But, what.
"Might be?"
Those to, and those for.
"Or those for an."
Y, or for an.
Other, or.
For all others, and.
"Quite a bit?"
Also, and.
"Too, like."
Wise.
What might be those.
"To, and for, me."
As well as, also?
"Are these."
And, are those.
For, and to, me.
As much as, and.
"Also?"
Quite so similar, is.
Here, for.
"And to me, also?"
There, for.
"And, or."
To them, and?
Also, likewise.
"Is?"
What is.
"There, to."
Or, for them.
"Here for."
And, to.

"Me, and."
You, and.
Also, and.
If not, also.
For me, and.
"Too, like?"
Wise.
What is there.
For, and to, me, also?
"More than most likely, and."
So, probably, is?
Here, to.
"And for them, and."
Whosoever they are, if.
Also.
Not you, and.
"Of course?"
And, also.
"So as?"
To be.
"Most thorough, and most rigorous, too."
If what is to be.
Here for, and here to, them.
Is.
"To be."
There for, and there to.
Me, and.
"And?"
Because.
Of course.
Quite so very often.
"I must choose."
Or, must I choose?
Except, really.
Whether to be here.
And, except, actually.
For me.

Need I, or must I, and.
Or?
Can you, or.
Whether to be there.
Rat.
For, or to, them.
Her might you be able, to.
Be both?
Because.
Here, and.
Because, there.
"Of course."
And there, and here.
I cannot be both.
Or in?
More than one place.
At once.
Or?
At the same time.
Or?
In the same time.
Or, times.
Or?
"Can I be."
Both.
And, or.
"But, either way."
Also, of course?
"Must I choose, at least."
Some things, like.
"To know?"
Or like.
"Not to know?"
Or, like.
To know what, or.
What is.
Like not to know, or?

"And, what is not?"
For, and.
Or, by?
Myself, or.
"Rather, or?"
To let.
Another, or others.
Know.
You, or.
"For me?"
What, or.
"Who, or."
Who, or what, is.
True, or.
True, or?
What.
"Or, who."
And, Who.
Is real.
Or, Real?
"Or, what."
And, who?
"Or, who."
And, what.
Is false.
And, or.
"What, and who."
Who, or What.
Or who, and what.
Or What, and Who.
"Is un-real, un-true, surreal, or ideal."
Or, Ideal?
And, of course.
"Likewise?"
What, and who.
"And who, and what."
Are not.

"Of course."
And?
Too, also.
"And, also?"
And, too.
Must I, also.
"Choose, or decide."
Decide, and.
"Or, choose."
Or else?
What to think.
"Of course."
And what.
"Be decided, or."
Or who.
"Else, of course."
To believe, or.
"Be chosen for."
Who, or.
"And?"
What, to.
"Or, so."
Believe, in?
"Or."
Of course?
"Rather, to be."
Told what to think.
"Or, what to believe, or."
Who to believe, or.
"In Whom, or."
In What, in what, or in whom, to.
"Believe."
Or?
"Because, of course?"
What, or.
"Who is."
Or who, or what.

Might be?
True, or real.
"Real, or true."
For, or to, whom, or w.
Un-real, un-true, ideal, or sur.
Hat, or.
Real?
Except, what.
"Or, except?"
Who I do think.
Is, or.
"Who, or."
What I do.
"Decide, or."
Choose to think.
"Or, what."
Or, who.
"I do choose."
Or, decide?
"To believe is."
Or, is not, and?
"Or, rather."
What, or.
"Who, or."
Who, or.
"What, I do."
Choose, or.
Decide, or.
"What, or who."
Is most real, is, al.
So, most true, and.
Or who, or what.
"I do decide."
Or, choose.
To permit.
"Or, to let?"
Be true.

Or, True?
Real, or.
"Un-real."
Ideal, surreal, or.
"Fake or false, or?"
And, because.
Even if?
Some things are false, and fake.
"By def?"
In.
It.
Ion, like?
"Art, and like?"
Love, which.
"Of course?"
Are both im.
It.
At.
Ions, and lies, ill.
Us.
Ions, and de?
Lus.
Io.
Ns, not life, and not necessary, to, or for it, but.
To differing de.
Gre.
Es, of course?
Are such works, acts, thoughts?
Or feel.
Ings suc.
Cess.
Ful de.
Cep.
Ti.
Ons.
Or, are they.
"Of course."

And, too.
What might be true.
Or, are they, and, too.
Or, real?
Or, Real.
Or, ideal.
For some.
"Might, or more than might, be."
Fake, or false.
Or ideal, or surreal?
To, and.
Or.
For others.
"And, too."
Because, of course.
"Likewise, and?"
Too, because.
"Similarly?"
What might be.
Less than most true.
"Real, or ideal."
Ideal, or real.
"Ideal, or Real."
False, or fake.
Or fake, or false.
For others.
"And, too."
Because, of course.
How so ever many things.
Or, people?
And, truths?
Or, People.
Which once were true, or which.
Once were.
"Believed to be true."
Or be.
Or, real.

Lie.
"Or, un-real, or."
Ved, by whom, or by what, and.
Fake, or.
False, are.
No longer, and.
Or be.
Lie.
Ved by whom, or by what, and.
"Are not anymore, and."
Because.
Of course?
Once was.
Not the earth flat, too?
And, because.
Did not the sun, once.
Also?
And, too.
Revolve around the earth?
And, too?
Or was that, *or is this?*
The moon, or.
"Or?"
Was that the stars?
Or?
Whose stars, and?
Or?
"Whose moon."
Too, and.
Or, rather.
And, so?
And, too.
Because?
Of course.
"What does matter."
Is matter, and?
"Because, of course."

What does mat.
Ter, and, so?
What is true.
Is what, or is who.
"Can be shown to be."
Or, is.
Who, or.
Is what.
Can be proven to be so.
"True?"
Or, false.
Though, too.
Of course.
Which does not mean.
At least.
Not necessarily.
"That what."
Or, that whom?
"I cannot see."
Is not true or.
True?
Or, that whom.
"Or, that what."
I cannot see.
"Is not real."
Or, Real?
But, is, or is not?
"None, or."
Never.
The.
Less far less mys.
Teri.
Ou.
S, than what, or than whom?
"I can see, or."
Than What, or than Whom?
"I can see, or."

Or, than whom.
Or, Whom?
"Or, than what?"
I cannot see, is.
"Not most real."
Or, not.
"Most true, that."
Or, this is.
"If?"
What, or.
Who, is.
"Most true."
Is, also, most real, or.
Most Real, or.
"Of course."
This, or.
"That is."
If who.
"Or, if what."
Is most real is most true, and.
"Too, of course?"
Also, assuming, that.
"Who, and that."
What, and.
"That what."
And, that who.
"Is, or."
Are real.
Or, Real?
Or, true.
Or, True?
Can be so.
"Comparably, and relatively."
Rather than.
Absolutely, or.
"That can be, being."
Or, Being?

True, or real.
"Or real, or true."
Or, both?
Be.
So, or not so?
"In degrees, or."
In varying, or in vari.
Ou.
S, am.
Ou.
Nts.
"Or me."
As.
Ur.
Es, or.
To different, and.
"Or, to differing."
Extents, levels, or scales, or.
"To differing."
Or, to.
"Different amounts, and."
Even if.
"That, or this, or."
Even if.
This, or that, is not.
"Is not."
Necessarily?
Most simple, or.
"Most easy, and."
Even if.
Or, not ea.
"It does."
Sie.
"Complicate things."
St, or simp.
Is it.
Lest.

"Most true, and."
Of course.
Because?
Who is to think.
"Or?"
Who, or.
"What?"
Without thinking.
"Who would."
Or?
"Who might like."
To try?
"To assume, or."
To presume, that.
Who, or.
"That?"
What is most true.
Or, that?
What, or.
"That who?"
Is most real.
Or, that?
What is most True, or.
That what?
Or, that who.
"Is most Real, also, is."
And is, also.
Most simple, or.
"Most easy, or?"
That what.
"Or?"
That who.
"Is most simple."
Or am I, also, not?
As you are not.
"One crazy enough to think, or."
To believe.

Or to think, that.
"Who, or."
That what.
"Is most easy, is."
Also, most true.
"Or, also?"
Most True, or.
"Also, most Real?"
Or, also.
"Most real, or."
That, of course.
What.
Or, who?
Is, or does.
"Stay?"
Or, that.
"Who, or."
That what?
"Does remain hidden."
Or un-.
Seen, or.
"That what."
Or, that.
"Who?"
Does re.
Main.
"Or stay."
Hid.
Den, or.
"Un-see."
Able.
Or, in.
Vis.
Ible?
Is not.
"What, or."
Is not who, or Who?

Is.
Necessarily.
"Most true?"
Most True.
"Most real."
Or, most Real?
Or, that.
"Who, or."
That what.
What, or.
"That what?"
Or, that.
"Who does."
Remain, or stay.
Or stay, or remain.
Un-seen, hidden.
"Unknown, or."
Un-know.
Able, or.
"That what."
Or?
"That who."
Does stay.
"Or that who, or that what, does?"
Remain un.
Provable.
And so un-.
See.
Able, or?
Un-see.
Able, and, so, un.
Prov.
Able, or.
"Is any."
Less than.
"Most true?"
Or, is any.

"Less than."
Most real, or.
That what.
"Or?"
That who.
Can only be known.
"Or, shown?"
To be.
"By its."
By his?
"By her."
Or, by their effects, is.
Any less powerful, or potent, or poig.
Nant, or is.
Any less than.
"Most true, or?"
Any less than.
"Most real, but?"
Or, any more, or less, than most.
Or, any less than true, or real.
Real, or True, or.
Than what, or than who, can be seen.
Or, heard?
Measured, or proven, or.
Because, too.
"Of course?"
People do.
Tend to see.
Or not to see, or do they.
Tend to ig.
Nore.
What do they want to.
"And, not what."
And, not whom.
They will, or do not.
Want to, or.
Who, or what, W.

Think they need to, or have to, or think they must.
Hat, or Who.
As much as?
"Do people."
Tend to think?
"To assume, or to."
Presume, that.
"They find, or."
That they do.
Do cre.
Ate, or.
That they have found?
"To believe."
What do they want to.
Or?
"Who, or."
What, or.
"What, or whom?"
They do want to believe in.
"Or?"
What, or.
"Who they do need to?"
And, so, quite so very most of.
Ten.
"So?"
Unreasonably, and.
"Too, also?"
Quite so often, and.
"Quite so irrationally, too."
Though, but?
Of course.
"Is not the point?"
Of faith.
"Or of belief, or."
Of disbelief, to?
Believe in.
Or?

"To decide not to."
Believe in?
"What is past."
Or, in what, *or in whom, or Whom,* is beyond?
Human comprehension, understanding, and logic, so?
"Or, is the point."
In what, or in whom, is past, and be.
Yond all human limits, and?
And the pur.
Pose, of.
"Be."
Lief, and, or.
Of faith?
To realize.
"The limits of ord?"
In.
Ary human logic, reason, and rationalizing, and?
Even if, in.
Deed, what is vis.
I.
Ble, in.
Deed, might, also, be.
Most mys.
Ter.
Io.
Us, and.
Because, of course.
"Is not."
The point.
"Of faith, and."
Of belief, and.
"Of believing?"
In miracles, or.
"In what is possible, past."
And, beyond.
"What is."

Humanly logical, comprehensible, attainable, or logically, reasonably,
or rationally do.
Able, and, so?
"Is not."
The purpose, or.
"The point, of."
Faith, or.
"Of be."
Lief, or.
Of believing?
Because, of.
Course, can, do, and will not mira.
Cles, hap.
Pen, if.
One does not let them, and.
"Of course?"
Cannot mirac.
Les hap.
Pen if one does per.
Mit, or let, de.
Tails get in the way, and.
Of course?
Can, and will.
Not miracles hap.
Pen, if.
One does not be.
Lie.
Ve in them, or.
In, at least, a bit.
Of ma.
Gic, and.
Also, is not the point?
Of believing, in.
"What."
Or, in whom is pa.
St, and in.
What, or in whom, is be.

Yon.
D what, or who, is merely, just.
"Or un."
Justly?
So small-.
Ly, and so sim.
Ply hu.
Man.
"And, so?"
Is the point.
"Of faith, or of belief?"
To believe.
"At least."
A bit?
"In the ma."
Gic.
If not, ne.
Of what.
Ces.
Or, of.
Sarily, al.
Whom?
So, in the ma.
Is past.
Chine.
Or?
"Of whom."
And, or?
"Of what is be."
Yon.
D.
Quite so simply.
"And qui."
Te so simplistically?
Or, beyond.
"And, past?"
What, at first.

"Does seem to be?"
Most simply.
"And, most elegantly?"
Rational, or reasonable.
If not, necessarily, most correctly.
Because?
"Of course?"
Has not ever, or has.
"Not always."
The point?
"Or the purpose, of."
God, or gods, if not, also.
The point, of.
Myths, science, and stories, to explain.
"What."
Or, who?
Or Who.
At first sight, or glance, at?
Least, does not ap.
Pear to be.
"Logical, or."
Who, or what.
Is not sensible.
"Reasonable, rational, or."
What is not rational, or.
"What, or who."
Does not seem.
At first sight?
"Or."
Who, or.
What, at first glance.
"Does not?"
Seem to make much sense, but.
Who said being, or to be?
That the mind of God, or of God.
Rational, reasonable, sensible, or logical, or?
Des.

"That the mind, most di?"
S, or.
Vine, is.
Merely, only.
Or, just?
Or Just.
Most simply.
"Logical, rat."
Ion.
Al, rea?
Son.
Able, or sens.
Ib.
Le, "Or?"
That only, that me.
Rely, or that just?
Who is log.
Ic.
Al, rat.
Ion.
Al, rea.
Son.
Able, and sens.
Ib.
Le, might real.
Ly, "Or?"
Might tru.
Ly, or.
Might actually, also?
Be unknowable.
Or knowable, or.
"Or?"
Controllable, or?
Known, already, or?
Already known, or ought, or should, remain.
Or, stay un.
Known, or.

Because, is.
Or, is not?
All.
Everyone, or everybody?
Meant.
Or, in.
Tended?
"To be known, or."
If intended, or.
Is all already known, or?
If meant.
To be known by whom, by Whom, or.
"Are some things."
By what, or by What, or.
By whom, or.
Some people, or.
By what, or.
"Some beings, or."
By what, or.
What, or.
By whom, or.
"Who, or."
Why, or.
Who, or.
"What is yet to come?"
Meant to stay.
Hidden, unknown, undecided, undetermined, or un?
Destined, or.
"And unknowable, or?"
Rather, of.
"Course?"
Did God—*or G-d, or God.*
Dess—once come down.
"To be known, and?"
Or, rather.
Is that, or is this?
God, or god.

Or G-d, or g-d.
Or savior?
Or Goddess, or god.
Yet to come, or.
Dess.
How to know?
"Who, or what."
What, or Whom.
Or, what.
"Or, if who?"
Has come, already, and.
"Gone again, if?"
One is not ready, or prepared, or?
If one does not have the eye.
S to see, or the ear.
S to hear, or?
If one is not an Eye, or?
How to know if one, two, or more.
Are coming at all, or.
How to know if the one, or The One?
Has come already, or.
"If one?"
Is not waiting, or.
"If one does not know."
Or, recognize when.
"Or, where."
Or, where.
"Or, when."
The savior has.
"Come, and gone."
Again, or.
Is that.
"Or?"
If where, or.
If when, one.
Or, One.
Does not know who, or know what.

One is waiting, looking, seeking, or.
Searching for, or?
If is this savior.
"Yet to come, again."
As if?
Or, for.
"The, or a se."
Con.
D, or.
Second time, as in.
The, or.
As in a.
Se.
Cond co.
Ming, or.
Is that.
"Or, is this?"
Or, is this.
God, or gods.
Or, is that.
Meant to stay?
Also, this.
Or, meant?
"To come down, or."
Meant, or?
Intended, to.
"Become one of us, or?"
Intended, or meant.
"To stay."
Unknown, and unknowable, or meant, or intended, by whom, or by
what, if not by Himself, if a Him at all, and?
"So, feared, or?"
Is this, or.
"Is that."
God, or gods.
"Meant to be known?"
And so, loved.

"Or?"
Rather, what.
"Does loving."
Have to do with knowing, because?
"If is."
Knowledge, power.
"Is knowing."
Power, too?
And, is knowing.
Power, over.
"The known, and."
Or, rather, ought it be me.
Rely, over the know.
Er, and so, over one?
Self, because.
Is not?
"To know another, to."
Objectify another, and?
Of course.
Is not love objectification, and.
So?
"Cannot love be a."
Bout.
Too, of course.
"Is not objectification."
Having, or.
"Love, too."
Or, about.
"Wielding, power."
Over another, or.
Is not love, also a.
Bout ne.
"Over all others?"
Eding.
Or, over.
Want.
Or, is me.

Ing, or ha.
Re curi?
Ving to know, or.
Os.
It.
Y not ever, or?
Not al.
Ways in.
No.
Cent, be.
Cause.
"The known, but."
Does love re.
Spec.
T boun.
Dari.
Es, and lim.
Its, and it does not need to know, and.
Of course?
To be love, or Love.
"Because."
Must it trust.
Who is to say.
Does love, so-.
Cal.
Led, not use know.
Ledge wrong.
Ly, mis.
Use, or a.
Bus.
E it, or.
"That all of this."
Use it a.
Gain.
St the know.
N, or?
"Or, that all of that?"

But, rat.
Her, of.
Course, must love, and lo.
Ving, be a.
Bout trust, and a.
Bout trust.
Ing, which is not all a.
Bout ha.
Ving to know every.
Thing, or all, as well as can.
Not a re.
Lat.
Ion.
Ship be with.
Out trust, too?
"And, so."
Or, but?
Who did say, think, ass.
Um.
E, or pre.
Sume, that?
"All of that, or all of this?"
Is about love, or is about lo.
Ving.
But if not a.
Or is a.
Bout.
Bout re.
Lov.
Lat.
In.
Ion.
G, w.
Ships, or?
Hat is it ab.
Be.
Out, an?

Cause, of.
D.
Course, must people be trusted to be loved, and.
"Because?"
Of course.
"Would, and does, only a fool, idiot, or moron, trust?"
Or dare.
Who, or.
"What, or."
Who is not.
"To be trusted, but?"
Of course.
"And, yet."
Again, what.
"Such great."
Or, such grand.
Questions.
"Ei."
Ther.
With, or without.
Answers, *what do.*
"Or, what might they have to do?"
With to.
Day, or.
"With this morning, or."
With these hands, or?
"With the task at hand, and."
So?
"But, of course."
Because.
"I am."
As yet.
And, still.
Still waking, and.
"So to?"
Not to rush, and.
Or?

"So, not to."
Hurry myself?
With such great questions.
Of such gre.
At im.
Port.
If not of ex.
Por.
T, to?
O.
And, so.
"Of course."
I cannot move on.
"Or, I need not, without."
First, exploring.
"These hands, these palms?"
Or these, or those?
Quest.
Ions, of be.
Lei.
F, of be.
Liev.
In.
G, of be.
Lie.
Ving, in, or of?
Fa.
It.
H, or of t?
Rust?
Or, though might so.
Because.
Me be.
"Of course?"
Lie.
Though some might believe.
Ve.

"In some great being."
Or?
"In some great Being, or."
In something, or in someone, greater, higher, and.
"Or, in?"
Someone, or in something, far past, or.
"In someone?"
Far beyond.
What, or who, is me.
Rely, just, only, or sin.
Gu.
Lar.
Ly, human.
"Whether?"
That, or this, thing, or.
"Being, is?"
Or, might be.
"Found within."
Or without, or?
Which, of course.
"Is not some."
Thing, that.
Can necessarily be shown, or proven, but.
"Because, of course."
Quite so very often.
"Do people believe, because?"
Others do, and.
Not because?
"What, or."
Who, or.
"Who, or."
What is, is.
Know.
Able, or prov.
Able, and.
"Even if?"
Some beliefs might, or.

"Even if?"
Some believing, might make.
Life worse.
Or better.
Less pleasurable, and.
Or more so, or.
"More painful, and?"
Or less so, or.
"Or more difficult, but?"
Or easier, of course.
Of course.
Though some might like, or en.
Joy pain, or choose?
"Pain."
Or pains?
Over pleasures, but.
Or power, or con?
Trol, over.
Pains, or over plea.
Sure, or over pleas.
Ures, or?
"Which, once again."
Does prove.
"Just, quite."
And, exactly.
Because, of course.
"Would some rat?"
Her mast.
Er an is.
Sue, or a pro.
Ble.
M, how.
So.
Ever plea.
Sur.
Able, or pain.
Ful, and re.

Gard.
Less of the con?
Se.
Quen.
Ce.
S, and.
"How unreasonable, how illogical, how irrational, and how insensible
people can be, and."
As well, of?
Course, do some.
Seek pain, or pains?
And find, in the.
M pleas.
Ure, while?
Do they a.
Void plea.
Sure, and plea.
Sures, for.
"Whatsoever rea."
Or, for no reasons, at all, lacking.
Son, or rea.
Reason, as a faculty, in gen.
Sons, and.
Er.
So?
Al, and, or.
"Once again."
Failing to use it, and.
Should, and ought.
I not, and you not.
But, who are you?
"Be shocked, or surprised?"
That do, quite.
Or, which are you.
So very often.
Their beliefs, also.
"Seem to be?"

Quite so unreasonable, and.
"Quite so irrational, and."
Quite so illogical, and.
"Quite so insensible, too?"
Which, of course.
"Is to be?"
Expected of, or from, ones.
"So merely."
Human, but.
Of course.
"Cannot one be expected."
To have.
"Any amount."
Of infinite patience, for.
Such non.
Sense, or.
For the truth, or for the Truth?
"Or for whose, which, or what truth, or truths, or."
For such.
"Illogical irrationalities, or."
For such?
"Magical thinking, or."
For what?
Or for whom.
"Cannot with certainty, be."
Known, or shown.
"To be?"
Real, or True, or.
"Because, if?"
Might many versions of the truth exist.
"And?"
Because they do, and.
As much as.
"Too, might?"
Or, as much as.
"More than most certainly, do."
Possibly?

"An infinite number of ways of reaching."
Of finding, of getting to, or?
"Of achieving the Truth, exist?"
Even if.
"Of course."
Which does.
"Or, even if?"
What might.
"Cause, and create?"
Much confusion, but.
Because, of course.
Quite so.
"Most reasonably, or."
Because?
"Quite so."
Most rationally, and.
"Because, quite so?"
Sensibly, or.
"Because, quite so?"
Logically, too, if not.
Necessarily?
"Most prac."
Tic.
Ally, most real.
Is.
Tic.
Ally, or most prag.
Mat.
Ic.
Ally, too.
"I cannot trust any."
Or all?
Who do claim to have found the Truth.
Or the truth, as in.
The only one.
Finally, or forever, or.
"Any, or."

All, or.
"The most, or."
The many, who?
Might try to claim, that.
They might have, possess, or own the tru.
Th, *or the Tru.*
Th, and.
"Or?"
As, if.
"One Truth, or one truth, ever."
Was, always.
"Or will ever."
Forever?
Or for always, be.
And, if.
"Ever, forever."
And, for always?
For everyone, everywhere.
Was such a Truth.
Or is one.
Or such a truth.
Or One.
To be.
"Of course?"
Would it not be, a.
"Or the."
Truth, which.
"Can be known, or grasped."
Wholly.
Totally, ever.
"Entirely, or."
Completely, and.
"Too, of course?"
Will it.
"And, can it."
Ever, not be.
"The, or."

A truth.
"Which?"
Can, ever.
"Wholly, always."
For.
Ever, every.
Where, for eve.
Ry.
One, for all, for eve.
Ry.
Body, or for al.
Ways, every.
Where, and.
"For everyone."
Or, for everybody.
Always, or ever.
Be told, shown, spoken, or known.
"Finally, or completely."
Or?
Might it be, or.
"If can it be?"
Or is knowing.
A pro.
Cess, as is revel.
At.
Ion, too.
Told, shown, known, or spoken, wholly, entirely, or completely.
"Would it not, already?"
Be, or have been, tho.
Ugh, per.
Haps, re.
Veal.
Ed, in an in.
Stant, or ins.
Tant.
Ly, or.
"Only in, via, or through?"

Via reason, or Rea.
Time, or.
Son, or.
"Of course?"
Which does me.
An that, rat.
Her, per.
Haps, known in an inst.
Ant, or in a flash, on.
Ly by, or in.
"The mind of God?"
Or G—d, or.
Which mind, or.
"Whose G—d," or which god, or gods, or.
Or is it now, pre.
Or which, w.
Sent.
Hat, or w.
Ly, or cur.
Hose, god.
Rent.
Des.
Ly, eve.
S, or god.
R, and al.
Des.
Ways, e?
Ses.
Tern.
Ally, in the mind of the God.
Dess, while.
"Or this?"
In the mean.
Time, must be.
Re.
Vealed to us, me.
Re hu.

Man mor.
Tals, trap.
Or in real.
Ped, or stuck.
It.
Down in time, grad.
Y, or?
U.
In the re.
All.
Al, or Re?
Y, and on.
Al, or in who.
Ly lit.
Se vers.
Er.
Ion of it, or.
Ally, and so.
In the mean.
Time, must we.
Or 'we.'
"But, all?"
Live so part.
I.
Ally, or.
So sub.
Ject.
Iv.
Ely, or?
"That must we?"
Live so un-.
Objectively, or?
Of cour.
Se, so un.
Fairly, or?
"Do the best with."
So pre.

Judicially, or?
"What we do have, and."
With, or.
"In, or?"
Play.
Ing such fav.
Or.
It.
Es, or.
"Or?"
That, or.
This is.
"Or, is this, or?"
Is this.
"That must we?"
To be partial, also?
Strive, or struggle?
Necessarily, to be?
"To be."
Subjective, and.
As happy.
If to be subjective, is?
"As joyful?"
Necessarily, to be.
As thank.
Ful, and.
Pre.
Ju.
Dice.
D, or.
Prejudicial, or.
"As real?"
Un.
Fair, or?
And, as.
If is?
To be.

Part.
I.
Al, al.
So.
"True, and."
Merely, just.
As au?
Then.
Tic?
Or, un-.
Just.
Ly as we can be, too.
To be?
"Or?"
Less than most ob.
Ject.
Ive, which.
Is, also, most hu.
Man, most nat.
Ur.
Al, and to be ex.
Pect.
Ed, too.
As much as.
Some do, of.
Course, pre.
Fer some over.
Ot.
Hers, and.
"We do want?"
Who, or what.
Is to say, decide, or ass.
Ume to have the right.
To de.
Cide w.
Hat, or to de.
Cide whom.

To pre.
Fer, or.
Who, or what, not to, or.
Who, or what.
Is fav.
Or.
Ed, or.
What, or who?
"Is a fav."
Or.
Ite, or.
What, or who, is not, and.
Or, as much.
Who, or what.
"What, or Who?"
Does get to know, choose, or de?
Cide what, or who.
"Who, or What?"
Is best, right, cor.
Rect, or just, or.
"If one, two, or more?"
The most, or the man.
Y, are.
Al.
Ways be.
St, right, cor.
Rect, or most just?
As.
"'We' do choose to be."
Or.
And, or?
Which, might.
Or who, or what, must.
"Also, mean?"
That might 'we,' also, be.
"As fair?"
As caring.

"As jealous, and?"
As ven.
Ge.
Ful, or.
As loving?
"Or as forgetting."
Or as for.
Giving, or.
As kind.
As we do choose to be, or.
As kind.
"As forgiving."
As loving.
"As vengeful."
As de.
Ceit.
Ful.
"As forgetful."
As jealous.
"As caring."
As fair, and.
"As understanding."
As we do want to be, and.
Not how who, or.
How what, *or What.*
Says, dic.
Tates, de.
Cides, or deter.
Mines, that we must be, or.
How who, or how what.
Do.
Es de.
Ter.
Mine, or de.
Cide, or choo?
Se.
I must be, think, do, say, feel, or be.

Lie.
Ve, or.
"Of course."
As well as might we.
"Or, as."
Well as might 'we' not?
Choo.
Se to be.
Lie.
Ve.
"Or decide not to believe?"
In.
Some sort of hi.
G.
Her be.
Ings, or Be.
Ing.
Or be.
Ings, so, al.
So, can.
Not such rules, man.
Dates, or dic.
Tat.
Es, be.
Dic.
Tated, im.
Posed, or for.
Ce.
D, if in.
Deed, they are.
To be True, real, or au.
Then.
Tic, or.
Which does?
"Or which, but which not ne."
Ces.
Sari.

Ly, must.
Al.
So, in.
Clu.
De.
Be.
Lie.
Ving in.
"Lower beings, or."
In a lower Being, too.
"Because?"
Of course.
How might what, or.
Who is hig.
Her, or high.
Est, be with.
Out whom, or what, or What, is.
Lo.
Wer, or.
Lo.
West, and.
How might, or.
How does w.
Hat, or.
Who is high.
Est, or high.
Er go, or be, do, or co.
Me, come, or go, be, or do, with.
Out what is lo.
Wer, or.
Without whom?
Is lo.
West, and like.
Wise?
Or, rat.
Her what does who, Who?
What, or what.

Need, want, or care for, what.
"Or for whom?"
Is low.
Er, or.
For who.
M, or for what?
Is low.
Est, though, of.
Course, not quite like?
Wise can the low.
The low.
Er, or the low.
Est, qui?
Te do with.
Out what, who.
M, or who?
M is high.
Er, or high.
Est, and.
"Which might, or."
Which might not, be?
Fo.
Und with.
In, or.
"Found with."
Out, or.
Which, or.
"What, or."
Who might.
"Or might not be?"
Ot.
Her than me, or.
"Which, and."
What, or.
"Who might?"
Also, be.
Omni.

Po.
Tent, om.
Ni.
Pre.
Sent, om.
Ni.
Sci.
Ent, and e.
Tern.
Al, or.
"Who, or."
What, also?
"Might not be, too."
And.
Whose name.
"Or, whose names?"
Might be known, know.
Ab.
Le, spoke.
N, un.
Spoken, un.
Speak.
Able, or.
Not, or.
"Who is ever."
And whatever will be?
"Past, and beyond."
All human.
Know.
Ledge, and com.
Pre.
Hens.
Ion, though.
T, think.
Ing, and lan.
Guage, and?
"Because, of course."

What are words, if not thought, or if not thoughts, or thinking, or
the product of it?
Or of them, and be.
Cause what is thinking, if not words, and.
Because, of course, thought and thinking.
Are not everything, or all, and.
Because, of course.
What happens when, and what happens where.
One does reach the end of thinking, or of thought, and.
Because what are names if not, also, words.
And meaning, meanings, intents, intentions, promises, associations,
and connotations.
Experiences, and interpretations, too?
"And, because."
What is the process of naming, if not?
"The process of trapping, or."
If not?
"The process of entrapping, in."
To, or?
"By human thinking."
By planning, plots.
Connotations, and agendas, thought, and meaning, which.
By definition, is.
And are.
Limited, and.
Or rather, by naming, is one set free.
From me.
An.
Ing.
Less.
Ness, and, so?
En.
Ab.
Led, and, so?
Em.
Powered, or.
"Because."

Of course?
"As much as meanings are names, are they?"
Also, intentions.
"And promises, too?"
And.
"Because, of course."
Who, or what.
"Or what, and who."
Limitless, endless, eternal, omniscient, omnipresent, and omnipotent.
Can not be so trap.
Ped, or so.
En.
Trap.
Ped, or.
But, of course.
"Why, now."
This morning.
"Con."
Fuse, or con.
Cern my.
Self, with.
Such huge, or with.
Such great, or with?
"Such grand."
And, even if?
"With what might be."
Qui.
Te such im.
Port.
Ant, but.
"What inevitably, and what ultimately, are?"
Un.
Answer.
Able quest.
Ions.
"Wanderings, or musings, and?"
Rather, might I.

Focus, here.
"And, on the now?"
And, in the now.
And, on these hands.
And, in these hands.
"And, on these palms?"
And, in these palms.
Which I can see, and.
"Which can be seen, and."
Which I can know, and.
"Which can be known, and?"
Or, in so far.
"As can I, or."
At least.
"In so far?"
As can we.
Or as can 'we.'
Or as can we.
Or as 'we' can.
"Or as do we?"
Know, or.
"See them, now."
Even if?
"Of course."
Whosoever 'we' are, and.
"How."
Soever in.
Clu.
Sive, or ex.
Clu.
Sive.
"'We' are."
Too, and.
"Howsoever like, or."
Unlike 'I' am 'we' are, and.
"Howsoever 'we.'"
And 'I,' are.

"But, ideas, or."
Con.
Structions, and.
Or de.
Con.
Struct.
Ions, second, first, third, fifth, or next, first, or last, later.
Before, or after.
Con.
Side.
Ring, or ans.
Wer.
Ing, or.
"If whether."
Or, if not?
"'We' all do know, can know."
Do see, or can see?
Or do, or can, or will, hear.
"All the same thing, or all the same things, and."
Or all the Sam.
E, or all at on.
Ce, or.
Of course.
"Too, if."
Whether, or not.
Knowing is seeing.
"And, too?"
If whether.
"Or not."
Seeing is knowing.
Or, rather?
If first, must one.
"Believe?"
In order to see, or.
"In order to know."
"Too, and."
Too, and?

But, of course.
"Why go on."
Or why con.
Tin.
Ue, on.
Or for.
Ward.
"With such questions, without answers, or."
With such que.
Sti.
Ons, that might.
"Or which, also, might not have?"
Answers, which.
"Might, or."
Which might not be?
"The same today as they are, or."
As will they be, to.
Mor.
Row, and.
"Or."
With questions.
As they were yes.
Ter.
Day, and as the.
Y we.
Re the day, and the day.
S be.
For.
E, and, which.
"Might also, or not, have?"
The same ans.
Wers.
For all.
"And for everyone, and."
Or, for every.
Body, or.
"Which, also?"

Might not, and.
"Or."
Or?
"Rather, why not."
Concern myself, here.
And, now.
"And, with the now?"
Or, with the here.
And with these hands, which.
"Of course."
Are mine, and.
"Too, which?"
Are, but two.
"And, which have always been?"
And, which.
"Of course."
More than most likely.
"And, so?"
What.
"More than most probably."
Will so ever, be.
"But?"
Two, and.
"Also, which are?"
Right, and left.
"And left, and right."
To me, though.
"Which, of course?"
Quite so oppositely, are.
"Right, and left."
And left, and right.
"To, and for."
And for, and to.
"Another, or all others, but."
Of course.
And, which.
"Also, might?"

Be left, and wrong.
"Or wrong, and left."
To, or.
"For, or."
For, or.
"To others, but."
But?
"If when, and."
If where.
Or if where, and if when.
Must I choose?
"Between them, and be."
Twe.
En me.
Of course?
"And, or."
Between, their, his, its.
Or, her.
"Per."
Spec.
"Tive, point-of-view, or mine?"
Most cer.
Tain.
Ly, and.
"Of course?"
Most sur.
El.
Y, and.
"Of course?"
Most reasonably, and.
"Of course?"
Most rat.
Ion.
Ally, and.
"Of course?"
Most sen.
Sib.

Ly, and.
"Of course?"
Most logi.
Call.
Y must.
"I choose myself."
And?
My own per.
Spec.
Tive, and.
"My own point-of-view, and?"
Accordingly.
"My own rights, and."
My own needs, and.
"My own wants, and."
My own points-of-view, and.
"My own hopes, and."
My own dreams, and.
"Because, of course."
If I am not my own ad.
Vocate, or.
If you are not permitted to be, or.
If I am not permitted to be, be.
Cause?
Not per.
Mit.
Ted by who.
M, or by w.
Hat, and.
Who.
"Can, who."
Will, or who would be, and.
"If I do not stick, or."
Stand up.
"For myself?"
Who can, and who will, and.
"Because, of course."

Is not what is ex.
Pec.
Ted of me.
"To be?"
A rat.
Ion.
Al e.
Go.
Ist, and.
"Because, of course?"
I am not one.
"Crazy, foolish, or out of my."
Right.
Or, left?
Or, wrong?
Mind, e.
No.
Ugh.
"To choose."
To select?
"Or to put."
Any, or.
To put?
"All ot."
Hers be.
Fore?
Me, or.
"Before myself, or."
One to choose, or?
One to favor, or.
"One to ad."
Vocate, for?
Any, or.
"For all ot."
Hers'.
Ho.
Pes, dre.

Ams, ne.
Eds, or w.
Ants.
"Other than my own, un?"
Less, of course.
"I do."
For some?
"Oddly masochistic reason?"
Or, per.
Haps, al.
Tru.
Is.
Tic re.
As.
On?
Choose to favor others.
"And?"
Or their, his, her, or its?
Wants, hopes, needs, and dreams.
"Over, or, rat."
Her than me, my.
Self, and.
Rather than my own.
Which, of course.
"Would be?"
Far from rea.
Son.
Able, and, too?
"Which, of course."
Would, also, be.
"Far from rat."
Io.
Nal, far from sens.
Ib.
Le, and far.
"From logical, too."
And.

"Even if."
Of course?
"Might thinking of others."
Which, of course.
"Is not, necessarily, thinking for them."
Be?
"At least."
One way, of.
"Escaping myself."
And?
Even if?
"Thinking of."
Or con.
Side.
Ring others'.
Or Others', or the Other's, or the Others'?
Or the other's, or the others'.
Miseries, needs, wants, hopes, and dreams.
Might be?
"One, if only one."
Way of es.
Caping.
"My own mise."
Rie.
S, or.
Your own faults, or.
My own fail.
Ings, or.
Ures, or.
Your own wor.
"My own self-hatred, or?"
Ri.
Your own needs, wants, hopes, dreams, am.
Es, or.
Bit.
Ions, or de.
Sires, and.

But, rather.
"If do."
Or if might I?
"Choose to."
Accept, and.
"Love?"
Myself, as I am.
And.
"All of your faults, and."
All of your failings, too, and.
If rat.
Her, "I do choose?"
To be hap.
Py, and joy.
Ful, rat.
Her than miser.
Able, and.
"If I do not let?"
Them, him, it.
Or her.
"Drag, or."
Keep me down?
In.
To, or in.
His, her, its, or the.
Ir.
Miserable company, might I not.
"Need to?"
Escape my.
Self, or.
Put them.
"Or?"
Might I, also, not need.
"To put him?"
It, or her?
Any, or all, or.
"All, or any?"

Ot.
Hers, be.
For.
E.
"Me."
Even if.
Might so.
Me think?
Or, even if.
"Might some like?"
To try to con.
Vin.
Ce me, that.
Love is?
"Or, that."
Or, this?
"Is love caring."
More for, or putting.
And, caring for your.
Self first, or.
For.
The wants, hopes, dreams, needs, wishes, and desires.
"Of an."
Other, or of.
Any, or.
"Of all others?"
Before.
Or, in front of?
"Your own?"
Or your own.
"Or my own?"
But on.
Ly if you want to hur.
T for.
Ever, and.
"Or be."
Cause love, true, or love, real?

Does not hurt, so.
"Fore."
If it hurts it is not love, and, so?
"My own, or?"
Before your own, or.
Might, or more than might?
"Al."
So, love.
"Be?"
Caring as much for your own needs, wants, wishes, hopes, and dreams, as for those.
"Of another, or."
As for those.
"Of all others?"
Might.
Be love most true.
Or True, but, or.
"Most real."
Or, Real.
Or, love most f.
But who cares for, or a.
Air, too.
Bout love, or for, or a.
Or, love most sin.
Cere, or.
Because?
If not sincere love would, and love could, it not be, and, or?
Because how to love an.
Ot.
Her, if.
"Love most au."
One does not, can.
Then.
Not, or will.
Tic, and.
Not love one.
Or.

Self, fore.
"Love most fair?"
Most, and first, or.
Because, of course, one can care too much, as well as too little, especially when, and especially where, caring is for the wrong reason, or reasons.
Or when, and where.
And where, and when.
It is for the wrong person, persons, or peo.
Ple, and.
Or when, or where, it is not re.
Because, of course, cari is.
Cip.
Ng too much as bad as caring too litt.
Ro.
Le, and.
Cat.
Because, of course.
Ed, and be.
Quite so very.
Cause.
Often one does try, pre.
Tend, or por.
Tend to care.
Ed, and.
In order, to.
Es.
Cape one.
Self, and.
Does one often try to care for any, or for all, ot.
Hers.
Rather than caring for one.
Self, and.
Or in or.
Der, not.
To have to care for, or a.
Bout.

One.
Self, or.
Or, because, of course, quite so very of.
Ten it is.
Easier to love, or to care, or to think, or to be.
Lieve, one does.
Care.
Rat.
Her than to per.
Mit one.
Self to be cared for, or loved, as well.
As, of course, do so man.
Y con.
Fuse lust, need, want, desire, or con?
Cupi.
Scen.
Ce, with love, which, of course.
Is quite rare, and.
Which, of course.
Is rare.
Ly true.
And which, when, or where.
It is real.
Or, Real.
Is us.
U.
All.
Y not, also, true.
Or True.
And, which.
Where, and when, it is re.
Al, or pur.
Porte.
Dly so, is it, and it is.
Us.
U.
Ally opposed.

Or in opposition to what, or to whom.
Is true, *or True,* and.
Too, though.
Of course.
A bit like war?
"And, too."
What fool, idiot, or moron.
"Who is?"
Too good for their.
"His, or its."
Or, her.
Or, my.
Own good.
Or?
"Good for."
Or, good to.
"Or, good."
Or, Good.
According to whom, or according to what.
Does not know.
"That, but?"
Of course.
"Love is not fair."
Or, is it?
And, but.
Or can it be, though.
Or?
"Of course."
Fair to, fair for, or fair.
Ac.
Cord.
Ing to whom, or to what, and.
What idiot, fool, or moron, does not know.
Not must, or need it not be, be.
That in love all is fair, or.
Cause, of course, can.
Not love be.

If where, or if when, it is for.
Ced, or co.
Er.
Ced, or.
Though, who said.
Of course?
"Thou."
Gh.
T, pre.
Sum.
Ed, or.
What, or.
Who.
Ever as.
Sum.
Ed, that.
Who does cease to love, or what, or whom, does cease to be loved.
"All of this?"
Where, and when.
That, or the other.
And when, or where.
"Or that?"
It is for.
Ce.
D, or.
Er.
Ce.
D, or.
All this, or that.
Where, or when.
"The other?"
Or w.
Hen, and w.
Here.
Is.
It, or she is.
All about love?

Not free.
Ly chose.
N, and.
Though, if.
Too, of course.
"Of course."
Does not love ever fol.
Low the rules.
Where, and when.
Or, whose rules, or?
"And when, and where."
Which, or.
If?
What rule, or.
"Which Rule, and."
If.
It is not about love, what is it about, or.
If it is not about love, Love, or lo.
"What can it?"
Ving.
Or.
"What must it be about, or?"
But, of course.
"Is not."
Here, and there.
And, too.
"Is not."
There, and here.
A time for thinking.
"A time for doing."
And.
A time for act.
Ing, and.
A time for lo.
Ving, and.
Of course.
"Is here."

A time, and a place, for for.
Getting, and for re.
Membering, and.
Is there.
And, here.
"A time."
And, a place?
"And a spot, for."
Thinking, past.
"Or for thinking beyond."
Or, past.
The here, and the now.
"The most immediate."
And the most present.
"And the most material, and."
The most tang.
I.
Ble, as much as.
"Of course?"
Also, here.
"And, also."
There, is.
"A spot, time, and place."
For meta.
Physics, and for.
Meta.
Physical thin.
Kin.
G, and.
For abstract.
Thinking, or
For feeling?
Or, for.
Feelings, or sentiments, or.
"Or?"
For metaphysical.
Thinking, and.

"As much as?"
Is there.
And?
"As much as."
Is here.
A time.
And?
"A spot, and."
A place.
"For."
Abstract thinking, and.
"For."
Abstract thought, and.
As much as?
"Of course, also."
Is here.
"And, is there?"
And, is there.
"And, is here."
A spot, a time, and a place.
"For thinking."
Or for con.
Temp.
La.
Ting, or.
"For considering?"
Big, great, grand things, or ideas, as.
Well as, is.
"A time."
A spot, and.
"A place, or."
A spot, or.
A time for.
Fo.
Cu.
Sing, and.
For the de.

Tails, and?
"For con."
Cent.
Rating, on.
How to make happen?
The here, and the now, and.
Such great, and.
Such grand id.
Eas, be.
Cause.
"What is, or be."
Cause.
What might, or what can.
"Be the grandness, or what could, or what might, be."
The great.
Ness, of.
"What are what."
Cannot be implemented, or.
"If great, or grand, ideas, can."
Not be made to work, or.
Depending?
"On what is just."
Or, on what.
Or, on whom?
"Is un."
Justly?
Right here, before me.
Or?
"And, be."
Cause.
Of course?
Is, al.
So.
"A time."
And, a place.
"For great."
And, for grand.

"Ide."
As, as.
Wells, as is.
"A place, and a time, for."
The de.
Tails, too.
"And?"
Even if.
"Of course?"
What id.
I.
Ot, fo.
Ol, mor.
On, or chump.
Too good?
"For her."
For his.
"For its?"
Or, for the.
Ir, hi.
S, he.
R, or its.
Own good.
"Does not know?"
That, but.
"Of course."
Is the de.
Vil.
"In the de."
Tails, though.
And, so?
"Of course."
Who would voluntarily, so choose.
"To be?"
One of those, or.
One of these dev.
Ils, or.

The dev.
Or, the Dev?
Il?
"Him, or."
Her.
Or, it.
Self, though.
Too, of course.
Un.
Less she, he, or it.
"What, or."
Is made to be, or?
Who, or.
"Who, or."
What, is.
"Not a."
Or the?
"Devil, to one."
But?
"A god."
Or, God?
"Or, the God?"
Or the, or a, god.
Dess, or God.
Dess, or.
Godness.
To another, and.
"Or?"
Too, of course.
"What id."
Io.
T fool, moron.
"Ape, chump, or monkey."
Does not know?
"To his."
To her.
"To its?"

Or, to their.
"Own great."
Or, to?
"Their, his, her, or its."
Own grand.
"Demise?"
That, but.
"Of course."
Is an ide.
A on.
Ly as good.
"As great?"
Or, as grand
"As its pos."
Sib.
Le im.
Ple.
Men.
Tat.
Ion, and.
Of course, without the, or a.
Will, or with.
Out one, two, or more.
"The most, or?"
The many, willing.
"Is no way, and."
So.
Of course?
What good.
"Or, how true?"
Or, how True.
Or, how real.
Or, how Real.
Are pro.
Mises, as long as.
"And in so far as?"
They do re.

Main, or stay.
Promises, and.
Or as long, or.
In so far, as.
They can.
Not be im.
Ple.
Men.
Ted, or.
"But, of course."
All of which.
"Is far from my con."
Cern, now.
And, here?
"Or here."
And now, because.
When, and where.
"And, be."
Cause.
Where, and when.
"Are not my hands ra."
Is.
Ed, here.
Before me.
"Now."
In this sky.
"But, rat."
Her.
What are.
None, and.
Nevertheless.
"Here, in."
This house.
Ran.
Dom, or.
And, here in.
This House?

"Or, herein."
This house?
Random, or.
"Otherwise, or."
This, which is.
"More like air."
Than like sky, and.
"Or, which?"
Al.
So, is.
"A bit?"
Or, more than.
"A bit."
More air than sky, and.
"So, which?"
And, so.
"What hands."
Are, al.
So.
Beneath this ceiling.
Which is.
"More like a ceiling, than."
Like a roof, and.
Which hands, are.
"Also, and, too."
Beneath my ceiling?
And, be.
Neath yours, and.
"Or."
Where, beneath the ceiling.
Do eyes, as.
And not I's, as?
Knots of wood, un.
Seeing.
And not, as in: an eye for an eye.
Or, where knots of wood.
And not, as in: an I for an I.

Or?
"And."
Where.
On the planks above me.
Of course.
Only an I for an I, can be.
And.
Where are.
Knots, and.
Where are.
"Not not's."
Of course.
Or, where.
"Are called?"
Or where.
"Are so-called."
Eyes, which.
"Of course."
Are not.
"To be."
Con.
Fused with.
"I's, though."
Of course.
"Do, or."
Might they.
"Both sound."
Alike, or.
"The same."
Are they.
"Of course?"
Not quite.
"Or, are."
They, too.
"And, also?"
Not the same, or the Sam?
E be.

Cause.
Of course.
Are not.
"Things that are."
Or, things?
"Or, words."
Or, names.
"That do."
Sound sim.
Ilar.
"Not necessarily the same, and."
Or the Same, and.
Because, of course.
"Is a huge."
Big, great.
Or, grand.
"Dif."
Fe.
Ren.
Ce, be.
Tween.
What, and.
"Between whom."
Or, bet.
We.
En who.
Ms.
Are similar.
"And, between."
Who, and.
Or, bet.
We.
En.
What, and who, are the same, and.
"Be."
Tween.
"What are."

Me.
Rely a.
Like, and.
"Because?"
Though might.
Words, or.
Though might lan.
Guage, and though.
"Might some words."
Which, how.
Ever.
"Of course."
Are not the Word.
Or, which.
"Of course."
Are not whose.
"What, or."
Which Word, or words.
If not the word, or the Word.
Clar.
If.
Y so.
Me things.
And?
Though, too.
"And, also?"
On occasion.
Might some words be necessary.
Even if might, or might not, the Word, or His?
Word be, or yours, be.
Because, of course.
What civil.
Iz.
At.
Ion.
Or, whose?
And, too, be.

Cause.
Of course.
What, or.
"Whose?"
So.
Cie.
Ty, can.
Or could, or.
What might be?
With.
Out words, and.
Without language, and.
"Without lan."
Guage, and.
Without words, and.
Too, because.
"Of course."
Even if.
Names are not, nor.
Is lan.
Guage, as.
"Words are not."
Just, or.
Necessary to call things.
Only, or.
"Or, to call people?"
Be.
Cause, of.
Course, they are.
Me.
Rely, and.
On.
Ly words, and.
Because, of course.
People, and things.
Are, re.
Gard.

Less of the.
Ir na.
Me.
S, which do not ei.
The.
R make, or bre.
Ak the.
M, and.
Be.
Cause, of.
Course.
Words are not necessary to make things, as.
They are not, be.
Cause, of course, words do not make, or un.
Make people, things, worlds, or possibilities, or.
Do they, or can they.
Change, make, break, create, or destroy.
Reality, or realities, or?
"Beca."
Use, too.
Not all words do.
"Of course?"
And.
Are not words.
And, or.
Names.
Mastery over people, over things, over chaos, over the void, and.
Over the abyss, and.
"Don't they?"
Make for a lan.
Guage, and.
"Too, be."
Cause?
"Be."
Cause.
Of course.
Do not all words.

Belong in, or to?
A language, and.
Or.
Because is not the Word.
Necessarily about words.
Or about language either, and.
"Even if?"
No moron, idiot.
"Fool, or ot."
Her.
Wise, of course.
"But, who."
And, of course.
"But, what."
Or, which.
I am not?
Does not know.
"That, but."
Of course.
Is the word.
"Or that."
Is the Word?
"Or, that."
"Is whose Word."
Or, that.
Which Word.
"Or, that."
Whose words.
"Or, that."
Whose words, and which Word?
"Or."
That are the words.
Not the thing.
And not a thing, and.
Of course.
"Are they, al."
So, not.

The Thing, and.
Whose, or what, or which thin.
G, or Thing, or.
"Are they, also, not."
The thing, and.
"Too, of."
Course.
Would only a fool.
"Id."
I.
Ot, or.
Moron, confuse.
Or, conflate?
The words.
Or, the Word?
With the concept.
"Or, with the Con."
Cept.
Or, with which Con.
Cept, or with which con.
Cept, or with the ide.
A, or with which id.
Ea, or with whose Ide.
A, or.
"With the Ide?"
A, and, too.
Of course.
"Quite so similarly."
"Would on."
Ly.
Would just?
Or, would un.
Justly.
Or, would me.
Rely?
"A fool."
Id.

Io.
T, or mor.
On con.
Fuse.
The Ide.
A, or the idea, or.
"The id."
Eas, with the con.
Cep.
Ts, or.
With the Con.
Cep.
T, "Or with the con."
Cep.
T, *or.*
What is precisely.
"Exactly, the."
Difference, between?
"The idea."
And be.
Tween?
The con.
Cept, or.
"Between?"
The Idea.
"And, the idea?"
Or, between
"The con."
Cept.
And the Con.
Cept, or.
"Between?"
Whose, what's, or which.
Concepts, concept, Concept, Idea, idea, or ideas, or.
The Idea, and.
"An idea, or."
Between?

"A concept, and."
A Concept, or.
"Between?"
A concept.
"And an idea, or."
Between.
"The Idea, and."
The Concept, or.
"Between?"
An idea.
"And the Concept, or."
Between.
"A concept, and."
The Idea, or?
"Is the more."
Im.
Por.
Tant, or.
"Is the most?"
Essential difference.
"Between?"
The thing.
"And, the concept."
And, between
"The idea."
Is the point, that.
And the thing, or.
What must fol.
"Most es."
Low, logi.
Senti.
Cally, of course, is that what.
Ally, be?
Or, is that, or is this, who.
Cause, of co.
Or Who, or What.
Ur.

Or What, or Who.
Se, is.
Does not change.
"What is es."
Ab.
Sent.
Out a per.
"Ia."
Son, ab.
L, what.
Out a con.
Does not change, and.
Cept, or.
"Because."
About an idea, is?
Words are.
Or ab.
Not ei.
Out the Ide.
The.
A, is?
R the.
What is who, or.
"Con."
Who is what, or What.
Cept.
Is most es.
The idea.
Sent.
"The thing."
Ia.
The things, or.
L, or most fun.
"The ideas, or."
Da.
The con.
Mental, and.

Cepts, them.
Selves, but?
"Of course."
How ea.
Sily.
"And most sim."
Ply?
Might one get lost.
"In the thin."
Kin.
G, or in.
The words?
"Or in the lan."
Guage, ass.
Um.
Ing that words?
"Are the things."
Or, that.
They are.
The idea, or.
That they are.
The Idea, or.
"That they are the concept, or?"
That they are.
"The Concept?"
Or, that might they.
"Truly, really, or."
Actually create, or.
"Make?"
Worlds of their own, or.
That might they, that can they, or that do they, ou.
Gh.
T, or should they?
Break, or destroy, worlds, too.
If so only in order to make space to create new ones, and, or.
"Too, how."
So easily.

"Might one."
Or, might more, or.
"Might the most?"
Or, might the many.
Or might all, or might the all.
Or, the All.
"Quite so easily?"
Forget that.
"Words are."
Merely, just.
"Or, only?"
Representations of reality, and.
So, rather, instead.
Might they, *as in, peo.*
Ple, or.
The Peo.
Ple, or.
As in.
Every.
One, or.
As in.
Ever.
Y.
Body, be.
Gin to re.
Member, that.
"Also?"
Might words create.
"Idea."
Lit.
Ies.
"Heavens, or hells."
Or real.
It.
Ies, or.
Hells, or heavens.
U.

Topias, or dys.
Top.
Ia.
S, or.
So, also.
Might, can, or do.
Words, also, destroy would-be heavens, and hells, too, as well.
As perfections, or.
"Imperfections, or."
Suit.
Abilities, and, or, un.
"Suit."
Abilities, non.
Suit.
Abilities, or.
Flaws, or.
"Un-flaws, fa."
Ults, non-fa.
Ults, or.
Un-fa.
Ul.
Ts, or.
Utopias, or.
Practicalities, or.
"Impracticalities, or."
Ulti.
Mates, or.
"Non-ulti."
Mates, or pen.
Ult.
I.
Mates, or un.
Ulti.
Mates, or.
Su.
Prem.
It.

Ies, or.
Absolutes, or.
Ex.
Trem.
E.
Ties, or.
"In."
Ab.
So.
Lutes, or.
Less than ab.
Solutes, or.
Un-, or non-.
Absolutes, or.
Realities, perfect.
"Imperfect."
Happy, or.
"Hellish, pleasant."
Painful, or.
"Miserable, sensible."
Insensible, illogical.
"Or logical."
Rea.
Son.
Able, rat.
Io.
Nal, "Or?"
Ir.
Rational, or un.
Reasonable worlds, or.
"Universes."
Pure, or.
"Impure, or."
Mostly, or.
"Leastly, or."
Slightly less than pure, or.
"Universes, worlds."

Hells, or.
"Heavens, u."
To.
"Pias."
Or dys.
Topias.
In which.
"One, or."
More, or.
"In which."
The many, or.
"In which."
The most.
Or, in which.
The all.
"Might, also."
Get lost, too.
Or.
"Are not words."
Reality it.
Self, as well as.
"Are they."
Also, no.
Thing more, or less, than.
A sign of be.
Ing, or of Be.
Ing, or, of.
Course, of.
The Thing?
Or, of.
The idea, or.
Of the Idea, or?
Even of a thing, or of.
An idea, or.
That, also.
"Of course."
Not to forget.

That, also.
They are not.
"The Word, either."
Or.
Any more, or any less?
"Than they are."
The spaces in between the.
M, ei.
The.
R, of.
Course, though.
"Without which?"
Spaces.
Of course.
Would, and could, the words.
Not make much sense.
But which those who are in too much of a rush, or a hurry, to fill.
Do not quite get.
As, also, they do not quite get.
That the space, or that the spaces, so essential, are the air.
Into which the spirit does, and must, escape, and which.
Is the space, and which are.
The spaces.
Not me.
Ant, or in.
Tended to be filled, or.
They are.
But me.
"Not quite."
Ant, or in?
Me.
Ten.
Ant to be fil.
Ded by w.
Led with, or by.
Hat, by who.
What, or by.

M, or by Who.
Or with, whom.
M, or.
Or with, or by, what.
Or What.
One is not, or.
By what, or by whom, I do not per.
Mit, or.
By whom, or by what, is dark.
Or by, or with.
The wrong kind of light, or qui.
*Te so very ironically without what, without which, or without whom,
such things.*
Such objects, such forms, such posi.
Tiv.
Ists, and, or.
Such mater.
Ia.
Lists, or such words?
Could not do, and.
Would not be, and.
Would not make any sense, or.
"And?"
Though, too, quite so very ironically.
Were, and are?
Such spaces exactly, and.
Precisely, those which he.
And, those which they?
And, those which you.
Did, and do, so need.
"And, do so rely on?"
Without quite knowing, realizing, and without quite getting.
It, or the.
M, as we.
Ll as were they the ones that he, and that they.
And, that you.
Did, *and do.*

Rely on, but.
Who he, *and who you,* also.
Did, *and do.*
Not quite have the time, or the patience for, but.
"But?"

*   *   *   *   *

Of course, he was.
"And, I am."
Not one like that, or one like the.
M, and, so.
"And, so?"
If had he been up, off his back, and if had he al.
Ready?
Been out of his bed.
Or if, already, you had been up, and out, of our bed, and.
"And?"
If, already.
He had been.
"Out of my bed."
Might have he have knelt on one knee, to.
"And?"
In or.
Der, to?
Genu.
Flec.
T, to?
"That Other."
Or, to?
This other?
Or, to.
"This Other?"
Or, to.
That, higher.
Or, to this higher?
So, called?

"Or to that, Highest."
Or to this, Highest.
Or?
To the other, Other, higher, or to the high.
Est, or.
To whom.
Or?
To what.
Might, or.
"Might not be?"
Or, Be.
"Or at the mention of the name."
Or, Be?
Or, at?
The mention of whose, which, or what name, or.
Names, or.
At the thought, of?
"Or."
Or?
"At the men."
Tio.
N, or thou.
Gh.
T, of?
That, or.
"Of t."
His most?
Sac.
Red, high.
Est.
Or to yours, or.
"And ho."
Ly, or?
To your idea, of.
At the thought, or at.
"The mention, of."
The Word.

Or at the mention, of?
"Which, what, or."
Whose Word, or whose, which, or what words, or na.
Me.
S, if.
"What is, and if what are."
Not necessarily.
The Word.
But, because.
As yet?
"I am not ready."
And, because.
"As yet?"
I am not ready.
To get up off my back, or.
"Ready?"
To get up off his back, or.
"Ready?"
To sit up, or.
"Ready?"
To stand, or.
"Ready?"
To genuflect, or.
"Ready?"
To bow, or.
Ready?
"To kneel."
Or?
"Re."
Ady to wor.
Ship.
Any.
One, or.
Any.
Body, every.
One, or every.
Body, or.

Ever.
Y.
Thing, any.
One.
Anybody, or someone.
Or, somebody.
Other than my.
Self, or.
Other than himself.
Or, other than yourself.
And, so?
Rather, he did.
"And, rather, did I."
And, rather, did you, an.
D, rat.
Her, he did.
Continue on, lying.
"On his back, and."
If not staring, at least.
"Looking up?"
At the ceiling, and.
Without looking down, too.
"He did."
Or.
"I did."
And.
Did he.
"And, did I."
Pick up, and.
"Kiss."
The gold, or sil?
Ver, but.
Ver, was it.
If gold.
Is it, or.
Of co.
Will it.

Ur.
Ever.
Se, mu.
And al.
St it go.
Ways, be?
But go w.
Or, rat.
Her.
Her, per.
E.
Haps?
A bit of both, sil.
Ver, and gold.
Cross, *or cre?*
Scent, that from a chain, was.
Or, is it a s.
That you willl never show, or.
Tar, or S.
But why, of.
Tar, or some.
Course, hide.
Thin.
What, from whom, and.
G el.
Be.
Se al.
Cause, of.
To.
Course, do not.
Get.
Sec.
Her, or en.
Rets make you sick, or.
Tire.
Are so.
Ly, or.

Me en.
If a s.
Tit.
Tar, a.
Which does elevate me, and.
Led to so.
Five, or.
Which does make me bet.
Me sec.
A six-poin.
Ter, above, and set apart, from.
Ret.
Te.
All of the rest of them, and.
S, and, or.
D, one.
"To so."
Me *pri.*
If so, to?
Vacy, whi.
Ch one.
S, and.
And is, as it al.
As in, or l.
Ways has been.
Ike.
And as it al.
A cres.
Cent, or.
Ways, and as.
If was, or if is.
It ever, will be?
It a cross, at all, or?
If eve.
R has it be.
En, and if.
Ever will it be, but?

If it is not a cross, cir.
Cle, or squ?
Are might it be, has it be.
En, or?
Ever will it be, sac.
Red, or holy, or not.
And, or.
To, or for who.
M, and?
Or for, or to w.
Hat, and?
Ever, or al.
Ways, or?
Per.
Haps, more.
Im.
Port.
Ant.
Ly, what does it me.
An, or re.
Pre.
Sent, to who?
M, or to w.
Hat, and.
Still, and.
If a sym.
Bol, of w.
Hat?
Or if, per.
Hap.
S, a pe?
Arl, or pe.
Arls, or me.
Rely a cir.
Cle, or squ.
Are, or?
If really, truly, and actually, is.

Or, is it not his.
But mine, and.
And, mine?
A gold cross.
Silver, but not for.
Second, of course, and.
If a cross, a cir.
Cle, squ.
Are, or pen.
But not the cross, of cour.
Se.
Dan.
As in.
T, an.
The only one, or.
D not on.
As in.
Ly, ju.
The most im.
St, or me.
Port.
Rely a neck.
Ant one.
Lace, but, rat?
Hang.
Her a ring.
Ing a.
And if a ring, on.
Round his neck.
What fin.
As was it us?
Ger, w.
U.
Or.
All?
N, and a.
Y.

Dia.
And.
Mond, ru.
As it was, al.
By, or em.
Ways.
Er.
Or.
Ald, or?
"Or?"
Perhaps, a square.
At least?
Black, of course.
Or?
And, as it is.
"And, as it has been, for."
As long as?
"I can, or."
For as long as?
He did.
Care to.
"Remember, or."
At least?
"In so far, as?"
He, "I," *or you.*
Did, or do, care to remember.
"That, or."
This, or.
"This, or."
That is.
Or, rather.
How.
So.
Ever long you have to, or must, or.
Rather than.
"As he would have?"
But, who is he.

Or, rather than.
"As I would have?"
If had it been later, or.
"If had I, or."
If I had been one willing, or one wanting.
To?
"Wake, and sit up."
Right away, as.
"If in a rush, or."
As if.
"In a hurry, or."
As if.
"Having been?"
Jump started, or.
"As if?"
Having been wakened, by.
"Another, or."
By any, or by all, others?
"For some point, or."
For some purpose?
"Other than my own, or."
Either, before.
"Later, or."
After, or.
"Either too soon."
Or too late, or.
Too early, or too late.
For what though, or.
Than I would.
Or, than you would, or.
Who gets to say, choose, or decide.
Too late, or too early.
For what, or.
"Or than I would?"
Or than he would.
Wake, or.
"Than he would have wakened."

Himself, and.
"And?"
Or, than I would have, if.
I was waking, only.
Just, or only.
For me, but.
"Or, if I were only waking."
Alone, or.
"Even if?"
This morning, I was.
Ready, or.
"Willing, or."
Even if?
This morning I was.
Or, you were.
"Willing, or."
Ready with.
Or, by?
"A hop, leap, and a jump."
To get up?
"And, or."
To get out of bed, right away.
"Or?"
Even if I were in a rush, or in a hurry.
"Would I?"
"And, would he."
"And, I would."
Not necessarily.
Do so.
"In or."
Der, to?
Right away, or.
"In order, to?"
Most immediately.
Genuflect, to.
Some altar?
Or, to some.

"God, or."
To some gods, or.
"To some god."
Dess, or.
To so.
Me God.
Dess, un.
Seen, but not un.
Seeing, and.
But, not necessarily?
To one.
Merely, mir.
Ror-ly.
"Just, unjustly."
Or?
"Only."
Imagined, but.
Of course?
Or only created, or known.
Only by you, or.
"To one."
Unseen, because.
"Of course?"
I am not one.
"To bow, or."
One to try to wor.
Ship?
"Idols, or."
Any objects, or.
"Any other beings, as?"
Gods, or.
Of course.
"As goddesses, but."
Of course.
"Because."
He was.
"And, because."

I am.
"Still, and."
As yet.
Not up?
"So could."
And, so I cannot.
Now, quite.
"Kneel, or."
Genu.
Flect, and.
Because.
"As yet?"
And because, still.
He, or.
"I was."
And, be.
And, still am.
Cause.
As yet?
"And am, still."
Taking his time.
Or, taking your time.
Waking, and rising.
If is not one time, or.
"And, taking my time."
Because, of course.
He was.
"And be."
Ca.
Use I am.
Or, because.
"Of course."
I am.
"And, am I."
And, because, you are.
"I am."
Not one.

To rush.
"Or, one."
To be hurried.
"Or, one."
To be hurried.
"Or, one."
To be rushed.
By anyone, by someone, by no one, by nobody, by everyone, or by everybody, else.
"With a plan, with an agenda, with a point, with a purpose, or with a mission, for me."
And, because, he, also, was.
Not one.
"To be."
Wakened, rushed.
"Or, one to be."
Hurried, by.
The most, or.
"By the man."
Y, or by.
The all, so?
Eager to use.
Or, by.
"The many, most."
The all, or.
"By everybody, or?"
By everyone, or.
By anyone, far.
"Too eager, to?"
Pos.
Sess, to use.
And, to ab.
Use me, and.
"Because."
Of course.
"I am not here."
Or, there.

"And because I am not there."
Or, here.
"Or, here."
Or, there.
"To be used as a tool."
Or, as.
A means to some end.
Other than my own, of course.
"And, so."
As he.
"And, as I."
And as you do, and.
"As do you."
You?
Still lie in his own.
"And, in my own."
And, in your own.
Bed.
Or, in ours?
For then, and.
At least?
"For there, and."
At least?
"For here."
And?
"At least?"
For now, and.
"For as long?"
As will I.
"And?"
For as long as.
"I do."
Want, or.
"Wish to?"
Because, of.
"Course, and."
Even if.

Of course.
"I do not owe anyone."
Or, everyone.
Everybody.
"Or someone, or no one."
Or no.
Body, or so.
Me.
Body.
Or, any.
Body, or every.
Body.
"Anything, or?"
An ex.
Plan.
At.
Ion, or.
A just.
If.
I.
Cat.
Ion.
For myself.
Or, for yourself.
For living, or for being, *be.*
Cause, of course.
Life does not need to explain, or justify.
It.
Self, or.
If it does, to whom must it, or.
Why, and how, can it, or.
"And, so?"
I will lie, as.
"Long as."
I do want, and.
"As long as."
I do wish to.

And?
"Because."
He was.
"And, because?"
I am.
As yet.
Still waking.
And, or?
"Because, I am."
And, because?
He was still.
And, as.
"Yet, in."
The process, of.
Waking, and.
"Because."
Of course.
He was not interested in.
Being rushed or in being.
Hur.
Rie.
D, or.
In being.
Hurried, or rushed.
Or, in.
Being waked, a.
Wakened, or.
Woke.
Ned, and?
Or, in being woke, or?
In being awakened?
By anyone, by.
"Anybody, by."
Everyone, or.
"By everybody, or."
By nobody, or.
"By no one, or."

By some.
Body, or.
"By someone."
Be.
Fore I am re.
Ad.
Y.
"To wake, and."
Or, be.
Fore.
"I am ready."
To be awakened, because.
"Of course?"
I am not one.
"Wanting, willing, or one."
Wishing.
To be used.
To, or for, so.
Me point, or.
For, or to.
Some pur.
Pose.
"Ot."
Her than my own, or.
Other than his own.
Or, other than my own, but.
"Or, other than my own, but."
And?
As I have said.
"Or?"
As I have written.
"Or?"
As has been written.
"Or?"
Written by what, or by whom, or.
As I have thought, before.
Or thought by whom, or by what.

"Because?"
Or by What, or by Whom.
Of course, is not what is said.
Or, what you say.
"Or, what I say."
Or, what is thought?
Or, what you think.
"Or, what I think."
Or, what you write.
Necessarily what is written.
Or, what you have writ.
Ten, or.
The same, or the Same, as.
What I do write, or.
"And, because."
Of course.
What is writ.
Ten.
Ex.
Cept, by whom.
And, where?
Or, when?
Is not necessarily what is said.
Or, what you say.
Or, rather?
And, too.
"Because, of course."
What is thought, is.
But thought by whom.
Not necessarily.
Or, by what.
Or, by What, or.
By Whom, or.
"What is said."
By whom, or by what.
And, too?
"Because, of course."

What one thinks, or.
"What one does think."
Or, what you do think.
Or what all do think, or what.
Do all, or what All, every.
One, or every.
Body does, or.
Is not necessarily.
Or, suf.
Fi.
Ci.
Ent.
Ly?
"What one says."
Or, what you do say, or what.
Every.
One, or what eve.
Rybo.
Dy, or what all, or All, *do, or.*
What one writes.
Or what one does, and.
Or, what which one, or One, does, and.
Because?
"And, too?"
Because, of course.
"Might some."
Do without thinking, first.
And, too?
Because.
"Because."
Of course.
Might some others, also.
"Say?"
Or, do.
"Without, first, thinking."
And, though.
Too?

Of course.
"Might others say."
Or, might Others.
Or, just say?
Or, might some ot.
Or, unjustly say.
Hers, or so.
"Or do, and."
Me Ot.
Apparently?
Hers, or.
Or.
"Most simply, and."
Or.
Apparently?
"Most easily."
Without thinking, first.
Or?
"Without, first, thinking, but."
"Because?"
Of course.
"I am no fool."
And, because.
Often what is said is less im.
And, because.
Port.
"I am not a f."
Ant, than.
O.
Who does get to say it.
Ol, ex.
Or, than who is list.
Cept that you are.
En.
And, be.
Ing, or than who, Who, w.
Cause.

Hat, or What, is he.
Of course.
Aring, or.
"I am nobody's fool."
And, because.
Of course.
"I am not everybody's, or anybody's."
Fool, too.
And, because.
"Of course."
I, also, am not one willing?
"To be."
Or one willing to be?
"Made to be."
Such a, or.
"Anyone's, everyone's, no one's, someone's, or."
Somebody's, or.
"Nobody's, or."
Because, of course.
"Also, is."
Nobody, a.
"Someone, too."
As much as?
"Is, or."
Might, or.
"Might not?"
E.
Very.
One, or.
Eve.
Ryb.
O.
Dy, be.
"Too, and?"
Or.
Everybody's, or.
"Anybody's, or."

My own fool.
And, too, because.
"Too, and?"
Because, also?
You are not one.
"And, too."
Be.
Cause, of?
Course.
"Also, am I not one to go, or."
One willing to re.
Peat my.
Self, ti.
Me and a.
Gain, or.
Sim.
Ply.
Or, not.
Be.
Cause they were not list.
En.
Ing, or.
One to rush a.
Ro.
Und do.
Ing.
Or sa.
Ying, without.
First thinking.
Too, and.
"As much?"
As, also.
Am not I one.
"To say, or."
One to do, or?
One.
"To think?"

Anything I do not mean, or.
"As much as, al."
So.
I am not one.
Not to.
"Or one?"
To fail to say what I do mean, though.
"Of course?"
Even if, most ideally.
And, though.
Of course?
Only in a.
Or, only in the.
Or, only in whose?
Which, or what.
Ideal world.
Heaven, or uni.
Verse.
Universe, or he.
Aven.
U.
Top.
Ia, or para.
Dise.
"Which?"
Of course.
"By de."
Fin.
It.
Ion.
Is not.
"The real?"
One, or.
"The Real?"
World, *or.*
Can one.
Or, does one.

Get to say ex.
Act.
Ly.
"And, or."
Precisely, what.
"One does want, or pre.
Cise.
Ly, or ex.
Act.
Ly.
"What one does need to say."
When, and where.
Or where, or when.
"And where, and when."
Or where, and when.
Or, to whom?
Or, to what, or.
One does need, or.
To What, or to Whom.
Or.
When, and where.
Where, and when.
And, to whom, and, or.
To what, to What.
And, to Whom.
One does want to, and.
Because, of course.
"Because, of."
Needs are not ever, ne.
Course, must, at times?
Ce.
One be.
S.
At le.
Sar.
As.
Il.

T, a bit.
Ly w.
Dis.
Ants, too.
Creet, or.
If not, al.
So.
Necessarily dis.
Crete, too.
And.
"A bit?"
Because, too, are not, ne.
Sub.
Cessarily w.
Tle, or.
Ants, ne.
"A bit?"
Eds, too, or.
Re.
Strained, which.
"Does, also, mean?"
That, too.
"Quite so very."
Often, must one.
Quite so?
"Wisely, and."
Quite so prac.
Tic.
Ally, and.
"Quite so prag."
Mati.
Call.
Y, and.
Quite so far more far.
"Sigh."
Ted.
Ly, than near.

Sight.
Ed.
Ly, and.
"Quite so judi."
Ci.
Ou.
Sly?
Be.
"A bit less than most hon."
Est, in order to be?
"More, or."
Most kind, or.
"In or."
Der to be?
Nice, or.
In order to be?
Kind, or.
"More, or."
Most pru.
Dent, or, and, too?
Similarly, though, too.
"Which, and."
Of course.
Is not the same as the Same.
Or the Same as the same, as well, as.
"Of course."
Is not the Same the Same as the same, or as the Same, or.
The same as the Same.
Or, the Same as the same.
"Or, the same as the Same."
Or, but.
"Be."
Cause, but.
"Too, like?"
Wise, must one.
"Of."
Ten, al.

So, be?
A bit less than most honest.
In order to be?
Kind, or?
"In order to be."
A bit.
More, or most?
"Judicious, or?"
In or.
Der to be.
"A bit more pru."
Dent, or.
Nice, or.
In order to be?
"A bit w."
Is.
Er, or?
In order to be.
A bit shrew.
Der, or?
"Even though?"
Per.
Haps, or even though.
More than?
"In some idea."
L world, or uni.
Verse, or, and.
"Even though?"
In.
Some per.
Fect para.
Dis.
E, or u?
To.
Pia, or?
"Even if."
And, even though.

"In some."
Perfect.
Dream world.
"Which does not exist."
Of course.
And which, of course.
"Is not real, or Real, by."
Def.
In.
It.
Ion, of.
Course.
Can, and would, one, al.
Ways and eve.
R, be?
"Able to be."
Both most honest, and most kind.
"As well as."
Most prudent, and.
"As well as?"
Most judi.
Ci.
Ou.
S, and.
"As well as?"
Most practical, and.
"As well as?"
Most reasonable, and.
"As well as?"
Most prag.
Mat.
Ic, and.
"As well as?"
Most rat.
Ion.
Al, and.
"As well as?"

Most real.
Is.
Tic, and.
"As well as?"
Most sensi.
Ble, and.
"As well as?"
Most true, and.
"As well as?"
Most real, and.
"As well as?"
Most sin.
Cere, and.
"As well as?"
Most genu.
U.
In.
E.
"All at once."
And, all.
At, and.
"All in?"
The same time, or.
Times.
And?
Also, and, too.
"As well as?"
The most ideal?
Or, though.
"But, though?"
Or, the most sur.
Real, or?
"Of course."
And, too?
Real, or ideal.
"Ideal, or real."
Or, surreal?

"Or, perfect?"
To, or for.
Or, for.
Or, to whom, and.
"Or, rat."
Her? Of.
Course.
Most real, and most true.
"Or?"
More, or most.
Kind, or.
Most, or.
"More honest."
Sincere, au.
Then.
Tic, or gen.
Ui.
Ne?
Or more, or less.
Or less, or more?
"Real, or ideal."
Or less, or more?
Ideal, or real.
Per.
Fect, or im.
Perfect heaven, or.
"Hellish."
For, or to, whom, or.
"Or to, or for, whom, or."
But, and.
As I have said, or.
"And, as I have thought."
Again and a.
Gain.
So, too?
Or.
More of the same.

"Or?"
More of the Same.
"Or?"
More of the same, of.
"What, or?"
Of which.
Or?
"According to whose."
Same, sam.
E, or id.
Ea of the same, or of the Same, or.
So, again, and, again?
"Or."
And, too?
"But, of course."
Or, according to what, which.
Or, whose.
Or, Whose.
"Stand."
Ards, and mea.
Sur.
Es, or.
"According to what?"
Or, according to whose.
Or, Whose.
"Me."
As.
Ures, and stand.
Ards, or?
Per.
Fect, or im.
Per.
Fect.
"In whose heaven."
Ideal, or real, or.
In whose hell, or.
Honest, and kind, or.

"In whose paradise?"
True, and genuine.
Or, in whose utopia.
Genuine, and authentic.
"Or, in whose dystopia."
Or?
Because, of course.
"Is not heaven to, or for, one."
Hell for others.
And, too?
"Of course."
Is not.
"Hell for some."
Heaven for any, or for?
All others, and.
Because, also.
"Too, might?"
Heaven be.
"For the most, or for the many."
Hell for one, or for some.
And, too.
Because?
Of course.
Cannot one's, his, her, its, yours, or their.
Idea of heaven be imposed, on.
"Any, or."
On all others, or?
"Of course, when, and where."
Where, and when.
It is.
So imposed, or.
"It does cease to be."
So invaded, it does cease to be.
Heaven, and be?
Come hell, and.
"Is not hell for some."
Or, for one?

Or, for One.
"Heaven for the most, or for the many."
But?
And, be.
Cause, "But, any."
Way.
Though, and.
"Because, of course?"
Not every way, but.
Because, I am.
"Not in."
Te.
Rest.
Ed in being ru.
Shed, or.
In being hurried.
"As I am waking."
Or, as you are.
"Or, as I am, or."
And, be.
Cause?
"Of course."
I, also, am not.
And, because, you are not.
"Interested in being?"
Waked, or.
Woken, or.
Wakened, and.
Or woke, and?
Or.
"In being?"
Awakened, as.
I am waking, or.
As you are, or.
As he was waking.
And, so.
"And, so?"

Did he keep, on.
And, so you did.
"And, so did I."
And so did you.
Continue, on.
If not, necessarily, forward.
Or, backward?
Or, forwards.
Or, backwards?
Lying on his back.
And, on yours.
"Staring, and watching?"
And, of course.
"Not on mine."
Watching, and.
"Sta."
Ring, and.
Looking.
Up at the ceiling, or.
"Up at my ceiling."
Or, up at your ceiling.
Where did the eyes.
Or, where the eyes, do.
And where do not the I's, of.
Course.
"And, where do the knots."
And, where the knots, do.
And, not the nots.
"Of wood."
On the ceiling, above me.
"Not see me back."
Of course.
Because?
"Of course."
They are not eyes.
Like that, or.
"Like this."

For seeing.
And, "Be."
Cause.
Of course.
"They are."
Not eyes like that.
Or, like this?
"Or I's like that."
Or like this.
And, too.
"Because, also."
They are not eyes for seeing.
Though, of.
"Course, for."
Seeing what, or.
"For seeing whom."
Or?
"And, even if?"
Of course.
"Is not seeing necessarily watching."
As much as.
"Is not necessarily."
Watching, seeing.
And?
"As much as?"
Not necessarily is to be seen.
"To see."
And?
As much as.
Not necessarily.
"Is not watching to be watched."
And, as?
Much as.
Is not, necessarily, to watch to be wat.
Ched, and.
As much as.
"Not necessarily."

Is to be watched.
"To watch?"
And, as much as.
"Not necessarily."
Is to watch, to see, or.
Is to see, to watch, or.
As much as, is.
To see.
"To be seen?"
Because.
Some do watch with.
Out seeing, while some can see with.
Out watching, while.
Still others can see without being seen, and.
While others can be seen without being seen.
And while others can be seen without seeing, and.
"Be."
Cause, of.
Course.
Can some see more.
Longer, or.
Further.
"Than others."
And, because.
"Of course."
Can some see, and.
"Because, too."
Some can see further.
"Or, better."
Or, past.
"And be."
Yond the simple, and the obvious, and be.
Yon.
D, and past.
What is right.
Or be.
Yond, "And past."

What is just.
"Or past?"
And, beyond.
What, or.
"Who is."
Un.
Justly?
Before them.
Or, be.
Fore.
Her, or.
Before him, or.
"Before it."
And.
Too, be.
Cause.
Who does not see.
"What will they."
Or, what they will, and.
"Or?"
What will she, or.
"What will he, or."
What she will, or?
What he will, or?
What you will, or.
And, not what, and not whom.
Or, Whom.
It, she, he, or they.
Will not, and.
"Too, be."
Cause?
Who does rather see?
Just, or.
"Unjustly?"
Merely, mirr.
Or-ly.
"Or, only?"

What will they, or.
What they will, or.
What she will, or.
What he will, or.
"What will it, or?"
Just, or.
Unjustly, or.
"Merely, or."
Mirror-ly, or.
"Only?"
What does she.
"He, it."
Or they, *or you,* choose.
"To, and?"
So, of.
Course.
"Not what."
And?
"Not whom."
They, *she,* he, it, or you choose, or decide, not to, and.
"So, be."
Cause, of course.
"Can some."
Or?
"Do some only see them."
Selves, and their own needs, wants, hopes, dreams, and de.
Sires, or ot.
Hers as functions, or as ex.
Tensions of them.
Selves, do.
Others, only, seek to see themselves in others, too.
While ot.
Hers will, or?
"Can, or."
At least?
Try to see.
Others, too.

Though, of course.
"Past and be."
Yond.
Whom, or.
Or?
What, or.
"Be."
Yond, and past.
But.
Who does not know.
"And, while."
Who, or what.
What, or who.
Really, or.
That, of course.
"Others, are."
"Or what, or who."
But, trapped?
Is not trying.
Actually, or.
Succeeding, or.
"In themselves, and in."
Truly, doing.
"The, or in."
Or, being?
"Their house of mirrors, and, so."
Or, Being, or.
Consequently?
"Do not necessarily."
Too, of.
Course, as much as.
Al.
Most is not is, and.
All see.
Or, hear.
"The same, or."
The same things, or.

"The same people, or."
The same people, in.
"The same way, or."
In the same ways, or at, or in.
The sam.
E time, or time.
S, or.
"Too?"
Of course, and.
"Also."
Do.
Not all.
"And, does not everyone?"
And, does not everybody.
"Necessarily?"
See all.
"Of the same."
Thing, or.
"Things, all."
In the same way, or.
"All?"
In the same ways, or.
"All at, or."
All in?
"The same time."
Or times, and.
"So?"
Do some.
"See more, while."
Or, hear less, while.
Others, me.
Rely?
"Just, or."
Unjustly?
"Only."
See less.
Or, hear more.

And, so.
Also, while.
"Or, whereas, too."
Of course.
"Are some, or?"
Some are.
Scared of what, and of.
Whom is different, too.
"As well?"
As of the Difference, or?
Of deference, or of the Dif.
Fé.
Ran.
Ce, or.
Are some.
Far more interested in being seen.
Or, in hearing.
"Than in seeing."
Or, than in being heard.
And, too.
"Because, of course."
Some are, also.
Far more interested in se.
Ein.
G.
"Than in being seen."
And, in being heard.
While others are.
"Far more?"
Interested in watching.
Or, in listening.
Than in seeing.
Or, than in hearing.
"While others?"
Are for more interested.
In watching, or in listening, or.
In seeing than in watching, while.

"Others are more interested in being seen."
Than in being watched.
"While others."
Are.
More interested in hearing, than in listening, while others are.
"More interested in being watched, than in being seen, or."
While others, are.
More interested in being heard, than in listening, while others are.
"More interested in watching than in being seen."
While others, are.
More interested in being listened to than in being heard.
And, so on.
And, so forth.
"And, but."
Because, of.
Course.
"I am not one."
Stupid, or.
"One de."
Spe.
Rate, or.
One in.
Se.
Cure, or.
One scared e.
No.
Ugh to.
Though, of course?
"Scared of."
"Want, or."
What, or.
To need to.
"Scared of whom, if."
"Be seen."
Not of themselves, or.
Or, heard.
If not of it.

And, be.
Self, or if not of him, her, or your.
Cause, also?
Self, or.
"I am not one who does need to be seen."
Or, heard?
In order to be.
Or in or.
Der to k.
Now that I am.
"And, too."
Because, of course.
"Need some be watched."
Because they cannot be trusted.
"And, because?"
Also, and.
"Of course?"
Of course, can, ought, and should.
Not all, everyone, or everybody?
Be trusted, and.
Too.
Do some, or.
Some do de.
Serve to be the watchers.
While others must be watched, and.
"While others do not."
Deserve, either.
While still others do like, want, wish, will, or hope.
Or, both.
To be watched, but.
Or, to watch.
Which, of course.
Is not to say, not say, suggest, or im.
Ply, that.
The self-de.
Sign.
Ate.

D watchers do deserve to watch, or.
Ought, or should, or.
Have some right to watch, and, be.
Cause.
"Of course?"
While some can see.
Others can.
Not, will not, and.
Do re.
Fuse to, and.
But, though.
Too, of?
Course.
"Some can see."
What, and.
"Or?"
Whom, or.
"Whom, or?"
What ot.
Hers can.
Not, and.
"So?"
So?
"Even if, so, per."
Haps?
And while, and can, and do.
Some others, also, hear bet.
Ter.
Than others, and.
What is all so much, and?
"So, too."
Now.
Is this, and is that, e.
No.
Ugh a.
Bout.
"The eyes."

Which, of course?
"Are not to be con."
Fused with the I's.
As well as?
Also, en.
Ou.
Gh a.
Bo.
Ut.
"The knots."
Which are.
"Of course."
Not to be con.
Fused with the I's.
Or, with the nots, and.
Whoso.
Ever.
"And, where."
Soever.
All those.
"Or, all these?"
I's might.
Be, and.
Though, then.
"And, because."
Now, too.
Here, and.
"Because."
Once again, he did raise his palms.
And, you did.
"And, I did raise."
And, which are raised.
And, what are, now.
"And, here?"
Pre.
Sent.
Ly, and cur.

Rent.
Ly, raised.
And, so, also.
What were, and.
"What are raised."
Are.
"My hands, and."
Too, are.
"The hands."
Both right, and left.
"And."
Of course?
"The hands which are."
Both left, and right.
To, and for, me.
And for, and to, you.
"And for, and to, me."
And.
"Too, both?"
Which are raised, now.
And, here.
"Into what."
Is more air.
Or, the air?
Than sky.
Or, than the sky?
And, too.
"Which are raised."
Into.
And, or?
What are raised, now.
And, there.
"Before me."
And, in front of me, or.
"Before my face, or."
Before my chest, and.
Which are a bit a.

Bov.
E me, too, and.
"Of course."
As one.
"Or, as?"
More might.
"Wonder, or."
Ask, or?
"As would."
As would, and as do.
Any, or.
"All reasonable?"
Per.
Son, or per.
Sons.
"Ask why?"
What are.
"Now raised?"
Because, of course.
Why do.
What, or.
"Anything, or."
Everything?
Without reason.
"Or, without Reason?"
Or, without reasons.
"Or, without a reason, or."
Without whose Reason?
"Or, without whose reasons."
Or, rather.
Why do anything, something, nothing, or everything.
Without a good reason, or.
Without good reason, or.
Why do?
What.
"Anything, or."
Everything, un.

Reasonable, at all?
"Or?"
Or, why does any.
Why do.
Thing ex.
"Or, why?"
Ist, at all, or.
Continue, on.
"Without finding."
The reason, or the Reason, or without finding the rea.
Sons, and.
"Or."
Also, without creating?
Or dis.
Covering one, two, or more.
Rea.
Son, or rea.
Sons, or.
And, if so, and be.
Cause, I am a reason.
Able man, of course, or.
"So, what are raised for."
Whatsoever reason, or.
"For whatsoever reasons, or."
For whose reason, reasons, or Reason, or.
For no reason?
"At all, and."
Or?
"Because, rather."
As I was saying, or.
But saying to whom, or to what, or.
"Rather, as I was thinking, or."
To What, or to Whom, or.
As, rather?
"As was I both."
Thinking, and saying, that.
"Or be."

Fore?
Being in.
Ter.
Rupt.
Ed, though.
"Of course?"
Interrupted by.
"Whom, or."
By what.
If not by me, and.
"Or, if."
Not by my.
Self, and.
"If not in this hand."
And, if not in this palm.
"Then, in."
Or, now?
"Or, then on?"
Or, now on?
That one.
Palm, or hand.
"Hand, or palm."
Which is.
"Of course?"
Left, or right.
Or, which is.
"Right, or left."
To, or for, whom?
"And."
If, per.
Haps.
"Not, just."
And, or.
If not only.
Left, for.
Or, right for?
Or to, me.

Or, wrong to?
"But, also."
Or, wrong for.
What might be?
Left for, or to, her.
Or for, or to.
"Or, to."
Or, for whom?
He could not.
"And, or?"
To, or.
"For, or."
To whom.
"Or, to."
Or for whom, too.
"I can, and."
Too, I could?
"Not be."
Bot.
Her.
Ed to remember, or to see.
"Who was the one?"
Or, who is the one.
Or, the One.
Who might have been.
Or, who is the one?
Or, Who is.
"Or who was the one?"
Who could have been, or.
Who is.
The one who has always been.
"Or, the one who was."
Or, who is?
Or, Who is.
"The one?"
Or, the one.
Or, which one, or.

Whose one.
Who did.
And, the one who does?
Still lie.
By his side, and.
"By my side."
In the bed.
And, in my bed?
Or, in our bed.
Still sleeping.
"And, still dreaming?"
As she had been.
And, as I have been.
"And, as she has been?"
And, as.
"Ever she has been?"
And, or.
"As she ever will be?"
Or, and.
And, or.
Who?
Of course.
He did ignore.
"As us."
U.
Al, and as al.
Ways.
And?
So, who.
"And?"
Who so.
Also.
"And, who?"
Likewise.
I.
"Did ignore him."
Too, and.

Or, me?
And.
"As always, and."
As usual.
She did continue, on.
"Sleeping, and."
Snoring, and.
Either dreaming.
"Or, not dreaming, away?"
Or a way, or.
"Except."
As she was, and.
"As was she?"
And, as I am.
Not quite snoring, but.
And as I am, and.
"As if?"
Because, of course.
Do, or.
Do not?
Peaceful souls.
Or, minds?
Snore, and.
"So, as?"
She was.
And, so.
As ever?
As I am, and.
"Because?"
Or, rather, as?
"I ever have been, or?"
As I ever will be, or.
As ever will I be, or.
As ever I will be, or.
As I am, and.
"As."
Or, rather?

She was?
And as ever I will be.
"Either more."
Or will I be, or.
Or, less.
"Or, less."
Or, more.
"Than apparently."
Will I not be, and.
"Or, more than apparently, so?"
Because, of.
Course.
"What id."
I.
Ot, fool.
L, or mor.
On, and, or.
"What fool does not know."
That but, of course?
"Is not being, seeming."
And that being is not seeming.
And, that.
"Is not seeming, being."
Too, and.
That seeming is not being, or.
"But, be."
Cause is it, that?
"Or, be."
Cause is it, this?
That peaceful, or that dead?
"Souls do, or do not?"
Snore, though.
Of course?
"Is it rather?"
It?
Not all dead souls are pea.
Ce.

Ful, and.
Snoring souls.
Of course?
"Are either dead, or peaceful?"
Too, also, are.
Or, both.
Not all peaceful souls dead, either.
"And, or."
And?
Is it.
It?
"Or, how am I to know."
How it is, or how it is not, or.
Why should I care.
"If her right is, also, mine, or."
If my left is his right, or.
If her left is, also, my left, or.
If my right is his left, or.
"If, rather."
Might her right by my wrong, or.
If might my wrong be his right, or.
If, rather.
"If what is right to, or for, her."
Is, also, left, or wrong, to, or for you, or.
Is, also.
Similarly?
"Or like."
Wise right, if not, necessarily, correct?
Pro.
Per, or ac.
Cur.
Ate, for.
Or, right.
Or, Right.
"To her, or."
If, rather?
"What, or."

Who is?
Wrong for, and.
"Wrong to."
Me.
"Or?"
If, rather.
"Quite so far more absolutely, is?"
Or, is not.
"My right the right."
Or, the Right.
Or?
"If is the right my right, or."
The Right your right, or.
Or?
"If is the right her right."
Or, my left.
Or?
"If is her right the right, or."
My left, or the Left, or.
Or?
"Of course?"
How to know.
If am I wrong.
Or, if you are.
"Or, if I am."
Left, or.
Or?
"If she is."
Wrong, or.
If can we both be wrong.
Or, right.
Or?
Left, or.
"If can we, or?"
If might we.
"Both be right, or?"
If, rather.

"Might we both?"
Be.
"Left, or."
If, rather?
"Of course."
Might we both.
"Be wrong."
Or, right.
Or, be left?
Or, Left.
"About some things, as?"
Well as.
"Might we both."
Be wrong?
Or, right.
Or, Right.
"About other things, too?"
And, also.
"Might she be?"
Or, might I be.
Right about some things, and.
"Wrong about others, and?"
Too, of course.
"Also, might."
Or, also?
"More than might."
She be.
"Wrong about other things, and."
Or?
Left about some other things, be.
Cause.
"Of course?"
Does not anyone.
"Get to be."
Right about everything, or.
"Right about all things, all."
Of the time, and.

In all places.
"But, and."
Even if.
"Of course."
Always being right.
"Is easier, and."
Is more convenient, and.
"Is more simple, but?"
Or, simpler.
Of course.
"Simple, or."
Easy, or.
"Most, or."
More convenient, to.
"Or, for whom, and."
Even if?
"Rather, what might be easier."
Or, more simple.
"Or, more simplistic?"
Of course.
Is, or is not?
"To have to consider anyone."
Ever.
Yon.
Every.
Body, or all, other than one.
Self, or.
Rather, what is.
"Or, rather?"
What might be.
Most simple, most easy, or most obvious, is.
What is, or?
"Is what is."
Easier, simple, more, or most.
Convenient.
To, or.
"For, or."

According to whom, or?
"According to what, or?"
Is everyone's, or.
Is.
"Everybody's?"
Or, is some.
One's?
"Or, is some."
Body's, or?
Is any.
Body's, or?
Is.
"Anyone's."
Point, or.
Perspective, or.
Point-of-view.
Other than my own.
"Better, or?"
Of course?
Though better to.
Or, for whom, and?
"Or."
What is most simple, or.
Who is?
Simplest, or.
"What is most easy, or?"
Easiest, or.
Who is, or.
"What is most obvious, too?"
Or, just.
"Or, rather."
Quite so un.
Justly, and.
"Rather."
Or, rather.
Quite so un.
Fairly, too.

"What is simple."
Only, or.
"Merely, to."
Or, for.
"Or, to."
The simplistic, who.
Can.
Not, or?
"For those, or."
For these, who?
Cannot be bothered, to?
Have to consider, or.
"For these, or?"
For those, who.
Do not want to, or for.
"Those, or."
For these, who.
Do not want to have to be bothered.
"To consider."
Any other point-of-view.
"Or any, or."
All other?
"Points-of-view."
Other than your own.
Other than my own.
"Or."
Other than their own.
"Or?"
Other than your own.
Quite so unfairly.
"And, quite so unjustly."
For the simplistic, who.
"Do not want to have to be bothered to consider."
Any other right.
Or, Right, or.
Any other wrong.
Or?

Any other left, or.
Left, or.
"Anyone's."
Or?
"Everyone's."
Or?
"No one's, or."
Nobody's, or?
"Somebody's, or."
Someone's?
"Rights, or."
Lefts, or.
"Wrongs."
Other than my own, or.
Or?
Ot.
Her than your own, or.
Other than their own, or.
"To have to consider."
Or.
"To have to remember?"
Anyone's.
"Someone's."
Somebody's.
Nobody's?
Or, everybody's.
Or, everyone's?
Or, no one's?
Wrongs, or rights?
Other than my own, and.
Or, other than your own, or.
"Because, of course."
Though rights, do.
"Of course?"
Exist.
"As much as do wrongs."
As, too, does.

"The Right."
Exist.
As much as does The Left.
Though?
"Of course?"
Which does not necessarily mean.
That.
"Does the wrong?"
Or, that the Wrong does.
Exist, or.
At least.
"In so."
Far as you do know.
Far as I do know, and.
Or as far, or as long?
As I say, or tell.
"But?"
Of course.
None, and.
Neither, or.
Both of which.
"Are not mine."
Of course.
And, if.
Because.
"On occasion."
Like eve.
Ry.
One, or?
"Like all, and."
So?
"Who could, or."
Who might, or?
"Who would."
Try dare.
Or, dare try.
"Blame me for?"

Choosing one, both, all.
None, or neither, because.
Of course.
At times.
"Must one choose?"
As you must choose.
As must I choose.
"And, as I must choose."
Now, and.
"Always, and?"
Ever, or.
My rights.
Or, mine.
"Or, my interests?"
Or.
My own happiness.
"And my own well-."
Being, of.
Even if.
Course.
And, even though.
Be.
Is not some.
Cause.
Thing, surely.
Rather than.
And certainly, and.
Of course.
Even more than.
Hers, or.
Surely, so?
Theirs, or.
Wrong with one, or with ones, who.
Its, or.
Do re.
Why care a.
Fer to him.

Bout, or for.
Self, as a 'we,' or.
Any one, two, or more.
As more than one, or.
Who do not care for, or about.
With those who do try to speak for an.
"His, or."
Ot.
My happiness, either.
Her, or for any.
"Or."
Or all ot.
Rather than.
Hers, and.
"Its, or."
With those who do try to put words, in.
Theirs, and.
The mo.
And?
Ut.
"Because?"
Hs of an.
Of course.
Y, or all ot.
"Why care about, or."
Hers, or.
Why care for.
"Any, or."
For all, or.
"For?"
The most, or.
"For the many, who."
Can, or.
"Who will, or who do not?"
Care back, be.
Cause.
Of course.

Every.
One, is not a some.
One, or a some.
Body who can care, and.
Be.
Cause, of course.
Ever.
Y.
Body is not.
A some.
Body, who can care, ei.
The.
R, and.
Is not caring, like.
So much else?
"In an ideal world."
A choice, and.
Para.
"Dise, or in."
A decision, that.
"A per."
Must one, and.
Fect, one.
That one must.
"Make for."
And, by.
"One."
Self, be.
Cause?
Of course.
"Not necessarily."
Is caring.
"To be cared about, or."
For, in.
Spite, *or de.*
Spite, of what might be, and.
De.

Spite, and in.
Spite, of.
What, or who?
"Or. Who."
Or, what.
Might seem to be most simple.
Simplest, or?
Most expected, and easiest, and.
"Too, of?"
Course, not.
"Necessarily, is."
To be cared about?
"To be cared for, and."
Too, be?
Cause.
"A u."
Top.
Ia.
Of course.
"Is not caring."
Either an.
"Entitlement, or a right, and?"
Or, rather.
Is it that being.
Cared for, is not, necessarily?
A right or an entitle.
Ment, while.
Is not caring a duty, or an ob.
Li.
Gat.
I.
On, or.
Because, of course.
"Must one?"
Or, be.
Cause.
"Should, or."

Ought one care?
"In order to get a care, and."
But, of.
"Course?"
But, too.
If one does give a care on.
Ly to get one, or only be.
Cause one should, ought to, or must.
Is not that, and is not this, not really, truly, or actually caring, or.
Caring, in.
Whose, which, or what.
Ideal heaven.
"Or?"
In whose, or.
"In which, or."
In what.
"Idea."
L world.
Hell, heaven.
"Heaven, hell."
Dystopia, or.
"Utopia, and?"
Or.
"Of course."
Must, or.
"Might, or?"
Must.
Might my own interests.
All care.
"Happiness, and well-being."
For all?
Also, be.
And, or.
"His, hers, its, and theirs, too."
Or, and.
And.
For everyone, or.

"But?"
For everybody, the.
Of course.
Same as.
Might, ideally.
One is cared for, and.
Their, its, hers, and his.
Or?
"Happiness, well-."
Being, and in.
Te.
Rests, also, be.
And, so.
Mine, too.
On.
Ly in.
An ideal world, or.
Universe.
"Can all win, but."
Of course.
What, or.
Do not all, every.
One, or eve.
Rybo.
Dy.
"Is not?"
De.
Serve to be happy, or.
At what cost, or costs, or.
"This, here."
Well, or.
"Real world."
Of course?
So, is it, or.
It is not.
Ideal.
"By definition?"

Or, by whose.
"Or, by what."
Or, by which def.
In.
It.
Ion, "Or?"
Rather, is not life—real life, if not a, or if not the, or if not whose, or if not which real.
Or, Real One? — what happens.
When.
"What is real?"
And where, or when.
Or what is real.
Ized, and, not?
"Because, of course."
And, not?
"What is not realized, and."
Or, what is not man.
If.
Est.
Ed, real.
Iz.
Ed, or.
Made real, or Real, or what.
And, not what.
What, who, or Who.
Does stay, or re.
Main, as a me.
Re ide.
A, or Ide.
A, or.
Too, because.
"Of course."
What idiot, moron, or fool.
Fool, idiot, or.
"Moron?"
Does not know.

"That real."
Or, Real?
"Life is not."
What does not happen.
Could, or me.
And, not.
Rely what might.
"And, that."
Happen.
And.
"Is not this."
And, not what.
"And, not who?"
Or, Who.
We might dream of happening, and.
"Or?"
And, not what who does dream of happening?
And, or.
"And, not just."
And, not me.
Rely.
"And, not on."
Ly, just, or me.
Rely what who, or what.
"What?"
Does want to happen, or?
What who, or what what does want, or.
The, or.
Does want to hap.
What, or.
Pen, or.
"Whose life?"
Might, rather.
"Or might, also, be?"
An ideal.
Or?
World, but.

Or?
What reality, or whose?
Reality is.
"Not?"
Ever, or always.
"But one more idea of it, or?"
What, or of whose.
Reality.
"Is ever more."
Or, less.
Or, is ever?
"Less, or."
More than.
"One's?"
Idea, or im.
Position, of.
Their, his, her, or of?
Its id.
Ea, or Idea?
Of the real, of the Real, of what is real, of who is, or.
Of real.
It.
Y, or.
"Or, of?"
The, or.
"Of its?"
Or, of.
"Her, or?"
Of his.
"Real?"
Or, reel?
Or, rather.
"Whose, or."
What's im.
Po.
Sit.
I.

On, of.
"Reality, is?"
But one more way.
To make.
"Really miserable?"
Or, really miserly?
"Though, of."
Course, miser.
Ly, or miser.
Able, in.
"What way, or."
In what ways, or?
According to whom, or ac.
Cord.
Ing to what, and.
Or?
Is not the imposition, but.
One more at.
Tempt to make real.
Or, Real.
Ly miserable.
"All those, who?"
Are not already, or.
"All those, who?"
Have man.
Age.
D to find.
"Or, all those who?"
Have managed to make.
"A bit of happiness, in."
And, de?
"Spite of it, all."
And.
"Or?"
Rather, is it.
Or, rather.
"Is this?"

Or, rather.
"Is that?"
The real one.
Or?
The Real one, or.
"The real world, or."
The Real world, or.
Who's real.
Or, whose.
"Which, or."
What Real.
"World, or?"
Rat.
Her, of.
"Course."
Who's, or what's, real, or Real, idea, or Idea, or vers.
I.
On of it, or.
Rather, is it?
"Or, rather, is what."
Or, rather, is who?
"Or, rather, is whose."
Idea, or.
Version.
"Imposition, or."
Certainty?
Just, or.
Only, or.
"Only, or just?"
Or un.
Justly, of course.
Which, by definition.
Of course.
"Is but one more idea of real."
It.
Y, of the real, or of the Real, or.
Which, of course.

"Is not."
The, or.
"Whose ideal, or."
Which, or.
"What is."
Whose.
Not?
Sur.
Real one?
"Or."
Un-one, but.
"Of course?"
Because.
Whose idea of the real.
"Or, of?"
The Real.
"Is yet one more idea it, that."
And, which?
"Can."
Ought, or should.
Not be im.
Pose.
D, on.
Any, or.
"On?"
The most, or.
"On the many?"
Or, on.
"All, or."
On everyone?
"Or, on."
Everybody, as.
Much as some?
"Might like to try, but."
Which?
Of course.
"Is only."

As real.
"Or?"
As Real.
"As do?"
We, or.
"As does?"
She, or.
"As does?"
He, or.
"As does it?"
Or, as.
"Do they?"
Or, as.
"Do the most, or?"
As do the many, or.
"As do the all?"
Choose to let it be, and?
"As much as?"
Might the many, or.
"As much as might?"
The most, or.
"As much as might the?"
All be.
Lie.
Ve it.
"Is real, or?"
Does.
"Not believing it?"
To be real, or Real.
Make.
The Real, or the real.
Un.
"Make the real, real."
Or?
"Make the real, Real, or."
Make the Real, real, and.
"In spite of?"

Or de.
Howso.
Spite.
Ever real.
"Real, realistic?"
Realizable?
"Rea."
Son.
Able, or un.
Reasonable, pre.
Dict.
Ab.
Le, ex.
Pec.
Ted, un.
Ex.
Pect.
Ed, or un.
Pre.
Dict.
Able, be.
Cause.
"Of course."
As much as.
"Do the more?"
Not necessarily make.
"The merrier, too?"
Does not.
"Believing, or."
Does not f.
Ailing to be.
Lie.
Ve, or?
"As, also."
Do not more believing, or.
"Does not the all?"
The most, or the man.

Y?
Failing to believe, me.
An?
"That is something."
Or, that something is.
Or, that is someone?
Or, that someone is.
"More, or."
Less than.
"True, or."
That one, two, or more.
The most, or the many, are.
"One, or."
More.
Real, or.
"Ideal, or?"
Less, or.
"More than."
Ideal, or.
"Surreal, and?"
Because, even.
"Can the most."
Sin.
Cere, and.
"Too, also?"
Can the most.
"Gen."
Ui.
Ne be.
Lief, or be.
Liefs?
"Also, be false, be?"
Cause, of.
Course.
"Howsoever many."
Have so ever fallen?
And, do fall.

As did the one great?
"And, great."
Est.
Liar, dec.
Ei.
Ver, and be.
Tray.
Er.
"For their own lies, and."
Because, of.
"Course, even?"
If the e.
Go's lies are, or.
Might be.
"Most evident, and."
Most obvious, at?
Least to, or for some, or?
"At least."
For, or to, others, or Ot?
Hers, do.
They, also.
Of course, also from.
Quite so very of.
The mo.
Ten.
St om.
"Hide from?"
Ni.
The most all-knowing, and.
Sci.
"Also, from?"
Ent, or.
The oh-so-well.
"And, from?"
The most, and from.
The best, and most.
"Well-in."

Tent.
Io.
Ned, and.
Because, of?
"Course, who."
And, what?
"So obsessed, or."
What, or who.
So trapped?
"Down in."
The real world, or in?
"The Real World, or."
In whose real, or Real?
World, does.
"Not demand?"
At any.
"And?"
Or, at all costs.
"Company, and."
But, of.
"Course, what?"
Or, whose.
"World, Real."
Ideal, real.
"Or sur."
Real?
Is only.
"As sur."
Real, as.
Real, or.
"As ideal?"
As heavenly, or.
"As hellish, or."
As ide.
Al, or.
"As u."
Topic, or.

As dys.
Topic, or.
"As hor."
Rib.
Le?
Or as miser.
Able, or.
"As fan."
Tas.
Tic, or.
As joy.
Ful, as?
"One does choose."
To let it, or.
"As one does choose?"
To make it, or as one.
Does de.
Cide to per.
Mit it to be, in.
"Spite of, or?"
De.
Spite all those, and de.
Spite the rest of them, so.
"Deter."
Mined, to?
Make it.
Or, me.
"As miser."
Able, as they can, as pos.
Sib.
Le, or?
As they are, or in?
Spite of all those.
And, these.
"And?"
Or de.
Spite.

"The most, or."
In spite of the man.
Y, or?
"In spite of the all, or."
In spite of eve.
Ryb.
Od.
Y, or?
"In spite of every."
One, who?
Are all so.
"Determined to make you?"
Or me, or one?
"And, all."
As miser.
Able, but?
"As real, or."
As Real?
"As they are, be."
Cause, of.
Course?
"Cannot some be hap."
Py, un.
Til all are as Real, or as real?
Ly miserable as.
"They are, or."
Un.
Happy, or.
Til all.
Are.
"Beneath them, or."
Until all have been.
"Shot, or."
Kept down, or?
"Until all."
Have, also, or.
Also, have.

"Been en."
Slaved, too, be.
Cause?
Might some.
"Rather, con?"
Trol all others, or, at le.
As.
T, try to?
"Rather than?"
Have to learn.
To con.
Must some master any, and, or all.
Trol them.
Others, rather than thems.
Selves, and.
Elves, and.
"Because?"
Cannot some be, or stay.
Up, without.
Keeping all others down, and.
"Because, of?"
Course, can.
"And, will?"
Not some be.
"Happy, or sat."
Is.
Fi.
Ed, OK, or all.
Right, un.
Til all ot.
Hers are as miser.
Able as they are, or un.
Til they do have.
"Com."
Plete, to.
Tal, en.
Tire, and.

All con.
Trol.
"Over all ot."
Hers, but, of.
Course.
"Does not free."
Dom con.
Sist of, and.
Is it.
Not, and.
"It is not."
Ha.
Ving to ask, or beg.
For it, or.
Having to have complete, total, or en.
Tire con.
Trol, or power, over all others, as.
Well as.
"Are none, who."
Do seek to give it, or.
"Any, who."
Do seek to take it, or.
All, or any.
The most, or the many.
Who do seek, pre.
Sum.
E, or ass.
From any, or fr.
Ume.
Om all ot.
To have the power to give, or to take, freedom.
Hers, or.
"Ever free, and."
Because, of.
"Course."
Is not true, real, last.
Ing, or en.

During.
"Freedom ever had."
By en.
Slaving any, or.
By at.
Tempting to en.
Slave, to im.
Prison, to have, own, or pos.
Sess, any.
"Or, all?"
Others, but.
"While, of?"
Course.
"Do some."
Seek all power.
"And, all control, do?"
Ot.
Hers, only.
"But seek?"
To be free from, or to be rid of?
"Such types, and."
But.
Of course?
Are not the only.
Two choices, between.
The real and the ideal, and.
Or, between the Ideal, and the Real, or.
"Between the real, and the Real, or."
Between the Ideal, and ideal, or.
Between the Real, and the real, or.
Be.
Between the i.
Tween the ide.
Magined, and the I.
Al, and the idea.
Magi.
L, or.

Ned.
Between master or slave, enslaving or mastering, or.
"*Or?*"
Imaginary, or.
"Because, of."
Course, who?
"Does not know, that."
But, of course?
Is not either.
"The Real, the."
Real, or.
"The ideal, or."
Even?
The sur.
Real, what.
"Will, or."
What does set one free, but.
"Of course?"
What, or who?
Se id.
I.
Ot, and.
"What."
Or whose, moron, or.
What fool?
"Also, does not know."
That, but?
"Of course."
As ob.
Vi.
Ou.
S, and.
"As common?"
And as sensical, as.
"Such truths?"
Might be.
"What fool."

Idiot, or.
"Moron, also?"
Does not know, that.
"Too, of?"
Course.
"Is not what."
Does seem, or does appear, to be.
"Or, what."
Is so-called.
If not whose is.
Com.
Mon know.
Ledge?
"Or sense."
Necessarily all so.
"Com."
Mon, be.
Cause?
Of course.
Though, while.
"Might some."
Crave reality.
"Might others crave to a."
Void, or.
To es?
Cape it, and.
In so do.
Ing, be?
Come a, if not the.
Void them.
Selves, while.
"Might some."
Prefer to live in a dream?
"Do others prefer to live in the woken world, or?"
In the waking, woke, wakened, or woke.
Ned world.
Or, in the so-cal.

Led.
Real world, or.
And, because.
"Of course?"
While some.
Do seek to a.
Void themselves.
"And, so?"
The Truth?
The truth.
Or, the Truth.
By blaming any.
Or, all others, too.
Are others?
"Brave enough."
Or, so bullied.
Or, for.
Ced, right?
E.
Ou.
Sly.
"Or, rightfully."
If for.
Ce.
D can eve.
R be.
So, right.
Ful, or so right.
E.
Ou.
S, or.
To face themselves, and.
"The Truth?"
Which, of course.
Is not an option for some, and.
Which?
"Does not care much for."

Truths, or.
"For whose, or."
For which, or.
"For different truths, or."
For what.
"Is true."
For one, or.
"To, or."
For the most, the man.
Y, or the all, or for?
What might be true to, or.
For whom, where?
"Or when, and."
Which does, also.
"Not much care, for."
Time, or.
"For place, or."
For place, or.
"For time, and."
But, of.
"Course, I."
Am not.
One of them, or?
"One like the rest of them, and."
Be.
Cause, of.
"Course, are."
We not.
"All different, too."
And, because.
Of course?
You are, also, differ.
Ent, too.
"And, so."
Because, I am.
"Not one of them, and."
Because, they are?

"All not."
One just, ex.
Act.
Ly.
"Completely, or."
Totally, or?
"En."
Tire.
Ly, pre.
Cisely quite like me, and.
"Be."
Cause, if are we not?
All different.
"And all in."
Divi.
Duals, then?
Or now, and now.
Or, there.
"Or, here?"
And, now.
"Then, what."
Or, now what?
"Are we, and."
How bo.
Ring would things be, if we we.
Re, or if we.
Re we.
All co.
Pies, all the same, all the Same, or all de?
Riv.
At.
Ives, or if, in.
Deed, we were.
All pro.
Hib.
It.
Ed from be.

Ing our.
Selves.
Though, even if?
"What is true."
For, or.
To one.
"Is not?"
Necessarily true.
"For all, and?"
Even if.
"What is most true."
Might, or.
"Might not be?"
What feels good, or.
"What feels best, or."
Most com.
Fort.
Able, or most fam.
I.
Liar, or.
What all?
"Are willing."
And, so, able.
To hear, or.
"What all?"
Or, what everyone, or.
"What everybody is?"
Willing to accept.
"As true, or."
As well as is.
Not the truth.
Necessarily what the most, the many, or the all.
Would like to believe it is, but.
What is most true is what is true.
For one, for all, for all time, and in all places.
For everyone, and, or.
For everybody, as.

Well as, of course.
Is not the Truth, or the truth?
More often than not, what, or who?
Is believed, or.
What, or.
"Who is grea."
Test?
All-knowing, or.
"What is loudest, or."
Who, or.
Who, or.
"What is."
What has the most bo.
Mightiest, or.
Mb.
"What, or."
S, or g.
Who is.
Uns, or.
"Most silent, or."
Even if?
"Might, or."
Might it not be?
"More, or."
Less than real, or.
"Less, or more."
Than Real, or.
"Less, or more."
Or more, or less.
"Than i."
Deal, or.
Less, or.
"More than sur."
Real, and.
Whether, or not.
"The truth does change, or."
Even if?

"It does not, and."
Whether, or not?
"It is, was, ever will, and ever."
Does, and will.
Stay the Same, or.
"The same, or."
And.
"Whether, or not."
It is the same.
"Or, the Same?"
For all.
"In all places, and."
For all?
"Everywhere, and."
Or.
For all?
"For all times, and."
In all places, and.
"Or, if?"
Rather.
Whether, or not?
"The truth."
Or, the Truth.
Can be spoken, or.
Spoken by whom, or by what.
When, or where.
"Or where, or when, and."
Whether, or not?
"It is."
What, or who, is.
"Most correct, most right."
Most left?
"Most wrong, most proper, most accurate, or?"
Whether, or not.
"It is."
What, or.
"Who is?"

Most ap.
Pro.
Pri.
Ate, or.
"Even if?"
Might, or.
"Might it not be?"
Known, or.
Knowable, and?
"Even if?"
Must it stay, and.
Even if.
It must.
"Remain un."
Known, and?
"Or un."
Know.
Able, or un.
Known by, or to, who.
M, or.
Even if?
"Can it be seen, heard, or."
Shared, and.
"Even if?"
It is.
"Not easy, and."
Even if?
"It does make one."
Or, more?
"Or, even if."
It does make.
"The most, or."
The many, un.
"Comfortable, and."
Even if.
"Might, or must."
It be?

Told, or.
But told by what, or by whom.
"Even if?"
And told to whom, or to what, and.
Rather, might.
Or, must it be.
Kept secret, and.
"Or?"
Even if.
"It is, or."
Is not?
That, or who.
Which does.
"Seek to be."
Exalted, or.
"Even if?"
It, *she, he, or the.*
Y, do.
Demand to be wor.
"Choose to re?"
Ship.
Main hum.
Ped, fol.
Ble, and.
Low.
"Whe."
Ed, or.
Her, or?
Idol.
Not.
Ized, or.
"Known?"
Already, or?
It, *she, he, or the.*
Y, is, *or are.*
"Known already, or?"
Whether, or not.

"It is yet."
To be known, or.
"Whether, or not."
It is.
"Yet to be revealed, and."
Whether, or not.
"One is."
Logical, reasonable, or.
"Rational, or."
Rather, if.
"Is it."
Or, are you.
Irrational, unreasonable, and illogical.
Enough to believe it, or to believe in it, and.
"Whether it is."
To be known.
"By one, or."
By all, or.
"Whether all?"
The most, or the many.
Are ready for it, *hi.*
And whe.
M, he.
Ther.
"Or, not?"
R, or them.
All, everyone, or every.
Body are, or is.
Is, or are not?
Expecting it, and.
But, because.
"Of course."
I am not them.
And, too.
"Because, of course."
I am not one of them.
Or,? are you, and?

Too, because.
"Of course."
Are we not.
All different.
"And, too, be."
Cause.
"Of course?"
Or, one of whom, or one of whose, or one of what's, or?
"Because."
Of course.
Or, because?
"They are not me."
But, who are you?
And be.
Cause they are not me, and be.
Cause?
"If not just, and."
If not only.
"And, if not them, which."
Would, but.
Make you.
One more not, or.
As if some.
But one m.
Thing is wrong with the no.
Ore no.
Thing, or.
Things, with the no.
But one more no.
Bodies, or with the ap.
Body, and, or?
Parent no ones, and.
"But."
Too, be.
"If not one of what?"
Cause, of course, no one and no.
As much as.

Body, is.
And, too, be.
A some.
Cause.
Body, and.
"Of course?"
A so.
And, also.
Me.
"I am not it, or them."
One, to.
Or them, or it.
O, an.
Or it, or them.
D.
And, too.
Of course?
"As much as."
It is not me.
And, too?
"Because, of."
Course, what, or.
"Who, or, be."
Cause, what.
Or, because, whoso?
Ever it is, and.
Who, or what, so.
Ever they are, and.
"Too, because?"
Of course.
As much as.
"I am not her."
And, as much as.
"She is not me."
Who, or what.
Whosoever she is, and.
Soever you are, and.

Too, because.
Of course?
"As much as."
He is not me.
And, also?
Who, and what.
So.
"And, as much as."
Ever I am, and.
They are not me, and.
I am not him.
"Or, but."
And, he is not me, and.
Am I?
Or, but?
"I am, or."
But?
"You are, and."
Or, though.
And, though?
"Or, but."
Because.
Of course.
If am I who they say I am, or.
"If I am?"
Rather, who I do know I am, *already,* or.
Are you, rather, or, too.
And, so, not?
Who you have been, or.
Or so, either.
"Who you will be, or."
"More, or less?"
Who you do think you are, or.
"If, rather?"
Am I just, me.
Rely, or.
"Only?"

Who they, who he, or who it.
Or, who she, or.
"Does need, or."
Who it, or.
"Who he?"
Or, who she, or.
Do ex.
"Who they?"
Pect you to be, or.
Do want me to be, or.
Who, or what.
Or What, or Who.
They have made me.
Or you, or.
What, or who.
Soever they, he, she, or it?
Have turned you into, or.
"Made me be, or be."
Come, or.
Rather, am I.
"Who I do know that I am."
Because, of.
"Course, is."
Not knowledge, and.
"Too, because?"
Of course.
"Is not knowing, power."
And.
"So?"
In spite of what.
Is knowing, or.
Is choosing.
"And, in spite of whom?"
"Or, in spite of whom?"
And, so?
To know?
They say I am, or.

Or, despite what?
Oneself, choosing.
They might think, want, or need.
To have power, over.
"Me to be?"
Them.
"So?"
Selves, and.
So?
But.
Though, might.
Is not knowing, being.
"Course, though."
And, one need not know, to be.
And, or?
But what is a life, or one?
Will I al.
Un.
Ways.
Known, or.
So, and.
One un.
"And, ever?"
Ex.
Eve.
Am.
N if?
In.
Be a me, or.
Even if.
And?
Some might rat.
Her.
Try to know me, for me, and.
"Am I?"
Even if some might like, to.
Try to know all.

Or everything, about all, or.
"About you, or."
About an.
A me to me, will.
Y, or all.
Others, so?
I, also, be.
As to have.
"Or?"
So as.
"To obtain?"
All pow.
Er, and all con.
Trol over them, rat.
Her?
A 'he' to them, which might.
Than having.
"On occasion?"
To know, and.
Match, or.
Rather than having to?
"Be the same, as my 'me' is to 'me,' but."
Take.
Which, also?
Responsibility for.
"Might not be the same, or a match, and."
Oneself, or.
For my.
Self, or for them.
Selves, if not for.
You, and.
Too, be.
Cause.
"Of course?"
Is not knowledge, or.
Is not knowing, just, me.
Rely, or on.

Ly.
Power.
"'Me,' 'he,' and 'I.'"
But ide.
As, or cons.
Truct.
Ions, which.
"Always, and."
Which ever?
Responsibility, too.
"Are changing, and."
Because is one's idea of one.
And?
Self, necessarily, all who, or.
Because is, or can.
Who, What, or what.
All id.
One is, and.
Entity, or merely e.
Go, or self, be?
A construction, and?
So fake, and false.
All do have.
Because, of course.
"Their own?"
Opinions, and.
"Their own interpretations?"
And means, and ways, and.
Of whom, or.
"Of what?"
One, another, or of.
Whom, or of what.
Or of What, or of Whom.
All others are.
"Or, of?"
What they, or.
"Of?"

What she, or.
"Of what."
He, or.
"Of what?"
It does.
"Perceive, or."
Ex.
Per.
Ie.
N.
Ce, and.
"Too, of?"
Course, are.
Not any.
"Perceptions, interpretations, or."
Experiences, ever.
"All identical, and."
Or all ex.
Act.
Ly, or all pre?
Cise.
Ly the same, or the Same?
Or of the sam.
E, or of the Sam.
E, or un.
Less, in.
Deed, the, you, or 'we?'
Are all rep.
Li.
Cants, or co.
Pies, or all.
Art.
If.
Ici.
Al mon.
Sters, and?
So, eit.

Her, if not both?
Good, or bad.
Little, big, or huge?
Machines, or agents.
Created by some machine, or?
"And."
So, too?
"And, of."
Course, also.
"Does?"
Not always, and.
"Does not ever."
And, does not ever.
"And, does not always?"
For all, or.
"For everyone, or."
Only for the select.
Elite, chosen, or spe.
Cial, or.
For everybody, or.
Only for a few.
"For all?"
In all places, and.
"Or, for all times."
Does not the, or.
"Does not?"
My id.
Ea, or.
"Does not?"
My con.
Struct.
Ion, of.
"'Me,' or."
Of 'I,' or.
"Of 'I,' or?"
Of 'me.'
What you are, and.

Of whom, or.
Who you are, and.
Of what.
Of whom, you are not, be.
Of What, or.
Cause.
Match a, or.
Of course, who is not, also.
Match the id.
What, and who.
Ea, or match the idea, or.
They are not, as well.
What, and who.
They are not, as well.
"Match theirs, or."
Its, his, or.
Her.
Idea, construction, or interpretation, of.
Me, as.
Who, or what.
"Much as?"
What, or who?
Of course.
Is on.
"Does, and."
Ly part, or part.
Can, and.
Ial with.
"Can, and?"
Out his, her, its, or the.
Does not.
Ir own shad.
"Ever, or."
Ow, or shad.
Does not al.
Ows, though.
Ways?

Which does not ne.
The 'I."
Ce.
Match, or.
Sarily, me.
"Meet up with?"
An.
The 'he.'
That one, two, or mo.
The 'it,' or.
Re, or that.
The 'we,' and.
The man.
As much as.
Y, do.
"Also, does?"
Not more of.
Not ever.
Ten than not, pre.
"And, does?"
Fer to try to pro.
Not al.
Ject the, his, her, or its?
Ways.
Own shad.
"The 'we.'"
Ows, is.
Meet, or.
Sues, faults, and fail?
The 'he,' the 'it,' or the 'we,' and.
Ings, on.
As much as.
Any, or on on all.
"Also, does?"
Ot.
Not ever.
Hers, or.

"And, does?"
Not al.
Ways.
"The 'we.'"
Meet, or.
"Match up, with?"
The 'I,' and.
"As much as?"
Too, also.
"Does, and."
Can, and.
"Can, and."
Does not?
"Ever, or."
Does not al.
Ways, the.
"We?"
Absorb, or.
"Include, all."
'I's, or.
As much as.
"Ever, or."
As always?
"Do not 'they.'"
Match, meet up.
"Or accept?"
The 'we,' or.
"The, or."
My 'I,' and.
"Of course?"
As much as.
"Also, and."
Too, does not.
"The 'I' seem to match, or."
See.
M to me.
Et up with, or.

"Seem to co."
In.
"Cide, with."
The 'we,' or.
"With the 'they.'"
Or, with the 'she,' or 'he.'
Because.
Of course.
"I am just, and."
Because, I am.
"Only, but."
One man, and.
"Because, of."
Course, I.
"Am not."
A 'we,' royal.
Or, are you, and?
"Or otherwise, and."
Or, do.
Which is?
Me.
As much as?
Stic, or.
But one more reason, why.
"Also, and."
Boundaries are necessary.
Too?
Because.
"Am I, also, not."
As well as.
Of course.
Also, I am not.
And, you are not?
"But."
As well as, of course, also.
I am not.
When, and.

"A 'they' either, and."
Or?
Because, where.
Though, of.
Does not one, or.
"Course, at."
Where, or.
Times, need.
When, do not the.
"And, must?"
More, the.
One think of, and.
Most, the.
Do for, and.
Many, or.
"Do with, and."
The all, not.
Consider others, also.
Know, where.
"And?"
They do start, and.
At times, too.
Or, where?
"Must one."
Or, when.
Think of.
Another, or all.
Others, or others?
Do end, or.
"And, do."
Where, or when.
For, and.
Or when, or where.
"By?"
One, all.
Oneself, be.
The mo.

Cause.
St, or.
"Of course."
The many.
Though, can some things.
Do end, and.
"Only be done, or."
Where one does start, or.
Only be?
When, or.
Reached, or.
Where, one.
"Only be."
Does end, or fin.
Is.
H, and.
"Or, where?"
Another does start, or be.
Gin, or where?
And when an.
Ot.
Her does end, or.
"Accomplished together, too."
Though whose ver.
Sion of ac.
Com.
Pli.
Shed, and.
Whose vers.
Ion of to.
Get.
Her, or.
How to.
Get.
Her, or.
By, or at, whose word, Word, words, command, dic.
Tate, or man.

Date, and.
Who gets to de.
Cide, or choose.
What is accomplished, and what is not.
By whom, when, or where, and.
Who does get to decide, or determine.
What, or who, is successful, and.
Who, or what, is not, and.
And, also?
"Can other things, only."
Be done, reached, or.
Accomplished alone, and.
Because, other.
"Though, of course."
Wise, of course.
Do not the un.
How to know.
Able, and.
Who thinks, or who feels?
"Do not the un."
Willing, and.
What, or how?
Also?
To know.
"Do not."
Whose arm is whose, or?
"Whose leg, is."
Whose lips, or whose hips, are?
The crip.
Whose feet are, or?
Pled ones, or.
Whose eyes are whose, or.
"The blind."
Which ones, are.
Ones, "But?"
Or, whose cheek, is whose.
Seek to get others to.

To turn, or which one.
To, or.
"Which one is to be, or?"
Whose teeth are whose.
White, dark, missing, filled.
"With silver, or?"
"Walk, or."
Gold, or.
To see.
"For them, or?"
Whose ears are whose, or.
Seek to.
Which ones do hear, and which ones do not, or.
"Drag, or keep, the rest down, and."
Which ones do hear what.
"From whom, or of whom."
From what, or.
What from, via, or through.
"The left ear, rat."
Her, or as opposed to?
"The right one."
Or?
How to know, which.
Ears, or which eyes.
Which arms, toes, fin.
Gers, hands, or palms.
"But seek to."
Do belong to.
Get the able, or?
Whom, or.
"To get."
To what, and.
The willing.
"To do for the."
"Of course."
M, what?
What, or.

The blind, or what the.
"Whose, or."
Crip.
What will?
Pled.
"Does not necessarily."
Will not do, or.
Make for.
"What they do not want?"
A way, and.
To have to do.
"Because, and?"
"For, or."
Too, as.
By the.
"Much as."
Ms.
Do the blind?
Elves, because.
"Quite so very often."
Without knowing, and?
Even, if.
Without intending?
Do.
Seek to blind the seeing, and.
Who do?
Quite so very of.
Ten, without.
"Intending, to?"
Do succeed, and.
"As much as?"
Because, of.
Quite so often, do.
Course, where?
"The crippled, seek to."
Quite so very often, do.
Cripple, also?

The best of intentions, lead.
"The walking, or."
If not straight, or.
"If not directly."
To hell, but?
The run.
Hell to, or hell for.
Whom, or for what, and?
"Or, according to what, or accord."
Ing, or.
Ing to whom, and.
"Those still?"
Or, hell of whose, or hell of what's?
"Those who are."
Making.
As yet?
And, or.
Able to stand, and.
Rather, called?
"But, of."
Perdition, or.
Course, I.
"Am not."
One, who.
"Or one, that?"
Can.
Not, or.
One who will not, or?
"One, that."
And, or, one?
Who will not, so.
One who can.
Not, or?
One who can.
Not, so?
One who will not, or.
One, who?

"Does, so."
Seek to.
"Blind, to."
Cripple, or.
"To deafen?"
But, of course.
The hearing, the.
"What else, can."
Walking, the.
The blind, crippled, or deaf.
Running, or.
Do, but?
"The seeing, or?"
One willing.
"Or, one."
Wanting, or.
"One needing, to."
Be so crippled, so?
"Blinded, or."
One.
So deafened, or?
One.
"So muted, or."
As much as?
"Of course."
I am not.
"One who."
Can, or.
"One who."
Will, and, so, one who can?
"Not tolerate himself, his."
Own thoughts, or.
Your own thoughts, or.
"My own."
Feelings, *or your own,* or.
His own, *or your own.*
Needs, wants, hopes, dreams.

Or desires, so that.
I cannot tolerate, or.
"So that?"
I will not tolerate, those.
Or, these?
"Of any?"
Or those, of.
"All ot."
Hers, or.
So that?
I cannot be a.
Lone, with.
"Myself, or."
With my own.
"Thoughts, or."
With my own.
Feelings, or.
"As much as."
Of course.
"I am not."
One un.
Willing, or.
"One un-."
Wanting to do.
For, or.
"To do by, or?"
To do by, or.
"To do for."
Myself.
"What, and."
When, and.
"When, and."
Where, and.
"What I can do, for."
Or, by.
"Or, by."
Or, for.

"Myself, and."
Too.
"Also?"
Of course?
Am I not one.
And?
"Dumb, one foolish, one stupid, one moronic, or one."
You are not one.
"And, I am not one."
Id.
Io.
Tic e.
No.
Ugh, not.
"To know."
For me.
"When, and."
Where I do need he.
Lp, and.
"Where, and."
When I do not, and.
Or, with?
"As much as?"
What, or.
I am not one.
With whom?
"Dumb, one stupid, or."
Or with.
One foolish, or.
Whom, or.
"One moron."
Ic, or.
With what?
Idiotic enough, to?
You might need help, or.
Think, or.
One idiotic, one moronic, one dumb, or.

One stupid.
"Enough, to?"
Assume that.
All help.
So-called.
"Does in."
Deed help, or.
One na.
Ive en.
Ou.
Gh.
To ass.
Ume, or to pre.
Sum.
E, that.
"All help?"
Can, or.
"Does help, and."
Also, because?
"Of course."
Also, am.
"I not."
One to.
Fail to know, or.
"One who does not know."
What I should, and.
Or.
"What I ought know, which."
Now, and.
"Which he."
Re, and.
Which?
"This time."
Is that.
"Quite so very of."
Ten does 'help,' so-called.
Not help, but rat.

Her does it need help, or, rather.
Does it.
Seek to make it.
Self needed, wanted, or use.
Ful when, and where, it is not, or.
Does it.
Rather, seek.
"To be helped, rather."
Than does it help, or.
Even if, of.
Course, of.
Ten can, or of.
Ten will not.
The so-called, or self-dec.
Lared.
"Strong, not."
Deem them.
Selves low.
Enough to ask for, or to.
Need help.
"And?"
Too, rather?
"Quite so often, does help."
Seek to make it.
Which, of course.
Self needed, or.
Is but need it.
"Seek to make it."
Self, and.
Self want.
Ed, or.
Which, of course.
"Is, but."
Want, it.
Self, and.
Or, does it.
Seek to make it.

Self use.
Ful, rather than.
"Truly, or."
Rat.
Her than real.
Ly, or.
"Rather than actually."
Helping, and.
"So, of."
Course, am.
"I most."
Wise.
Ly, and.
"I am."
Most rat.
Ion.
Ally. and.
"Most lo?"
Gic.
Ally, and, also.
"Of course?"
Most sens.
Ib.
Ly sus.
Pic.
Io.
Us, of.
"All of."
The so-called 'we's', 'us's,' and 'they's,' and.
Of.
All of.
"The so-called."
Goody-goody.
"Types, of."
So, good.
"And, of?"
Good.

"Helpers, and."
Because, of.
"Course, as."
Does any, and.
"As do?"
All wise, all sen.
Sib.
Le, all logi.
Cal, all rea.
Son.
Able, and.
"As, also?"
Do all.
Rat.
Ion.
Al men, know.
"When, and."
Know where, and.
"Know what, and."
Or, if?
"One does need help, and."
Also?
"Like any."
Rational, reasonable, sensible, logical, wise.
"Or en?"
Light.
En.
Ed man?
Or ma.
Chin.
E, which.
"Of course, can but."
Think it.
Self en.
Light.
En.
Ed, but?

"Which, of."
Course, is not act.
U.
Ally, real.
Ly, or tru.
Ly, so?
Or Be.
Because, of course.
In.
Is not thinking, living, or being, and.
G, and.
"Because, of course."
Is not think.
Ing all that is, and.
"Because?"
Of course, does not thinking, or is not be.
Lie.
Ving a thing, a person, a will?
Or, a way?
To be, or to be true, or to be real?
"Or Real, or True, not."
Make the per.
Son, thing, idea?
Or be.
Lie.
F, or way?
True, or.
Real, so?
Do I, also?
And you do, also.
"Know where, and."
Know?
"When does one."
Or when, or where.
"One does."
Or, when?
"Or, where."

You do, or.
I do.
Need, or want.
Or want, or need.
"Help, and."
When, and.
Where, rat.
Her.
"One, or."
I am?
"Better?"
Off, or on.
Hel.
Ping my.
Self, be.
Cause, of course.
As all do, ought, and should.
Know, does.
Can, should, and ou.
Ght gen.
I.
Us he.
Lp it.
Self, and.
"Of course?"
And, too.
"Because?"
Does the, or.
"Because, of?"
Course, does.
"My Lord, tend."
And tend to help, and tend.
To choo.
Se, and.
"Tend to favor?"
Those who can, and.
"Those who do, and."

Because, of course.
Is self-re.
Though, of course, is not.
Li.
The 'thou,' the you, the ot.
An.
Her, or.
Ce the best way, means, and policy, and.
The Ot.
Those who will?
Her, still fav.
"Help the."
Or.
Ms.
Ed, and.
Elves, without.
So, is the self, or even.
"Without seeking."
The Self?
Help, un.
Eve.
Necessarily, and.
R, and al.
Without wanting.
Ways, lower, and older?
"To cripple, to."
And, so, less.
Maim, to.
Er, and?
"Blind, to."
Though might the Self, if not necessarily the self, be.
Mute, or.
More sac.
"To de?"
Red, but.
Afen?
Who, or what.

By, through, or.
Does care about whom, or about what.
"Via helping, or?"
Is sac.
Via, thro.
Red, or.
Ugh, or.
What, or who.
"By?"
Does care for, or a.
Trying, or.
Bout What, or whom.
"By, via, or."
Whom, or w.
Through at.
Hat is hi.
Tempting?
G.
To help.
Her, lower, older, or.
"The seeing, the."
Les.
Fine, the?
Ser, or young.
Standing, the.
Er, ex.
"Speaking, the?"
Cept, per.
Hearing, the.
Haps, the low.
"Able, or."
Er, the high.
The willing, even though.
Er, the young.
"Of course?"
Er, and the old.
I, also.

Er them.
"Am not one."
Selves, or.
To try.
"Of course?"
I, also.
"Am not one."
To try.
"To deny, that?"
But, of.
"Course."
Even though?
Sometimes.
"Must 'we.'"
Do for.
"And, do by?"
Ou.
Rs.
Elves, and even.
If you do not want.
And, eve.
N if you do not w.
To have to, and eve.
N if you do not l.
Ike, or w.
Ant to have to h.
Ear, or accept, "No," and.
Also, and.
"Too, at."
Times, must?
"'We' do."
For, and.
"With others, and?"
As much as.
And, too?
"Likewise."
Also, at.

"Times, must?"
We need to.
"Be alone, and."
While, at.
"Other times?"
Need, or.
"Must 'we?'"
Need, or.
"Want to be."
With an.
Other, with some, with any.
"Or, with all others."
But, which.
"Not necessarily?"
Does mean, for an.
Y, or for.
All others, or for all.
Others, and.
Be.
Cause, of.
"Course, is."
Not being.
"Too much."
For others, as.
"Bad as."
Be.
Ing, too.
"Much for."
One.
Self, and.
"As much as."
Too, also.
"Is doing too much."
For others, as.
Bad as.
"Not doing enough, and."
As much as.

Is doing, or.
"As much as?"
Is thin.
King, of.
"Or, for?"
Oneself, too.
"Much, as."
Bad.
"As not?"
Thinking, for.
"Or, of?"
One.
Self e.
No.
Ugh.
As much as.
"Is doing?"
Too much for.
"Oneself, as."
Bad as?
"Not doing?"
Enough, for.
"Oneself, but."
Of course.
"What, or."
Who is.
"Or, of?"
Course, who.
"Or, what."
Is per.
Fect, if.
"Not the ba."
Lance, which.
Is in the mid.
Dle, but.
Or which, is in.
What, which, or.

Whose mid. Dle, or.
"What life?"
Or, whose life, or.
"Whose world, or."
Which world, or.
"Which, or."
What real.
It.
Y, is.
Just, or.
Is on?
Ly, or on.
Ly, is.
"Or, is."
Me.
Rely is.
Perfect as.
"One does choose?"
To let, or to per.
Mit it to be, and.
"Be."
Cause, of.
Course, is.
"Not my."
Job, or.
"My re?"
Spon.
Sib.
Il.
It.
Y, to.
Make perf.
Ect for.
"Him, for it, or."
For her, or.
For the.
M, any.

Thing, as.
"Much as?"
Also, is.
"Not my responsibility, to."
Make the.
M, to make it, or.
Or, to make me happy, or.
To make him hap.
If whether, is.
Py, eit.
Or, if is not.
Her.
To be hap.
Or, to make her happy.
Py to be per.
Because, of course.
Fect, or.
Is not one's happiness.
If w.
One's own re.
He.
We all find?
The.
Or be ab.
R, or?
Le to agree on?
If not.
Or, about.
Is to be per.
"What, or."
Fect, al?
About whom.
So, to be.
Is perf.
Happy, or.
Ect, or.
If what?

"Also, might?"
If most per.
We be ab.
Fect, also?
Le to.
Is what, or.
"Find?"
Al.
"See, or."
So, is who?
Or?
Or Is Who, is.
In.
Most hap.
Ter.
Py, or.
Pret, as?
If who, or.
"Per."
If.
What.
What is.
Or who.
Most hap.
"Or how?"
Py, al.
One is, or.
So, is what.
"What, or."
"What, or."
Or, al?
So, who, *or Who.*
Is, and.
Is who.
"As much as?"
Is most perfect.
Too, also.

Too, and.
"At times?"
Might we.
"Though, of."
Course, who.
Also, and.
Again.
"So ever."
Might 'we' be, but.
"Of course."
At times.
"Might my happiness."
Or?
My per.
Fec.
Tion, or?
Your per.
Be the.
Fection, also.
Ir.
S, and.
"Also?"
Be.
"His, and, also?"
Hers, and.
"Be its?"
While, also.
"And, too?"
While, at times, too, and.
"Also."
Might its, might his, or might their?
Or, might her.
"Happiness."
Or, perfection?
Also.
Or, con?
Tent.

Ment.
Be mine, too, but.
"Of course?"
If, al.
So.
"At times."
Must one choose.
"One's own happiness, or."
One's own per.
Or, one's own per.
Fect.
Fect.
Ion, or.
Ion.
"One's own version of it, or?"
Is.
Another's, or.
One's own sat.
Is.
Faction, or content.
Men.
T.
"All others, must."
And, and.
Or?
"Must all."
Rat.
I.
On.
Ally self-in.
Te.
Rested, and.
So must one, and, or.
So must all.
Rat.
I.
On.

Ally, and.
"Rea."
Son.
Ably, and.
Logically, and.
"Wise, and."
Enlightened?
"Sane man?"
Or, men.
Naturally, most.
"Reasonably, and."
Na.
Tur.
Ally?
Or to, or.
Most logically?
For whom, and?
Choose my own hap.
Pin.
Ess.
My own per.
Fection.
My own san.
It.
Y.
My own rea.
Son, rat.
I.
On.
Ale, and self-.
In.
Te.
Rest, and.
Regard.
Less of what it does, or what it might?
"Mean, for."
All of the rest, or for.

"All of the others?"
Or for all Ot.
For the Ot.
Hers, or.
Her, or.
"For an?"
Other, or.
"Because, of."
Course, I am.
Not one.
"To choose?"
Or, one.
To pre.
Sum.
E, or.
One.
"To ass?"
Ume, the.
Right to have some right, or some?
Ability to choose.
For an.
Other, or.
Some privi?
Lege, to.
"For all others?"
So.
Must I, also.
"Let them choose."
For, and by.
"Themselves."
Because, of.
"Course, if."
One is to remain, or.
"If one."
Is to stay, in.
"Good faith, of."
Course, can.

"One not?"
Choose, or.
"Decide?"
Or, know.
"Or, try to know?"
For another, or for.
Any, or for.
All others.
But, rather.
"One must."
Or, rat.
Know, and.
Her, must.
"Or, what?"
One.
One must.
Or, which.
Choose, or.
"Which one?"
Or, what must all.
"Decide, or."
What one?
Or, what must all.
"Or, what must every."
One, or what must e.
Very.
Body.
"Must know."
For, and.
"By oneself, and."
Or by, and.
"Or, for."
Them.
Selves, and.
Because, if.
"I do not."
Know me.

"Or, know for me."
Who might?
Who will, or.
"Who will try to."
Know me.
"For me?"
Or, know for me, and?
Because, of.
"Course, I."
Am not one.
Co-dependent, or.
"One?"
Trying, or.
One?
"To try?"
To know.
"For any."
Or, for all.
Or, All.
Other than myself, as.
Much as I am not one?
"To try."
To take responsibility, for.
Anyone's, or.
"For everyone's, or."
For everybody's.
"Happiness, other."
Than my own, and.
As much as.
"I am not one?"
Willing, or.
"One to try?"
To make.
My happiness, your hap.
"Eve."
Pin.
Ry.

Ess, anyone's.
One's, or ever.
Body's re.
Sponsi.
Bili.
Ty.
"Other than my own, though."
Too, of.
"Course, on."
Occasion, and.
"In some places, and."
At, or in.
Some.
Times, might.
"For some."
Another's happiness, be.
Or, might the hap.
Pin.
Ess of any, or of all ot.
Hers, be.
"One's own, and."
Too, also.
"Might the happiness of another."
Or, of.
Any, or of all, others, also, be.
One's own, but.
"Of course."
Because, is.
"Not happiness a choice, and."
If it is not one's own choice, to be.
"Made for."
And, or.
"To make by."
Oneself, then.
Or, now?
Whose.
"Might it be."

To make, to.
"Take, or."
To try?
"To give to another."
Or to any, or.
"To all others."
But, of.
Course.
"Because I am not one."
To stay, to re.
Main, or to try to hide in.
"In anyone's, in."
Everyone's, in.
"Every."
Body's, or.
In any.
Body's good faith, if.
"Not in my own, be."
Cause, of.
Course.
"If, and where."
And where, and when?
"One does choose."
To stay.
"In good faith, with."
Oneself, does.
"One, also?"
Naturally, or.
Naturally, for?
Or, naturally, to.
Whom, or.
"To, or."
For, or.
"According to what."
And, or.
According to whom.
"Automatically, also?"

Or, necessarily?
Stay in good faith, with.
"All of the rest, and."
With all.
"Others, or?"
At least.
"With those."
Who are, also.
"And, with those?"
Who also, do.
"Stay, or."
Remain, al.
So, "In good faith?"
But in whose, or in what's, or how good, and.
Because, of.
Or, in which way, or ways.
"Course, I am."
Bad, or good.
Not one.
Good, or Bad.
"To choose."
Bad faith over the good, or.
Over the Good, or.
"One foolish, one stupid, or one idiotic."
Or, one mo.
Ron.
Ic e.
No.
Ugh.
"To choose."
The, or.
"Anything, or."
Anyone bad.
"Over anyone, or."
Over anything.
"Good, even if."
Might 'we' not all agree, on.

"Or, about."
What is good, or.
"About, or."
On what is bad, even.
Or, on what is Bad, even.
"If, of?"
Course, is.
Only.
"The good, quite necessarily."
And only good if, or in.
So far, as.
It is uni.
Vers.
Ally, so, which, of.
Course, also, does mean.
Only in so far as it is not singularly, and not wholly, entirely, or completely, but only, or merely.
Particularly, or specifically good, or.
Even if?
"What, or."
Who is.
"Good, does."
Or, can?
Not de.
Pen.
D on comp.
Lete, or on to.
Tal a.
Gree.
Ment, *or una*, and.
Nim.
Even if.
It.
"What might be good for one."
Y, whi.
Might not ne.
Ch, if not en.

Cessarily, be.
Tire.
Good for all, or.
Tire.
Good for everyone.
Ly, whol.
"For everyone, or."
Ly, whol.
Ly, or com.
Plete.
Ly im.
Pos.
Sib.
Le, is.
Un like.
Ly, and, or.
For everybody, *ever.*
Y.
Where, in, or at, all ti.
"Even if."
Me.
Of course.
S, or.
Most simply might the good, or.
The Good, or.
The idea, or the Ide?
A of it, be ab.
Solute, of.
Course.
"What is good for e."
Go or for the ego, or.
"For whose ego, or."
For e.
Very.
Body, or.
Who is to as.
Sume, or pre.

Sum.
E that what, or that who, is.
"Is most simple, or."
Is simplest, or.
Even if.
"What is good for everyone."
Might, or.
"Not necessarily, is."
What is good for all, and.
As much as?
"Once what."
Or once, who?
"Was good."
Might no longer, be, or.
Might not be any.
More, or any.
Longer, or.
"And, even?"
If what.
"Is good here, might."
Be, or.
Not be?
"Good there, and."
Even if.
"Of course."
What, or.
"Who, once?"
Might have been bad.
"There, is."
Now good, or.
"Even if."
Of course?
"Who, or."
What, once.
"Was bad here."
Was good there, and.
"Even if?"

Once what, or who.
"Was bad there, is."
Now?
"Good there, and."
Even if?
"Of course."
What, or.
"Who."
Was good here, is.
"Now bad here?"
And, or.
"Even if."
Of course.
"As much as."
One must know.
"For, and by."
Oneself, what.
"Is good for one, and."
What, or who.
Is bad, and.
All the same?
"Or, like?"
Wise.
As, also.
"Can, should, and."
Ought not one.
"Try to know, try."
To choose, or.
"Try to decide, what."
Is, or.
"What might be."
Good for another, or good for all others, because.
Of course.
"Is knowing."
Some things.
Or, is knowing.
Some people, or?

For some people.
"Good for some, while."
Is knowing.
"The same things?"
Or, the same people, or.
For the sam.
E people.
"Bad for others, and."
Because, of.
"Course, and."
Do not all, and.
Too, is.
Does not every.
"Knowing some things?"
One, or ever.
Or some people.
Y.
Or for so.
Body ever, or al.
Me peo.
Way.
Ple.
S, w.
Bad for some, but.
Ant to h.
"Good for others, and?"
Ave to k.
Because.
Now, or ad.
"Of course."
Mit?
Cannot every.
They do k.
One, or eve.
Now, for, or by, them.
Ry.
Selve.

Body.
S, or.
Cannot every.
One, or eve.
Ry.
Body.
"Know everything, and."
Too, be.
Cause?
"Of course."
Cannot e.
Very.
One, or ever.
Y.
One.
"Know all, and."
Be.
Cause, of.
"Course, also?"
Even if, are most fas.
Cin.
Ating, those who.
"Do know everything, as well as."
Those who?
"Do know all, as well as equal."
Ly, as fas.
Cina.
A.
Ting are those who do know no.
Thing at all, though?
"Of course."
Might, in.
Deed, the lat.
Ter be the wis.
Est, be.
Cause, of.
"Course."

Is not.
"Part of knowing, al."
So.
Knowing what.
Or, What.
And, knowing?
"Who."
Or, Whom.
One does not know, and.
"Is it, also."
Knowing how to know what, or whom.
Can be known, or how.
Not to know whom, or what.
Or, whom.
Ought, or what should, not be known, or.
"Also, too?"
Is part of knowing.
"What, or."
Who, or.
"Who, or?"
What?
"Cannot be known, or."
And, too?
"Also, is."
Part of k.
No.
Wing.
How one does know, as well.
As is.
"Part of wis."
Of course, that wis.
Dom?
Dom, and en.
Or part of being en.
Light.
Light.
En.

Ed?
Ment are not the same, or.
Knowing what should, and.
The sam.
"Knowing what ought."
E thing, and knowing, that.
And, knowing what, or who, can?
Or Who, or What.
Not be known, and knowing.
"So, if."
Is it.
"But, of."
Course, what?
Is it.
"About both."
Knowing, and.
Also, at?
"Not knowing, too."
Once about.
Also, is.
Not knowing, too.
"Or, can."
And.
Or, should?
"And, ought."
It not.
Be about.
"Being known for, or."
And, also.
"Should?"
And, also.
"Ought it."
Not be.
"About."
Trying?
"Or, about."
Assuming, or.

Pre.
"About?"
Sum.
Presuming, to.
In.
"Know for all, or."
G, or as.
To know?
Su.
"For any others, be."
Ming.
Cause, as much as.
"I am not one."
Wanting, or.
"One willing, or."
One?
Needing to.
"Be known for, too."
Also, am.
"I not."
One needing to.
"One willing."
Or, one.
"Wanting to."
Have to know for.
"Any, or."
For all.
"Others, either."
Or, even if.
Of course.
"Might, as."
Also?
Or, also, as.
"More than might."
One, or.
"Some, or."
Some, or.

"One like."
To try?
"To assume, or."
Like to?
"Try to."
Presume to.
"Know for."
Another, or.
"For all."
Others, rather.
"Than having?"
To know.
Oneself, or.
"Rather than having."
To know.
For.
"Oneself, too."
But.
Of course.
Because might not one.
"Or, too?"
Because, also, might.
"Not another, and."
Too, also.
"Or?"
Might not all.
"Want to have to know?"
For, or.
"By them."
Selves, or.
Themselves at all?
"And, because."
Of course, rather.
"Might, or."
Rather?
"More than might, some."
Also, like.

"To be able, to?"
Escape having to know themselves, or.
"Having to know?"
For, or.
By themselves, and.
"Because, also?"
Is not.
"Knowing, and."
Is not knowledge?
A right, and.
"If not yours, then."
Or, now?
"Or, now."
Or, then.
Whose, and.
"So, also?"
Is it.
"My responsibility, as."
Much as it is?
Also, my.
"And, also?"
A, and.
"Also, power, and."
Because, would?
"Not some, rather."
Like to es.
Cape both power.
"And re."
Spon.
Sib.
Ili.
Ty, too.
Because, of course, would so man.
Y like po.
Wer with.
Out re.
Spons.

Ib.
Il.
It.
Y, or wit.
Hou.
T ac.
Count.
Ability, or with.
Out having to be held.
Accountable for what does work, as well as for what.
Or, for whom?
Does not, and.
Though, also.
And, of course.
"Who, or what?"
What, or Who.
Would not like to take credit for what does work, and, or?
"Of course."
While blaming, any.
"Or all?"
Others for what does not, and.
As much as.
"Too?"
Also, might.
"One, more."
Or, some?
"Like to seize, or."
Like to take?
"The power, or."
The apparent power, of.
Knowing, or.
The assumption, of.
Knowing, or.
"The presumption of knowledge, or."
The assumption.
"Of knowledge, without."
Also, having?

To deal with, take.
Have.
"Or hand."
Le, also, the.
"Responsibility of it, too."
And.
Also?
"As much as?"
Also, too.
"Might, or."
More than might?
"One, or."
More, or.
"Some, also."
Like, to?
"Escape the responsibility of choosing, or."
Of having to choose, or.
"Of having to decide, or."
But, of.
"Course, if."
Is not life.
"Necessarily, about."
Or, all?
"About knowing, or."
All about having to know, or.
"All about?"
Needing to know, or.
"All about?"
Not knowing, or.
"All about?"
Escaping having to know, or.
About what one does know, or does not know, or ab?
"All about?"
Out who one does not, or does know, or.
"All about?"
Power, or.
"All about responsibility, but."

Also, and, too?
"Might it be."
All?
About choosing, and.
Or, all about?
"Choices, and."
Or, all?
About decisions, and.
Or, really?
"Not necessarily?"
All about?
Just, or.
Anything, or.
"Only, all."
Really, truly, or.
About one decision, or.
Actually?
"All about one choice, or."
About anyone, or.
Also, and.
Because, really?
"Too, might?"
And, because.
Or, more than might.
Truly, and.
"It be?"
But what is it, or It, and.
Because, actually.
"Might, or."
More than might?
"Also, it."
Be not.
Or, not be.
"So black-and-white, or."
Also, not.
"So all-or-nothing, and."
Or, so.

So, also.
Over.
Might it.
Ly-simp.
"Also, be?"
List.
A bit more complicated, than.
Ic.
"That, or than."
This, or.
"Than this, or."
Than that, even.
"If, also."
Of course?
"Which is not."
Necessarily, to.
Say, or.
"Not to say, or."
To think.
"That, rather."
Necessarily, it is.
"Or, is it?"
About shades of gray, or.
"Of grey?"
Either, or.
That it is.
"A series of choices."
Though, too.
And, or.
Of course?
Or, rather.
Is gray, or grey?
Or, are the greys, or the grays?
But a mix.
Tur.
E, and so, a blend.
Of black-and-white, and, or.

"Of white-and-black, and, so?"
All mixed up, and, so.
A sign, of.
A lack of proper, necessary, or correct.
Differ.
En.
Tia.
Tio.
No, or.
Bound.
Aries, and, so?
Not good, or Good, at all.
And.
Rather, can.
"Or, and?"
Not beggars, be.
"A series of decisions."
Choosers, or.
And, so.
Deciders, either.
"If one does choose."
Though, beggars.
Not to decide, or.
Why, or.
"If one does decide?"
For what reason, or rea.
Sons, or.
So-mad.
E by whom, or by what, and, so.
Not to choose, does.
Beggars, or.
"One, also?"
Slaves, to.
Choose not.
Whom, or.
"To live, and."
To what.

If not to live is.
And, or.
"To die, then."
Or there, or.
"Here, or."
Now, or.
"If, rat."
Her?
Is, or.
"Could be?"
Not to live, also.
"Merely?"
To exist, or.
"Merely, to."
Think about living, or.
"Is thinking enough, or."
Is it sufficient?
"Or, is it equivalent to living, or."
Is thinking.
Merely, just.
"Or, only?"
Be.
Ex.
Ing, or be.
Cept, of co.
Ing.
Ur.
Se, thin.
Kin.
G be.
In.
G, or Be.
In.
G, or Thin.
Kin.
G Be.
In.

G, or be.
In.
G, is not act.
U.
All.
Y, real.
Ly, or tru.
Ly be.
In.
G, or Be.
Ing, and.
Or, too, of course, not quite so sim.
Ply, is it, also., un.
Like be.
In.
G, and un.
Like Be.
Ing, too, be.
Cause, of cour.
Se is, and could not Be.
Ing, or be.
Ing, be with.
Out thin.
King, thought, or thoughts, and, or?
Could, and would.
Not beings, be.
Either, or?
Is not thinking, not.
At all, ever, or al?
Ways necessary, as well as.
Of course.
Does not one need to think, to live.
Or, must one not be thought.
Or, thought of?
By whom, or by what, to live?
Or, to be.
Or, to Be?

Though, of course.
"Is it."
Far better to be forgotten by the Devil.
And, by his de.
Mons, or agents.
"Than by God."
Or, his, His, Her, or her.
Angels, and, of.
Course, be.
Cause to be for.
Gotten by God, is?
To be for.
Gotten by life, or.
Which, or what.
God, or God.
Dess, and.
To be for.
Gotten by the Dev?
Il, is.
"To be for."
Gotten by death, and.
Or, by?
"Because?"
Of course, is it.
And, it is.
Far better to re.
And, so, to be.
Member the an.
Re.
Gels, than?
Membered by them, than.
To forget them, as well.
"As is it?"
And, it is.
Far better, to.
Forget the devils, or the de?
Mons, than the an.

Gels, be.
Cause, of course?
To forget the angels, is.
"To be forgotten by them, while?"
To forget the de.
Or, the De.
Vil, or his de.
Mons, not ne.
Cess.
Ari.
Ly to be for.
Gotten by them, or?
"Rather, does not God ever for."
Get, or.
"As well?"
As is not living, or being.
Or, Being.
Only, or all.
About thinking, or about thought, or about thoughts, any.
More, or any.
Less than living.
Or, life.
Does need thought, or does need.
Thinking, *though.*
Of course, do some.
Still, and.
As yet.
Think, and be.
Lie.
Ve.
"Believe, and think?"
They, he, she, and.
Or it, are.
Only because they think they are, or.
Also, too, of course, do some.
As yet, and still, believe, or think?
That because they think, they, he, she, or it, are.

As well.
As do some.
As yet, and still.
Believe that, or believe this?
That they.
He, she, or it, only are.
In so far as they, he, she, or it do think, *or do be?*
Lieve they are, so, still.
Could, and would, thinking.
Thought, or thoughts, not be.
Without life, without living.
Or?
Did thought, or did con?
Scious.
Ness, or.
Whose thought, or whose conscious.
Ness come first, or.
Does Being, *or does be?*
Coming persist, even as beings do die, pass, come, and go.
And, even as beings do pass away, and.
So, too, will the Thought, if not necessarily will thinking, or.
I.
Gin.
Al, if here.
Or, if there?
Was, is, and ever?
Will be one, would, will.
And, does?
Continue on, after thoughts, thought, and thinking, have gone, and
after they have passed away, too.
Or, is it God, or the gods, the im.
Mortals, or.
Belief, or be.
Lie.
Ving in the.
The machine, or in.
M, or in.

Its little machines.
Either good, or bad.
Or Bad, or Good.
That does, and that do, go on, and on.
For.
Ever, and e.
Tern.
Ally, or.
"And, is."
Living more.
"Or, less than."
Being, or.
"Less, or more, than being, and."
Or.
As well as, of.
Course, is not thinking.
Of li.
Ving, or living, *or life,* as well.
As is not the id.
Ea of living, or me.
Rely ex.
Ist.
Ing liv.
Ing, eit.
Her.
Now, or.
Is living?
"Also, something."
A bit more, which.
"Also, does include."
Be.
Coming, too.
Which is.
Of course, not just.
"Not only."
And, not me.
Rely thinking, and.

Which, also, is?
"Not just, or un?"
Just, and.
"Here is."
Which is.
Failing to choose, or.
Not only, or me.
Rely.
"Is choosing not to choose, or."
Being who.
Is deciding not to decide, or.
Or, being what.
"Is choosing not to decide, or."
One is, but.
"Is deciding not to choose, for."
Does, also, living include.
"Whatsoever reason, or."
Becoming who.
For.
Or, also?
"What."
Soever reasons, if.
Becoming what.
Not for more, or.
One will, also, be.
Later, so, also, is be.
Ing be.
Coming, too.
If it is, or is.
Not necessarily.
Or can, should, or ought, not be?
Falling back in.
To whom, or in.
To what, on.
E was, or.
Into the eternal return, or.
"If not for less than."

Too, and.
In order to try.
"To escape."
Both oneself, as.
"Well as."
One's own power, and.
Or, accountability, or?
"As well as."
One's own responsibility, and.
One's own free.
Dom, too.
"So, failing to choose, and."
Which, of.
So, is.
Course, is.
"Choosing not to choose, and."
Also, a responsibility, too.
So, too.
And.
Also, is.
"Deciding not to decide, and."
Too, so?
"Also, is."
"Deciding not to choose, as well as."
Is?
Choosing not to decide, also, actually?
"Choosing, or."
Really, or.
"Truly, choosing?"
To die, how.
So ever pas.
Sive.
Ly, but.
Or on.
Ly as long as.
Choosing not to live, is.
Also, sim.

Ult.
Ane.
Ou.
Sly, or not, al.
So, choo.
Sing to die.
"Of course."
Did I not come, and.
"Was I not necessarily?"
Just, or.
"Only, or."
Merely born, only.
"Or, just?"
Or, only.
"Or, merely?"
Unjustly.
"To die, and?"
So not to act, not to do, not to say, not to be.
Lie.
Ve, or not to be.
Li.
Eve, in.
So, because.
Or, does to so choose, or to so.
Fail to choose, to live, and, so?
To choose to die, either act.
Iv.
Ely, or passively, have.
Nothing at all to do with just.
Ice, or rat.
Her.
Is the choice not to choose, or the decision not to de.
Cide, or.
The choice not to say, not to think, or not to be.
Lie.
Ve.
In what, or in whom?

The most just, and brave, act, *or non-act,* of all, and.
"Also, of."
Course, I am.
"Not one?"
So co.
War.
Dly, or.
One?
"So ir."
Responsible, so.
As to?
"Try to."
Escape.
"My own."
In.
Divi.
Duality, which.
Of course, my.
"Own decisions, and."
Which, of.
"Course, my."
Own choices, do.
"Make, or."
Which?
"My own?"
Responsibility, or.
"My own power?"
Over me, and.
Or, your?
"Own freedom, or."
Your own?
Power.
"Over my life."
And, over your death.
"Because."
And, over your life, your future, your fate, and your destiny, if not, also, necessarily, over.

Of course.
Your past, because.
Or, over my own, unless.
I do, too, choose not to be.
Cause, of course, al.
So, I am not.
"I am not."
One interested in.
"Con."
Troll.
Ing, or.
In having?
All power, or.
In having, or.
In taking.
"All control?"
Or, all power.
Over all others, rather.
Than having, or.
"Rather than."
Ob.
Taining, such.
"Pow."
Er, or.
Such con.
Trol, over?
Yourself, or over.
"Myself, and."
Though, of.
"Course, which."
Might not?
"Necessarily be."
The on.
Ly.
"Two opt."
Ions, or.
The only?

"Two choi."
Ces, either.
And.
So.
Though, of.
"Of course."
Course, quite.
Because, I, also.
So often.
"Am not one?"
Do those.
Willing, one wanting.
Who do not want.
"Or one choo?"
Sing.
To have.
To accept responsibility for.
To control themselves, seek.
"Everyone, for."
Rather, to.
Eve.
Ry.
Body, or.
Control the.
"For all?"
World, and.
Rather than.
"Or?"
In ad.
Di.
Tion to.
Having to.
"Accept?"
Responsibility, for.
To control.
"Myself, as."
All.

If I?
"Am some."
Others, around.
"Sort of."
Them, and.
Grand, master.
"Daddy, or."
As if?
I want, or.
"As if?"
I would like to be.
"Some sort of."
Grand, master.
God?
"Pa."
Pa, or.
Pap.
I, or.
Fat.
Her, or.
As if?
I want, need, or.
"As if?"
I would like.
"To be."
Or to be made.
To be?
Or to be for.
Ce.
D to be?
"Some sort of God, savior, mar."
Tyr, or.
Mast.
Er, or.
And, so.
"Of course."
As much as I.

"Do choose."
To choose.
"For me, and."
Also, as?
"Much as."
I do.
"Decide to."
Choose.
For myself, too.
"I, also?"
Do choose, and.
"Do decide, to?"
Do, act, say, believe.
Not say, not do, not act, not believe.
Just, only, and me.
Rely for you, and, to.
Decide for.
"And, to?"
Choose for.
"No one other than myself, and."
Too, so?
"As much as, also."
I do, and.
"As much as?"
Also, do I.
And, so, too.
Do you.
"Choose, and."
As much as, also?
"I do decide to."
Take responsibility for.
My own choices, and.
Or, for?
"My own de."
Cis.
I.
Ons, and.

Or, for?
"My own f."
Ail.
Ures, or.
"For?"
"My own de."
Cis.
Io.
Ns.
Not to choose, and.
Which, of course.
Is, also, a choice, or a de?
Ci.
Sio.
N.
"Or, for?"
My own choi.
Ces.
And, for.
Your own act.
Ions, words, be.
Liefs, fee.
Lings, and for.
Your own failures.
To do, say, act, or believe, as well as for.
Your own decisions.
"Not to decide, as."
Well as?
For.
"My own life, and?"
For my own happi.
Ness, and.
As well as?
"For my own in."
Divi.
Duality, and.
As well as?

For my own freed.
Om, and.
As well as for your own, but.
"For?"
My own liber.
Ty, too.
But not for mine.
"Because?"
As well as.
For what.
You do decide, or do choose, to do, say, feel, think, or be.
Lie.
Ve, and.
For what you do choose, and decide not to, and.
Of course.
As well as for what you do not decide, or do not choose.
To do, say, feel, think, or believe, and.
Once again, not for their, his, her, or its.
Actions, words, silences, betrayals, omissions, beliefs, thoughts, or.
Failures to think, or failures to believe, or.
"Is not."
My life?
"Mine, to."
Make the.
"Most, or."
Mine, to?
"Make the best, or."
Mine, to?
"Make the least, or."
Mine, to?
"Make the worst, of."
And, because?
"Of course."
Is not the, or a.
Boss, one.
Who must?
Take responsibility, for.

Those beneath *her,* or him.
For what does work, as we.
Ll as for what does not, and.
As I have said, or.
Not said, or.
"As I have thought, be."
Fore.
Just now?
Because, I am un.
Willing.
Or be.
Fore that, or be.
Fore this, too.
"To choose, or."
To decide, for?
"Any, or."
For all?
"Of the rest of them, too."
And, also.
Because you are un.
Willing to say, to do, to be.
Lie.
Ve, not to be.
Lie.
Ve, not to do.
And not to say, too.
Must I?
"Also, let them."
Choose, and.
De.
Cide, do, say, not say, not do, not.
Think, think, be.
Lieve, or not be.
Lie.
Ve, and.
"Decide, for?"
And by them.

Selves, and.
"So?"
To make.
"Of their lives."
The best, the.
"Least, the."
Most, or.
"The worst, of."
Them, and.
"So, also?"
Must I.
Let them.
"Choose, and."
Decide, and.
"So, of."
Course, also?
"Must I."
Decide, and.
"Choose to."
Let them.
Be who?
Or what, and, so, also.
Who, and what?
What, and who.
They are not, as well as.
What, and who.
Who, and what.
They are, and.
"Also, of?"
Course, must.
"I choose, and."
Must I de.
Cide to let, and, so.
To per?
Mit them, to.
"Take responsibility, for."
Them.

Selves, and.
"For their."
Own freed.
Om, and.
"Or, for?"
Their own.
Liber.
Or, for their own slave.
Ty, and.
Ry, and?
For their own thoughts, words, actions, beliefs, or fee.
Lings, or.
Failures to believe, failures to act, or fail.
Ur.
Es to feel, and, or.
For the.
Ir, his, her, or its.
Failures to say, or to think, and.
"Because, of."
Course, I.
"Also, am."
Not one?
"To try to."
Deny, or.
"One to try to es."
Cape?
Reality, or.
"What is, without."
Wanting, or.
"Without needing?"
Or, without hoping for better, and.
"Or, without?"
Ho.
Ping for more, and.
"Or, without?"
Hoping for the best, even.
"If, of?"

Course, is.
Hope not finding.
What is, to be.
Enough, or.
To be suf.
Fi.
Cie.
Nt.
Or, is hope, or.
Is hoping.
Being brave, or being cour.
Age.
Ou.
S e.
No.
Ugh, to?
Believe in some.
Thing bet.
Ter, in some.
Thing high.
Er, or in some.
Thing more, even if.
Is.
"Hoping not a crime, and."
Even if?
Might it be as re.
Or.
As.
"I do mean, that."
On.
Or, this?
Able, as.
Is hoping, or is be?
Lieving not a crime, or is.
"Failing, or."
Is choosing?
"Or, is deciding not to hope, or."

Not to be?
Lieve, eit.
Her, or?
And.
"Of course."
Hope is.
Or, is it.
"A necessary."
Panacea, or.
"A necessary?"
Anti, or ante?
Dote, to, or for?
"Des."
Pair, though.
Even if?
"Hope, or."
Even if ho.
Ping, is.
"Or, even if?"
Hopi.
Ng might be.
What does?
Make one, or.
"At least?"
Some na.
Use.
Ou.
S, and.
Even if?
Hoping, or.
"Hope is."
What does?
"Give one heart."
Aches, and heart at.
Tacks, be.
Cause, of course.
Is hope, or.

"Too, and."
Because, of.
"Course, is."
Hoping, but.
"Wishing, or."
But wanting?
"For what."
Is not yet, and.
Or, for what, very well, might not ever be, and.
"Because, too."
Of course.
"Is hope."
And, hope is.
"But lack of faith, and."
Or, but only?
Because, of course.
"Is faith finding."
And, because.
"Faith is."
Finding acceptance, and.
Certainty, in.
What, or in whom?
Or in Whom, if not, ne.
Ces.
Sa.
Ri.
Ly, in what.
Is, and.
Or, in?
What is, in what has been, in what will be, and, or?
In what has been promised, but?
Of course, promised.
By whom, or by what, and.
Or, to who.
"So?"
M, or to what, and.
In reality, or in Reality?

By what, which, or whose.
If not, necessarily, in.
God, or Goddess.
The real, or in the Real, or.
State, or politician, or.
Because, is.
And, so?
"Is because."
Hope failing to find certainty.
In what is, here.
"And, or."
In what is now, or.
"In what is, al."
Ready, and, or?
In what will be, or.
In what, or in whom.
Is to come, or?
Also, is.
"And, is."
Also, hope.
"Failing to be certain."
Though, of.
"Course."
Failing to be.
"Certain, about."
What, or.
"Failing to be?"
Certain about whom, and.
Because?
Of course, how to know.
Who, *or Who,* or what, *or What,* is to come, or?
"Too, also."
Of course.
Is hope, and.
"Hope is, and."
Too?
"Of course."

Hoping, is.
"And, is hoping."
Also?
"Failing to."
Be?
OK, or all.
Right?
"With what is, and."
Because.
Of course, is.
To ac.
Cept what is.
As enough, and.
As sufficient.
"Far better than."
Always, and far bet.
Ter than ever.
And, far better than?
"Eve."
R, and al.
Ways.
Hoping, wanting, wishing, willing, needing, for more, or.
Better?
"Than?"
Demanding, or.
Better than?
"Longing?"
Or, better than trying, or better than at.
Tempting to demand.
For more.
"Or?"
Far better?
Than longing.
"For what, or?"
Than longing.
For whom.
Is not yet?

"Or, for."
Whom, or for what.
Is yet to come, or.
One does not, and cannot have, or.
"For what, or."
For whom.
Is yet to come, or.
For whom, or for what.
"Has never been?"
Or, for whom.
"Or, for what."
Never will be?
"Or, for whom, or for what."
Can.
Not, and so will not.
Ever be had, or.
"For?"
What, or for whom.
Has, already.
Or, for what, or.
"For whom?"
As yet.
Might not come, or go, at all, or.
"For whom, or for what."
Has, already.
Come and gone, or.
"For what, or."
For whom?
"Is not possible, or."
For whom?
"Or for what."
Is impossible, or.
"For what, or."
For whom?
"Is either."
Probable, or.
"Improbable, but."

Of course.
"Not for both, or for all."
That is probable, improbable, impossible, and possible, and.
Or, of.
"Course?"
But though.
For what, or?
When, and where.
For which, or.
"And where, and when."
For whose savior, or?
For whose, or.
"For which?"
Savior, or.
"Where, and when."
Or when, and where, some?
Do, or.
"Do not know."
For whose, or.
For what.
"Or for whom, or."
For which?
One is waiting, looking, seeking, or searching, or.
For what Sa.
Vior, has.
Because.
"How."
Already?
Can one know when that one.
Or, One?
Has gone, and.
Come, and.
"Has come, and has gone."
Already, or again?
Or where, and when.
For which, or.
"When, and where."

For what, or.
That one, or.
"Where, or when."
Or when, or where.
This one?
For whose Lord, or.
"Has gone, and has come."
Again, and.
Or.
For whose lord, or.
For whose Lord, or.
For which lord.
For which Lord.
"Or lords, or?"
Or Lords, or?
And.
Too, though.
Or.
For whose?
"Of course."
Lords, or?
For which, or.
What idiot, fool, or moron.
For whose ladies have.
"Does not know."
Already?
That, but.
Gone, and.
"Of course."
Come, already, or?
Can.
Not one real.
Ly, truly.
Actually, truly, or.
"Really?"
For what, or.
"Ever be saved."

By any one, two.
Three, or more, or.
More, or.
"By?"
Some other than one.
Self, and.
For whom?
That, too.
"Of course?"
Or, for whose.
"Cannot any other, really."
Is yet to come, or?
"Truly, or actually."
Save any.
One other than one.
Self, and.
Much less everyone, or eve.
Ryb.
Ody, un.
"Too, that."
Less, of course.
That one is Je.
Sus Christ, Him.
Self, in His Se.
Cond Coming, *or in He.*
R fir.
St, or Fir.
St, who, of.
Can.
Course, can only.
Not any.
Save those who do choose, or those.
Body, oro one, every.
"Who do decide."
One, or body.
To be saved, or.
Those who do want to be.

Saved, or.
Those who have chosen.
To believe they do need to be saved, or.
Those who have chosen to be saved, or.
"Some."
Body, or some.
One, or no.
One, or no.
Body, or.
"Be saved."
Who does not wish, want, or need.
"To be, and?"
Quite so sim.
I.
Liar.
Ly, or?
And, also.
"Quite so."
Likewise.
I can.
Not find.
Have, or find.
"Faith for another."
Or, believe for another.
As much as can.
Not another have, or.
"Find."
Faith, or be.
Lieve, for me, *or for you,* as.
"Much as, also?"
Do you, or do I?
Not expect them to, or.
Of course.
"Can."
Not an.
Other, or.
Can.

Not any, or.
"Cannot all."
Others be.
Lie.
Ve for me, as.
"Much, as."
Also, too?
"Cannot I be."
And can you not.
Lie.
Ve for.
Any, or for all?
Others.
"And?"
As much as, also.
"Quite so."
Reasonably, and.
"Also?"
Quite so most.
"Rationally, and?"
Also, quite.
"So most logically, and."
Also?
"Quite so most sensibly, can."
And, will.
"And, do I?"
Also, not.
"Expect any."
Ex.
Pect all?
"Or ex."
Pec.
T the most, or.
"Expect the man?"
Y, or ex.
Pect any ot.
Her than.

"My."
Self?
To have, or.
"To find?"
My own.
"Faith for me."
Or, to find faith.
In yourself.
Or, my?
"Own be."
Lief, or.
My own beliefs.
For me?
"As much as?"
Or for you, because.
Of course.
Can.
Not an.
Other, any, or.
"All others?"
Or, the Other, or.
"Can I not."
Let, or.
Tell you what, or?
In whom, or in what.
Or in what, or in who.
M, you do, ou.
G.
Ht, or should, be.
Lie.
Ve, or.
"Permit, or."
Expect any?
"Other, or."
All others, to.
"Tell me."
What, or how?

To be.
Lieve, or in.
What, or.
"In whom."
To believe, or.
"As much as?"
Also, can.
"And, also, will."
I, also, not.
"Permit, or."
Let, another.
"Any, or."
All others tell.
"Me, or."
Decide for me?
"Or, choose for me."
In what, or.
"In whom, to."
Have faith, or.
"What to think?"
Or, what to say, or.
"How to feel, and."
Also, of.
"Course, as."
Much as.
Every fool, should.
"And, as every idiot, and."
As every moron, ought to know.
Can.
Not one.
"Or, cannot all?"
And, can.
Not the most, or.
"Can."
Not the many?
Have faith in me.
"If I can."

And, if I will, or.
"If I do not?"
First, also.
"Or, simultaneously?"
Have.
"Faith in myself, and."
Or, if I do not, or.
So, of?
"Course, also."
As I would not expect them, to.
Believe in me, or to.
Believe in you, or to.
"Have faith in me?"
Or, to have faith in you.
If I do not.
"Also, and."
Too, first.
Second, or.
"Simultaneously, also."
Believe in myself.
"And, so?"
Too, of course.
"Quite so similarly, or?"
Too, also.
"Of course?"
Quite so.
Likewise.
"Can I not."
Have, or find?
Faith in another, or.
In any?
"Or, in all others, or?"
In the most, or.
"In the many, if?"
I do not have faith in myself, and.
Also, of.
"Course, can."

I not.
"Have faith."
In any, or.
"In all, of."
The rest of them, if.
"They do not, also, have."
Second, first, after, before.
"Or, simultaneously, have."
Or, find?
"Faith in themselves, but.'"
Of course.
And, though.
Even if.
"Faith is, and."
Even if.
"Is not faith, generally, preferable to hope, and."
Generally, or.
"Universally, preferable, also?"
Is certainty.
To hoping, too.
"And, also?"
Is not hoping, or is not hope, also.
"But a righteous fear?"
Of, or.
"In the face of the unknown, or?"
Rather, can.
"And, or."
Rather, should.
"Or, and?"
Rather, ought.
"All, and."
Or?
Every.
Thing, and.
"Or, all?"
Be known, or.
Is, already, and.

Or, rather.
"Too?"
Already, is.
And, rather.
"And, or?"
Are all.
Every.
Body, and.
"Is every?"
One, and, too.
"Is every?"
Thing al.
Ready known, and.
"Too, because."
Of course.
"I am not one."
To let, or.
"One to per."
Mit?
Another.
Or, all?
"Or, any."
Others?
To know for me.
Or?
"Will I."
Or?
"I will."
Also, not.
Permit them to know?
"Or per."
Mit them to?
Decide for me.
What, or.
"Who, or."
Who, or.
What, to.

"Know, or."
What to know.
"Or, whom to know."
Or, whom not to know, or.
"What not to know, or."
What, or.
"Whom should be known, or."
Whom, or what, can.
Or, can.
Not be know.
N, or.
Who, or.
"What, should not be known, or."
What, or.
"Who, or."
Whom.
I do, or do not know, or.
"What, ought."
To be known, or.
"What, or."
Whom, or.
"Whom, or."
What ought not be known, or.
In what to believe, or.
In whom to, or not to, or.
"What, or."
Whom, or.
"Whom, or."
What not.
"To believe, or."
In what, or.
"In whom, or."
In whom, or.
"In what to be."
Lieve, or.
What, or.
"In whom, or."

In whom, or.
"In what to hope, or."
Who, or.
"What, or."
What, or.
"Who, to."
Hope for, or.
"What to know, or."
Whom to know, or.
"Whom not to know, or."
What not to know, or.
"As what, or."
Who will make me hap.
Py, or.
Who, or.
"What will."
Sat.
Is.
Fy me, or.
"Who, or."
What, or.
"What, or."
Who will.
"Make me."
Un.
Happy, dis.
Satisfied, or.
What is plea.
Sur.
Able, or.
"What is painful, what."
I am to know, and.
"Or, whom?"
Or, what.
I am not to know, or.
What is important?
Or.

"What is not, or."
What matters, or.
"What does not matter, or."
Who does matter, or.
"Who does not, to."
Or, for.
"Me, now."
Or, when.
"Or, here."
Or, where.
"Or there, or."
Then, or.
"Later, or."
Part.
Ic.
U.
Lar.
Ly, or.
"Universally, or."
Generally, or.
Objectively, or.
"Subjectively, because."
Of course.
"Even if?"
Of course.
"As who, or?"
As what, does.
Know, or.
"What, or."
As who?
"Does not know?"
That, but.
"Of course."
Is not matter.
What, or.
"All that matters?"
Or, too.

"Also, that?"
Is not matter, all.
"That is."
Here, or.
All that is.
"There."
Because, of course.
Now, too.
"And, also?"
Too, does.
"Anti-."
Or, does.
What is dark?
Or, does.
"Who, or."
Does what.
"Is invisible?"
Or, also.
What, or.
"Who is?"
Not matter, also.
"Matter, too."
As least as much, if not.
"More than?"
What, or more than who?
Is visible, or.
"More than?"
What, or who.
Who, or what.
Is seen, or.
Known, or more than.
"Material matter."
Because, of.
"Course, as."
Much as things, and.
As much as people.
Are.

Too, are they?
Also, not.
And, too.
"Also, are."
They not.
"What, or."
Not who.
Or, whom?
"They are."
Too, and.
Because?
"What, or."
Because who?
"Might they be, and."
Without?
"What, or."
Without?
"Also, who."
They are not.
"Too, and."
Because?
What, or.
"Even if?"
Who, or.
"What is."
Important for.
Or, to.
What does matter, anti?
Dark, or un-
Matter, for.
Or to, some.
Or?
"Even if."
What, or who.
"Who?"
Or, What is re.
Levant, to.

"Or, for some, is?"
Not necessarily, what.
"Is relevant, or."
Important?
"Or, is."
What does matter, or.
"Is what."
Does not matter, to.
"Is not necessarily?"
Or, for others, or?
What is.
Important, to.
"Or, for all."
And, even if?
Is what does matter, to?
Of course.
Or, for all, and.
"Is not all."
Is not necessarily?
Or, always?
What is all, and.
"Or?"
What is necessarily.
"What is."
Important, or.
What is ex.
Port.
Ant, of im.
Port, or of ex.
Port, or.
What, or.
Who is.
"Relevant, or."
What, or who.
"Who?"
Or, what is ir.
Relevant, or.

What does matter, to.
Or, what is anti-, or.
"What is dark."
Mat.
Ter.
"Or for all."
And, because?
Of course.
Also, and.
"Too?"
Not ever.
And, not always?
"And, not ever."
And, not always.
"Or eve?"
R im.
Port.
Ant.
Or, rele.
Vant, or.
"Material."
For, or.
To all.
"Or."
Important to everyone.
Or, to every.
Body.
And, too.
"Or."

*　*　*　*　*

And, so.
With a sigh, and with a bit of a turn, did he con.
Tin.
Ue.
"Or, did I."

And, so, as did I, and, so, or.
As did I con.
Tin.
Ue, and, so.
As did he, too, and, so.
As much as.
If in the same thought, idea, dream, or night.
Mare, or.
What is.
Important, relevant, or.
"Material, to."
Or, for one, is.
"Not necessarily."
What is.
For everyone, for.
"All, or."
For everybody, everywhere, or.
"For all."
All at, or all in, the same time, or times, or.
"Or, for everyone, or."
For everybody, for.
"All of the same reasons."
Or.
"For the same reason?"
Or, for all the right rea.
Sons, or.
For all the wrong reas.
Ons, or.
But, of course.
"Wrong, or."
Right, or.
Left, or wrong, or.
"Right, or left?"
For, or.
To whom.
"Too, and."
Because, of course.

"And, too, if."
Because, of course.
"When, and where."
And where, and when.
Choices must be made.
And.
"When, and."
Where, one.
"Or, more?"
Must know, choose, or.
"Decide?"
What is important, what.
"Is material, what."
Or, who?
Does matter, and.
Who, or?
What does not.
"Must one."
And, must all.
"Choose, and."
Decide, and.
Know, for.
And, know by?
Themselves, and.
And.
Because, of course.
In order to know, by.
"And, in order to know, for?"
One.
Self, *or your.*
Self, must.
"One know one."
Self, and.
Because, of.
Course?
"I am, and."
Because, of.

Course, also.
"Am I not one."
Willing to know.
"Another, or."
All others, for.
"All others, or."
For an.
Ot.
Her, and.
"Too, also."
Because, of.
"Course?"
I am not.
"One willing."
One wishing, one needing, or.
"One wanting?"
Or, one de.
Siring?
To choose, to de.
Cide, to act, to say, to be.
Lie.
Ve, to think, not to think, not to be.
Lieve, not to say, not to act, not to de.
Cide, or not to choose for anyone.
"Or, for everyone."
For everybody, or.
"For all?"
Or, for any.
Body, other.
Than myself.
"And, too, because."
Of course.
"As much as."
I am not one.
"Willing to know."
What is right.
"Or, what is wrong."

What is wrong.
"Or, what is right."
To, or for.
"Or for, or to."
Anyone, or everyone.
"Everybody, or anybody."
All, or any.
Other than my.
Self, and.
Too, because.
"Most fairly."
Or?
"Of course."
Fair to, or fair.
For whom, and.
"Or."
As if fair does matter, or.
"As if life is?"
Or, as if is death.
Only, as.
Fair, as.
"We might hope, wish, want, or dream it to be, and."
Or?
As if what is fair to, or.
For one.
"Might be."
Fair for.
Or, for to all.
"Or?"
As if.
Might fair.
"Or, as if?"
Might always.
"Or, ever."
Fair be.
A, or.
"The Rule?"

Or.
The way, or.
The Way, ever, or al.
Ways, for all, everywhere, or.
As if what is fair, also, is.
What is.
"Most easy."
Or, what is.
"Most obvious."
Or, what is.
"Most simple."
Or, what is.
"Really, or."
Truly, or.
"Actually, real?"
Or, Real.
"Or, reality."
For everyone.
"Or, for everybody?"
Or, for all.
"Or."
What, merely.
"Just, or."
Only, what is?
Merely, ideal.
"Or."
And, too.
"Because?"
And, as if.
What is fair to, or for, one.
"Might always."
Or, ever might.
"Everywhere, and."
Or, always?
Be.
"What is fair for, or to."
The most, or.

To, or for.
The many.
Or to, or.
"For the all, and."
Or?
"Of course."
How to explain.
Why, or the fairness, of?
Good things happening to bad people, or.
"Bad things happening to good people, or?"
Merely, or only.
Only, or merely.
And, if so, not quite so justly?
Do seemingly bad things.
Merely, only, or.
Just, or.
"Unjustly, seem?"
Or me.
To happen to seemingly good people, and.
Re.
Just, or un.
Ly seem.
Justly, or what kind of God, or God.
Dess caring, or good, and?
"Only, or merely."
All-power.
Ful, and all-.
Knowing, could.
Would, or might?
Let, or per.
Mit such things to happen, or.
"Why?"
Do seemingly good things happen to.
"Or, happen for?"
Seemingly bad people, and.
Or, rather.
"Is all of this, and."

Or, rather.
"Is all of that."
Mere, and more.
"Rationalizing, or."
Justification, and, or?
Or.
"Because, of course."
As every idiot, fool, or.
As each, and as every.
"Moron should."
And, ought know.
Is not seeming, being.
"As is not appearing, either?"
And, so?
Because, "Of course."
Who, or what?
What, or Who.
Is to say, that.
Or, this?
Or, that this, or.
What, or who.
Or, Who?
Is good.
"Or, that."
Who is, or that.
What, or Who.
Or, who?
Is bad?
Or, that who, or Who?
Or, that what, is.
Good, or bad.
To, or for, whom, or.
Bad, or good.
For, or to, whom.
Is, so.
"Absolutely, for?"
All, for everyone, or.

"For."
At, or in.
Everybody, everywhere.
In, or at.
Because, too.
All time, or ti.
"Of course."
Me.
Who is to assume.
S, and.
"Or, who is to presume?"
That life, is.
"Or, that it is meant to be?"
Though, of course.
"Meant, or."
Intended.
"By whom?"
Or, in.
Ten.
Ded.
"Or, meant."
By what?
Or, for who.
To be fair, or.
M, or for what.
To be good, or.
"To be bad, or?"
To be ideal, or.
"To be real, or."
To be whose version, of.
Any, or of all.
Of those, or of.
"The real, or."
The Real?
To be.
"Whose version of the ideal, or."
Of the Ideal?

Because, too.
"Of course."
Is not.
Love fair, either.
Or, rather.
As much as is not war.
Is all fair in both, or.
Though, too.
If not ne.
"Of course."
Ces.
So is not life, or dea?
Sari.
Th ei.
Ly, in.
H ei.
Every.
Ther.
Thin.
"All love, or."
G, or in all, or.
All war, and.
"Too, of."
Course, is not.
"War, or."
Is not love.
"All of life, or."
Too?
"Though, and?"
Too, do not.
Either love.
Or, war?
"Ever, or not al."
Ways.
Play by the rules, or.
By which rules, or by which R.
"Play by whose rules, and."

Ules, or.
Or, by whose.
Rules for whom, or for what, and.
So, who?
"Or, so, what."
Is to say, that.
"Life does."
Or, that?
All of life, is about.
Does death, love, or war?
Love, loving, or a.
"It, or they."
Bout being loved, or.
Does, or do.
Not, and, so?
"And, though."
But, so.
"And, but, so?"
Of course.
Who, or.
What, or.
"What, or whom?"
Or.
All about death, or war, or.
"Who, or what?"
Pea.
Is to say, speak, choose, or decide.
Ce, or.
What is fair?
To, and, or.
For whom.
"And?"
Or for, or.
To whom.
"And?"
Because.
And, so?

"And, too."
Because.
Of course.
"Do things."
And, does life?
"Get a bit more complicated, when."
And, where.
"And, where."
And, when.
What.
Or, who?
Is fair.
"Is, also, not."
What.
Or, who?
Is good.
Or, who, or what, *at least?*
Does see.
M, or does ap.
Pear to be so.
What? And.
"Where, and when."
Who, or what.
Does seem to be good, or.
What, or who, does pretend.
To be, try to pose as, or appear to be.
Is, also, not who, or what, does seem, or pretend, or appear to be.
Fair, or.
And when, and where.
What, or.
Who?
Is just.
Or, fair.
"Is, also, not necessarily."
What, or.
Who?
Is good.

Or, where.
"Or, when."
What is fine is, also, not what is best.
Or good, or great, or even all.
"Or where."
Right, at all.
Do, and can, not all agree on what, or about whom.
Is best, fine, good, or fair, or. About whom, or a.
Bout what is un.
Fair, bad, *good*, not fair, *not great,* or not best, and so the worst?
Or, Worst.
Or, when.
What, or.
Who is.
Good, is, also, not fine.
"Or?"
Where, or when.
"Or when, or where."
Who, or what.
"Is fine."
But for, or ac.
Is, also, not what, or.
Cord.
Also.
Ing to whom, or ac.
Is not who.
Cording to what, What.
Or Who.
Is good, or.
What, or what, who, or Who is great, or.
"Where, or when."
Or when, or where.
Or where, or when.
"What is fine, is, also, not."
Who, or what.
"Or what, or who."
Is best, or.

Worst, or?
Who, or what.
Says, things, feels, believes, chooses, or de.
Cides is fine, or good, or.
Also?
Is not who, or is not what.
Is best, or fair, or.
When, and where?
"Or past both, or."
Where, or when.
What, or who.
"Who, or What?"
Is.
Best is not necessary what, or.
"Who is."
The greatest?
Or who gets to say, choose, or de.
Cide?
What, or who, Who, or What, is best, greatest, good, fine, bad, or good, or?
Whose greatest?
Or where, or when.
"Or when, or where."
What does work for some.
"Or, for one?"
Does not work for all.
The best?
"Or, when."
Or, where?
What does work for all.
Or, for the All.
Or, for the worst?
Does not, necessarily.
"Work for some, or."
Where, or when.
"Or when, or where."
What does work for the most.

Or, for the many?
Or, for the best?
"Does not work for the all, or."
For all, or for All, or.
Where, and when?
Or when, and where.
What does work for the all.
Or, for All.
Or, for the greatest.
Does not work for one, or.
"For the one?"
Or where, or when.
"What does work for all is not what is good, best, greatest, or fine."
To, or.
"For one?"
Or, for One.
Or when, or where.
Or for the one, or for.
"What does work for one."
The One.
Is not what does work for all, for the all, or.
"For the most, or for the many, or."
Rather, but.
"What to do."
When, and where.
"Or where, and when."
Most reasonably.
Or, most rationally.
Or.
"Where, or when."
Or when, or where.
"Most rationally, or most reasonably."
Cannot una?
Nim.
It.
Y be ex.
Pec.

Ted, de.
Man.
Ded, for.
Ced.
Or en.
Forced?
"Or?"
Can it, or must it be, which.
Is un.
Real.
Is.
Tic, and um.
Prac.
Tic.
Al, *at least,* in the free wor.
Ld, or in?
A free so.
Cie.
Ty, or?
Where, and when.
Or when, and where.
Be?
Ca.
Use, of.
Ur.
Se, do not dis.
Agree.
Ments, ne.
Cess.
Ari.
Ly me.
Nt off.
En.
Se, or ne.
Ed me.
An of.
Fen.

Ses, and be.
Cause, of course, can.
Not every.
One, e.
Very.
Body, or all, agree a.
Bout every.
Thing, all of the time, as we.
Ll as, be.
Cause I do know, that?
Or, do you.
Those who are wil.
Know what?
Ling, or to.
O re.
Ady to a.
Gree, as are all the 'yes,' men, and wo?
Men be.
St mis.
Trust.
Ed, and.
"Most rationally."
But, rat.
Or, most rea.
Son.
Ably.
Her, qui.
Most sensibly, most logically, or.
Te so very most, and mo.
Because, but.
Re real.
"Of course?"
Is.
"Except where, or ex."
Tic.
Cept when.
All.

And when, and where.
Y, are most peo.
"Or what?"
Ple em.
People ever are.
Ot.
Most reas.
On.
Able.
Ion.
Most sensible.
Al, to.
"Or most."
O, whi.
Rational?
Ch is, at le.
Most logical.
As.
Or, most agreeable.
T, part of w.
And, be.
Hat doe.
Cause.
S ma.
"Of course."
Ke the.
What to do.
M hu.
"Where, or when."
Man, so.
Or when, or where.
"Agreement, or agreements, can."
Not be for.
Ced, or en.
Forced, so.
Where, or when.
"Or when, or where."

Can una.
Nim.
It.
Y not be, either.
"Too, where."
Or, too, when.
"Do all."
Agree, quite.
"So, or."
Quite, too?
Easily, where.
Or, when.
"Or, when."
Or, where.
"Can any, or."
Where, or.
"When, can."
Any, or.
All be?
"Trusted, and."
Or, too?
Who, or what, is bet.
Te.
R off, or bet.
Ter on, mis.
Trusted, or.
And, so.
"And, too?"
So, and.
"And, but?"
Of course.
What are quest.
"Ions, di."
Ions.
Lemmas, and pro.
Blems.
Timeless, end.

Less, and with?
Out.
"Ans."
Wers, eternal, lasting, or en.
During, or.
Even ones tempo.
Rar.
Y, im.
Per.
Man.
Nent, or ot.
Herwise.
For e.
Veryone, for al.
Ways, or for ever.
Ybody.
Uni.
Ver.
Sally.
"Or, for every."
Where, but?
Because, of course.
"Too, and."
Once again?
As much as I am not one willing to choose for anyone.
"Or, for eve."
Ry.
One.
Or, for everybody.
For somebody.
"Or, for no?"
Body.
For someone.
"Or, for no one."
Other than yourself.
"Other than myself."
And, too.

"Because, of course."
As much as.
And, also.
I am un.
Willing to choose.
To know?
For any, or.
One will.
To take responsibility.
Ling.
For all.
"Other than myself, too."
Am I, also, un.
Willing to.
"Be chosen, or."
To be?
Known, or.
Chosen?
"For."
As much as I am.
Also?
Un.
Willing, to.
"Take responsibility, for."
Anyone, or.
For everyone, or.
For everybody, or.
Anybody.
"Other than myself, and."
Also?
As much as I am, also, not one.
To try?
"To speak for another."
Or, for any?
"Or, for all others, and."
As much as I am, also.
And, as much as you are?

"Not one."
Willing to be spoken for.
Or.
"One willing."
Or, one.
"Needing, or."
One ex.
Pec.
Ting to.
"Be able?"
To escape.
"Myself, so."
As?
"To be taken."
Responsibility, *or known?*
For.
Or?
As much as.
So as to blame another, for.
"Of course?"
Doing, saying, not doing.
"Not saying?"
Thinking, be.
Lie.
Ving, or.
I, also, am not.
For not believing, or for.
Not thinking, or.
"One willing."
To blame any, or all.
Ot.
Hers.
For feeling, for not feeling.
For being, for becoming, or for.
"To be?"
Not be.
Ing, or for.

Not be.
Coming.
"Mastered, had."
Who you are, and.
"So con."
Trol.
Led, so en.
Slaved, or.
Or, for?
Becoming, or.
For being.
"Taken, or played."
What, and who; who, and what, you are, also, of course, not.
By, or for.
"Or as a fool, and?"
Too, because.
"Of course."
I am not one.
Dumb, one foolish.
One pos.
Ses.
Sive, one can.
Trolling.
One fas.
Cist, one de.
Spe.
Rate, one.
"Dev."
Ili.
Sh, one de.
Mon.
Ic.
Or one bar.
Bar.
Ic? Enough.
"To have to try."
To ow.

N, or.
To try to have.
"Or, to think?"
For, or that.
Another, or.
"That any."
Or, that all.
Others.
"Can, or should, or ought."
Or ought, or should, or can.
Be had, taken, or.
"Possessed, be."
Cause, of course.
I am not such a player.
Game, or.
"Otherwise, and."
Too, because?
"Of course, and."
Also?
"I am not one."
Quite like that.
Or, one.
"Quite like this?"
Or, one.
Quite like them, ha.
Ving?
Willing.
"Wan."
Ting, or?
Needing to win, at.
"Any, or."
At all costs, and.
"Because, rather?"
I do know.
"Think, and be."
Lieve.
Be.

Lieve, and.
"Think, and."
Also, know?
"That, but."
Of course.
"Ought, and should."
And, that?
"Should, and ought."
Not others, be so.
Ma.
Ste.
"Or?"
Red, so con.
Trolled, so en.
Slaved, or.
"Attempted to?"
Be had, possessed, taken.
"Or?"
Objectified.
Or, because.
"And, too."
Because.
"I am, also."
As as I have said, and.
"As I have thought, before?"
Too, of.
"Course, I."
Am not one.
To want, one to need.
Or?
One to try to know for any.
Or, for all.
Other.
Or, others.
"Than myself."
And, too.
As much as I am.

"Not one."
To need, or one to want.
To be known, for.
"Because."
Of course, is to be known.
"To be objectified."
By the know.
Ers, or.
"By?"
The subject.
If.
Ie.
Rs, too.
"And."
Because, of course.
"Knowledge is power, of."
Course, and.
Because to know another.
"Or, to presume to know?"
All others.
Or, to presume to know another, is?
"An attempt, or."
Is?
"The want, or."
Is?
"The need."
Or, is to ob.
Jec.
Tif.
Y.
Another, and.
"Too, because?"
Of course.
Is not love ob.
Ject.
If.
I.

Cat.
I.
On, and.
People are not things.
Of course.
Even if, most simply.
They might be.
Pre, or as.
Sum.
Ed to be, and.
But, of course, by whom, Whom, What, or what, and.
Even if.
You might like to so.
Be able to re.
Duce, and to so con.
Trol them, and.
Too, because?
"Of course."
Is not love, or.
"Loving, also?"
About controlling, or.
"About, power?"
Either, and.
"Too, so."
What does, or.
"What can?"
Or, what must.
"Loving, or."
Love, have?
"To do with knowing an."
Other, or.
With knowing?
Any, or all.
Others, or.
With knowing?
"In general, or."
With having to know, as.

Can one love, without knowing, or.
"Well, as."
Be loved with.
Of course?
Out, or in, or de.
"Can love not be."
Spite of be.
About, or.
Ing know.
"To be?"
N, or?
Objectified, and.
"Too, because."
Even, if?
Might ob.
Jec.
Ti.
Fi.
Cat.
I.
On, be.
"Most ea."
Sy, most simp.
Le, and?
Even if.
"Of course?"
Might objectification, also, be.
"Most natural, or?"
Most obvious, and.
Most simple, and most easy, *but.*
Or, even if so?
"Of course."
What fool, id.
Io.
T, or mo.
Ron.
"Does not know?"

That, but.
Of course.
"What is most simple."
Or that who, *or Who,* is simp.
Lest, or.
That What, or what, is, or.
That who, or t.
Hat what, at le.
As.
T, does seem, or do.
Es app.
Ear to be, or.
And, that.
"What is most easy."
Is not, necessarily.
"What, or who?"
Who, or what.
Is most right.
Or, that.
"What, or who?"
Who, or What.
Does but seem.
To be?
"Most simple, does."
But seem?
"To be, and."
Or, that.
"What does but seem?"
Or who, or Who, does seem.
To be most easy, or ea.
Si.
Est, is.
"Not really, not truly, or."
Is not actually, or.
"That what?"
Is most easy, or.
"That what?"

Or, that who.
"Is easiest, or."
That who, or.
"That what?"
Or, What.
Is simplest, or.
"That what, or."
That who?
Or, Who.
"Is most simple, is."
Also, what?
"Or is, also, who."
Is most simp.
List.
Ic, or.
"Is who, or."
Is what, is.
Most correct?
Most right?
Or, what is.
Or ,What is.
Or, who is.
Or ,Who is.
"Most proper."
Or, what is.
Or, who is.
Most ap.
Pro.
Pri.
Ate, or.
"Or?"
But, which.
Of course.
"Either, is."
Or, is not.
Or, is it?
Also, or.

Not.
"To say, that."
Of course?
To be objectified, is.
"Also, to?"
Objectify, or.
"That to objectify, also, is?"
To be objectified, or.
"That to objectify is but asking to be?"
Ob.
Jec.
Tif.
Ie.
D, or?
"That to be objectified is, also, to earn the right to objectify."
Because?
"Of course."
Are not some OK, or all.
Right un.
Til all are un.
At least, un.
Der con.
Til one is un.
Trol, or be.
Der the.
Neat.
M, or?
H the.
Un.
M, or?
Til he, she, it, or the.
"And, too, who?"
Until all are re.
Y, do h.
Duced to be.
Ave, at le.
Ing thing.

As.
S, or ob?
T, one to r.
Jects, or.
Ide, or.
Is not.
To say.
"That not wanting to be objectified."
Or, that.
"Not willing to be?"
Does mean.
"That I am willing."
Or, that you are.
Or, that I am wanting?
Or, that one.
Or, that all?
Is, or.
Are, also?
Willing, wanting, or.
Needing?
"To be sub."
Jec.
TI.
Fi.
Ed, ei.
Ther.
Because, of course.
"I would not pre."
Fer.
Though, of course.
"I cannot speak."
Know, or.
"Think, or."
Think, or.
"Know."
Decide, or.
"Choose, or."

Choose, or.
"Decide."
For the most.
"Or, for the all."
Or, for the many.
"Or, for any, or for all."
Others, but?
"At least, as for me."
I do prefer.
To be both know.
Er, and known.
And, so?
"To be, both."
My own.
"Object, and."
Subject, and.
"Both, my?"
Own sub.
Ject.
"And ob."
Jec.
T, and.
So?
"And, to."
Know for, and to know.
By myself.
"Than to."
Be known for, or by, any, or all, others.
"Or, than to?"
Presume.
"Or, than to."
Assume to be known.
By, or for.
Any, or all, ot.
Hers, or Ot.
Hers?
"And, too?"

Because.
"Of course."
I would prefer to know myself.
"Than to be presumed?"
Or, than to be assumed.
"To be?"
Known, or.
Than to be?
Studied, by.
"Or, than to be?"
Known by.
"Another, and?"
Too, because.
"Of course."
How to be.
"Oneself, or."
How to be?
"At all, where."
Or, at all?
"Or, wholly, or."
Completely, or.
"Entirely, if."
Where, or.
"If when, or."
If when, or.
"If where."
One is al.
Ways.
"Being watched, studied."
Objectified, stalked.
"Or at?"
Tempt.
Ed.
To be known, had.
"Con."
Troll.
Ed, take.

N.
Or, pos.
Se.
Sed?
"Captured, mastered."
Enslaved, or.
"Controlled, and?"
Because, of.
"Course."
How so far much easier.
"Is it."
Or, it is.
To know another?
"Or, to presume."
Or, to assume?
"To know another."
Or, to assume, or.
"To presume?"
To know for a.
Not.
Her?
Or for any, or for all.
Others, or.
"Than to have to know for."
One.
Self, or.
By one.
Self, "Or than?"
To have to know one.
Self.
"Too, because?"
Of course.
Who does have.
Pos.
Ses.
S, or ow.
N.

Or, because?
"Who does, or who can, find."
The courage.
Or.
"And, the strength?"
Or, the strength.
"And, the courage."
To know oneself.
"And, to know for oneself."
Might ever care, or.
Want, or.
"Need, or."
Need, or.
"Want?"
To be con.
Cern.
Ed.
Or, to be.
"Bothered by, or."
With having to know for any, or for all.
Ot.
Hers, and.
"Or?"
Who does know one.
Self would ever ass.
Or, pre.
Sun.
E, "Or?"
Need to know for any.
One else.
And.
Too, of.
"Course, who."
Does know oneself.
"Need not worry about."
Knowing any.
"Or a?"

Bout.
Knowing all.
"Or, about?"
Knowing for.
"Any, or."
About?
"Knowing for."
All others, or?
"Too, of course."
Because, is.
"Not needing to know?"
Or, is.
A fail.
Needing to know.
Ure to t.
Rust, and.
"Is not too much curiosity, too?"
A sort of violation, and.
"Because, of."
Course.
Who.
Or, what?
Or What, or who.
Does know oneself.
"Does not need to try."
To know for.
"To master, or to control?"
Any, or all others, and.
"Because?"
Of course.
Though all know.
Ledge is po.
Wer can know.
Ledge be wrong.
Ly used, and, so, ab.
Used, and.
"Can, and should, and ou."

Gh.
T not.
All things.
Or, all people?
Or, all the People.
"Or, all things."
A.
Bout all people?
Or on.
"Or all things."
Ly ab.
About all things?
Out so.
Be known.
Me, or.
By all.
And, if so, a.
And, too.
Bout which ones, or.
"Because?"
By ever.
Of course.
Yon.
"Cannot all."
E, or by every.
Know, or.
Body, or.
"Get, or."
Under.
Stand all.
Everyone, everybody, or every.
And.
Thing, about every.
"Too, be."
Body, ab.
Cause, of course.
Out every.

Rather, who.
Y.
"And, because?"
Thing, a.
"And, because?"
Bout all.
Rather, who.
So, un.
Cert.
Ain.
"And, be?"
Cause.
Rather, who.
"And."
Because, who?
So, un.
Sure.
"Of whom, or."
Who so.
"Un."
Sure?
Of what.
"They are?"
Is far more ur.
Gently concerned.
"With imposing who they are?"
Or, with.
"Im."
Posing.
What they are not.
"On any, and."
Or?
On all others.
Because?
Of course.
"To know who one is, also, is to know?"
And, does re.

Qui.
Re knowing, also.
What, or who.
"Or, also, is to know?"
Who, or what.
What, or Who.
"One is not."
Too, and.
"Because."
Who does know who they are.
Until they.
"Or un."
Til she, he.
"Or, it."
Also, does.
"Know who."
Or, also, does know what?
"One is not, and."
Because, too.
Who.
Must, also, know.
"Who, and."
That.
"Also, what?"
Or, this.
But, of cour.
Is if one ever is.
Se, on.
To be, or.
Ly in.
If one ever.
Sofar, as.
Is to find, be, or stay.
This is not t.
At peace, or.
Hat, and t.
"They are not."

Hat is not t.
And, too?
His, or.
"Because, of course."
Who does not know who they are.
"Also, and, too."
Does not know who they are not.
"Too, and."
So?
Who does know who, and Who, they are, al.
So, does know.
What, and what, if not, al.
So, who, or Who.
They are not, and, so.
Who does not know who they are.
"Will continually, ever."
And will, always?
"Consistently try."
To be someone, or.
"Try to be?"
Something else.
Or, who does not know.
"Who, or what."
What, or Who.
They are will.
Always, and.
"Will ever?"
Try to.
"Pretend to."
Be something, or.
Try.
To be?
"Someone who."
They are not.
And, too.
"And, but, though."
Of course.

Even if?
Might they, he, she, or it.
"Convince themselves."
Of himself, or.
"Of herself, or."
Of itself, for.
"A bit, or."
For a while, of.
"Their own lies, and."
Or, of.
Their own ill.
Us.
Io.
N.
S, and.
"Or, of?"
Their own de.
Lusions, and.
Least, for.
"A bit."
Or, for a while.
Will they, will.
"He, will."
She, will.
"It, and."
Will you?
"Also, and."
Quite so inevitably be un.
"Able to con."
Vince all.
Or, to con.
Vince every.
One.
"Everywhere, or."
Everyone, or.
"All, for."
Or, all in.

All time, *or ti.*
Me.
S, and, still.
What is.
"And, what still."
Will, and what.
Or, who?
"Ever will be."
Who, and.
Or?
"What will be."
And, what is.
Only, just.
"Or, un."
Justly?
Merely, or mirror-ly.
"Only pretending."
And, on.
Ly po.
Sing.
Or mirr.
Or-ly, just.
"Merely, or."
Justly, only.
Imp.
Ost.
Ering, and.
"Even though."
Because.
Who would not rather be.
"True, and real."
Or real, and true?
Rather than false, and fake, or.
"Rather than?"
Fake, and false, and.
Which is quite dif.
Because.

Fi.
"Who would not rather?"
Cult.
Be an or.
And ti.
Ig.
Ring.
In.
Al, or.
"Unique?"
Or dis.
Tinct.
Themselves, or.
Rather than a copy, or.
"Rather than?"
Fake.
False.
A clone, a ro.
Bot, or.
Another, the same, one of the same, or one of the Sam.
E, or, rather, than one of the 'we's,' or.
"Rather than?"
A repli.
Who would not, rat.
Cant, and.
Her, be?
Or, rat.
Who they are, rat.
Her than a liz.
Her t.
Ard, or a dino.
Han who, or w.
Saur, or.
Hat, they all do w.
Who would.
Ant, or ex?
"Not rather, be?"

Pect you to be, or.
Genui.
Ne, and.
Or, rather than a poser, pre.
Tend.
Er, or im.
Post.
Er, and.
Who would not rat.
"Authentic, or."
Her be.
Au.
Then.
Tic, or.
"Gen."
Ui.
Ne?
Rather than.
A pre.
Tender, though.
"Of course?"
Might it, or might one?
Be better.
"To be a good?"
Or, great.
Fake, or.
"A good?"
False im.
Poster, than.
"A real?"
Or, than?
"A truly bad."
Real, aut.
Hen.
Tic, or genu.
Ine per.
Son, or.

Rather than a true, real, genuine, or au.
Then.
Tic replicant, or lizard, tho.
Ugh.
"Of course?"
Bad, or.
"Good, or."
Good, or.
Great, or.
"Bad, according."
To whom, or.
"According to what, or."
In what way, or.
"In what ways, and."
For whom, or for what, and.
Because.
When, and where.
"And where, and when."
So ever have.
All agreed.
On, or about.
About, or on.
What, or whom, is true, or.
On, or a.
Bout.
Whom, or what, is true, or.
About, or on.
Who is most tru.
E, or true.
"Or on what, or about whom, is false?"
Most ob.
Or about, or on.
Vio.
What, or whom, is fake.
Us to one, and to all, and.
As well as do all.
Or for all, or for one, and, or.

Does everyone, and does everybody.
Ex.
Who do not.
Cept, of co.
Lie, so.
Ur.
All.
Se, what is ob.
Who are ho.
Vi.
Nest with, and tru.
Ou.
E to.
S to, or for, on.
The.
E, or so.
Ms.
Me, is not ne.
Elves.
Ces.
Just know.
Sar.
Who, and what.
Il.
Is fake, and.
Ly, so.
What, and who.
For all, for ever.
Or, for every.
Is fal.
One, every.
Se.
Where, or for ever.
As well as.
Y.
Do.
Body.

Such types, know.
Without needing to think.
Or be told, or shown.
What, and who, and Who.
Is true, and.
Who, and what, or Who, and What, is not.
And.
Without needing to be told, or shown, or.
"Or about, or on."
Who is?
On what, or about.
What, or who, is real.
"Or on?"
Or, about.
"What, or who."
Is true, or.
"About whom."
Or, about what?
"Is un—"
False, or.
And, so true?
About whom.
"Or, about what?"
Is un-.
Fake, or.
And, so, about who, or a.
Bout what?
Is true, or.
"About whom, or."
About what?
Is un.
Real, sur.
Real, or ot.
Her.
Wise.
"Or?"
About what is being real.

Or, Real.
"Or, about?"
Who is, or.
"About what?"
Is being true, or.
True, or.
"About what, or."
About whom?
"Is genuine, or."
Ab.
Out who, or.
"About what?"
Is authentic, or.
"About who, or."
About what.
"Is in."
Authentic, or.
About what, or.
"About who?"
Is not genuine, or.
"If?"
Being real is, also.
Being true.
Or, True.
"Or, if."
Being true is, also.
Being real.
Or, Real.
"Or, if."
Who is being real, is.
"Also, who."
Is being true, or.
True, or.
"If who."
Is being true, is.
"Also, who."
Is being real, or.

Real, or.
If, rather?
"Quite so far more easily, and."
Or, if rather?
"Quite so far more simply."
Or, not.
Do some just know.
Without knowing why.
"And, or."
With.
Out know.
Ing how.
And, without needing to know how.
They do know, or do not know.
What is real.
Or, who is real, and.
Or, Who is Real, or.
"What is Real, or."
Who is Real, or.
Who, or.
"What is not."
And, because.
"Of course?"
Cannot one know.
"What is true, and."
What is real, or.
Real, or.
"Who is real, or."
Who is true, *or True,* with.
Out.
"Also, knowing?"
Who, or.
"Without, also?"
Knowing what.
"Is not, or."
Also, without?
"Knowing who, or."

Also, without?
"Simultaneously knowing."
What is fake.
Or, Fake.
"And what is false."
Or, who is.
And, without.
Or, Who is.
"Also, knowing?"
Who is false.
Or, False.
"And, who is fake."
And, also, without knowing.
Who, or what, is lying, and.
Without knowing, but not necessarily without caring.
What, or who, is being real, or true, because.
"Of course."
How to be true, or real.
Or Real, or True.
With any one, two, or more.
Who are not, and.
How to know who, or what.
"Is fake, or false?"
Or False, or Fake.
Without first, knowing.
Or, at least?
Without first, at the same time, know.
Ing.
"What, and who."
And, so, who, and what.
"Is true, and."
Or True, and.
Though, but.
"And, even if."
But, because.
And, too.
"Because."

Of course, while.
"Do some."
Crave the truth, do.
Others seek.
"To do all, and."
Everything?
"They can, to."
Escape it, and.
Or, to a.
Void it.
"Because, of."
Course, while.
"Some do crave."
Reality, do.
"Others seek to?"
Escape, and.
"To avoid?"
It, at any, and, or.
At all costs, and.
"While some."
Do crave, want, need.
"Thirst, or."
Hunger, for.
"The truth, or."
For?
The Truth, do.
"Others crave lies, de."
Lus.
Ions, and, or ill.
Us.
Ions, and.
"Be."
Cause, while.
Of course, do some.
Have the courage.
"To face the truth, and."
While, are.

"Only, some?"
Brave enough to.
"Face?"
Them.
Selves, and?
"To accept themselves, and."
To accept the truth, do.
"Others, ever."
And always, need.
"To try."
To run from it, or.
"And, or."
From them.
Selves, be.
Cause.
Of course.
Is not the truth, ever.
"Or, of?"
Ten.
Or, always.
Nec.
Ess.
Ari.
Ly, what, or who.
Is simp.
Le, or simp.
Lest, but.
"Of course?"
Or, is it, but.
Is it not necessarily, ever.
Or, always.
"What is?"
Most simp.
List.
Ic, or.
What, or who.
Does but seem, or appear to be, or.

"Because?"
Can.
Not ever.
"And, cannot always."
All in.
All places.
"Or, all."
At, or.
"All in."
All times.
Be whol.
Ly, be comp.
Lete.
Ly, be en.
Tire.
Ly, or be to.
Tally.
"True, and real."
Or genuine, and authentic?
Or real, and true.
Or True, and Real.
"Or authentic, and genuine, with."
All, or.
With all?
With every.
Or, with ever.
Body, or.
Yon.
"All of the time."
E.
Or, with everyone, or.
"With all, and."
Because, of course.
How can one?
"Be true, or."
True, or.
Be real, or.

Real, or.
"Be?"
Or, how can you be.
Au.
Then.
Tic, or.
"Genuine?"
When, and.
"Where, or."
Where, or.
"When, is."
With, or.
"When, or."
Where, or.
"Where, or."
When one.
"Is surrounded by?"
Those who are.
"Not real, not."
True, or.
"By those?"
Who are.
"Not genuine, or."
By those?
"Who are in."
Aut.
He.
N.
Tic, be.
Cause, of course.
Do so.
Me in.
Sist.
On being false, and on.
"Being fake, or."
False, or Fake, or.
On being poser.

S, pre.
Ten.
Ders, or im.
Post.
Ers, as if.
So being is being at all, or.
To, and.
"With others."
Because they are false, *and False.*
Fake, and fake.
With them.
Selves, and, too.
"Because, how."
To be.
"True with."
Or, to.
"All others, if."
One is not true.
Or, True.
"To, or with."
Oneself, and.
Because, how.
"Not to lie to any."
Or, to all?
Others, if.
When, or.
"If where, or."
If where, or.
"If when."
One does in.
Sis.
T, on.
"Lying to."
One.
Self, be.
Cause.
"Of course."

Or which is, but.
Do some.
A me.
Ins.
Re.
Ist on pre.
Ly, and in.
Tending.
Cre.
Because?
As.
"And, on."
In.
Pla.
Gly, pat.
Ying ga.
He.
Mes.
Tic ex.
They do know no other way, or.
Cuse to ke.
Ways, ot.
Pin.
Her than t.
G on be.
Hose of the e.
Ing so ir.
Go, and of its lie.
Ration.
S, and lim.
All.
Its, and?
Y, and de.
Which far too of.
Man.
Ten is de.
Din.

Luded by its own de.
Gly self-in.
Lus.
Te.
Ions, and which.
Rest.
Far too ea.
Ed, or.
Sily, does.
Also?
Which does not like, or want.
Fall for its own ill.
To have to to.
Us.
Ler.
Ions, and.
Ate any.
Which far too easi.
Thing, or an.
Ly, does.
Yon.
"Also."
E it is not, or.
Be.
Any.
Lie.
One, two, or m.
Ve its own lies, while?
Ore, the mo.
From the side.
St, the man.
Lines, the self, or.
Y, the all, or?
The Self, an.
Can.
Y thin.
Not help but laugh at.

G, t.
Its ga.
Hat it can.
Mes, at its lie.
Not con.
S, at.
Trol, or.
Its ill.
Us.
Ions, and at its de.
Lus.
Ions, and.
"And, on."
Or, because?
In.
Vent.
Ing a self, fa.
Ke, and fal.
Se.
"They do not know."
And, in?
"Any other way, or ways, and."
Believing in a self.
"Because they."
Or, be.
That is not.
Cause, you.
"Do in."
Sist on, or up.
On.
"Denying the truth, and."
Because, do not?
"Some insist."
On sticking, to.
Or, on.
"Or, with?"
An idea of who they are.

"Or, on."
Or, of?
"An idea, of."
Who, *or what,* they should be.
Or, on.
"Or, with?"
A cons.
Tru.
Ct.
Ion of both, or of ei.
Ther, or of.
Course, whose idea, or.
"Of course."
On, with, or.
"Of?"
Whose ideal, *or whose idea?* Of.
Who they ought to be.
"So, are."
They ever.
And, so.
Are they.
"Always?"
Doomed to be.
"Not quite good enough, as."
And, because.
The ide.
By def.
Al, ever be.
In.
"Just be."
It.
Yond, or just?
Ion, of.
Past.
Cour.
The real, or.
Se, the Re.

Al, or?
Real.
It.
Y, or.
"Just out of reach?"
So.
What, or whose.
"Or, whose."
Or what, or.
Which identity.
"Is not?"
A construction, or an idea, until.
"Of course."
One does reach.
Or, un?
Or, en.
Til?
Counter.
"One's true self."
Or, one's True Self?
Where, and when.
"Or when, or where."
One is no one.
"And, no?"
Body other.
Than who one is.
Because.
Except.
"Of course?"
Is one's true self, also.
Not the Self, too?
Or, and.
"Because, also."
Is not.
"Who, or."
Is not?
"What is."

One's own true.
Or, True.
Self, also.
Not who, *or what.*
Or What, one is not.
Except?
Though, of course?
"Might one's real."
Or, Real.
Self be.
"And, also, because."
Might one's real.
"Self, also?"
Include, what.
"Or, whom?"
And, Whom.
One is not.
And, not.
"Who, and."
Not what.
"One is not, and."
So one's shadow, too, as does the big Self.
And the small selves it does incorporate, dissolve, destroy, and, or swal.
Without having to deny, project, try to run from.
Low.
Or es.
Or, one's shad.
Cape the shadow, and.
Ow, or.
Because, of.
Your shad.
Course.
Ow, or.
"Who, or what."
Or, what.
I do spit out.
"Or, who."

Is does not need.
"What, or who."
Or, who.
"Or, what."
One is not.
"To be, and."
Because, who.
Or, Who.
"Is, also."
Does not need.
"Anyone."
Anybody.
"Everybody?"
Or, everyone.
"Nobody, and."
Or, no.
"One, or who?"
Or, what.
"One is not, so?"
As to.
"Be, and."
Because, of.
"Course, who."
Is, is.
And, can.
Not be.
What, or with.
One is not, and still be, be.
Cause.
"Not anyone."
Not anybody, not.
"Everybody, not."
Everyone, and.
"Not no one, and."
Not nobody, who.
"They, or."
Who she, or.

"Who he, or."
Who it is.
"Is not, and."
All, of.
Which?
Of course.
Might seem.
To be.
"Quite so."
More than ob.
Vi.
Ou.
S, but.
"Of course?"
What is.
"Or, what."
Is not?
More, or less.
"Or less, or more."
Than obvious, to?
Or, for.
"And for, or to?"
Whom, *or what,* and.
"Because, of course."
Might, or might not?
Also, or.
"Rather?"
Might.
One be.
"Both who one is."
As well as, who.
And.
"As well as what?"
Or, as well as what.
Or, What.
And, as well as who.
If not, necessarily, Who.

"One is not."
Too, and?
Or, rather.
"And, too?"
Or, if rather.
Who, or what.
"And what, or who?"
Is not.
Both who one is, and.
"Also?"
Who one is not, and.
"Because, also."
Of course.
Most simply, most easily, and most ob.
Vi.
Ou.
Sly.
"Is not who one is?"
Good, and.
"Is not?"
Who, or.
"Is not?"
What one is not.
"Bad, or."
Is it?
"Rather, quite."
The op.
Po.
Site, be.
Cause, of.
Course.
"Might some, also."
Choose, the.
"Or choose to be?"
Bad, and.
"Because, also."
Of course?

"And, too."
What is good, or.
Good, or.
"What is bad, and."
Or, who is bad, or.
"What is bad, except."
Bad, or.
One's idea, of.
Or, rat.
What is?
Her, is it, who.
Or, ex.
The mo.
Cept, one's ide?
St, the man.
A, of?
Y, the all, or.
So, of.
Who, or what, the mob?
"Course, is."
Or, who.
Not what, and.
Se, or w.
"Is not who?"
Hat, or whi.
And, is not Who, and.
Ch, mob.
"Is not what?"
Does de.
Is go.
Cide, is go.
Od.
Od, or bad, or.
"Bad."
Not absolutely, so?
But, of course.
Because what, or be.

Cause who, is not.
"Relative, and."
Or, rather?
In order to stay sane, OK.
"Or all?"
Right, might even.
"The bad rat.
Ion.
Ali.
Ze.
Their, his, her, or its.
Bad.
Ness as go.
Od, and.
Or, because?
"Of course."
Who can.
Not rat.
Ion.
Ali.
Ze them.
Selves.
"Or, what they are doing?"
Or.
What he, she, or it.
Did, or did not do, or.
Saying, thin.
King, fee.
Said, did not say, be.
Ling.
Lie.
Or, what they are.
Ved, did not be.
Fail.
Lieve, thought.
Ing to do, fail.
Felt, did not fee.

Ing to say.
L, or did not think.
Or choo.
K, or.
Sing, or de.
Did fail to do, or did.
Ciding?
Fail to say, or.
Not to be.
Did choo.
Lie.
Se, did not choo.
Ve, think, or fe.
Se, de.
El, or.
Ci.
Who they are.
Ded, or did not de.
"As good?"
Cide.
Or, as having.
"Good," or.
At least some.
"Reason to be, is."
The cog.
One bound to go in.
Nit.
Sane, due to.
Ive dis.
"For those who do not mind ad."
Son.
"Mit."
An.
"Ting."
Ce, and.
Or, con?
Fes.

Sing.
Though admitting to whom, or to what?
Of course.
To themselves, that consciously.
They are bad.
Or, who is.
Or, even evil.
Or, what is.
"Too, and?"
Because, of course.
Who is not whole who does try to den.
Y.
His, her, its, or the.
Ir own shad.
Ow, or shad.
Ows, and.
Who, or what.
What, or Who.
"Because, of course, do such denials."
Which, quite so inevitably, and.
"Which quite so far more often than not, do."
Result in pro.
Jec.
Tions, or in.
De.
Flections, in.
Ac.
Cur.
Ate, and un.
Fair, and.
Or.
"Or what, or whom?"
But.
Is not a bit.
Un.
Of both.
Fair, to, or for who.

Good, and bad?
M, or ac.
And bad.
Cord.
And good.
Ing to what, or What, and.
Good, and Bad.
Bad, or Good.
And, also?
"And, both?"
A bit.
True, and false.
And false, and true?
Or True, and False.
"And real, and unreal."
Or?
"Unreal, and real."
And?
"False, and true, too."
And, as.
"Well as?"
Also, gen.
U.
In.
E, and.
"Ingenu."
Ine, and.
As well as?
"Also, both."
Inau.
Then.
Tic, and.
"Authentic, too."
And.
Or?
Because.
Rather, who.

"Or, what?"
Is.
Ab.
So.
Lute.
Ly goo.
D.
"Is not, also, who."
Or, what.
"They, he, she, or it are not."
Or?
And, too.
"Because?"
Of course.
"Because, rather."
And, too?
What 'I' is, also, not, at least, a bit of a 'we,' too.
"And, or?"
Even though.
"Of course."
Is one but one.
And, one is but one.
And, One.
Or, One.
"Of course."
As is two, two, too.
As two are two, too, and.
"And, too?"
Because is, or be.
Cause, in.
Deed, some.
By wrong.
Thing is wrong with.
Ly re.
Try to re.
Pla.
Fer to them.

Cing the ne.
Selves, in.
Ces.
The third per.
Sary 'I,' or.
Son, as a 'we,' or.
As if they are part of some?
As if.
Thing more than them.
They are.
Selves, or?
More than one, be.
Ex.
Cause how to say.
Cept part of what, and?
Those who do pre.
For what rea.
Sum.
Son, or reas.
E, or those who do ass?
Ons, if not.
Um.
In or.
E to spe.
Der to try to es.
Ak for more than them.
Cape them.
Selves, as if?
Selves, or.
They, he, she, or it.
Can take the words from, or put?
Words in the mouth of an.
Other, or.
"As if?"
He, she, it, or they.
"Indeed?"
Might know an.

Other, an.
Y, or all, ot.
Hers, bet.
Ter than that, *or this?*
Ot.
Her does know?
Him, her, or it?
Self, or?
"As if."
The so-.
Called, or self-?
De.
Clared, 'we?'
Might know what an.
Ot.
Her, an.
Y, or all ot.
Hers, do.
Need, or w.
Ant, or?
As if so.
Me, 'we,' im.
Per.
Son.
Al, and col.
Lec.
Tive, mi.
Ght k.
Now you, or me, on.
E, all, every.
One, or every.
Body, bet.
Te.
R than he, she, it, or they.
Do, or can.
K.
Now the.

Ms.
Elves, or.
"As if."
That one 'we?'
Need not list.
En to any.
Or to all ot.
Hers, or.
As if.
Think, or believe.
"That might one, and one."
Or, One?
Not add up?
Or, not make two, and.
"Because, of."
Course, who?
"Is, or."
"Who is not?"
More than one, and.
"Because?"
Or, of course.
"Because?"
Rather, a bit more.
And.
Rather, too.
Mys.
Tic.
Ally, or myst.
Er.
Io.
Us.
Ly, might?
"Or, also?"
On occasion.
Too, of course.
Except those?
Who do insist, that?

"They are all."
Part of some 'we,' and.
But, of course, part of which one, or who.
Se, and.
"Except, of."
Course, to, and for.
So.
Me, and some.
Times , one and one do, in.
De.
Ed, ma.
Ke thre.
E, a.
Nd, of.
Course, for.
"Those who do?"
Think, assume, or.
"Presume, that?"
They are some sort of royals, w.
He.
The.
R with crow.
Ns, real, act.
U.
Al, or not, and.
"Of course?"
Except those.
"Who do still talk of themselves, as."
If?
Part of?
"Some 'we,' but."
Of course, what kind of 'we,' and.
Including, and ex.
Clu.
Ding, what, or whom, and.
Of course.
Who is more than one, oneself, and.

Who, or What.
What, or Who.
Does get to de.
Cide.
Who is in, and who is out, or.
Who gets to choose, or.
"Are not those, who?"
Are least, and.
"Those who are?"
Least true, but.
"Of course?"
Un.
Less one does know, of.
Course.
"How to be true."
Un.
Or, at least?
Less, or un.
Or, real?
Til.
With, or around.
"Around, or with."
One has eaten the apple, or.
"An?"
Apple—whether if.
Gold.
En, red, gre.
En, Fu.
Ji, de.
Lic.
I.
Ci.
Ou.
S, or ot.
Herwise, or.
Those who are not real.
Or, Real.

"Or?"
Those who, as yet.
"Might?"
Around, or with.
Believe.
Or with, or around.
Or, those who.
"More than might."
Or, True.
Believe, that.
One and one.
"Those who are not true."
Do, or can?
To, and with?
Make three.
Themselves.
To, and with, themselves?
Because, of course?
So, who.
What is life, without.
Cannot be.
At least a bit?
True with, and.
Of mystery, or intrigue, or.
True to others, because?
Without?
At least, a miracle, or two, and?
Of course.
Without, at least, a bit of intrigue, or myst.
Ic.
Be.
Is.
Cause, of course.
M, whi.
Ch, of co.
Ur.
Se, sim.

Ple, and ba.
Sic mat.
H doe.
S des.
Troy, and.
Is the big.
Might some be able.
Gest, great.
To fool themselves, for.
Est, and most grand.
A bit.
Fool, the one who is.
"Or for."
And, the one who does.
A while, and.
Think, try to think, ass.
Too, eve.
Ume, or pre.
N, if?
Sum.
"Of course."
E, with.
Might some.
Out thin.
"Be able."
King.
To fool some.
"People, some."
Times, and.
"Though, even?"
If, of.
"Course, might."
Some be far too easy to fool, and though might.
Some be wil.
"To believe?"
Ling.
And, far more than apt.

Their own lies, their.
"Own illusions, and."
Their own de.
And, so.
Lus.
Al.
I.
So, t.
On.
Hose of an.
S, if.
Y, and, of.
All ot.
Hers, too, an.
D, if?
"So, only?"
Might, or can.
He, she, it, or they?
At le.
As.
T, a bit, or for a w.
Hi.
Le, de.
Lude, or ill.
Ude the.
M, hi.
M, he.
R, or its.
Elf, t.
Hat the.
Y can, or do.
Know all.
Or, every?
Thing.
"If, so, only?"
Or, the.
"One, or the ones, who."

Do assume, or.
"The one?"
Or, ones.
Who do.
Es pre.
Sume, that.
"All ot."
Hers, are.
The ones, or On.
The fools, or.
Es, who.
Do know no.
Thing, or are the k.
Now no.
Things, and.
For a while.
But which does, or can.
Or, only?
Only work.
For a bit.
"Or, for a while."
Or, only to a certain extent, or.
"Only as long as they are able to."
Or, only for so long, or.
"Only, so as?"
Long as they are permitted to.
But, of course, per.
Mit.
Ted by whom, or by w.
Hat, and.
Or, be.
Cause.
And, too.
Because, of course.
What, or which, or.
Who.
Se e.

Gos.
Are so good at hiding.
But, of course.
From thems.
Elves, and, so, good.
"At lying?"
What idiot.
And, at de.
Cei.
Ving one.
Fool, or moron.
"Or two, or more?"
Does not know.
The most, the many, or some.
That, even if.
"Some of the time."
Might e.
Though.
Go, be.
"Of course?"
Most simp.
But though.
Le, mo.
And.
St ea.
"Even though?"
Sy, and most ob.
And.
Vi.
Even so.
Ous, to.
"The all, the."
Or for so.
Every.
Me, and.
Thing, the.
"End all, and."

The be all.
"For some."
And, even if.
Of course.
But, though.
Is not ego, all.
"Necessarily, all."
For all, and.
Or, for ever?
Or at, or in, all ti.
Yon.
Me, or ti.
E, or for eve.
Me, or ti.
Ry.
Mes, and.
Body.
"Too, because."
Of course?
Can.
Not one.
"Or?"
Are all not all.
"Necessarily, ever."
Or al.
Ways, all?
Ego, and.
"Can?"
Not one, or.
"Cannot all?"
Too, and.
Fool, all.
"Or, everyone?"
Or, everybody.
Or, all?
"All of the time."
And, so.

"And, though."
But, of course.
And, too.
"Because?"
Of course.
"And, too."
Because.
Of course?
How to be tru.
E to, and.
With, and for, one.
Self.
"If one has ever."
And, if.
"Where, and."
If when.
And if, and where, and when.
One has never been able.
"Or permitted to, or."
Let be to let be, or.
Let be to plea.
Se.
One.
Self.
"And, too."
Where, and.
"Too when, or."
When, or.
Where.
"One has al."
Ways, and ever?
Had to please.
Another, or any.
"Or?"
All others, first.
Or fore.
Most, sing.

Ul.
Ar.
Ly.
"Or, only."
And, too, be.
Cause?
Of course.
"Howsoever."
To be pleased.
With, and by.
And by, and with.
"Or by, or for."
Or for, or by.
Oneself, where, and when.
"And when, and where."
One has always been sur.
Ro.
Un.
Ded, by.
"The un."
Pleas.
Able, and.
Or with, and by.
The un.
Ap.
Pea.
Sable, and.
Of course.
Should, and ought.
"And, too."
Ought, and should.
One first.
Please oneself.
"Because, of."
Course, where.
"And, when."
One cannot please, or ap.

Pea.
Se? One.
Where, or when.
Self, or.
One is not per.
How.
Mit.
"Might, or."
Ted, to.
How can.
"One please."
Another, and.
"Because, of."
Course.
"In order to please oneself."
Must one know oneself, first.
Or se.
"Last, or."
Cond, thir.
Simul.
D.
Tane.
Ou.
Sly, and.
"So, first."
Should, and ought, and.
"Ought, and should, and must."
One.
"Know, and please."
And, please.
Or app.
Ease.
"And, so, know?"
Oneself, before.
Or, first?
"Or, first."
Or, before.

"And."
Or.
Simultaneously?
"In order to be able to please, and."
In order to be able to know.
"Or, in order to be able to know, or."
In order to be able to please?
Or, in order to be able to ap.
Pea.
Se, or.
Any, or.
"All others, or."
Though.
"More than most likely."
Never, and.
Not all.
Will ever, all.
"Or, ever will?"
Everyone, or.
"Will everybody, ever?"
Be pleased, or.
Appeased, or?
"Be?"
Ap.
Pea.
Sable, or.
Pleas.
Able, and.
"Because, of course, would only a fool."
Moron, or.
"Idiot, or."
Would, and.
Could, and.
Can, only.
"An idiot, or."
A moron.
Try, or think.

As.
Su.
Me, or pre.
Sum.
E.
Sume.
That all, or.
"That can."
Everyone, or.
"That can everybody, ever."
All be pleased.
All at.
"Once, all."
Together, or.
Altogether?
"All at."
Or, all.
"In the."
Same time.
"Or, all."
In, or.
"All at."
The same times, and.
So.
"And, so?"
But, of course.
"Most sensibly, most."
Rea.
Son.
Ably, most.
"Rat."
Ion.
Ally, and.
Also, most.
"Logi."
Call.
Y, and.

Of course.
But, ne.
Ces.
Sar.
Il.
Y phe.
Nom.
Eno.
Logically, or?
"Also, most."
Wisely, and.
"Of course."
Also, most.
"En."
Light.
En.
Ed.
Ly, one.
"Must please one."
Self, fore.
Most, and.
"First, and."
Because, of.
"Course, need."
One know.
"One."
Self, in.
Order to.
"Be able to."
Please oneself.
"And, in."
Or.
Der, to.
"Be able to."
Know how.
"To please any, or all, ot."
Hers, or.

In order to.
"Know how."
To make oneself happy, or.
"In order to."
Know what.
"Or in."
Order to.
"Know who."
Will make one happy, though.
"Of course."
Cannot another.
Any, or all ot.
Hers.
"Or, Ot."
Hers make you.
"Make me, or."
Make one happy, if.
"I can, or."
If I will not.
"Make my."
Self happy, or.
If I.
"Will not."
Let myself.
Or, yourself.
"Be happy, and."
Like.
Wise, too.
Whether, or not, wise is, also, en.
Light.
En.
Ed, but.
Of course.
It is not, for whom, or.
For what.
So.
Ever does not care, or.

Though, *of course,* it is dif.
Fi.
Cult to be happy, at rest, or at pea.
Ce, when, and where, or.
Where, and when.
One is waiting for the next.
Per.
Son, vamp.
Ire, liz.
Ard, or vul.
Tur.
E to come a.
Long to try to take *your, or* my, or one's.
Happiness, con.
Tent.
Ment, or peace, be.
Cause, of course, *cannot one be happy, or con.*
Tent, as long as, or if?
One does l.
Ive in fe.
Ar, or an.
Xi.
Ety, whether re.
Ason.
Able, ir.
Rational, rat.
Ion.
Al, or un.
Reason.
Able, as well as.
"Or?"
Of course.
"And, also?"
Need one know others in order to please them?
Or.
"Need one know oneself in order to be pleased by them?"
Or, is knowing.

"Over-rated, or in."
Deed?
Is knowledge, and is kno.
Wing power.
"Or?"
Too, like.
"Much else, is."
Knowing too much, or.
As then, he did turn.
Off, or from?
His back, and.
Away from her, and, so, to?
And, to.
War.
Ds the le.
Ft, or?
To.
War.
Ds he.
R, who, as yet, he co.
Uld, or did?
No longer see.
"Is trying."
To know too.
"Much, as."
Bad as not.
"Knowing enough, or."
As bad as.
"Not wanting, or."
As bad as.
"Not needing."
To know enough, and.
"Too, of."
Course, also.
Necessarily—what does power have to do with pleasing, or pleas.
Ing with po.
Wer, or.

Is cur.
Io.
Sit.
Y, also.
What does power have to with appeasing, or with being appeased, or.
"As?"
Over-rated, as.
Power, is.
"Or, as?"
It might be.
Or, rather.
What, or whose, power.
"Over?"
Or, under.
"Who, or what."
Or, under?
"Or, over."
What, or.
"Who, if."
Not first, or.
"If not?"
Fore.
Most, over.
"Or under, or."
If not.
"Fore."
Most, or.
If not first, un.
Der.
"Or, over."
Oneself, and.
"Of course?"
Or, rat.
Her, do.
"Some seek."
To have.
Or, to take?

"Power, over."
Another, or.
"Over all."
Others, rather.
"Than see."
King.
To have, or.
"To have it?"
Which, of course, as.
Over them.
So.
Selves, or.
Me, mi.
"Over their own?"
Ght say, or.
Un.
As so.
Ruly, or un.
Me mi.
Ruled p.
Ght h.
Ass.
Ave sai.
Ions, and.
D, are.
Though, too.
The op.
Of course, does.
Po.
And, can.
Site, of.
Any, and, or.
Rea.
All ot.
Son, and lo.
Hers only have.
Gic, but.

As much power, over.
What do such ty.
You, over me.
Pes, care.
As I do choo.
Se, or as I do de.
Cide, to give the.
M, and.
"Too, of course."
What, or.
"Whose power."
Is only, as.
"Long as."
And, is.
Only as.
True, or.
Only is.
"As real, as."
Delusional, or.
"As illusional, as."
Ill.
Us.
I.
On.
Al, or.
"As de."
Lusi.
On.
Al, as.
Realized, or.
"As real."
Iz.
Able.
In so.
Far, as.
"One, or."
Only, in.

"So far, as?"
All, or.
"Only, in."
So far as.
"Do the most, or."
Only, in.
"So far as, do."
The many.
Choose to believe it is, or.
"Only, what."
Is only.
"So real, or."
What is.
"Only, so."
True as.
Does everyone, or.
As does.
"Everybody."
Choose to.
"Let it be, or."
Only as.
"Real, or."
As true, or.
"As act?"
U.
Al, as.
Do you, or as do I?
Or as you do, or as it do.
Es, or as.
"Does one?"
Or, as.
Do you, or.
As?
"Do the all, or."
As does everybody, or.
"As does everyone."
Choose to permit, or.

"Choo."
Se to let, or.
Choose, or.
"De."
Cide, to.
Believe it is, and.
"Or?"
Is my be.
Lie.
F.
"In my own pow."
Er eno.
Ugh?
Or suf.
Fi.
Cient, to.
Legit.
Im.
Ize it.
"Or?"
And, rat.
Her, too, is.
My own belief in it.
Sufficient, and.
"Too, is."
It enough, to.
"Seize, it."
And, or.
Enough to take it, or.
Enough.
To seize it, once.
Again, for the first time, or back, and.
Or?
Is.
To know too much.
About whom, or about what?
"As bad as?"

To know too little.
"And?"
Or.
Too, is.
Also?
Knowing what, and.
Knowing who, and.
Knowing what.
Should, and knowing.
What ought to be known.
"As important, as?"
Knowing what need.
Or, as im.
Port.
Ant, as?
Knowing what I.
And, as knowing.
What I do need, can, ought.
Or, do have some right to know, and.
As kno.
"What ought."
Wing.
And, knowing.
What should, and.
"As knowing what."
Ou.
Gh.
T, and, or, what, and who?
Can.
Not be known.
"And?"
Because, of course.
"Are some things?"
And are some people.
"Better, being?"
And better, staying.
"Unknown, and."

Or, are some things, and.
Are some people, simp.
Ly, or not quite so.
Simply, or.
Not quite so un.
Know.
Able by, via, or through.
Ord.
In.
Ary, or nat?
Ur.
Al.
Human logic, brains, minds, reason, or.
Due to.
Norm.
Al, ord.
In.
Ary, hu.
Man limits, or.
Rather?
Are some people, or some things.
Sim.
Ply, or not.
Un.
Knowable here, or un.
Know.
Able now, in the present.
As e.
Ternal as the pre.
Sent might, or might not, be.
Though, of.
Course knowable why, *by whom, how,* or for.
What reason, and.
Or for.
What rea.
Son.
S, and.

"Would, and does."
Only an id.
Io.
T, mo.
Ron.
"Or, fool?"
Refuse to know.
"What can be known."
What should be known?
And, or.
What ought to be known, and.
"Or?"
Does only a smart *wo.*
Man know what.
And, or.
To know what she knows, and.
Know who, or whom?
Who, or what.
As well as does only, a.
Smart wo.
Man know.
Whom to tell, what to share, and what, and with whom, not to share,
or tell, and.
Because, of course.
"Is to try to know what."
Or, whom?
Should, or.
"What, or."
Whom?
"Ought."
Not be known.
"Blas."
Phe.
Mo.
Us, or?
Fu.
Tile, or.

Foolish, or.
Yet one more.
Game, and.
"Or, because?"
Of course.
Who, or.
"What is."
To say, choose.
"Or de."
Cide, what.
Or, who.
Or, Who.
"Gets to know, what."
Or gets to know whom, or.
"Who is to decide."
Or, who gets to choose.
"What does get to be known, and."
What does not, or.
"What should be known, or."
What ought to be known, or.
"What ought not to be known, or."
What should not be known.
By whom, or by what, and.
"And, too."
Because, of.
Course, you.
Are, and.
"I am not one."
To be played as.
Or, one.
Or, One.
To be taken as a fool, and?
Too, be.
Cause.
Of course.
"Is it bet."
Ter, to?

Know, or not to know, and.
"Or?"
Better to know whom, or to know what, or.
Rather, is.
"Or, rather?"
What might be.
"Far more important, and."
Far more cru.
Cial, is.
To know the dif.
Fe.
Ren.
Ce, bet.
We.
En.
"What can be known?"
Or who, *or Who,* can be known.
And, bet.
We.
En.
What can.
Not be known, and.
Or, be.
Twe.
En.
"Who cannot be known."
Or, the.
Or, The?
Dif.
Fe.
Ren.
Ce, be.
Twe.
En.
What one does know.
Or, who one does know?
"And, or."

Between?
What one does not know.
Or, what one does know.
"Because?"
Of course.
"Is not the big."
Gest id.
Io.
T.
Fo.
Ol, or ron.
On.
Or, idiot?
"Mo."
Ron, or fool.
Or, idiot.
Who, or what.
"Or what, or who?"
Does think, presume.
"Or ass."
Ume?
That one.
Or, that you.
Does know all.
Or, can know all.
"Or, one who does assume."
Or presume, that.
One can.
Or, that you can.
Know all.
"Or, one who does pre."
Sum.
E, or ass.
Um.
E that one.
Or, that you.
Has, *or have,* some right to know all.

"About all."
Or, all.
A.
Bout ever.
Y.
Thing.
"About every."
Thing.
Or, ever.
Y.
Thing.
"About ever."
Yon.
E.
"And, because?"
Of course.
"Is not the want to know."
Or, the, or a, want to know is not.
The right to know, and?
"Too, because."
Of course.
"What fool, idiot."
Or, moron?
"Does not know."
That, but.
Of course.
"Did, and does."
And.
That.
Does, and did.
"Not curiosity, kill?"
Whose, or what.
Which, or what.
Or which, or.
Li.
"All."
On, or lio.

Cats, or.
Ns, or.
"At least?"
Or lion.
The cat.
Es.
The cat.
S, or.
"Or, rat."
Her?
Is the cat, or the Cat?
But one, or.
Of course.
If is there, or.
Here?
"Who does not know."
If is here, but.
Or, if here is.
One cat, or.
What does not know?
"That, but."
Of course.
Cats are not.
"And, that."
Cats can.
Not be owned.
And, too?
Or.
"That might they own you."
Or, you.
Or, might they try to, but, of.
Course?
Or, that?
What does knowing have to do with owning, or.
Might they try to adopt you, or me.
Everything, or.
Rather than are they willing.

Or, rather are they willing.
To sub?
Or, not.
Mit to being ad.
Opt.
Ed, or own.
Ed, or.
"Rather?"
What does owning have to do with knowing, or.
"And, that."
Everything, or.
How to own an.
Other, any.
Or, all ot.
Hers, if.
One does, or if one can.
Not know him, her, it, or them.
Selves, or.
If one is not per.
Mit.
Te.
D, or let know.
One.
Self, or.
Be.
Cause, of course, how to own, without knowing, or.
Is more, or is most.
Im.
Port.
Or.
Ant, or valu.
Since, by.
Able, to.
Then, or.
Own, or to know, an.
Since.
Other, an.

"By now."
Y, or all.
He had, and.
Ot.
"Since by now."
Hers, or.
I have, and.
Is far more, and, or.
"Since by now."
Is far most.
And, since by then.
Im.
He had.
Port.
Al.
Ant to know, and to own.
Ready, and.
To own, and to know.
Since by then, and.
One.
"Since by there."
Self, be.
Had he?
Or have you, be.
Fin.
Cause, of course.
Is.
What id.
He.
Io.
D, crump.
T, fool, or mo.
Ling en.
Ron.
Ough.
"Does not know, that."
Or, did you.

But, of.
"Or?"
Cour.
Sin.
Se, can.
Ce, by.
Not an.
"Now, and."
Ot.
Or, sin.
Her, an.
Ce, by.
Y, or all ot.
Then, he.
Hers be own.
"Or, now, I."
Ed.
And, now you.
Or, now, you.
Had he?
Or, have you.
Finished, crumpling enough.
Or, did you.
"Or?"
Sin.
Ce, by.
"Now, and."
Or, sin.
Ce, by.
"Then, he."
Or, now, you.
Had fin.
Is.
Hed crump.
Ling.
A suf.
Fi.

Cie.
Nt, am.
Ou.
Nt, or.
E.
No.
Ugh, or.
"A sufficient number."
Of newspapers from the stack alongside the brick-framed place.
Though from the place, red-.
Or, are you dreaming, here.
Or me.
Rely im.
Ag.
In.
G, or plan.
Nin.
G, or.
Grey, or gray-.
And, now.
Bricked, and.
"Or, was that then."
Except, of course.
Or, will that be later, or?
"What papers, and."
So.
"So, and."
By then.
And, so.
"By there?"
He had.
And, so.
"By there, and."
So, by.
"Then, I."
Had?
"Or, by now."

I have, or.
"By now, and."
Or, by here, now.
"He has?"
Or, by.
"Now, and."
Or, by.
"Here, he."
And, now you have, or.
Had, or have.
Begun to place, or.
Started?
To skip, to hop.
Or, to jump a.
Round, or be.
Gun to p.
Ut, or to p.
Lace, or.
"To pick, fir?"
St, a few.
To get a.
Head of your.
Self, or.
Of the slenderest, or of.
The most slender?
Pie.
Ces of kind.
Ling.
To be.
Gin to place, on.
The I.
Ron grates, which did lie with.
In the hole, or.
"Which did."
And, which do.
Lie hori.
Zon.

Tally, like.
"Or, as."
A rack, within.
"The vertical black iron gates."
Which had covered.
"The opening, or."
Those, which.
"Had previously."
Covered the.
Place, or.
The spot, for.
The fire.
"So, only, before."
He had, or.
"If, so, only, before."
I, *or you,* did.
"Pull, or."
Draw the grates back, but.
Of course.
"Were, and are."
And are, and were.
And, so?
"And, so."
Too, because.
"Though?"
Is it only, said.
Or does who, or does what?
"And, too, because?"
Say, or.
As, only, do they say.
Or, as they do say.
"Except, of course?"
Who so.
Ever they are, and.
"Because, too?"
Of course.
"What idiot, moron."

Or, fool does not know?
While lions, or.
That, but.
Lion.
Of course.
Es.
"Cats do have."
Ses, of course, as cats?
Nine lives.
At least?
Do have.
"And, that?"
Of course.
Are not nine.
"Better than."
One to have?
Even if, too.
"Is not nine, also."
A bit more com.
A fin.
Pli.
Ite num.
Cat.
Be.
Ed.
R, too.
And, though.
Of course.
"What, or."
Who is.
Because, of.
"Course, who."
Are you.
"Only saying, or."
Me re.
Ly speaking.
Or.

What is only saying.
Or, who is meta.
Phor.
Ic.
Ally, or?
Figuratively.
Saying, or.
That, but.
Thinking.
Because, of course.
"What, fool."
Idiot, or moron.
Would dare, con.
Fuse?
The 'like' with the 'is.'
Or.
"The 'al.'"
'Most' with the 'all,' or.
With the whole, or.
"The thing with the word."
Or, the.
Sign with the thing, or.
"Thing with the Word, or."
The Word with the sign, either.
Or.
The words with the thing?
Or.
"The words with the Word?"
Or.
The Word with the words, or.
"The thing with the idea."
Or, the idea with the thing, or.
"The Idea with the thing, or."
The sign with the idea, *or with the Idea,* or.
The thing with the Idea, or.
The things with the ideas?
Or, the concept with the words.

Or, the words with the concept, or.
"The concept with the words."
Or?
The word with the Concept.
"Or, the Concept with the word."
Or, the word with the con.
Cept, or.
"The Idea with the Word, or?"
The ideas with the words, or?
"The Word with the idea, or?"
Or, the ideas with the Word, or.
As, did he.
"And, as."
Did I.
"And, as I did."
And, as you did.
Have to.
Pause then.
And, must I.
And must you, or.
"I must."
Or you must, or.
And, you must.
Pause there.
Or here, and now, or now, and here.
"And, have to."
Pause here.
"And, as I did have to."
And, as you do have to.
And, as I do have to.
"And, as he did have to."
And, as did he have to.
And, as you do h.
Ave, to, "An."
D as I do have.
To pause, there.
"To genu."

Flect, though?
Because, he was, and.
Because you are, and.
"Because I am."
Already kneeling.
Before the.
"Fireplace, and."
Because he.
Was, and.
"Because I am, already."
And, because.
You are, already.
In my living room, kneeling.
Or, merely re.
"Before my fireplace, so."
Me.
Did he, rather?
M.
"And, so."
Em.
I did, rather.
As you did, rat.
Her.
Lift the silver?
Or, is it gold.
Or was, or is, and, or.
Of course.
As ever will it, al.
Ways be.
A bit of both gold.
And silver, which.
Did hang around his neck.
"And, which does hang, as."
Ever, and.
"As al."
Ways, has it.
To bless, and.

And as al.
Ways, and.
To keep me, and.
"As ever?"
Will it, or.
To kiss it.
As you must.
As, too.
Or, real?
Ly, act.
U.
Ally, and tru.
Ly, is it a cross, or.
"Rather, is it."
"Because, as must we."
Do what we must do, and, so.
"Did he, al."
So, and as.
You did, also.
"Because, of course."
Are some sym.
Bols too ho.
Ly to show, as we.
Ll as be.
Ca.
Use, of cour.
Se, are so.
Me name.
S too.
Sac.
Red to ut.
Ter, as we.
Ll as, be.
Cause, are?
Some thin.
Gs, or so?
Me peo.

Ple to pow.
Er.
Ful, and too-all.
Know.
Ing, and, too?
All-see.
Ing to re.
Pre.
Sent, and.
"As?"
Also, are.
Some beings, or is the Be?
Ing too po.
Wer.
Ful, and, too.
Omni-, in all ways, to?
Be know.
N by a me.
Re mor.
Tal mind, and, so.
"Did you?"
Or.
"Did I?"
And, do you do, what.
"And, as I must, and."
And, as you must.
"And, as I, also, did."
Do, and ever will?
Bless, himself.
As they do.
And, of.
"Course, or."
As do I me.
An, as did I me.
An, and.
As you do mean, and.
"As I do, also, mean, as."

I did.
As you did, as you do, and.
And.
As you ever have.
"And, as I do, with."
The, or with a?
Sign of the cross.
Which might me.
An some.
Thing, or?
Not, if not any.
Thing, or every.
Thing, at all, be.
Cause, of course?
If might it, or.
"If does it, or."
If can it mean.
Or, does it not mean any?
Any.
Thing, or.
Thing, or.
Does it me.
Every.
An no.
Thing, does it, not.
Thing, or.
Me.
Does it me.
An a thing, at all, and.
An no.
At the end, of which.
Thin.
But, be?
G, or.
Fore.
Or, on.
He did con.

Ly, what.
Tin.
You do be.
Ue, with.
Lie.
Fat.
Ve, it doe.
Her, Son, and Ho.
S, or.
Ly Spir.
It, or Ghost.
"Is it?"
But eit.
Her, and, if not.
"In both ways, at on."
Ce, of course?
Which does bring up the quest.
Ion, whe.
The.
R, or not, he.
Re, or now, you do, in.
Deed, want to think of it, but.
"Of course."
Or?
Does the or.
Der mat.
Ter, if, in.
De.
Ed, in time, we do live, or, if.
In.
Deed, we are li.
We?
Ving in time, but.
"Does what, or does who?"
Come first mat.
Ter mo.
Re, or mat.

Ter les.
S than what, than What?
Than who.
M, or.
Than who do.
Es co.
Me se.
Con.
D, or last?
And, after.
Be.
Cause, of.
Course, who do.
Es not k.
Now that the be.
St do co.
Me la.
St, at le.
As.
T, or this, or that, is un.
Til the last do co.
Me fir.
St, but that, in.
Deed, who.
"Does come se?"
Cond, or last, or who.
"Or, what?"
Or Who, or What, does.
Co.
Me sec.
Ond, or last, or who?
Does fol.
Low, or what does.
Fall be.
Hind is the one with the po?
Wer, if, in.
De.

Ed, po.
Wer does mat.
Ter, or does.
Ex.
Ist, and.
If, in.
Deed, mat.
Ter.
Ing more is bet.
Ter than mat.
Ter.
Ring less.
But, al.
Or, too much?
So, and, too?
Or, if who do.
Es fall be.
Hi.
Nd, or s.
Lack, do.
Es, by.
Ma.
King ot.
Her.
S w.
Ai.
T, h.
Ave, or t?
Ake, all of the po.
We.
R, or.
Only as long as, or.
"Only?"
In so far as, is.
One, two, or m.
Two more than, or bet.
Ore, do be.

Lie.
Ve, in.
The ill.
Us.
I.
On, or in.
The de.
Lus.
I.
On of.
It.
Or.
Ter than one, or?
That, of cour.
Se, is two hig.
Her, or?
"Only as."
More than one, of.
Long as.
Course.
One, quite so.
"And, or."
One?
Oh, so most ver.
Y fool.
Ish, does for.
Get, that?
Who does com.
E sec.
Ond, whe.
Ther mast.
Er, or slave, does s.
Till, and do.
Es, as yet?
Fol.
Low, or fall?
Un.

Der the law, that.
"More of."
Ten than not the serv.
Ant, *or se.*
Cond, is the one who rules, be?
Cause what ser.
Vant does not know his, her, or its?
Mas.
Ter bet.
Ter than the mast.
Er doe.
S know him.
Self, *or her.*
Self, and?
"Of course."
Be.
Cause know.
Ledge is, in.
Deed, po.
Wer, or.
As well?
Quite so very.
Simp.
Ly, or ob?
Vi.
Ou.
Sly, does what, or does who?
"Come first."
Matter most, and, so, is?
If matter does matter.
"Most imp."
Or.
Tant, and, so.
After.
"He had."
And, after you did.
"And, after I did."

Perform the sign of the cross, giving.
"All thanks, and."
All due praise, to.
"The Father, and."
To the Son, and.
"To the Ghost, so."
Holy, or.
If not?
"Of course, to."
Holy, the.
The Holy Spirit, or.
N, or the.
The Spirit, Holy, or.
Re, or he.
He did, too.
Re, or now, w.
And so, but only, af.
Hat?
Ter done, com.
Ple.
Te, and fin.
Is.
Hed, as do they.
Ever, and.
"As do the most."
Or, as do they?
Not quite, but.
Devout, kiss?
The hand, and.
"This hand, and."
That hand, which.
Or, which hand?
Had blessed him.
Self, though.
Or, your.
Self, or.
"My."

Self, of.
"Course."
Even though.
He was not a priest, but?
And, too.
"Because, of course."
Also, I am not, and.
"Because."
Of course.
"And, also."
You are not, too.
"But."
And, even.
"If."
He might as well have been, except.
Of course.
"For?"
Except that he had married once, though?
"Of course."
Ex.
Except that I did.
Cept, of co.
Once, and.
Ur.
Though, of.
Se, you are not Cat.
"Course, cannot."
Ho.
The married be priests.
Lic, ei.
Or, can they be, where?
The.
Or, what kind of priests.
R, or.
Or how, or.
But can the form.
Priestess, bow.

Erly, or pre.
Ing, or.
Vio.
Praying, to.
Us.
To what, or to whi.
Ly married, be, so, and.
Ch god, God, G-d, or god.
Though, now.
Because now, you are not.
"Married, and."
Des.
More, or a.
Ses, or.
Ny longer, or am I?
Or, are you, and.
Or?
So ever will you be?
But if, in.
Deed, you are not.
"A priest, but."
Could you, now, and here, be.
If married once.
"Am I for."
Eve.
R, or are you, forever.
"Of course."
But.
Because I am no longer.
Or, not anymore?
Because she is dead.
Married, but.
"Who was?"
Or.
Who is.
And, who had been?
Though you were, to.

The woman whose blood he had, al.
So.
"And, the blood I had, also."
Had to spill, of course.
Be.
Cause, in.
Deed.
"To be free."
Of course?
"I did me."
Re.
Do what I had to do, and, be.
Cause.
You did?
"And be."
Cause I did h.
Ave to be free, and.
Because?
Because.
Of course.
I did need to do, and.
What you did need to do, and.
To be able to do, what.
"I did need to do, and be."
Cause, of course.
"She would not, and."
Be.
Cause she had not, and.
"Because."
She would not stop.
Nag.
Ging him, or.
"Nag."
Ging me, or nag.
Ging you.
"Or nag."
Ging me, or?

Haunting me.
"And, because?"
She would not leave me alone.
"And, because?"
She would not get out of my way.
"And, because?"
She would not stop.
Being her, or.
"And, because?"
She would not stop.
Being me, and.
"Because."
Well, any.
Way.
I could not stop getting her.
"To oppose me, or."
To stop talking, or.
"To stop thinking, or."
To stop dis.
Agreeing with me, or.
To stop challenging you?
"To stop de."
Fying me, or.
To stop contra.
To stop trying to get away from me, or.
Dicting you, or?
"To stop trying to escape me, or."
To stop trying to leave me, and.
Or?
"Because I could not get her to, and."
Because I could not get through to her, and.
"Because, of course?"
What is one to do.
And, because.
"Of course."
What can one do, and.
"Or, because?"

What is one not to do, and.
Or, because.
Of course.
Must one do what one must, and.
"What are you to do, or."
What else were you to do, and.
"What else was I do to, and."
What else could you have done, and.
So?
"So, rat."
Her than remember such painful things.
Because, of.
"Course, are."
Some lucky enough to for.
Get what, and.
"To forget whom, when."
Or when, or where.
They do want to, and.
They do need to, and.
So did he, and.
So did I.
And, so.
Did you.
Continue, on.
Stacking, as I was.
And, as you are.
"And, as I am, and."
As he had been, and.
As you ever will be?
"Placing."
The twigs.
Qui.
Te so ex.
Act.
Ly, and.
"Quite so per."
Fect.

Ly, and.
Quite so pre.
Cise.
Ly, and.
"Quite so neat."
Ly, and.
As he would.
And, as he had to.
And, as I must, and.
And, he did.
And, as you did.
So, when.
"And, so."
Where he was finished.
And where, and when.
And when, and where.
He was done.
Or, when he was done.
"And, now that I am done, and."
There, and then.
Then, and there.
Since he was fin.
Is.
He.
D, and.
Because now you are, and.
Because you now are, and.
Because he, then, and the.
Re, was.
Where.
"And, when."
He was finished, did.
He, and.
Did I, and.
"I did, and."
Did I.
And, you did.

"And, did he."
And, did who?
And, he did.
"And, did I."
And, did you.
Next, move on.
And, you did.
"To light."
Beneath the twigs.
First, the papers, and, then, next.
Did he.
And, he did.
"And, next."
Did I.
"And, next."
I did, and.
"Next, he."
And, next you.
Did watch.
The flames, licking.
"For a bit."
Or, for.
"Some time, be."
Fore.
The flames from the papers did catch the kindling, or.
Before.
The kind.
Lings, or.
Before the flames did, next.
Move on, to.
"The small sticks, which."
He had, and.
"Which I had."
And, which you did, also.
And, which he did, and.
"Which I did, and."
Which he had.

"Stacked horizontally, on."
The grates with.
In, and.
Which he had, also.
Let burn.
"For a bit."
And, for a while, before.
Next he did.
And, be.
Fore.
"Next I did."
And, be.
Fore next you did.
Add one log.
And, before, next.
He did light, and.
Before you did, and.
"Next, before."
I did light, it.
As in the log, be.
Cause.
"Could I, and."
Because, I can.
Not, and, be.
Cause, you can.
Not trust, or.
"Let, or."
Wait for the.
"Flames to move."
On, from.
"The kindling, or."
On, from.
The small sticks, to.
"The big log."
And, be.
Cause, "Of course."
I can.

Not wait, or.
"Necessarily trust, or."
Necessarily be.
"Sure, or."
Necessarily, be.
Certain, that.
In.
Deed, the.
"Big log will."
Catch fire, by.
"It."
Self, or a.
Lone, and.
So, rather.
"Than wait, did."
He strike, yet.
And, be.
Fore you did strike.
"One more, and."
Yet, once.
"Again, a."
Match, a.
Long.
"One of the bricks, to."
Or, in.
"Or."
Der, to.
A.
Light it, be.
Fore.
He did touch it.
Or, before you did.
To the log, to.
"Help it."
Catch fire, again.
"And, before."
Once, again.

He did watch for a bit.
"And, for a while."
And, before.
He did begin to rub his hands together, before the flames.
And, before you did, and.
"Though, they."
Meaning, of.
"Course."
My hands.
Had not grown quite so cold, be.
Cause, of course.
"Cold hands."
Do mean.
A warm heart, *or he.*
Arts, but.
Of co.
Ur.
Se.
"Only if one does have one."
As in.
A he.
Or.
Art, or.
Only if they do, or.
Though, be.
Cause.
"He had not quite noticed."
Or, because.
I did notice.
"Or, because."
I had not quite noticed, though.
Or, because you did not quite notice.
And, though.
"Except, not yet."
Not yet?
And, ex.
Cep.

T, but.
Because.
"As yet?"
He still was.
And, be.
Cause, yet.
He was still, and.
"Because, as."
Yet, I.
"Am still."
In bed, and.
"Because."
As yet.
You are.
And, so.
"What has not happened."
Or, because.
And, because?
What was.
"And, because?"
Or, because.
What did hap.
What is not happening?
Pen.
Or, because.
And, because.
"What will not happen?"
Or, and.
And, or.
Because.
"What has happened, already."
Or, what is not yet, or al.
Or, be.
Ready, de.
Cause.
Cided, or.
So, now.

And, so, there.
"And, so, here?"
And, so, now.
What am I remembering.
"Or?"
What I am re.
Mem.
Be.
Ring, *or what you are.*
Or, are not, or.
So, what.
"Now, I am re."
Member.
Ing, and.
Or?
What is yet to hap.
Pen, or.
What has al.
Or, what might me.
Read.
Rely hap.
Y, hap.
Pen.
Pen.
Ed.
"Or, what did happen."
Or, what will happen.
Yes.
Ter.
Day?
Or, to.
Mor.
Row?
Or, the year before.
"Or, the one before that."
Or?
What was, already.

And, or, what.
"Yet, or, still?"
Is.
Happening, else.
Where, "Or?"
What might happen here.
Or.
"Or, what will happen here?"
Or.
What did happen here.
Or?
What never will, be?
Cause.
What is past, or be.
Cause.
What is the past.
Or?
Who will come, or.
"What is the future."
Or?
Who might come, or.
What is yet to come.
Or?
"What is now."
Or?
What is sure to come.
Or?
"What will come?"
Or?
Who will, or.
What might come.
Or?
"What might happen."
Or?
What will happen?
"Or, what is sure to happen."
Or?

"What has, already, happened."
Or, what is certain to happen, or.
What will not happen, or.
What has, already, been decided.
Again, or for the first time, or.
De.
Cided by whom, *or by Who.*
M, or.
Cided by what, or.
Cided by What, or.
"Or, what has, already, been determined."
Or, what has, already, been destined, or.
"What has, already, been fated, or."
Fated, de.
Or, for.
Cide.
What re.
D, or deter.
As.
Mined, by whom, or by what.
On, or for what rea.
For what, or for whom, and, so?
Sons.
What will, or.
What will not happen.
Again, or for the first time, or.
Or?
"Of course."
And, so.
"But, so?"
Of course.
What might happen.
"And, what might not."
And, what more.
Than might, already, not?
"Be decided."
By Whom.

Or, determined.
By whom, or.
Or, destined, and?
By what, and.
Because, of.
By What, and.
Course.
"So, but."
And, or.
"If, but, so?"
And, or.
If not destined, and.
"If not determined, or."
If not decided by me.
Of course.
Then, or.
"Now, decided."
Or, now.
"Or, then, decided."
De.
Ter.
Mine.
D, or de.
S.
Tin.
Ed by whom, or by what, and.
"If, because?"
Of course.
I can.
Not let them.
Who, or what.
So.
Ever they are.
Him, her, or it.
Who, or what.
So.
Ever he is, or.

Make me.
Or, let you.
"Get ahead of myself?"
And, too.
Because, of course.
And, too?
Be.
Cause, I can.
Not let them.
"Him, it," or her.
Any.
One, or every.
One, or.
"Eve."
Ryb.
Ody, or.
Any.
Body, write.
The, or write, my.
Story for me, and.
"Because, of course."
I can.
Not let, or per?
Mit any.
One, every.
One, or eve.
Ryb.
Od.
Y, else to de.
Cide, or to choo.
Se, for me.
Or, for me.
What, or who?
Who, or What.
Is to co.
Me, or.
Who, or What?

Is to hap.
Pen, or.
Let, or per.
Mit myself.
Or, your.
Self.
To get a.
Head, of.
Me, or.
Ahead of.
"Myself?"
Or, of.
Your.
Self, or.
And, even if.
Because.
"Of course?"
Might they like.
To try?
"To rush, or to hurry me, and?"
Even if.
Of course.
"Is, or is not?"
The, or?
My story.
Or your story, or.
Our story.
"Or the."
Or my.
Story, or?
My, or.
Whose story.
Or, your story.
Already written?
Or, already, determined?
Or, already, destined?
Or, if.

Rather, but.
"Of course."
If is it?
"Or if it is al."
Ready?
Writs.
Ten, de.
Tin.
Ed, de.
Ter.
Mine.
D, or.
"De."
Cide.
D, by?
Whom, or by what.
Is it.
"And."
If?
It is.
"Or, if?"
It is.
Not writ.
Ten, destined, decided, fated, or deter?
Mined by me.
But, rather.
"It is, or."
If, rat.
Her.
"It has been."
Determined, destined.
"Fated, or."
Decided, by.
What would-be.
Gods, or god.
Desses, or.
"By?"

What would-be.
"God."
Master, king, que.
En, em.
Press, prin.
Ce, prince.
Ss, or would-be emp.
Er.
Or, or.
By.
"Some would-be."
God.
Dess, or.
"By?"
Some ma.
Chin.
E, or by.
Some ma.
Chin.
Es, by.
What, which, or.
"By whose."
Ma.
Chine, or ma.
Chin.
Es, or.
"By?"
Which, or by whose.
Would-be mast.
Ers, or so-cal.
Led, or self-de.
Cla.
Red God.
Far.
Hers, or?
"By?"
What would-be Mis.

S, Mist.
Ress, or mis.
Tresses, of?
What, or.
"Of whom, of course."
Would this, or.
Would that?
No longer be.
My world, or.
My life, and.
"Or, if."
Rather.
"My life we."
Re to be de.
Cided, deter.
Mined, des.
"Tined, or."
Fated, by.
"Any, or."
By all.
"Others, other."
Than me.
What would no longer be.
"My uni?"
Verse.
Or, my life, and.
"Or, because?"
Of course.
"I am not one."
Willing to.
Let anyone.
Or, one.
"Willing to permit."
Everybody.
"Everyone."
No one.
"Nobody."

Somebody.
"Anybody."
Or, someone.
Else write?
My story for me.
"And?"
As much as, also.
Of course.
"I am, also, not."
One willing.
To let.
"Or, one."
Willing to permit?
Any, or.
"All others, the."
Most, the.
"Many, or."
The all, how.
"So ever, all."
Knowing, and.
"How so ever tyrannical, and."
How so ever mob.
Bish, to.
"Choose for me?"
To decide for me, or.
"To pick for me, or."
To se.
Lect for me, or.
To know.
Me, or to know.
"For me."
Or to know, or to try, or to at.
Tempt to know me for me, and.
"Or?"
To try.
To know.
For me.

Or, for you?
"What I do want."
Or, to try.
To know.
For you.
"What I do need?"
Or to try to know you, for you.
Or.
To try.
"To know for."
Me, what.
"Or, who."
Or, Who.
Is good for me, or.
To know?
"Who, or."
What is not, or.
"And, so."
Because, of course.
"To be known."
Is not nec.
Ess.
Ari.
Ly to know, and.
"Too, be."
Cause, of course.
To know.
"Is not necessarily to be known, and."
Though, of course.
"To be known."
Or, to know.
Or, to as.
Sum.
E to be known?
Or, to ass.
Um.
E to know.

Or, because.
"To presume to be."
Known, or know.
"Is to."
N, for?
Be made an object.
"Of another's possession, and?"
Of course.
And.
Who, or what.
What, or Who.
"Or what, or who."
Can be free, if.
And when, and where, possessed.
Though, of course, possessed.
By whom, or by what.
If not by, or with.
What, who.
Who, or What.
One is not, and.
"Or, had?"
Or, had.
Or, had?
And, if.
And where, and when.
When, and where.
"And when, and where?"
One is presumed, or assumed.
"To be known?"
To be had, or.
"To be taken."
But, who.
Is to think, not to thin.
K, to pre.
Sum.
E, or to ass?
Sume that all, or that every.

Thing is a.
Bout being free.
"And, so."
Even if.
"What, or."
Whose later, might have been?
Or, even if.
"What later might be?"
Is not now.
"And."
Because, of.
"Course."
Time is.
"As subjective, as."
All else, and.
"Because, as."
Yet, and.
"Because, as."
Still, he.
"And, be."
Cause still, and.
"Because, as yet."
I am.
Not fully wakened, and.
"Because I am not, and."
Because, as.
"Yet, I."
Am, as.
"Yet, and."
Still in the pro.
Cess, of.
Waking, and?
Because, of course.
"And, too, because."
Of course.
"As yet?"
I am still wa.

King, and.
"Too, because?"
Of course.
"Once again."
Am I.
And, you are?
"And, I am."
And, you are.
Unwilling, and.
So un-.
Wanting, and.
"Because I am un-."
Wanting.
So, am I, also, un.
Willing, to.
"Be rushed, or to be hurried."
And, be.
Cause.
"I am un."
Wil.
Ling, and be.
Cause I am un-.
Wanting to be hur.
Rie.
D, or to be rus.
Hed.
By anyone.
Or.
"By eve."
Ry.
One?
Or.
By some.
Body.
"Or?"
By any.
Body, "Or?"

By someone.
"Or?"
By no one.
"Or?"
By no.
Body, "Or?"
By every.
Body, or.
By all.
"Or, by."
The all.
"So far."
Too ea.
Ger to have me?
Or, by any.
Or, by the all.
Or, by all.
"Too ea."
Ger to use me?
And, or.
"By any, or."
By the most, or.
"By the many."
As if.
"People can, should, or ought."
Be.
Used at all, or?
"As if."
They can be.
Or, as if.
"They ought to be?"
Had, or used.
Or, ass.
Um.
Ed, or pre.
Sum.
Ed to be.

"Or a?"
Bused.
Because, of course.
"Is not use of another."
Abuse of another.
De.
Spite any, and, or de.
Spite all.
Rat.
Ion.
Al.
Iz.
At.
Ions, and.
"Because?"
Of course, is not.
Use of another.
As a means to some end.
Other than his.
Or, other than her?
Own, is.
"Abuse of another."
And, too?
Because.
Too, and.
"Because, of course."
To assume to have.
"Or?"
To presume to have.
Is?
"Not actually."
Real.
Ly, tru.
Ly, or ne.
Ces.
Sa.
Ri.

Ly.
To have.
And, too?
Because.
"Of course."
Who does want to be treated as.
"An object, as a pet, or as an an."
Im.
"Al, though."
And, even if?
Of course.
"What might be."
Perhaps?
Most eas.
Might some.
Y, and mo.
Like to have, own, or.
St simple, or.
Pos.
Easi.
Ses.
Est, or simp.
S, any, or all, ot.
Lest, to, or for, some.
Hers, and tho.
"And, though."
Ugh.
To be so mis.
Tre.
At.
Ed, is.
To be objectified, and.
"Because."
Of course.
"Who does not want to be."
Treated, better.
Or, as more?

"Than as an object, or."
Than as a pet, or than as a mouse, or than as a toy, or.
As a mere obj.
Ec.
T, or.
Who is.
"Not called."
By what, or.
"By whom, to?"
Treat better, so as to be.
Treated better.
Or not, or.
If so.
Be.
On.
Cause, of co.
Ly, by.
Ur.
The most fair, or.
Se.
If so, only.
Do so.
By the most.
Me de.
Equit.
Mand to be tre.
Able.
At.
Ed bet.
Te.
R, with.
Out tre.
At.
In.
G bet.
Te.
R, and.

Though, who.
Are not the ones that need be told, or re.
Mind.
Ed, be.
Cause they are the ones.
Who do get, that.
To be treated better.
Ought, should, or must one.
Treat others better, too, and.
That to treat others better, is, also, to.
Deserve to be treated better, too.
And, is.
"A most basic?"
Kar.
Mic rule, but.
Or a just, or Just one, or?
Which, of course, does seem to be.
Not more, and not less.
Than com.
Mon sen.
Se, and.
"Which does, or which might, in."
Deed, seem to be.
Most simp.
Le, and most ob.
Vi.
Ou.
S, if not eve.
R, or al.
Ways, most ea.
Sy, but.
Too, who.
Or, what.
Does not know, that.
Common sense is usually, hardly, and barely.
Ever common, or.
Ever.

Most simple, or.
"Called by?"
Every.
One, every.
Body, or all, no mat.
Ter who they are, seem to be, and, or.
Regardless, of.
Who they are not, or.
Re.
And re.
Gard.
Gard.
Less of who they do ap.
Less of who.
Pear to be, or.
M, or w.
By.
Hat the.
"Or, to?"
Y do thin.
Someone higher, or by?
K they are, and, or.
"Something bigger, or by.
Someone bigger, or by.
"Something greater, to?"
Also demand to be treated better, and.
Or, rather?
"Is not being."
A pet?
Just fine.
For some?
Or, at least, for those.
"Who do not mind?"
Being pat.
Ron.
Iz.
Ed, or ob.

Jec.
Tif.
I.
Ed, kept in a cage, or.
"And, too."
Even a li.
Or, might a cat be bet.
On, or.
Ter, or.
A li.
Might dogs, al?
On.
So.
Nes.
Be far wiser.
S, or.
"More humane, and."
If wiser does mat.
Most sens.
Ter, or.
It.
"Even if it does not?"
Ive, and, so.
Still, anti-, or dark.
More hu.
Does, and, so.
Mane, and, so?
What, and who.
More hu.
Is not matter.
Man, or?
As yet.
Even if still dog.
"And, still?"
S, or.
Does.
Are those who do claim to be most.

Cal.
Or, more?
Led to be more, as if?
Sensi.
Be.
Tive, more, or most.
In.
Hu.
G hu.
Mane, or hu.
Man, is.
Man, pre.
To be more, or.
Cise.
Ly, ex.
Act.
Ly, and more of.
Ten than not, those who?
Do, also, care.
A lot, or the most.
About their, his, her, or its.
Own feelings, and sens.
Iti.
Vit.
I.
Es, but.
Also, quite.
So very often are they, also.
So very often they are, also.
The ones who do not, like.
Wise, or re.
While, simul.
Cip.
Tan.
Roc.
E.
All, care for, or a.

Ou.
Bout the feel.
Sly, de.
Ings, or a.
Man.
Bout, or for.
Ding, to.
The sen.
Be care.
Sit.
D for, or ab.
Ivi.
Out?
Than might some hu.
Mans, be.
And than some, if not the mo.
St, the man.
Y, or all, hu.
Mans, are.
And, be.
Cause, "Of course."
Are not li.
Ons more po.
Wer.
Ful, and.
Or, only, are they.
Like most, and like much.
Else, only.
"As powerful as one does make, let, or per."
Mit, or be.
Lieve them to be, or.
"And?"
Too, of.
Of course, on.
Ly, are they, to.
The ex.
Tent that we are an.

Im.
Als, and.
Only.
Insofar, as.
This is, a.
Or, the jung.
Le, con.
Cre.
Te, or ot
Of cour.
Her.
Se, is this tow.
Wise, but?
N, or cit.
Too, of.
Y, not me.
Course, who.
Rely, just, or on.
Does not know?
Ly a jun.
"That lions, of."
Gle, or.
Ten be co.
Most esp.
War.
Eci.
Dly, as we.
Ally where.
LL, as is a li.
And, when.
On not much of a king with.
He does not have a heart.
Out a que.
En, and.
Do li.
Ons not eve.
R, or al.

Way.
S, ne.
Ces.
Sari.
Ly w.
In, as?
No.
Thin.
G les.
S, or as.
No.
Thing more than kin?
G of the be.
As.
Ts, be.
Ca.
Use.
As well?
Of cour.
Se, are we not all me.
Rely, j.
Us.
T, or on.
Ly be.
As.
Ts, so, too.
Do not em.
Per.
Ors, or emp.
Res.
Ses care much for queens, or kings, who are, of.
Course, far be.
Neat.
H them, if, w.
Hen, and w.
He.
Re pow.

"And who?"
Er is the game.
"Does not know."
Of the heart of ele.
Phan.
Ts, and.
"Of course?"
Who can forget.
"The memo."
Ries, of.
Them either, and.
"Too, because."
Of course can.
Not dol.
Phins.
S he.
Ar bet.
Ter, too.
"And what cats, of."
Course, must, or can?
Not, or.
Be.
"Admired, for."
Their selfishness, or.
Rat.
Is self.
Her.
Ish.
Ness quite so very most?
Simply very easy, and quite so very obvious, or.
For their steal.
Of co.
Th, or.
Ur.
Se, is?
Self.
Is.

H.
Ness on.
Ly cor.
Rect, and right?
"To a cer."
Ta.
In ex.
Tent, or?
"For their sly."
Ness, or.
For their skit.
Tis.
H.
Ness, or.
"For their hunting skills, or."
As well?
Can.
Not rab.
Bits be ad.
Mire.
D for.
Their softness, any.
"Or, all."
Of which.
"Of course."
Might de.
"Throne humans."
Or, at least the men?
If, of course, also, not the wo.
Who are the cruelest, or most cruel?
Men, too.
Of all animals, if anima.
L.
S might they, *or might we,* be able.
To lower them.
Or, your.
Selves to be, *or.*

As kings, or as queens?
Of the beasts, though.
If in.
Or, if eve.
Deed, he?
R, real.
Or they, ever we.
Ly, act.
Re, have be?
U.
En, or will be, of.
Ally, or tru.
Would man.
Ly, hu.
Y.
Man.
Like?
S have be.
To want, or.
En on top, even if.
"To con."
As do they ten.
Sider them.
D to thin.
Selves, far.
K, or to be.
Sep.
Lieve they are.
Sep.
A.
Rate, far.
"Apart, far."
Bet.
Ter, far.
"Past, and."
Far a.
Bo.

Ve the an.
Im.
Als, and.
Because, of.
"Course, even."
If, are.
"We not."
Necessarily, all.
"Just, or."
Only, or.
"Merely, or."
Qui.
Te so very most won.
Der.
Fully, or.
"Quite so miraculously, animals, and."
Even if.
"Qui."
Te so far more.
Mira.
Cu.
Lous.
Ly, might.
We all like.
"So far more glori?"
Ou.
Sly to thin.
K of our.
Selves, quite.
"So far more."
Fabulously, or.
"Quite, so?"
Far more flat.
Ter.
Ingly.
"As?"
Divine, rather.

"Than as beastly, but."
Is not the beast.
"In us?"
But, too.
"Our own cre."
At.
I.
On, rat.
Her than God's, a god's, or the gods', or.
Of course.
And, is it not.
"The Goddess's, or."
Some goddesses', or so.
Me, or the G-d's, or so.
Me Goddess's, or.
"Is not always, and."
Or, did Go.
D, the go.
Is not ever, how.
Ds, or.
"Or, what."
And, the God.
One does think of oneself, how.
Dess, and god.
"Or, what."
Des.
Or, who.
Ses, as su.
"One is, and."
Pre.
Be.
Me be.
Cause, quite so ver.
Ings, and Be.
Y of.
Ing, the Cre.
Not one's idea of one.

At.
Self who one really, actually, or truly is, either, and.
Or, and crea.
Because, of.
Tors, or.
"Course, is."
Not what, or.
"Is not who does."
Claim to be, or only do, or do on.
Ly good, or.
Those who do try to claim to be God, or gods?
Or all, or on.
All-power.
Ly, Good.
Ful, all-see.
Ing, and.
Omni.
Scient, ne.
Ces.
Sar.
Il.
Y, good, or God, or on?
Ly do goo.
D, *or Good,* or.
Are not.
Good, or.
"Those who do claim."
Or, those who do try.
"Or, those who do?"
Proclaim to be.
Better than ani.
Mals, or.
"Better than, or."
Wiser than, or.
"More enlightened, than."
Or past, or.
"Beyond the beast."

Or, the Be.
As.
T?
Or, the bea.
Sts, while.
"Forgetting, or."
While den.
While for.
Ying, that.
Get.
"But, so?"
Ting.
Of.
That.
That, of course.
"Do those who."
Do claim to be.
"Higher, better."
Or, more divine, or.
"Godlier, or."
More god.
Dess.
Ly, are.
"Quite so very of."
Ten?
Far crueler, and.
"Far more stupid, and."
Far stu.
Pider, and.
Far dum.
Be.
R, and.
"Far more ignorant, than."
The most basic of the beasts, and.
"Too, because."
Of course?
Are not god, gods.

"God, or."
Goddesses, created.
"Creators, destroyers, other, or."
Self-pro.
Claimed, or.
Self-de.
Clare.
D, of.
Ten.
"Far meaner."
Far more venge.
Ful, far more.
"Or less?"
Than apparently, just.
"Unjust, jealous."
Un.
Fair, foolish.
Pretentious, pre.
Sump.
Tu.
Ous.
"Idiotic, or."
More mor.
On.
Ic, than.
"Might, or than can, a cat, or."
Than might a dog, be.
Or, than.
"Might a dog, cat, fish, or."
Dol.
Phin, or drag.
On, ever be.
"Though, of course."
What, or who.
Who, or what.
Or, What.
"Or who, or what, is."

More selfish, or more self-centered.
More, or less, than apparently, or.
Less, or more, than actually?
"Than is a cat, and."
Whether if rat.
Ion.
Ally, or ir.
Rat.
Ion.
All.
Y, so.
But.
Too, of course.
"Who."
And, what.
And, What.
And, who.
And, Who.
Needs no excuse?
To so act.
"And, does not consider apologizing, for."
Acting, or.
From refraining from acting, or.
"For being, or."
For not being, or.
For doing, or.
For not doing.
"As no human being ever would."
Or, as?
No god, or.
"As no goddess, or."
As.
"No human being ever should, or as?"
No human being ever ought to, or.
"As no human being ever ought, or ever should."
Get away, with?
Being, doing, acting.

Or, non-acting.
"Though."
Of course.
Some might try to.
Act, so.
"Good, so."
Great, so.
"Fabu."
Lous, so.
All-knowing, or.
"So all-powerful, or."
So won.
Der.
Ful, and.
"Even if."
Of course.
"Might they try to."
Act, as.
"If, and."
Even if.
"Too, of."
Course, might.
"They, might."
He, or.
"Even if."
Might she.
"Have man."
Age.
D to con.
Vince them.
Selves, of.
"Their own good, or."
Of their own great.
Ness, or.
"Of their own fab."
U.
Lo.

Us.
Nes.
S, or.
Of their own fan.
Tas.
Tic-ness, or.
Of their own won.
Der.
Ful.
Ne.
Ss.
Too.
And, even.
"If, might."
They manage, to.
"Fool themselves, for."
A bit, or.
"For a while, or."
Partially, or.
Im.
"Even if."
Partially, and.
Of course.
Might they man.
Age, or.
"Even if."
Might they be able, to.
"Fool some, some."
Of the time, do.
"And can they, not."
Necessarily, fool.
"All, all."
Or, every.
One, or.
"Everybody, no."
Body, any.
"Body, no."

One, or.
"Nobody, all."
Of the time, and.
"Because, of."
Course, and.
Even if.
"What could, or even if."
What would never happen, but.
If were.
"And, or."
If when.
Or, if.
"When, or where."
Where, or when.
One were forced to be.
Or, if.
"Where, or."
If when.
"One, two, or m."
Ore, or all.
"We."
Re forced.
To live, like.
"Or, as?"
If we all were.
'We?'
Animals, as if.
"In me is nothing more, nothing higher, nothing more intelligent,
spiritual, or."
Otherwise, would one.
Or, would more, or.
"Would the most, or."
Would the many, or.
"Would the all?"
Be better?
Off, or on.
On, or off.

Helping my.
Self, be.
Cause.
Is the point, *or the point, is.* That can the mid.
D.
Le, or Midd?
Le not be own.
Ed, had, or oc.
Cup.
Ie.
D, or, at least?
Ou.
Gh.
T, and s.
Hou.
Ld.
It not qui.
Te be, and.
Choosing to be.
A cat, or a dog.
"Rather, than?"
Choosing, or.
"Rather than."
Being for.
Ced?
To be, or to be.
Come a dol.
Phi.
N, to.
"Hear, or."
To list.
En, or.
"Rather than."
Being for?
Ced.
To be a horse.
Or, to be?

A, or the, or.
Even the, or a?
Peg.
As.
Us, as.
If one can fly when all is i.
"When and where."
Ron, on the in.
Side, or.
Or where, and when?
All the all-too-heavy, i.
Ron men, and their wo?
Men, or pigs?
"Are they."
Do insist, demand, or keep trying?
To ride me, or?
"Even, if."
Of course?
As but one more opt.
I.
On, so gra.
Ci.
Ou.
Sly given, or en?
Do.
Wed by which, gods, God?
God.
Dess, or god.
Desses, or?
"By which ro."
Bot-ma.
Come a very quite so very spe.
Chi.
Cial, and un.
Nes, might be?
I.
Per.

Que uni.
Mit.
Corn, but still?
To be ridden?
And, so.
"Or, if so?"
But for such a good, or gre.
At, ride, but, as yet, and, still?
"To be used."
And, so.
Or, if so?
"To be petted."
Caged, and groom?
Ed, as if?
Cap.
Tur.
Ed, or, as if?
Owned, or.
"But, of course?"
What would, but, be.
"A worst case."
Or, a wor.
Se, or.
The worst-case scen.
Ari.
O, even if.
Of course, too, it is, or.
Might be.
The one who the de.
Men.
Ters, or is that, or is this?
Merely the D.
Evil? Him.
Self, the agent, the lover, and the cre?
At.
Or, of cha.
Os, or?

The des.
Tru.
Ct.
Or of all or.
Der, or?
"And, so."
Or, so?
Must cha.
Os be des.
Tro.
Yes, fir.
St, be.
For.
E or.
Der can pre.
Vail a.
Gain, or for the fir?
St time, or.
Is too much or.
As then, and as there, once again, did he turn in the bed, to reach for?
Der, and con.
The woman who was no longer his, or?
Trol, esp.
For the woman who was no longer there, so.
Eci.
"Must cha."
All.
Os be.
Y, of.
En got.
The wr.
Ten rid of, first?
On.
But what is, or.
G sort, or kin.
What might be?
D, as bad as not e.

Cha.
No.
Os to one, or.
Ugh.
Der to, or for?
All ot.
Hers, or?
"So, was this, or is this?"
Or, that.
Or, how to de.
The one, or me.
Stroy cha.
Rely one of his?
Os, or de.
Or, His.
Struct.
Which do, or which.
Ion, it.
Does try.
Self, or.
To create, make happen, manifest, or make true.
The wor.
St of the wors.
T, or?
"The worst of the w."
Or.
St-case sce.
Nar.
Io.
S, but, of course.
Or, is that, or is this you, or.
What is worst to, or for, some, or one.
But best for, or to, others, or.
To, or for.
An.
Y, or.
All others, and?

Because, of course, is not one man's heaven.
Or one wo.
Another's, or all others' hell, and.
Man's, or.
Because.
Of course.
"Though, even."
If what.
"Is not yet, but."
Of course, be.
Cause.
"Of course?"
What world, is.
More, or less, or.
"Less, or more?"
Than as it does.
Or as does, or as one can.
"Appear to be, though."
Imagine it to be, or, of?
"It does appear to be, to."
Course, as.
Or, for who.
M, or?
As who, or as what?
Does imagine, or plan.
"Or, rat?"
Her.
What world, or.
"Whose world, does?"
Tend to be, and tend to be.
Come?
What does one.
"Dream, or."
What one can, or what one does.
Or, who does it?
Ma.
Gine it to be, or.

What one, some, the most, or the many?
Or, you.
Do, or can.
Make of it, or.
Who, or.
"Do have night."
What, What.
Mares, of.
Or, Who.
It becoming, of.
Course, if is a.
Possibility, thought.
"Or dream of, can."
Or might, or.
"Might, or."
Can be.
Come real, or Real?
It.
Y, or.
Whose, or which, or what.
Ver.
Sion of re.
Al.
It.
Y, or?
Of the re.
Al, or of the Re.
Al, or.
Though.
Of course, be.
Cause.
"I am."
Also, what.
"And, also, who?"
And, Who.
I am not, and.
Also, what.

"And, who?"
You are not, too.
"Because, of cour."
Se, I, also.
Am who I was, and.
"Who I will be, and."
Because, of course.
"What is Be."
Ing, or.
What is being.
Or, who is.
Without Be.
And, Who is.
Coming, or.
With.
Out be.
Coming, or.
"Without No."
N-Being, too, or with.
Out non-be.
Ing, too.
And, be.
Cause, "Of course."
Who can be, or be?
Come without being, first, who they are, and be.
Cause, of course?
Who can be, or.
Who will be.
Come who they are with.
Out, also, being?
Or, leaving behind?
"Or, letting go."
What, or who.
Who, or what, and What.
They are not, and.
Be.
Or, how can be.

Cause, "Of?"
Ing, be.
Course.
Or Be.
I, al.
With non-
So, am.
Be.
Not one.
Ing, or with.
In.
Be.
Ter.
Co.
Est.
Ming, or?
Ed in owning.
Not one.
Interested in owning.
Or, one.
"Interested in."
Being owned.
Played, had, taken?
"Or, possessed."
By, or.
As if I am an ob.
Ject, or?
As if.
"A piece of prop."
You were.
Er.
Ty, as yet?
In the twenty-fir.
St.
Cen.
Tur.
Y, where?

"And, in which."
I think, or do be?
Lieve that, in.
Deed, most of us, or in which?
"We sane ones are living, or?"
Because, of.
Course, I am, also.
Far from interested.
In letting.
"Or, in permitting?"
Anyone, or everyone.
"Someone, or no one?"
Everybody, or anybody.
"Nobody, or somebody."
To write my story.
"Or, to run my life, or?"
To pre.
Destine, or.
"To pre."
Determine, or to de.
Termine, to.
"Decide, or."
To destine.
My life, for me.
"And, so?"
And, so.
Of course.
So as.
"Not to get ahead myself."
Of course.
But, also.
"Of course, so."
As not.
"To con."
Tin.
Ue, on.
And, on.

"In circles, again."
And again, without.
"Moving forward, and."
If not ne?
Ces.
Sa.
Rily up.
Ward, and.
Or, of.
"Course, without."
Moving for.
Ward, into.
What, or in.
Even.
To where?
If, of.
Though, or.
Course.
Ter than dow.
N, and.
Even if?
Of course, too.
Must mo.
Ving for.
War.
D, or for.
Wards?
Be bet.
Ter than mo.
Ving back, or back.
War.
Ds, and.
"Where, or."
Back.
In.
To what, or.
For.

"But, so?"
Ward, in.
Of course.
To where?
"So as."
Not to.
Have to.
Think again.
"And, again."
Around, and.
"Around, in."
Cir.
Cles, un.
"Pro."
Duct.
Ive.
Ly, and.
So as.
"Not to."
Keep re.
Pea.
Ting my.
Self, time.
"And again, and."
So as not to have to con.
Tin.
Ue.
Thinking, of.
Or, for?
"Or, about."
The same things, *or peo?*
Ple, again.
Or, per.
"And again, even."
Sons.
If, as.
Time does pass.

"Does time pass, and."
Because, as it does, and as.
Or, be?
Cause, of course, *you are in, and of it,* of.
Course, is.
"Not ever, or."
Is not al.
Ways, what.
Or, whom.
"I do think of."
Or, do choo.
Se, or do de.
Cide not to.
Not ever.
"Quite, exactly."
As is not ever one thought the same as the next, or as the pre.
The same, but.
Vi.
"Of."
Ous one, or.
Course.
Or, the Same.
Or, of course.
"Sooner, or later."
And, even if.
"Later, or sooner."
I might.
Indeed, need.
"Or, want?"
To get out of this bed.
Or, out of your bed, or.
"Because, of course."
Out of our bed, or.
Almost, more than most cert.
Ain.
Ly, and.
"Without needing to hope, without."

Finding the faith?
"That might, or."
That will, or.
"That, or."
Which does.
"Or which would?"
And, which will.
Re.
Lieve me of having to hope, or.
Or, in the pro.
"Of the ho."
Cess of be.
Ping, which?
Com.
Does trap.
Ing, with.
Or, which does keep.
Out qui.
"Me down, in."
Te be.
The trenches of thought.
Ing, or.
Or, in the trenches, of?
"Thinking, or."
In whose trenches.
Of un.
Certainty, though.
Or, of course.
Will I, in.
Deed, soon.
Er.
"Rather than later."
Who would.
"Get up, and get out."
Of this bed, when.
Or, who could.
And, where?

Be foolish enough.
"I am ready."
To try to be cer.
Tain about.
And?
What, most.
"About what, most."
Wisely, or.
Ration.
Ally, or.
"About, what."
Rea.
Son.
Ably, or.
"About what?"
Most logically, or.
"About what?"
Most certainly, can.
When, and.
"Where I de."
Ci.
De, to.
Will I not.
Where, and.
"Also, too."
Will I not ne.
Ce.
Ss.
Ari.
Ly, when.
They are ready for me to, and.
Or, a?
Not necessarily, where.
Bout.
"Or, when."
Or when, or.
"Where she is ready for me to, and."

What one should.
Also, of.
Ex.
"Course, not."
Cept, of.
Necessarily, where.
Co.
"Or when, or."
Ur.
When, or.
Se, who is she, and.
"Where, it."
Is ready for me, to.
Or, about?
And, also.
"Like."
Wise, and.
Of course.
"Also, not."
Where, and.
"Also, not."
When he.
"Does, or."
Also, not.
"When, or."
Also, not.
"Where, he."
Whoever he is, or.
"Whatsoever he is, or."
Whatsoever he.
Or, you?
Might want me to, and.
Ought not be certain, about.
"And, so."
And, too?
As did.
"And, as do."

Most of his mornings, start.
"And, begin."
And, like.
Wise.
"Of course."
As do mine.
Because, of course.
Begin, or.
"Start."
Either, slowly.
Is not.
Or, quickly.
At least.
Or, only as.
"Only, as."
Quickly.
A bit of hope necessary.
Or, only as.
To war.
Slowly.
D off.
"As slowly."
Des.
As one.
Pair, and.
Does, or.
As you do.
Choose, or.
As you do de.
Cide, to let them, be.
"Or appear, or."
Seem to be, be.
Cause.
"Of course."
And, as one must, and.
So, as?
As must one, and.

"Much like much else, of course?"
So as, must you.
Because, of course.
What, or who.
Who, or what.
Is most terribly, most hor.
Rib.
Ly, most cert.
Ain.
Ly, most won.
Der.
Fully, or most fan.
Tas.
Tic.
Ally, or.
What, or who.
Who, or What.
Is most ter.
Rib.
Ly, most hor.
Rib.
Le, most cert.
Ain, most fan.
Tast.
Ic.
Or, most fabulous
Is as subjective, as.
"Much else, is."
And, so.
"And, so?"
Did he wake early.
And, so, did you.
"Or, did he wake late?"
And, so, you did.
Or, did he wake.
Or, too late?
Or, just, right, on.

"Or, did I wake, or."
Time.
Or, too ear.
Ly.
"I did wake."
When, and where.
"And, where?"
And, when.
As do I, or.
"When, and."
Where, or.
"Where, and?"
When, as.
I do, usually.
And.
"And, so."
Where, and when, and as.
I usually do.
And, so, when you did.
"And, so, when I did."
Which, is.
"Or, which was?"
Most pro.
Bab.
Ly, if not nec.
Ess.
Ari.
Ly cert.
Ain.
Ly, or if not ex.
Act.
Ly, or.
If not pre.
Cisely.
"Around six."
Though he did not have.
And, though.

You do not have.
"And, though, I do not have."
A clock, or a watch.
"Which, also."
He did not need.
And, which, also.
"I do not need."
To know?
That most probably.
And, or.
That.
"Most likely."
Is it, or.
"It is."
Around, or.
"About six."
Though, even if.
"Did, or."
Even if.
"Had the grey."
Or, even if.
"Had the gray?"
Or, even.
"If have."
The gray, or.
"The grey."
But, of.
"Course, not."
The silver, because.
"Of course."
Can, and.
"Are, and."
Are, and.
"Cannot skies."
Ever be.
"Silver, and."
Because, of.

"Course, is."
Not what, or.
"Is not, who is."
Gray, or.
"Grey, is."
Not necessarily, what.
"Or, who."
Or, Who.
Is sil.
Ver, as.
"If, but."
Though, of.
"Course, people can be."
Or, ever.
"Are silver."
Or gray, or.
"Grey, or."
Ever are they.
Any color at all, un.
Less they, he, she, or it.
Is the, or a, tin man, all sil.
Ver, all gray, or all grey?
All mixed up, and all fuse.
D, but.
At least not all black-and white, or.
All white-and-black.
As if all things, and.
As if.
All people?
Mixed up, and con.
Fused, rather than.
Sep.
A.
Rate, are?
Any better, or any worse?
Than all se.
Par.

Ate, with bound.
Ari.
Es, pro.
Certain, and sure, or.
"As were?"
And, or, as.
Are the.
And, as are.
Skies outside his window.
Or, outside my window, or.
"As they are outside your window."
Out.
Or, as they are.
Side my win.
Out.
Dows, whi.
Side our win.
Ch, of.
Dow, or out.
Course?
Side my win.
If I can.
Dows, whi.
See out, can the.
Ch, if they can see, or if can.
Y see in.
Or, even.
Who, or what?
What, or Who.
"Soever."
They are, or.
"If has."
Or, even if.
"Have."
The gray, or.
"Even if."
My win?

Dow, which, of course, al.
So, is.
"My way out, and my."
Way in, if I do choose, and.
Even if.
Had the grey.
Skies, out.
Side my window.
Not changed much.
"Throughout the night?"
Though, now.
"Must, and."
Do I know, that.
"Must the day, have."
Started, or.
"Begun, as."
Can I not deny, *as you can.*
Not den.
Y, that.
"In."
Deed, the.
Morning has.
"Arrived, because."
Because?
"If the sky, and."
Even if.
"The skies are."
But the same, or.
The Same, or.
"Even if."
They are.
"But a similar, shade."
Of grey, or.
"Of gray, as."
They were yes.
Ter.
Day, and.

As the night.
"As they were, the."
Day, before.
"That, and."
Also, as.
"They were."
The day before, that.
"Too, and."
Even if.
"Might, or."
Might they not, also.
"Be, the?"
Same as.
"They will be, tomorrow, at."
Least are they.
And, at least they are.
"A bit less black, than."
They were, or.
"Than they usually are, during."
And through.
Out the night, and.
"Which is?"
More than most likely.
"The way they, also, were."
During the night, though.
"Of course."
I did not see them, and.
"Though, even."
If, of.
"Course, I could not see them, as."
I was sleeping, or.
"As I was dreaming, with."
My eyes closed, of.
"Course, and."
But, of.
"Course, what."
Were, and.

"What are."
And, what will be, even.
"Though I cannot see them, and."
What have been.
Even if.
"I am not watching them, and."
What will be, and.
Which, also.
"Is, and."
The way that more than.
"Most likely, they."
Will be.
"To."
Night, and.
The night, following.
And, following.
"When, and."
Where, and.
"Where, and."
When, once.
"Again, with."
My eyes closed, I.
"And sleeping, but."
Whether, or not, also.
Because, now.
You are dreaming.
"And, but."
Or, snoring, too.
Because, here.
And.
Or, but.
"Of course?"
Because there, and.
"Or, because?"
Also, of.
"Course, now."
Morning has.

"Now arrived, they."
Have turned, or.
"They are becoming."
A bit gray, or.
"A bit grey, as."
Is the wall.
"Across the way?"
Or, as.
"Is, the."
Wall, across the rather thin.
Or, across the rather thick?
Ice and snow-packed, path.
"Between my house, which."
Is between.
The brick wall, which.
"Of course, is."
Also, gray.
And, which.
"Also, is."
Composed, of.
"Grey, or."
Which, also.
"Is composed of."
Grey, or.
Of uniformly laid.
Or, uniformly lain?
Or, uniformly lying?
"Gray bricks, which."
Are as.
"Gray as."
Are the ski.
Es, also.
"Be."
Coming, and.
As is.
The wall, that.
"Does form."

The back side of my neighbor's house.
"Unit?"
Or, structure.
Or, a.
Part.
Ment.
"Or whatever it is, or."
What so.
What.
Ever it is called, or.
So.
"What."
Ever you do call it, or.
"Soever I do, or."
Whatsoever the most, or the man.
Y do, or?
"Whatever it is, which."
Is.
"Across the path, way, or trail, which."
Is.
"Between the wall."
And, the wind.
Ow, and.
"Which, also, is."
In between.
"The wall."
And my head, *and your head,* and.
"The path, trail, or."
Way, a.
Bove, which.
Also, he.
And, above which.
Also, you.
"Also, I."
Did not see evi.
Den.
Ce, of.

The sun having risen.
As us.
U.
Al, and.
"As al."
Ways, though, of.
Course.
The skies had begun to lighten.
And, to brighten?
So that.
"At least?"
He could see.
"That, at least."
The day had started.
"And, or."
That, at least?
And, or.
"That, at most?"
It had, or.
"Has?"
Indeed, begun, and.
"That, at least?"
Even if.
"I can."
Not see.
The sun, high up, above.
Which had not.
Yet?
Broken through the thick layer of clouds.
"And which has not, and."
Which more than most likely will not, though.
Who does need.
Could he still know?
A we.
Or could he still tell?
At.
"Though, of course."

Her.
Know, or.
Man.
Tell, what.
To know which way the wind.
"Or, tell whom, what."
Or, winds.
And?
Blow, do blow.
Even if.
Or, have blown, and.
To tell?
Is not, necessarily.
"To be told."
And, too?
Even if.
"Of course."
To be told, is not necessarily.
"To tell?"
And, even if.
Of course.
"Too, could he, also."
And, too, could you, also.
"And, too, can I, also."
And, too, can you, also.
And, even if.
Too, can he, also.
And even if, too, can you, also.
"And, even if?"
Too, I can, also.
Know that.
By seeing the effects, of.
"The sun?"
That the sun still was.
"And that it is."
Of course?
"Still there."

Or, still here, and.
"Too, that?"
Also, is.
"It."
Rising, and falling.
Or setting, and rising.
Or falling, and rising, or.
"Falling, and setting?"
Or rising, and setting.
Too, and.
That the earth?
Is, still.
And, as yet.
On its axis, rotating.
"And that it is, still, and as yet?"
Revolving.
As it does.
"And, as it will."
Of course.
Until we discover that no longer.
'We?'
Does it.
"And, or."
Until we discover.
That, or.
"This is."
Of course?
"Whosoever 'we' are."
And, or?
"Too, including."
Or, rather?
"Excluding."
What, or whom.
As do we not have kings.
"Or whom, or what."
Or queens, prin.
Also, 'we' are not.

Ces.
That it is not, any.
Ses, or prin.
"Long."
Ces, nor do we re.
"Er, or."
Cog.
That does it not, any.
Nize, or res.
Long.
Pect the.
Er?
"Or, any."
M, ei.
More.
Ther, as lor.
Though, of?
Ds, or lad.
Course.
Ie.
"Who."
S, of the cour.
So.
T, or Co.
"Ever."
Urt, or no.
We are.
Ble.
Whe.
Men, or wo.
The.
Men, ei.
R, if.
The.
Ro.
R, as ne.
Yal, or not.

Ver have we, an.
"Or?"
D, as ne.
But, be.
Ver will we.
Cause.
"This is America, and, so."
We do not do royalty, here.
Or, we do not have.
"Really, or."
Kings, or queens.
Queens, or kings.
Lions, or li.
On, or.
On.
Esses, or.
Actually, or.
Ex.
"Truly, in."
Cept, of.
Spite of.
Co.
"All of the self-de."
Ur.
Clared.
Se, the cour.
And, in.
Ts, of.
Spite of all.
A dif.
The self-crowned, self-.
Fe.
Anointed.
Rent so.
"Masters, kings."
Rt, or kin.
Queens, gods.

D.
God.
Desses, and emp.
Er.
Ors, *or emp.*
"Though, of."
Res.
Cour.
Ses.
Se, who.
"Are so only, as."
Royal, as.
"Powerful, or."
As important as.
"One, or."
As do 'we,' or.
As do three, four, two, the most.
The man.
Y, or the all, do.
De.
Cide, or do choo.
Se to think, or to be.
Lieve, they are, or.
"Who so."
Only are.
"As important, or."
As powerful as.
"'We' do."
Decide, or.
"As 'we' do."
Let, or.
"As 'we' do."
Permit them to be, and.
Or, as?
"All self-."
Declared, all.
"Knowing, and."

All powerful, and.
"Or, only?"
Or, just.
"Or un."
Justly, or.
As merely as.
All powerful, and.
"As all."
Knowing as.
"One, or."
As all, or.
"As all?"
Of the rest of us, me.
Re I's, or.
Me.
Re ones, or.
"As me."
Re sing.
Les, do.
"Permit them to."
Be, or.
"And, so."
And, so.
And, so, or.
"So, per."
Haps, rat.
Her, 'we' the peo.
Of, a dif.
Ple, or 'We,' the Peo.
Fe.
Ple, of course?
Rent, Dif.
Who are just, me.
Fe.
Rely, or on.
Rent, or dif.
Ly, a se.

Fe.
Lect, or an e?
Ring.
Lite few, and.
Kind, or so.
"Because, even if."
Democracy might have be.
Come fas.
Cism in some places, too?
Is it, or must it be?
"The best way there is, and, so."
Where, and, so.
When.
"And when, and where."
And where, and when.
It is no longer working.
But.
"At the end, must it."
Working for whom, or for what.
Start a.
Or, how not, and.
Gain, at the be.
Ginning, but.
"Or is it."
Rather, not democracy.
That does not work, but.
"Rather?"
But.
There, and then.
Or?
And, so.
And, here.
"Then."
And, now.
"And, there."
Or here, and now.
And, so.

Or, how to start over, or?
Or, so?
And how re-in.
And, also.
Vent the wheel, or.
"Here, and now."
And, so?
"Or, so."
Also, and.
Now, and here.
Was he, and.
"I am, and."
He was, and.
"Am I."
Done, and.
I am.
"Fin."
Is.
He.
D con.
Temp.
Lating?
His palms.
And, your p.
Alms, and.
My palms, and.
"His hands?"
And, my hands.
And, your hands.
Right, and left.
"And left, and right."
And wrong, and right.
"And right, and wrong?"
As if.
Never having seen them, before?
Or, as if.
"I have not, but."

For what.
So?
Ever reason.
Or, but.
"For what."
So.
Ever reasons, that.
Indeed?
He could, or.
"That, in."
Deed? Now.
"I can."
Not re.
Member.
Or, for?
"Whatso."
Ever rea.
Son, or.
For what.
"So ever?"
Reason, or.
For what?
"Soever."
Reasons, which.
Or, that.
I can, or.
Do not know.
Now, or.
"Here, or."
Here, or.
"Now, for what."
Soever.
"Reason, or."
For what.
So.
Ever reasons, too.
"And."

So, that.
"And, that?"
Because, if.
"Can I not know, here."
Or now, or.
"Now, or."
Here, then.
Or, for.
"What so."
Eve.
R, re.
As.
On.
"Reason, or."
Reasons, which.
"Are not, and."
Which.
Need I not know, or.
Which I do not.
Need to know, or.
Which you do not.
Need, or get?
To know, or.
For which.
Or, for what.
"So."
Ever.
Reason, or.
"Reasons, which."
Are not, then.
"Or, now."
Or, now.
Or, there.
And, there.
"Or, here."
And, here.
Can I not know, because.

Of course, is not knowing, being.
Or, Being.
Or being, knowing.
Any less, or.
Any more, or any more, or any.
Less, than is.
Thinking, knowing, or knowing, believing.
Or think.
Think.
Ing, be.
Ing, be.
Or know.
Liev.
Ing, thin.
In.
King, or.
G, or.
As is not thinking, saying.
Of course.
Or saying, doing.
Though some idiots.
Or thinking of doing, doing.
Mo.
Or doing, saying.
Ron, and fools.
Say what.
So what.
So.
You do not need.
Ever.
Want.
They are thin.
Care, or have.
King, and.
Any right to know, or?
Or.
"Of."

Say.
Course.
Ing, think.
Quite so rea.
Or writ.
Son.
Ing, say.
Ably, and.
Ing, think.
"Be."
Ing, or writ.
Cause.
Ing, or.
Of.
Think.
Course.
Ing, writ.
"Quite so."
Ing, or.
Logi.
Writ, thin.
Call.
King, or.
"Quite so logi."
Call.
Y, and.
Because.
"Of course."
Quite so rat.
Ion.
Ally, and.
"Be."
Cause, of.
Course, quite.
"So most."
Sens.
Ib.

Ly, why.
"Try, or."
Because, why.
"Need to know, what."
I can.
Not, or.
"What I do not, or."
What, or What.
Who, or Whom.
You do not know, or.
What, or who, can.
Who, or what, can.
Not be known, or.
Who ought not be know.
N, or.
"What is not, and."
Or who, or Who?
Is not, and.
So, be.
Cause.
"He, and."
So, because.
"I, also."
Did.
And, do?
Not need, or get?
To know, or be.
Cause.
"I cannot know, but?"
What, or who.
"Or, Who."
You can.
Not know, or.
Who, or Who?
Or what can.
Not be known, or.
What hands, and.

Or, whose hands, and.
"What palms?"
Did he, and.
"What pa."
L.
Ms, or.
Whose palms, and.
Did he, and.
Did I, and.
Did you, and.
I did, and.
"You did, and."
He did, and.
You did.
"Raise?"
Right, and.
"Left, and."
Because, what were.
And, because what are.
"But, not what are."
Not raised.
As if.
By another, or.
As if by any, or.
"As if?"
By all others, as.
If you are, or.
"As if I might be."
Some sort, or.
"Some kind of pup."
Pet, or.
As if?
Also.
"Both left."
And right, also.
He did.
"And."

What, also, I did.
And, what you did.
Drop, again.
"But, only."
And.
So, only.
"After, assuring?"
And, or.
"After, ensuring."
Or, only.
"So, only."
After en.
Self, or only.
Suring, only.
After as.
Suring him.
Self.
Or, if.
"So, only."
After en.
"Sur."
Ing my.
Self, that.
Of course.
"They are mine, because."
Of course.
If they are not mine, and.
"Because, of."
Course, if.
"Are they not mine."
Or, if they are not yours.
Who else's would they.
Or, whose.
"Or what's, else."
Could they.
"Or, might they be?"
And, so.

Even, so.
After having.
Ensured, and.
Even, so.
After having.
"Ass."
Ur.
Ed myself.
Of the.
Ir to.
Tal, and.
"Of their com."
Ple.
Te, and.
Of the.
Ir en.
Tire.
"Whole, and."
Genuine, au.
Then.
Ti.
City.
As mine.
"But, so."
Of course.
Or, if.
"After, having."
En.
Sure.
D, or.
If?
"Rather, after en."
Suring, or.
If, rather, after.
"Having as."
Sure.
D, and, or, if?

"After."
Assuring your.
Self, of.
"My more than sure."
Or, of.
My more than cert.
Ain.
"Possession of them, which."
Might sound, or.
"Which might seem, a."
Bit crazy, be.
"Cause, of."
Course, be.
Cause.
If not mine.
Then, or now.
Now, or then.
Whose might.
"Or."
Whose could they be.
Or, whose can they be.
And, be.
"Cause, if."
Not mine, and.
"Because, if."
I do not.
"Claim, or."
Seize, them.
Or, take?
And, own them.
"As my own, who."
Or, as my own, or.
As your own, or.
What.
If not as your own, or.
"Or what, or."
Who, is.

"Not me."
Or, not you.
"Might try."
To take them, or.
"Who, or."
What, might.
"Try to."
Seize them.
"Or, what."
Or, who.
"Might try."
To take them, or.
"Who, or."
What might.
"Try to."
Use them.
"As if."
They were theirs, or.
"As if."
They were hers, or.
"As if."
They were his, or.
"As if."
They were its.
Own, and.
"If, of."
Course, I.
"Do not."
Seize, take.
"Or use."
Them, as.
"My own, who."
Or what, or.
"What, or."
Who, might.
"Or, who."
Or, Who.

Or, what.
Or, What.
"Or, what."
Or, What.
Or, who.
Or, Who.
"Will try."
To take pos.
Sess.
Ion of them, to.
"Use them."
For, or to.
To, or for.
"Some point."
Or, for.
"Or, to."
Or, for.
Some purpose.
Or, to.
"Or, for."
Or, to.
"Some end that I do not know."
Or, to.
"Or, for."
Some point, purpose.
"Or end, that."
I do not want to know, or.
Do not want to have to know, or.
"For, or."
To, or.
"To, or."
For some purpose, end.
"Or point, with which."
I did, and do, not agree, or.
With which you do not agree, or.
"With which, I."
Do re.

Fuse, to.
"Collude."
Or, to.
"Or, for."
Some purpose, point.
"Or, end."
That I do not support, or.
"Of which I do not."
Approve.
"And, which."
Is not.
"Mine, for."
Me, or yours, for you, be.
Cause.
"Of course."
Who agrees, or.
"Who wants, or."
Be.
Cause, who.
"Needs to."
Be used, as.
An object, or.
"And, too."
Because, who.
"Or what, or."
What, or.
"Who is."
Or, does be.
Come.
"The id."
Io.
T, the.
"Fool, or."
The moron, who.
"Does agree, to."
Be so.
"Used, as."

Such a means to.
"Some end."
Other than one's own, or.
"Who is."
Or, who.
"Does become."
The, or.
"A, or."
One, of.
"The biggest, greatest, or."
Grandest.
"Fools, idiots."
Or morons, who.
"Does agree."
Or, who.
"Does let."
One.
Self, be.
"Used as."
A tool.
Or, as.
"An agent."
For change?
Or, as.
Or, otherwise.
A worker, for.
Or used at all, in any way, for, or as.
"Some boss, or."
For, or by, some so.
Ur.
Ce.
Other than oneself.
Or.
"As if?"
The agent of.
Or, for.
Some source other than oneself, or.

As if.
The agent, of.
"Some for."
Ei.
Gn so.
Ur.
Ce, of cour.
Se.
Who, or.
"Which, or."
What is not.
You, or yours.
"Me, but."
And, which are mine.

*   *   *   *   *

Too.
"Of course."
If these are not, and.
If are not those your hands, or.
"If are these not."
And, if those are not your hand.
My hands, or.
S, or.
"My own hands, or."
My palms, or.
"My own palms, then."
Or, now.
"And, here?"
Whose, or.
"What's."
Might they be, and.
"If I am."
Not talking.
"To myself."
Then, or.

Now, and?
Or.
"Here, or."
Now, or.
Here, to whom am I talking, or.
"To whom might I be talking, and."
To whom, or to what.
Might you be, and.
"Because, of course."
As much as, must.
These, or those, be my, *or be your*, h.
Ands, and your palms?
Must.
I, also, be.
Or un.
"Talking, just."
Justly.
Or only, or.
"Merely, or."
Mir.
Ror-ly, to?
"Myself, but."
Of course, can.
"They only."
Be mine, if.
"Where, or."
If when.
"They are not, all."
Swarming, black.
With black, all in.
"Or, with."
Black, all around.
"Them, and."
But, at least.
Do I still, and, as yet, know?
Or, can you still see.
What is black.

Or, ever could you.
What is not.
See, or.
Who is not, or.
Ever did you know?
And what is white, and, or?
Who is, or.
Of course, and.
And who, and what, is not.
In spite, or de?
Spite, or.
"And, will."
What, or who, is but gray, or grey?
And, are.
"They, only."
Mine, if.
"Where, and."
Or, if.
"When, the."
Black, of.
"Oil, or?"
If, only.
"When, or."
If, only where.
"The black of."
Snakes, or.
"If, so."
Only, where.
"Or, if."
So, only, when.
"I am without, or."
If, so.
"Only, when."
Or, if.
"So, only."
Where I am.
"Rid, or."

If, so.
"Only, where."
Or, if.
"So, only."
When I.
"Have rid myself, of."
The black.
Or, of the white, or White.
Of the devil?
Or, of the ma.
Or, of the De.
Chine, or of the be.
Vil, or.
As.
"Or if."
T, or of the Be.
So, on.
As.
Ly, w.
T.
Here.
"And, or."
If, so.
"Only, when."
I have been de-.
Bugged, or.
If so on.
Ly when, and where, or where.
And, when.
I have be.
On.
En.
Ly w.
"Dis."
Hen, or on.
Pos.
Ly w.

Ses.
Here, you have be.
Sed.
En dis.
If so.
Pos.
"On."
Ses.
Ly w.
Sed, tho?
Here.
Ugh, of.
And, or.
Co.
"If so."
Ur.
On.
Se.
Ly w.
Dis.
Hen.
Pos.
I have.
Ses.
"Got."
Sed, of w.
Ten rid of.
Hat, or.
The b.
Of who.
Lack, or.
M, or of W.
"Of all."
Hat, or.
Of?
Of W.
The whisp.

Hom, and.
Er.
Hat, or of w.
Ers, or.
Hom, and.
"What can, or."
Who can, or.
What will, only.
Be mine, and.
"Just, and."
Only, mine.
"Where, and."
When, or.
"When, or."
Where, I.
"Have rid my."
Self, and.
"This town?"
Of all.
"Of the secret keepers, or."
Only, when.
"And, only."
Where, I.
And, only where.
Do cease, or?
And, when you.
Do stop.
Hearing the.
"Whisp."
Ers, of.
The flakes, or.
"Of the snakes?"
Which do swarm, or.
"Of those?"
Which are.
"Merely, just."
Or, only?

"Flakes, which."
Do fall, or.
"Which are falling?"
And, which.
Do fall, as.
They do, and.
As they will, and.
"Just outside my window?"
Or, those.
Or, these?
"Flakes, which."
Of course.
"Are not snakes, which."
Are falling?
"And which do."
Fall, now.
"Quite silently, and."
Now, quite.
"Slowly."
Or, those of the whisp.
Ers of the snow.
Flakes.
So silent, or.
"Of those, rising?"
And, or.
Of those being risen.
Or raised, is it?
But, if.
But, if?
"Now, being risen?"
Or, now, being raised?
And, if, so?
Being risen by.
"Whom, or."
By what?
"If not."
Just, or.

"If not, only, or."
If not, merely, by?
"The wind, or."
If not.
By the g.
"Me."
Us.
Re.
Ts, or.
Ly, on.
By the g.
Or, j?
Ales, or.
Ust, or.
Unjustly, by.
"The winds, or."
Of course.
Of course.
Of course.
"By the wind, or."
By the winds.
"That can."
Not be.
"Had, or."
Seen, or.
Owned, or.
"Possessed, and."
Which are.
"No one's, and."
Which are no.
Body's, and.
"Which, of."
Course, are.
"Not con."
Her op.
Trolled by.
Po.

Any hi.
Site, of co.
H.
Ur.
Ger, se.
Low.
What.
Er, big.
Or, who.
Ger, gre.
So.
At.
Ever that, or.
Er, or.
This might.
Gran.
Be, if?
Er, or.
Op.
"All pow."
Po.
Er.
Site.
Ful, all.
Grav.
"Know."
It.
Ing, e.
Y, the.
Ter.
Re, or he.
Nal, or.
Re, and.
"Ever."
Now, what.
God, or.
Must be.

"Gods, god."
Anti-grav.
Des.
It.
Ses, or.
Y, go.
God.
Ver.
Des.
Ning ant.
Ses, ot.
Ti-, or dark, mat.
Her than grav.
Ter, ke.
It.
Ep.
Y, and.
In.
Like, or.
G thin.
Sim.
Gs a.
Il.
Part, as.
Ar, or.
Grav.
Off of the s.
It.
Now, and ice-.
Y do.
Pac.
Es gov.
Ked path out.
Ern mat.
Side of his win.
Ter, draw.
Dow, and.

In.
Or, rat.
G the.
Her, "Of."
M to.
Co.
Get.
Co.
He.
Ur.
R, and.
Se.
If, and as.
Just out.
Op.
Side my.
Po.
Win.
Site, far.
Dow, or.
More close.
Just out side your win.
Ly re.
Dow, or.
Late.
Off of.
D to her, than.
The s.
What is me.
Now, and ice-.
Rely a.
Packed, path.
Or, trail?
Just outside my window.
Or just outside mine, or.
If not.
"Necessarily?"

Outside ours.
Or way, just.
"Outside my window, or."
Rather, the.
"Silence, or."
Rather, the.
"Peace, of."
Those, falling.
And, or.
"Of those?"
Being picked up, and.
"Or, of."
Those being.
Blown all.
Around, and.
Or, of.
"Those, or."
Of these crystals.
"Forming around the edges, of."
The windows, all.
All of whi.
"Of which, are."
Ch, are.
All so dif.
Are all so.
Fe.
Dif.
Rent, and.
Fe.
Of course.
Ring, and.
"Of course."
All, of.
"Which, are."
All so spe.
Cia.
L, and.

"Of course."
All, of.
"Which, are."
All so in.
Divi.
Dual.
And, which.
"Of course, all."
Of which, are.
All so.
"Individualized."
Or individual, or uni?
Que, or dis?
Tinc.
T, and.
Which.
"Of course."
Are all.
"So spe."
Cial, and so spec.
Ia.
Liz.
Ed, and.
Though, but.
Or.
"But though, as."
If being different.
Or, as.
"If being."
Rather, is.
Dif.
Distinguishable the, or a, bet.
Fer.
Ter word, or Word?
"As if."
Or whose, or which, Word, or wor.
Ren.

Ds, or.
Being.
Per.
"One."
Haps, is.
From the ne.
Dis.
Xt, do.
Cern.
Es make one spe.
Able, the be.
Ci.
St, of all, or?
Al, or.
The be.
Do.
St, at le.
Es make one.
As.
More spe.
T, for he.
Cia.
Re, and.
L, and.
At le.
Or, as if.
As.
"Being?"
T, for now, and.
Different.
Does make one better.
Or, the best, but.
"Of course."
Who, or what.
What, or.
If op.
Po.

Sit.
E who, or Who.
M, or.
If op.
Posit.
E.
"Or, what."
Or, What.
Or, who.
Or, Who.
Is not as special as one does choose to be.
"Or, as?"
One does choose to feel.
Or, as one does choose to be.
Lie.
Ve one is, or.
And, or?
"So, not."
Necessarily, just.
"Or, only as."
Special as.
"One, or."
As more, or.
"As ot."
Hers, do.
Make one feel, because.
"Of course."
Can.
Not.
"Any one."
Two, or?
More, or.
The most, the man.
Y, or the all, or.
Another.
"Make."
You, me?

"Or, any."
One, body, or.
You, or me, or.
Ever.
Yon.
E, or every.
Body, feel.
Any way, or eve.
Ry way, without.
"One's own permission, or."
Without yours, or.
"Without mine, and."
Or, without my permission, and.
Too, be.
Cause.
"Of course."
Or, rather?
Perhaps?
"Is special is."
As special does, or?
If, rather.
"Of course."
I am not so dumb.
Or, one so stupid.
Or, one.
So crazy, so insane, or so demented.
Enough, to?
"Think, or."
Enough, to?
Believe, that.
"Might the snows."
Or, that might the flakes.
"Actually, or really."
Real.
Ly, or actu.
Ally, tru.
Ly, or act.

U.
Ally, or truly?
"Be whisp."
Ering, or.
That, out.
Side.
"My win."
Dow, in.
This we.
At.
Her, or.
"In this town, where."
Never have we.
"Had snakes, so."
Would 'we,' and do 'we.'
Have no.
"Re."
Aso.
N to.
Have them, no.
W, or here, or he.
Re, or now.
"And, which, I."
Would just, or un.
Justly.
"Or, only."
Be see.
In.
G, if.
I were hal.
Luci.
Nating, and.
Or, if I were i.
Magi.
Ning, or if you we.
Re, or if I we.
Re i.

Mag.
In.
Ing what is not true, or.
"What, or who?"
Who, or what.
Is not True, Real, or real, or.
"Because, of."
Course, are.
"Not whispers, things."
Which can be seen, and.
"So, rather."
Might the whispers.
Or, might the whisperers?
Be.
Or, in.
Deed.
"Most surely, or."
Indeed, most.
"Certainly, are."
They.
"Possibilities, options."
Or, ot.
Hers?
Who have been.
"Or, others?"
Who might be.
"Or, others?"
Who once were.
"Or, others?"
Who might have been, or.
"Others, who?"
Could have been, or.
"Others, who?"
Once might have been.
So, phant.
Flo.
Oms, or g.

At.
Host, or.
Ing the air, which.
Or those who have dis.
Of course.
Ap.
"Because."
Pea.
We are in.
Red, or those.
Side.
Who have been disappeared.
'We?'
"Or, because."
Or, silenced.
Of course.
Because?
Yet.
For trying to say, what.
"And, be."
They did not want to have to hear, or.
Cause?
The truth, or.
Still.
The Truth, or.
"I am but one."
Because, yet.
"That morning."
Or, this morning.
Or, because?
As usual, and, because?
"As always."
He did not consider.
"Or, think much about."
Or?
"Consider, or remember."
Or re.

Mem.
Ber to think about.
Or re.
Member to con.
Sider, or.
Remember, to.
"Think of?"
And, or.
Rather?
"To es."
Cape?
Thinker, and thought.
Thought, and.
"Think."
Er, al.
"Together, or?"
In fa.
Vor of be.
Coming a neu.
Tral ob.
Server, of me, of my.
Self, of?
And, of.
"My fee."
Lings, and, of.
"My thoughts, thin."
King, and, or.
"Of?"
Thought it.
Self, and.
Rather, preferring.
"Not to."
Have to.
Remember.
Or, remembering that, in.
Deed, all thought, and all thinking, is.
But me.

Mor.
Y, memo.
Ries, and re.
Mem.
Be.
Ring, and, that.
Thought, and.
That thinking, is, in.
Deed, the en.
Em.
Y of cre.
At.
Iv.
It.
Y, and of cre.
At.
Ion, and that, in.
Deed, too much thought, and.
Too much think.
Ing can, and of.
Ten does, lead to par.
Aly.
Sis, or to be.
Coming the new.
Est me.
Chan.
Ic.
Al man, or tin?
Wo.
Man, *all gra.*
Per.
Y, or all gre.
Son, or ma.
Y, or all si.
Chin.
Ver.
E, and.

"Because, of."
Course, who does not know?
That where thinking does start, or be?
Gin cre.
At.
Iv.
It.
Y, and cre.
At.
I.
On, does end, and?
"Or, not."
To have to think of?
And, of.
"Course, who."
Would he not.
And, you would not.
"Quite so."
Ever be.
"Able to."
Think for.
The woman who did lie in the bed alongside him, or?
At least, the one, who had.
Once.
And, even if.
"To think for another?"
Or, for an Other.
"Or, for the Ot."
Her?
Or, for a me.
Re ot.
Her.
Might be.
"Far easier."
Far simpler, and far more.
Simple.
Than letting.

"Or, than permitting?"
That, or.
"This Other?"
Or this, or.
"That other?"
Who, or what.
"Or what, or who."
Or who, or what.
So ever she, he, or it, might be.
Or What, or Who.
To think.
And, to be?
"For, and by, my."
Self, though.
"Or?"
By, and for.
Her, him, it, or them.
Selves, or?
But, of course?
"Even if."
Any.
Thing, or.
"All else."
Would be, and, is?
To vio.
Late my own.
"Free will, autonomy."
Liberty, and self-.
Determination.
"And, too."
Of course.
"What is, and."
What would be.
"And, what is."
Of course.
And, what is.
"Violating my."

Right to be?
"For me, and."
Of course, my right.
"To be for me, and."
My?
"Right to be."
Me, and.
For me, and.
"What, or."
Who, or.
"What?"
Because, of course.
Even if.
"Is not ob."
As are re.
Jectification, easi.
Duct.
Er, too.
Ions, and.
And, be.
As is over.
Cause, of.
Simp.
Co.
Li.
Ur.
Fi.
Se, and be.
Cat.
Cause, even.
Ion, too, if?
Only an idiot, moron, or fool.
Would try.
"Or, would dare."
Make more difficult, or more com.
Pli.
Cat.

Ed, what.
"Is, and what ought."
To be.
Simple, and easy, though.
Of course.
"Is not what is easier."
Or, who is.
Always what.
Or, Who is.
"Is best."
Or, always.
"What is."
Right, or.
Always what.
"Is greatest, grandest, or."
Always what.
Or, always Who is?
Most.
"Fabulous, or."
Always, or.
"Ever, what."
Is most fan.
Tas.
Tic, or.
"Always, or."
Ever, what.
Or, who?
"Is most."
Wonderful, or.
"Always, or."
Ever, what.
Or who?
"Is most."
Who.
"Has done so for as long as I do care to remember."
But who, or Who?
That, or.

Has done what, or?
This, is.
"Of course?"
If I do care to remember.
"Or, this, or?"
That is, if.
"I do care to choose to remember her."
And, too?
"Because, of course."
Can.
Not caring be for.
Ced, and.
"Because?"
Why would I.
Care, or.
"Choose, or."
Decide, or.
Remember.
Because?
"She has never been."
Here, or.
"There, or."
Good enough.
"Or, just."
Precisely, or.
"Exactly, as."
You would want, or.
"Exactly, or."
Precisely, as.
You would like, or.
And, or?
"Because, of cour."
Se, I will not be one.
"To be for."
Ced to re.
Me.
Mb.

Er, and be.
Cause.
"Of course."
I will not.
"Be one."
To be.
"Forced to forget."
This, or that.
Or that, or this, or.
"Who, or what."
Or what, or who.
As much as, too.
And, also?
"Of course."
I will not be one to be haunted.
Or, one?
"To be guilt-tripped."
Because, of course.
"She did have to go."
And, because.
"Is it my fault?"
And, because.
"Of course."
It is not my fault, that.
She would not stop.
"And, because?"
Is it my fault.
That she would not get out of my way.
"And, because."
Of course.
"It is not my fault that she would not get out of my way, and."
Because?
Of course.
Is it not my fault that she would not leave me alone.
"And, because?"
Of course.
"It is not my fault that she would not leave me alone, and."

Because, of.
"Course."
Is it my fault that she would not stop.
Driving me crazy.
And, too?
"Because, of course."
Was it my fault that I had to do what I had to do.
"Or, that?"
You did.
What I had to do, or.
"That?"
She made me do it, and.
"So, of."
Course, be.
Cause I am not one.
"Or, I am not one."
Or, he is not one, to.
Or, you are not one to.
"Be guilt-tripped."
Or, one.
To be made to feel guilty, for.
"Doing what I had to do?"
And, or.
"So?"
Because.
Of course.
Can she not be.
The one?
"Or, too."
Because, of course.
"She can."
Not be the one.
"Whispering, or."
The one?
Trying.
To haunt me?
"As much as."

Of course.
"I am not one."
To think, or one.
To seriously consider, that.
"The flakes of snow."
Might be the ones, whispering.
Or, that I might hear them?
Or, that you might hear them.
Outside, or on the other side.
"Of my window, or?"
That might the others, or that might?
The ghosts, or.
"That might the in."
Visibles, or.
That, might.
The dark.
"Invisible, or."
Anti-, or dark.
Mat.
Ter, or.
"That might."
What, or.
That might.
"Who is."
Not, or.
That might.
"The traces, of."
What, or of.
"Who might have been?"
Or, of.
"What, or of who."
Was.
Has been?
"Or, of."
Who, or.
"Of what?"
Could have been.

Be the.
One, or ones.
Hearing.
"Or, be."
The ones listening, or.
"Be?"
The ones slithering, or.
"Be the?"
Ones whispering, or.
That might, rat.
Her.
These hands.
Or, your hands?
"Or, these palms?"
Or, your palms.
Be the ones talking.
"Or?"
That might you be hearing it, or them, or.
That might their talking, or saying?
Her.
Be happening, at all, or.
"Going, on."
Around, or.
All around me, or.
All a.
At all.
Round you, or.
"Or?"
Is that, or.
"If is this, but."
Only me.
Or, only you, or on.
Ly.
Me, or.
"Or, my thinking."
Or, rather.
Might it all be in your head, or.

"Because, of course."
As if.
Might whispering, be.
Necessary, in.
"Places, or."
At times, where.
"Or, when."
Or, where.
One can.
Not say, what.
"One needs to, or."
What one wants to, to.
Who, or.
"When."
Or, where.
One does want, or need to, or.
When, or where.
Or where, or when.
"One does not."
Want to say.
"Or, have to say, or."
Tell what, or.
Tell.
Whom, what will, or.
"What can be."
Heard by.
Everyone, or.
"By all, when."
And, where.
"And, where."
And, when.
"One does."
Not want.
"All to."
Hear, or.
"All, or everyone, or eve."
Ryb.

Ody.
To hear, or.
"To know what is pri."
Vate, or to know.
What is per.
Son.
Al, or.
Real.
Ly, truly, and, also?
Actually.
What is none of their, his, her, or its busi.
Ness, or.
Is.
Actually, some.
"One else."
Or an.
Other, or.
"Any, or."
All others, other.
"Than me."
Either.
"Dead, or."
Living, but, also.
Is, or might.
The whispering, be.
"Not me."
And, is.
It not.
"Coming, from."
Me, eit.
Her, and.
"If the whisp."
Ers are.
Coming from.
"An."
Other, from.
Others, or.

From all others, or.
"From without, of."
Course, am.
"I not."
Quite crazy.
"Enough, to."
Think, or.
"To be."
Lieve.
That might.
"Gho."
Sts, or.
That might.
"Spir."
Its, be.
The ones.
"Whisp."
Ering, and.
Of course, I.
Also, am.
"Not one."
Crazy, or.
"One in."
Sane enough to think, or.
One.
"Enough to be."
Lieve.
That I do hear.
Or, one cra.
Zy en.
Ou.
Gh to be.
Lieve that I am he.
Aring, or.
"That I might?"
Hear them.
Or, her.

"Or, that I might."
Be hearing.
"Anything?"
Or, anyone.
Or, me.
"Or, everyone?"
Or, every.
Body, or.
Everything.
"Or, somebody?"
Or, someone.
"Or, all?"
At all.
"If they are not here."
Talking, or thinking?
Thinking, or talking.
Or, if they are.
"Not saying, or."
If they are.
Invisible.
"Not telling, or."
Telling whom, what, or.
Of course, or.
What, whom, or.
"If rather?"
Are the whispers, and.
"Or, rather, if."
Is the whispering, of.
"The secret-keepers, or."
If are not they.
Or, if they are not.
He, she, or it.
"Not talking, not."
Saying, and.
"Or, if they are not tel."
Ling, of course, though.
Telling whom, or telling what, what, or, of.

Course, how might I hear them, her, him, or.
"It, and."
Or.
"Be."
Cause, of course.
I am not one.
"In."
Sane, or.
One crazy e.
Nou.
Gh.
"To think that I might hear, or."
That you might.
To believe that I might be able to hear, or.
To think, or to believe.
"That I might know?"
What, or know whom, or What, or Whom, or.
What one, what more, what another, or what others, think.
"Or, are thinking?"
Or, do think, if.
"They do not say, or."
If they are not saying, or.
"If they are not telling, or."
If they do not tell me, be.
Cause, of.
"Course, I."
Am not.
One dumb, one crazy, or one in.
Sane enough, to.
"Think, or be."
Lie.
Ve, that?
The thoughts, or.
"That the thinking."
Of another, or.
"Of any, or."
Of all others.

"Might, or can."
Be heard, uni?
Vers.
Or, that it should, or.
Ally, by every.
Ought to be he.
One, or by all, or.
Ard, or aud.
That might I he.
Ib.
Ar the.
Le, or.
M, or.
That might I hear them, or.
That you might.
Know what he, or know what they.
Are thinking, if.
He does not say, or.
If she does not.
If they do not, or.
If you do not, or.
And, as if, I am.
One crazy, or.
"One in."
Sane, or.
One de.
Lusi.
On.
Al e.
No.
Ugh.
"To think."
To presume, or.
"To assume, that."
Might an.
Other, or.
That might.

"All, or."
That might.
Any other.
"Or, that."
Might, or.
"That can."
All others.
"Know, what."
I am thinking, or.
"That might."
They all have.
"Some right to."
Know, either.
"Though, of."
Course, also.
"Might some."
Body's.
Thoughts, or.
"Might some."
One's, or.
"Might some."
Thinking, or.
"Might some."
Possibilities linger.
"As traces, of."
What has been, or.
"Of what."
Could be.
"Or, of."
What might have been, or.
"Of who?"
Or, of Whom.
Has been, which.
"Of course."
Might just.
Or un.
Just.

Ly.
Or, on."
Ly, al.
So.
Be memories, or.
"Thoughts, or."
Possibilities, or?
"Traces, or."
Ghosts?
Of what might.
"Or."
Of whom, or.
"Of what."
Could be?
Or, of who has been, or.
What could, also, be.
"The whispers, of."
The angels, or.
Of what, or.
"Of whom is to come, or."
Or, of who?
Once were, or of those who are.
Yet to be, or.
Of those who?
Are yet to be, or yet.
Of those, who, are yet.
To appear, or.
Who are a bit less than most vis.
Ib.
Le, or.
"Of those, who?"
Are a bit less than material, or.
"Because, of course."
How to know, who.
"Or, how to know, what."
Is here, or.
"How to know."

Who, or what.
Or what, or who.
Is there, or is here, or.
How to know.
What, or.
"Who can."
Not be seen, or.
At least, not by those.
Without eyes to see, or.
What, or.
"Who can."
Not be heard, at least.
Not by those.
Without ears to hear, or.
Who is?
"Either there."
Or here, or.
"Both, or neit."
Her, and.
Or, of course.
"As do all know, that."
Or, as all do know, that.
Of course.
"Do not ghosts, spir.
Its, or an.
Gels, ex.
Ist, but.
"Only in."
Sofar.
"As does."
One choose, or on.
Ly in.
"Sofar as."
One does de.
Cide, to.
"Let them, or."
Permit them to, or.

"If so."
On.
Ly, in.
"So."
Far as.
One does choose.
"To let, or."
Only in.
"Sofar as."
Or, only.
"As long as one."
Does choose.
"To believe in them, and."
But, of.
"Course, be."
Cause can.
"Not one."
Most reason.
Able, or.
"One most rat."
Ion.
Al, or.
One most.
Logical, or.
"One most sens."
Ib.
Le, not.
Expect all.
Everyone, or every.
Body.
"To agree, on."
Or, about.
"The existence, or."
About, the.
"Reality, or."
About the being.
Or, about the Being, of.

"That, which."
Can.
Not be seen, or.
"Of that," *or who,* "which."
Or, Who.
Can.
Not be heard, be.
Cause.
"Of course."
As much as are we not all quite.
'We?'
"The same, too."
Also, is.
"Not one."
Way, for.
All, and.
"Because, of."
Course, not.
"Necessarily, are."
All for one, either.
"And, because."
Of course, far.
"More wisely, and."
Too, because.
"Of course, far."
More en.
Light.
En.
Ed.
Ly, too.
Is a way, for.
Each, and.
"For every, and."
Because.
To each his.
Or, to each, her.
Own, and.

"To every, and."
To each, according to.
"His."
Or, her.
Or, according to her.
Own taste, or tastes.
Even if.
But, of.
Course, with.
Out some found.
At.
Ion of com.
Mo.
Nal.
It.
Y, collab.
Or.
At.
Ion, or.
Coop.
Er.
At.
Ion, what would, or.
What will be.
Come of us, 'us,' or 'we,' and.
"Of course."
Is not.
"That, or."
Even if.
"Is not this, all."
Less, than.
"Most simp."
Le, or.
Less than.
"Most sim."
Pli.
Stic, and.

Even if.
"Might all of this, and."
Even if.
"Might all of that, be."
Or, is.
A bit com.
Pli.
Cat.
Ed, or.
"A bit con."
Fusing, but.
Which is OK, and.
"Which is all."
Right, be.
Cause, of.
"Course, on."
Ly would an idiot, fool, or.
"Moron assume."
That, but.
"Of course, what."
Is most simple, is.
Or what, or who, Who, or What, is simplest, is.
"Also, what."
Is, or.
That what, or.
"That who, or that."
Who, or that who is, is.
Or that Who, or that What, is.
Al.
So, sim.
Ple, or that what, or that who, is.
"Simp."
Lest, is.
Because, of.
Course, would only the great.
Est of fools, id.
Io.

Ts, or mo.
Tons, too cle.
Ver?
For his, for her, for its, or for their.
Own good, dare for.
Get that it is, or.
That is it?
The Devil, if in.
Who.
Deed, he, she, it, or they?
Is it the De.
Do ex.
Vil, and, or.
Ist, is the one, that.
"His de?"
Or, who.
Mons, or.
"Or, what does try."
Who do.
To over.
Es, or.
Comp.
"Who do try."
Li.
To over.
Cate thin.
Simp.
Gs, or.
Li.
Whi.
Fy thin.
Gs, or.
Ch do.
Peo.
Es try to con.
Ple, as thin?
Fuse the.

Gs, or?
M, or.
"Is what."
Ought to be, or.
"That what is, is."
Most sim.
Ple, or.
"That what is."
Ought, or.
"Should be."
Simp.
Lest, or.
"Of course."
That all.
Can, would.
"Should, or."
Ought to agree, a.
Bout.
"What is."
Most simple, to.
"Or, about."
What is most simple, for.
"Whom, and."
Or that what, or that who.
Does seem, or does appear.
To be com.
Pli.
Cat.
Ed, or dif.
Fi.
Cult.
Ought to be, or should be, dis.
Missed, or ig.
Nor.
Ed.
Because, of.
"Course, would."

Only, just.
"Or un."
Just.
Ly, or.
Would me.
Rely, a.
Fool, idi.
Ot, or.
"Moron assume, or."
Try to presume, or.
"Try to assume, that."
What is.
Or that Who, or that who.
Is.
"Is me."
Ant to be, or is.
Most simple, or.
"That what is."
Most simple, is.
"What is best, or."
Is meant to be, or?
That is.
What is simp.
L.
Est, or.
"That who is, is?"
Most correct, most proper, or.
"Most right, or."
Most left, or.
"Most wrong, or."
That who, or.
Great.
Who, what.
Est, or.
Or What, is.
"Grandest, or."
High.

Est, or.
That what, What?
Who, or Who?
Does seem, or does ap.
Pear to be.
Sim.
Ple, simp.
Lest, is, al.
So, gre.
At.
Est, most right, most cor.
Rect, most pro.
Per, or.
"Most fab."
U.
Lous, and.
Of course, who.
"Or, what."
Is to say, what.
"Way, or who."
Is best, great.
Est, or.
Grand.
Est, most right.
"Most pro."
Per, or.
Most cor.
Rect, for.
One, or.
"For all, be."
Cause, of course?
Who is to say, not to say, to think, to.
"Decide, or."
To choose, or.
"To know?"
For an.
Other, or.

"For all others, which."
Or, what.
"One way, is."
Best, greatest, most grand, or.
"Highest, most right."
Most cor.
Rec.
T, or.
"Most proper, or."
Most ap.
Pro.
Pri.
Ate, be.
Cause, of course?
If to each his own.
Or, if to each her own, of.
Course.
"How to know."
What, or.
"Which, is."
His, or.
"Which, or."
What is.
"My own way, or."
My own way, or.
How to know?
For, and by, or.
"By, and for."
One.
Self, which.
"Or what, or."
What, or.
"Which is."
The right, or wrong.
"Left, or right."
Correct, pro.
Per, best, or great.

Est, way.
With.
Out be.
Ing show.
N, or.
With ou.
T be.
Ing to.
Ld, or.
"Without copying another, or."
And, too?
Because, of course.
Do not all, and.
"Be."
Cause does not e.
Very.
One, and.
Because does not every.
Body, want.
"Or, need?"
Think, or feel.
"Need, or want, or."
Feel, or think?
"Desire, or crave."
Or crave, or de.
Sire.
"All of the same things."
All at.
Or, all in?
The same time, or.
"All in?"
Or, all at.
The same times, or.
"All in the same places?"
As can they, or as can we not, too.
Even if.
Have all of the same things, all.

"All wanting, or."
At on.
Even if.
Ce, or be.
"All ne."
All at, or be all in, the.
Ed.
Same place, or in.
"All of."
The same s.
The same things, all.
Pot, or pots, all.
At, or all.
At on.
"In."
Ice, ei.
The same time, or.
The.
Times, might.
R, or.
"Be most simple, or."
Even if.
"What might me."
Rely.
Seem to be.
"Most simple, or."
Most easy, is not that, or.
"Is not this."
Or, is not this, or.
"Is not that."
Not possible, of.
Course, be.
Cause can.
Not all have all.
"Of the same things, all."
At once, and.
"Too, of course."

Because, can.
Not more than one per.
Son, or one thing, be.
In, or oc?
Cup.
Y, or.
Or pos.
Sess.
"The same spot."
Or, the same place.
"All at, or all in."
Or all in, or all at.
"The same time, or times, and."
Too, because?
Of course.
As much as.
Cannot?
More than one, and.
Of course, as.
"Much as, can."
Not all, or.
Everyone, all.
"Have."
The same thing?
"Or the same things, all."
At, or.
"All in."
The same time.
"Or, all in."
Or, all at.
"The same times, or."
All at, or.
"All in."
The same places, or.
"Too, but."
Because.
Of course?

As much as.
"Of course?"
Can.
Not one person.
"Or thing, be?"
In more than one place, at once.
"Or, at?"
The same time, and.
Even if.
"Of course, can."
And.
Do some do.
"More than one thing at once, and."
So?
"And, so."
Too, so.
"Because, of course."
Even if?
"Might, and even."
If would.
"One way."
For all.
"And, even if."
All, for.
One way, would.
Or, might?
"Be?"
For some.
Most simple, or.
Most right?
At least, even if?
Or.
Might it seem to be.
"Most easy, or."
Most con.
Ven.
Ie.

Nt, and.
Or.
"Even if?"
What must be best?
But though, of course.
"If."
Not best for all, for ever.
Y.
One, or for every.
If every.
Body, and.
Body is not ne.
Then, for.
Ce.
S.
Sar.
Il.
Y every.
Or, now, for?
One, and.
"Whom, or."
If every.
For what, and.
One, is not ne.
"Or?"
Ce.
If ne.
Sari.
Ces.
Ly, every.
Sari.
Body.
Ly, or.
"Not, if."
What is best.
For the most.
"Or, for the many?"

Must, also, be.
"Best for the all, too."
Though, what.
"Is best, or."
What does work?
"For the most, or."
For the many, or.
"For the all, is."
Not necessarily, al.
Ways, or.
"Ever, what."
Is best.
"For one, as."
Like.
Wise.
"Too, of."
Course, what.
"Is best."
For one, is.
"Not ever, and."
Is not.
"Always, and."
Is not.
"Necessarily, what."
Or, who?
Or , Who.
"Is best for."
Or, best to?
"The most, or."
To, or.
"For?"
The many, or.
"For, or."
To the?
"All, or."
Must, also, be.
Or, can.

Not be.
"Or might, also?"
Qui.
Te so most con.
Ven.
Ie.
Nt.
Ly, al.
So.
"Be."
"What is easiest."
Or.
What is most ob.
Vio.
Us.
But.
"What is most cor."
Rect, but.
Correct.
To, or for.
Whom, or for.
"Or, to?"
What, and.
What is most right, be.
Cause?
"What is most simple."
And, beca.
Use what is most easy.
"And, be."
Cause what is most ob.
Vi.
Ou.
S, must, or might.
Be, or.
"More than most."
Likely, is.
"Not, also, most."

Probably?
For ever.
Y.
Body, or one.
"One, or body, or."
Not necessarily?
"For all."
Ever.
"Y, where."
Or, for.
"The most, or."
For the.
Many, or.
"For the."
All, ever.
Y, "When."
And, be.
Cause.
"What is most right, too."
And, so.
"And, so?"
Now, and.
"Here, and."
So, here.
"And, so?"
Now.
Enough with the whispers, and.
"Enough with the whispe."
Ring, and.
Because?
"Enough with the ghosts, and."
Because?
"E."
No.
Ugh with the spi.
Rits, and.
Enough, with, from, and about?

The ghosts.
Or enough, about.
"The angels, who."
Do not.
Care to, and, so, who.
Also, do not.
"Ever leave."
The, the.
Ir, or.
"A mark."
Though, of course.
As does the De.
Vil, and as do his de.
Mons, and.
"So?"
And, enough, with?
"The angels, who."
No one can.
"And, who."
Nobody will, ought, or should.
"Take seri."
Ou.
Sly, and.
But, of course?
"Without for."
Getting that no.
Body, and that no.
One, too?
"Is a someone, and."
That, nobody.
Is a some.
Body, too.
"And."
So?
Enough, with.
"And."
Enough, about.

"What could have been, and."
Enough?
About, or with.
What, or with, or a?
Bout who.
Might have been, and.
Enough with the voi.
The vo.
Ces, or with.
Ices, or.
"And, enough with, or a."
Bout.
"Any, or all."
Other ways, and?
Enough with the hardness?
"And enough with the difficulties."
And enough with the problems, because.
"What, or."
Who is.
Or, what life?
"Or, whose death, or."
What, or.
"Whose morning."
Or, whose.
"Or, what waking?"
Or, whose.
Woke-ness.
Which is, of.
"Course, the."
End, or.
"The death, of."
The night, or.
"Which is?"
The end, or.
Of course?
"The."
Death of.

"Sleep, and."
Or, of.
"Sleeping, and."
So, of dreaming.
Which is as it should, or.
And, so of snoring.
"Which is, as."
It ought to be, and which is.
As it ought to be, and.
Which is.
As easy as one does let it be, and.
"Or, and, if so?"
And, because.
Then, now.
"Or, now, then."
And, here.
Done, or com.
Plet.
E, and, or.
"Complete, or finished?"
Though, of course.
Finished?
"With what."
Or, done?
With whom.
"Too, and."
So?
"And, done."
And, finished?
"And, whole?"
Or, complete.
Or, if so.
"Or, if not?"
And, if rather.
To con.
Tin.
Ue, then.

"Now, and?"
On, and.
And, en.
Ou.
Gh.
With the all of the other ways, and.
"Enough with the traces, and."
Enough with the other opt.
Ions, and.
"Enough with the other choi."
Ces, and.
Enough with all of the other pos.
Sibi.
Liti.
Es, and.
"Because, of course."
Am I not one, and.
"Because, of."
Course, I.
"Am not one."
Or, the one?
To hear, or.
"The one?"
Hearing voices, and.
Because I am not one.
To think?
"That the eyes."
Or, that.
The knots of wood.
"On the planks above me, can."
Really, actually.
See?
"Or, that they are."
Actually, really, or truly.
Seeing, or watching me, and?
"Because, of course."
I am not one.

"Who needs to be."
Seen, or watched.
Or, one.
"Who needs."
To be.
Watched, or seen.
"In order to be?"
Or, in order to feel safe.
"Or?"
In order to feel OK, or.
"In order to feel."
All right, and.
Because, even if.
"Some do need to be watched."
Or, seen.
And, even if.
"Some do deserve to be watched, and."
And, to see.
Even if.
"Some do deserve to do the watching, and."
Even if.
Not necessarily is to watch to be watched, and.
"Even if not necessarily, is."
To be watched, to watch, and.
"Even if not necessarily, is."
To watch, to see.
"Or to see, to watch."
And, even if to be seen.
Is not, necessarily, to be watched.
"And, even if."
Of course?
"Is not, necessarily, to be watched."
To be seen.
And, too.
"Because?"
Of course.
Is not to watch, necessarily, to look out for.

"Or, to watch over."
Or, to be wat.
Che.
D, or.
And?
Because, of course.
"Is not, necessarily, to be watched."
To be watched over.
Or, to watch.
To be looked out for.
"And, so."
Because?
"Of course."
Is not, necessarily.
"To watch, to see, and."
Too, be.
Cause, of.
"Course, also."
Is not, necessarily, to watch.
"To see, and."
Because, of.
"Course, I."
Am not a.
"Or, the?"
One crazy e.
No.
But, see.
Ugh.
Ing what, or.
"To think."
Seeing whom.
That such eyes are seeing.
Or, that.
They are watching me.
"Because, of course."
I am not one.
"Of the para."

Noi.
Acs, or.
One of the crazies?
Hearing voices.
Or, whispers?
"Coming from the corners."
Or, from the shad.
Ows, or from?
"The demons."
Or, from the others?
"Or, from the Others."
Or, from the Ot.
But who do, rat.
Her?
Sing than whisp.
Or, from the an.
Er, be.
Gels, or from the De.
Hind hands.
Vil?
"They do not have."
"Or, from the d."
Evils, or from the spir.
Its?
"Or from the angels, or."
Of, or.
Or, if not in.
"From the ghosts?"
Your head, or.
Living, where?
If not in.
"If not with."
Your heart, or.
In me, and.
If not in your so.
Though, but.
Ul, gut, me.

Too, of.
Mory, or memo.
Cour.
Ries, or.
Se.
"As much."
As, too?
Of course.
"I am not one."
Crazy enough.
"To lie around, talking to myself."
As if I we.
Re more than one?
Person.
"Except, of course."
Who does not have, or.
"Need, at."
Least, a.
"Bit, or."
At least?
"Some sort of pri.
Vate life.
And space, or.
"Space, per."
Son.
Al, in?
Which one, or.
"In which?"
He can hear, or.
"In which?"
I can hear, or.
"In which?"
And, in which?
You can listen to yourself, or.
"In which."
I can list.
En to, or he?

Ar.
Or your.
Him.
Self.
Self.
"And myself, too."
And.
Of course.
"And, too?"
Is not, necessarily.
To hear.
To listen.
"As much as?"
Not, necessarily, is to listen, to hear.
"And, too?"
Even, if.
"Of course."
Is not, necessarily.
To listen to be listened to.
Or, to hear?
"And, too?"
Because, of course.
"Is not, necessarily."
To be listened to, to.
Listen?
Or to hear, or to be heard.
"And, too."
Because, of course, is.
"Not, necessarily, to be heard?"
To hear.
"And, too."
Because, of course.
"Not, necessarily, is to hear?"
To be heard.
"And, too."
Because, of course.
"Can."

Not one real.
Ly.
Truly, or actually.
"Hear another if one can."
Not hear, or listen to?
Oneself.
And, too.
"Because, of course."
Can.
Not one tru.
Ly, or act.
U.
Ally.
"Really, wholly, en."
Tire.
Ly, or.
Completely.
"Listen to another."
If one can.
Or, if one will.
Not listen to, or hear?
One.
Self, or.
If one is not per.
Mit.
Ted to, or let.
Hear, or list.
En to, one.
Self, or.
And, too.
"And, but?"
Of course.
"Cannot one, also, list."
En to.
Or, hear?
Another, if.
"One can."

Not listen to one.
Self, or?
"If where, or."
If when.
Or, if when, or.
"If where."
One is not let be, or.
"If where, or."
If when.
One is not given, or.
"If where, or."
If when one is.
"Not per."
Mit.
Ted one's own.
"Personal, or."
One's own.
"Pri."
One is not per.
Vate s.
Mit.
Pace, or.
Ted to, or let.
Thou.
List.
Ghts, or?
En to, or he.
If w.
Ar, one.
Here, or.
Self, or.
"If when."
When, and where, or.
"One is not per."
Where, and when.
Mitted, to?
Listen to.

"Or?"
If when, or.
If where.
"One is not per."
Mit.
Ted to hear one.
Self, "Or?"
If where, or.
"If when, or."
If when, or.
"If where."
Boundaries, spaces, and.
Privacy, are.
Or, if where, and.
"Or, if when."
Pri.
Au.
Vacy, and bo.
To.
Und.
No.
Ari.
My, in.
Es are.
De.
Not re.
Pen.
Spec.
Den.
Ted, can.
Ce, and self-de.
Not one.
Ter.
He.
Min.
Ar, or list.
At.

En to one.
Ion.
Self, and, so, can.
Not one real.
Ly, act.
U.
Ally, or tru.
Ly listen to, or hear, an.
Other, any, or all.
Others, or.
Know one.
"Which, of."
Self, ei.
Course.
The.
Is why.
R, or.
"I am."
And, too.
"Of course."
Which is why.
He was.
And, why.
You are.
"I am."
So thankful for the brick.
And a.
Walls around him.
Round you.
Whether gray, or grey, or rat.
Her, if.
Rust-colored.
But.
"And."
Which are they, and?
For those, and.
Which is it, and?

"For these, which."
Are around me, and.
For those.
"And, for these?"
Which do en.
Close me, and.
"Which do."
And, which.
"Are."
Cre.
At.
In.
G, and.
"Main."
Tai.
Ning.
My fort.
Ress.
"If not my cast."
Le, bec.
A.
Use, of course, here.
Do we not have, as never have we, and, so.
As never will we have.
Cast.
Les, *or moats?*
Even though, per.
Haps, *or more?*
Is not a man's.
Or a woman's?
House, or home.
Of course, also?
His.
Or her, castle.
And, also?
"Of course."
Whose, and which.

Walls which do pro.
Tect me, and.
"Which do keep me?"
And, you.
Safe, and.
"Sound, and."
Which, also, do?
"Keep the ot."
Hers, out.
Of course.
And, which.
"Of course?"
Also, do.
"Save, and."
Spare me, from.
"The we."
At.
Her, from.
The snows, from.
"The ice, and."
From the sleet, and.
From the ele.
Ments, as.
"Much as, also."
Of course.
"I am, as."
I must, also, be.
Thank.
Ful, for.
"The space."
Bet.
Ween him.
"And be."
Tween me, and.
"The next row of houses, and."
Because, even if?
"I might like my neighbors."

As much as I should.
"And, as much as I ou."
Gh.
Or, as much as.
T to.
They sh.
And, as much as.
Ou.
They ou.
Ld, or.
Ght to like me, and.
Ou.
"As much as."
Ght to, or.
They ought to like me, and.
And, as much as I might re.
Spect the.
M, or me?
And, or.
But, of.
Course, not too much, and.
"Not too little, and."
Not un.
Fair.
Ly, un.
Equally, or un.
Justly, and.
Or.
"In spite of."
How much.
"They should, or."
Ought to.
"At least?"
Respect me, am.
"I not them, and."
Are they not me.
And, you are not them.

"Anymore."
Than I do want to be them, to see them, or to hear them.
And, ought.
"Where, or when."
A person get to know her neighbors.
Or when, or where.
Before she is forced to love them.
"I do not want to, or."
Blindly, or unconditionally, or.
Where, or when, or.
Before she is forced to forgive them.
"When, or where."
Unconditionally, and unknowingly.
I do not choose to, or.
For everything, and for anything, or.
"Anymore?"
Than might they, or.
"Anymore?"
Are they like.
Ly to want to be, to see, or.
To hear me, all of the time, and.
Or, always.
Even if.
Of course?
On occasion.
"Might they?"
Or, even if.
"They might want to be me?"
Or know you, or love you.
And, even if.
"Might I, on."
Occasion.
Like, or want.
Or, need?
"To?"
Share some things, or some thoughts.
"Or, some feelings?"

With them.
"More than most certainly, and."
Past, and be.
Yond, and.
"Beyond, and past."
All hopes, and ho.
Ping, do I not want.
"And, I would not like."
To have to, or.
"To be forced to share."
All things with all people, and.
Or everything with everyone, or.
Everything with all, or.
All with everyone, or.
"Because, of course?"
Are not some things pub.
Lic, and.
Are some peo.
"Be?"
Ple, and.
Cause, of cour.
Be.
Se.
Cause, are, of.
Some is.
Co.
Sues, to.
Ur.
O, whi.
Se.
"Are other things pri."
As they ou.
Vate, and.
Ght, and as the.
Are ot.
Y sh.
Her peo.

Ou.
Ple pri.
Ld be.
V.
And.
Ate, and.
Because they ought to be, and be.
Cause they should be, and.
"Because?"
Of course, can.
Not all.
Be trusted with all, or.
With every.
Thing, and?
Too, because?
Of course, can.
Not every.
One be trusted with all, or with?
E.
Very.
Thing, and.
Or, with every.
"Too, be?"
One, or with ever.
Cause, of.
Y.
Cour.
Body, or.
Se, can.
Not every.
One be trusted with every.
Thing, and, too?
"Of course."
Are not, at least.
Some, if not all.
Bound.
Ari.

Es ne.
Ces.
Sary, and.
"Too, because."
Of course?
"Who does not know that do."
Good, *or great?*
Fences make for good, *or great.*
Neigh.
Bor.
S, and.
"Because, of?"
Course, are.
Some things meant to stay.
If not, necessarily?
Some people.
"Private?"
Because, of.
"Course, should."
And, ought.
"And, can."
Not all.
"Know all."
About ever.
Yon.
E, or.
"All about everything, and."
Because, of.
Course, can.
Not every.
One know every.
Thing about eve.
Ryb.
Od.
Y, eve.
Ryt.
Hing a.

Bout all, or all a.
Bout every.
Body, or all a.
Bout ever.
Yon.
E, which.
Of course.
"Does make."
Lines, and boundaries.
"Necessary, to."
Keep out what.
And, who.
"And, to keep out what?"
And, What.
I do want.
To keep out, and.
"So, to?"
Keep out what.
"And, who?"
And, Who.
I do need to.
Keep out, and.
"So as to feel, and."
So as to be?
"And, so to know that I am."
Safe, here.
"Within these walls."
And?
Because, of.
Course.
"I would like to be able."
To hear myself.
"And to know myself, and."
To be able to.
"Be myself, and."
Not to have to worry about, or.
For them, and.

"Not to have to hear them?"
Or, all.
"Of their wants."
Worries, needs.
Hopes, de.
Sir.
Es, or.
All of their gripes, and.
"Because I would like, not."
To have to rem.
Em.
Ber.
"All of the rest of them, or."
To have to think of them?
Or, for them.
"All of the time, and every."
Where.
And, be.
Cause, of.
Course.
"I would like to be able."
To know myself, without.
"All of them, or."
Without him, or.
"Without her, or."
Without it, trying.
To hear me, or.
"Trying to listen, in."
To my.
Or, to your?
"Private thoughts, and."
Or, without.
"Him, her, it."
Or them, trying.
"To invade?"
My most per.
Son.

Al thoughts, and.
"Space, and."
Or, without.
"Him, her, it, or them."
Trying to.
"In."
Vade, or.
Trying to im.
Pose them.
Selves, him.
Self, her.
Self, or.
"Itself, on."
Or in.
"My most per."
Son.
Al, and.
Your most personal, and?
"My most private."
Feelings, and.
"Thoughts, with."
Out having?
"To share everything, or."
All, with.
"All of them, to."
Use against me, as.
He would, or.
As you would, or?
"As they would, or."
As she, or.
"As it?"
Or, as he.
"Might like to, or."
As they would, and.
As they have, and.
"As she would, or."
And, as she has, and.

As he would, or.
And, as he has, and.
"As it would, and."
As they will, and.
"As she will, and."
As you have, and.
As he will, and.
"As it will, if."
I do let it, him, her, or them, and.
Or, if do you, and.
"As they, and."
As he, and.
"As she, and."
As it would, if.
They, or.
If she, or.
"If he, or."
If you, or.
If it could, be.
Cause, of.
Course, are.
Not all.
"Meant to be."
Best, close.
St, or.
"Most per."
Son.
Al, or.
Most pri.
Vate.
Fri.
Ends, and.
"Because, of."
Course, are.
"Some people meant."
To be closer than.
"Others are."

And, be.
Cause, of.
"Course, can."
Not all.
"Be trusted, and."
Because, of.
"Course, too."
Are not all things.
About all people.
Meant to be public.
As are not all people meant to be ei.
And, too.
The.
Be.
R, cause.
Of course.
Are not all things me.
And, not all thing are me.
Ant to be pri.
Vate eit.
Her, and.
Too, because.
"I would like to know."
Or, be able to know?
Some things and some people, at.
Or, in?
Some times, and.
Or?
In some places.
And?
Because, of.
Not ot.
"Course, what."
Her thing.
Fo.
S, ab.
Ol, id.

Out so.
Io.
Me, ot.
T, or.
Hers, or.
"What moron does not know."
That, do.
Or, that what, or w?
Se.
Hi.
Crets make you sick, and.
Ch se.
Morons, idiots, or fools.
"Because I would not like to have to know all, or."
Everything, everyone, or.
"About everyone, or."
About all, all of the time, and.
Even if?
Knowledge is power, too.
Would I not like to have to know.
Or?
To know of others, *or?*
Of all other things, *or?*
Of all other, *or Ot?*
Her, peo.
Ple, in other p.
Lace.
S, at.
Ot.
Or, in?
Her time.
Be.
S, or?
Cause, of course.
"Because."
Know.
Quite so very of.

Ledge is re.
Ten would I rat.
Spons.
Her, be.
Ib.
"Let be, and."
Il.
Because quite so very often would I prefer, to.
It.
"Be let be, and."
Y, too.
Quite so very most.
And?
Of.
Be?
Ten I would pre.
Cause.
Fer to be left alone, so as.
"To be?"
Able to know.
"Myself, without."
Having to know, or.
"Without?"
Having to know, for.
"All of the rest of them, because."
Quite so very most of.
Ten do I pre.
Fer the.
"Qui."
Et, or the.
Si.
Lence, where.
And?
"In which."
I can hear myself, and know myself, because.
"If I cannot, or."
If I am not permitted.

"To know myself."
Or, to be your?
How can I hear my.
Self.
Self, and?
"Because, of course."
If I can.
Not hear myself.
"How might I be able to know myself?"
And, because.
Even if?
Because one.
"Is part of knowing."
Who does not know who.
"Who I am, also."
Or Who, one is, also.
Knowing who, *or what, and What, you are not.*
I am not, and.
Must, and, so, do.
Or, rat.
Es k.
Her who does.
Now, to.
Need to know who, or what, or What, one is.
O, what, and W.
Not in or.
Hat one, W.
Der to k.
Ho, or who.
Now who.
One is not, and.
Or, rat.
One can.
Her, be.
Not be who, or Who.
Cause.
One is, as.

Who is ab.
Long as in.
So.
Vade.
Lute.
Ded, oc.
Ly, whol.
Cup.
Ly, en.
Ie.
Tire.
D, or plag.
Ly, and com.
Ue.
Plete.
D by, or with.
Ly.
What, or w.
In, and for.
Hat, W.
And by.
Ho, or who.
"One."
One is not, and, so.
Self.
"Oneself."
Does not need.
Want, like.
"Or, care for?"
What, or.
"For whom."
Or, for what.
He is not.
Or, of.
"Course, for."
Whom, or.
For what she is not.

"And, so?"
In, *and de,* spite.
Of their, his, her, or its.
Want to know, and.
Or de, or?
"In spite of all their curi."
Os.
It.
Ie.
S, too.
Of course, because.
Can cats be too cle.
Ver, and.
"Because, of."
Course, do.
"All, or."
As does.
"Everyone, or."
As does.
"Everybody, know."
Or, as they should know.
"That, of."
Course, did.
"Curiosity kill the cat, or."
The cats?
But, of.
"Course, how many times, or."
How many cats, or.
"Which is why I do keep my doors locked."
Oh, do you?
Too, and.
"Because, of course."
Does not a want to know.
"Make for."
A, or the, right to know, and.
"Because?"
Of course.

"I do not want to have to hear."
Or, list.
En, to?
"All of the rambling, or."
To all of the rumbling, to.
"All of the white, or."
To all of the black, to.
"All of the light, or."
To all of the dark.
"Nonsense, monkey."
Mind mutterings, or.
"To all of the drivel, bunk, hokum, hogwash, gibberish, twaddle, or."
Malarkey, of.
"Those who do tend to speak the most."
Who, also, most often are those who do have the least to say, and.
"Who, also, most often, are."
Those talking the most, quite.
A bit like, and.
"As?"
Much as are the know-it-all's, those.
"Who are?"
The biggest fools.
And, who.
"Are the ones, who?"
Do think.
"Or, those who do?"
Assume, or those who do?
Presume they do know all.
About all, or.
"That they do, or."
That they can know.
"Everything about everything, or."
That they can, or do.
That, in.
Know every.
Deed, they do have so.
Thing ab.

Me right to know, or.
Out everyone, or.
"That they can, or."
That they do know.
"Everything about every."
Thing, and who.
Of course, are?
"The ones."
Who I, also, must keep out, because?
Of course.
"Who does need."
Such know-it-alls.
"Trying, pre."
Sum.
Ing, or.
"Assuming to know."
For one, for an.
Other, for all others, or.
"For all."
And?
Because, of course.
"Who needs."
Such know-it-alls.
Up, and preaching.
"Without having a thing to say, and?"
Or, first without.
Listening, or.
Without, first.
"Having something to preach about, and."
Because, of.
Course, who.
Needs, or.
"Because, of."
Course, who.
"Wants."
Such know-it-all, blow-hards.
"Trying to come in?"

Or, trying.
"To force their way, or."
Trying to force.
Their ways, in.
"Or, on."
Me, "And?"
Because, of course.
"Would I rather, not."
Be me, and.
"Be for me, rather."
Than having, or.
"Rather than being forced."
To be them, or.
"Rather than being forced."
To be.
"For them, or."
Rather than?
"Striving, or."
Rather than struggling.
To be.
All that they do want, or.
"Rather than struggling, or."
Rather than striving, and.
"Or, rather?"
Than being forced.
"To be?"
All that they do need me to be, and?
"Without having to carry the."
Burden, or.
"The responsibility, of."
Having to be for all.
"Of them, or."
Rather than?
"Having to know for all of them, and."
Without having to.
"Handle the."
Burdens, or.

"The responsibilities, of."
Their needs, wants, hopes, dreams, wills, and wishes, and.
As if?
"Of course, would."
Some sort of saint, or savi.
I not, rather, be.
Or, or.
"Lighter, and."
Freer, *or?*
More free, with.
Out?
"Having to be."
Their, his, her, or its?
Prisoner, *ke.*
Ep.
Er, or savior, who, or.
"What so."
Ever, might.
He, she, it, or.
"They be, and, so."
Of course?
"If are."
The two.
"Options, or."
Choices, to.
"Know, or."
To be known?
"Of course."
Must I choose.
Because, who would not.
"To know."
Rather than.
"To be known, or."
Rather, most ideally, might.
"I like?"
Or, but, to be know.
To both.

N by who.
"Know, and."
M, or by w.
To be known, and.
Hat, and.
"Too, also?"
Of course.
Of course, would.
Or by What, or by Whom, and.
"I like."
To be.
"Both knower, and."
Known, and.
"So, of."
Course, most ideal.
Ly, and.
"And, most per?"
Fect.
Ly, too.
Rather, would I be.
"Both sub."
Ject, and ob.
Ject, and.
Too, also?
"In spite of the."
Responsibility of knowing, or.
"Due to?"
Or, because of.
"If, rather."
Would I rather, be.
"Both know."
Er, and.
Known, rather.
"Than being."
Staying, or.
"Rather, than.
Remaining un.

"Known, or."
Rather than being.
Or, Being?
"Known, for."
As much as, of.
"Course, would."
I rather.
"Decide, and."
Determine, and.
"Destine, me."
For me, rather.
"Than be?"
Deci.
Ded, or.
"Rather than being?"
Deter.
Mined, or.
"Rather than being?"
Desti.
Ned for, by.
"Any, or."
By all.
"Others, or."
By so.
As much as, of.
Me go.
"Course, too."
Ds, or god.
I would not like, and.
Des.
"Do not like."
Ses, Go.
Any.
D, God.
One, every.
Dess, the Go.
One.

D, or wo.
"Everybody, or."
Uld-be on.
And, every.
Es, or.
Body else.
Try.
Ing, or.
"As."
Sum.
In.
G, or.
Pre.
Sum.
Ing, *or.*
At le.
As.
T tr.
Ying, to.
"Know for me, or?"
Anybody, or.
"Everybody, or."
Everyone, or.
"Anyone, or."
Someone, or.
"Somebody, else."
As.
Sum.
Ing, or pre.
Su.
Ming, or.
"Trying, to?"
Know better than me, and.
"As much as?"
Of course.
"I do not like, need, or."
Want, any.

One.
"Everyone, everybody."
Any.
Body, some.
Body, some.
"One, or."
Even no one, or.
"Even no."
Body, trying to show me.
Or, pre.
Suming, or.
"Assuming?"
To be able.
"To show me."
Or, any.
"All, every."
One, or.
"Every."
Body, try.
Ing.
Ass.
Um.
Ing, or.
"Pre."
Sum.
Be able?
"To tell me."
How it is, or.
"How things are, or."
What is right.
Or, Right.
Or, left.
Or, Left, or.
Or, who is right, or.
What is wrong.
"Or, who is wrong, or."
"What is true."

Or, who is true, or.
And, what is fal.
Se, or.
Who is false, or.
"What is correct."
Or, who is cor.
Rect, or.
Without being told.
Or, shown.
What is proper, or?
Who is proper, or.
Without being told.
"What I should think."
What you should think.
Or, how I should think, or.
How you should think, or.
How I should feel.
Or, how I ought to feel, or.
How you ought to feel, or.
"How, or what, or who."
I can be, and.
Or?
Without being told.
"What, and who, or how, I can."
Not be.
And, too?
"Of course, as."
Much as, also.
"I do not need, want."
Wish, or.
Hope for?
"Anyone, or."
For anybody, or.
"For everyone?"
Or, for.
"Everybody, or."
For some.

Body, or.
"For so."
Me.
One, or.
For no one, or.
"For nobody?"
Trying to force me.
"To be."
One way, or.
"Another, or."
Without an.
Trying to force me.
Other, an.
To be, or to do.
Y, or all ot.
Their, his, her, or.
Hers, trying to force.
"Its way, as."
On me, as if.
Much as.
It is, has ever be.
"Of course?"
En, and eve.
I do not need, want.
R, and al.
"Wish, or."
Ways, will be.
Hope for any.
The on.
"For all, for."
Ly way, or.
The most, or for.
"The many, trying."
To force me.
"To do, or."
To be?
"Their, his, her, or."

Its way, and.
"As much as, also?"
Of course.
"I do not need any, one."
Two, or more.
"Trying to force me?"
To be.
"Too re."
As.
On.
Able, too.
Rat.
Ion.
Al, too.
"Logical, or."
Too sensi.
Ble, to.
"The point, of."
Absurdity, or.
"To the point, of?"
Insanity, or.
"More than does make sense, common."
Or, otherwise, or.
"More than?"
Is natural, or.
Except, of.
"Course, natural."
To, or.
"For, or."
According to.
"Whom, or."
For, or.
According to what, and.
"Of course?"
Nat.
Ur.
Al, as?

Opposed, and?
"As preferable, to."
Super-, or.
"As opposed, to."
Sub-.
Nat.
Ur.
Al, and.
"Of course."
Preferable, to.
"Or preferable, for."
Whom, or.
"Preferable for, or."
Pre.
Fer.
Able, to.
"What, and."
Of course.
"Who, or."
What, or.
"What, or."
Who is.
"To know, to."
Say, or.
"To decide?"
What is preferable, to.
"Or for whom, or."
Who, or.
"What, or."
What, or.
"Who is."
To say, decide.
"Assume, or."
Presume, to.
"Know what."
Is to be pre.
Fer.

Red, by.
"Whom, or."
By what, and?
Of course.
"Who is to."
Say, de.
Cide, "Or determine, what."
Or, who?
"Is all?"
Right, or.
Who, or.
"What is OK, or."
What, or.
"Who, or."
Who, or.
"What, is."
Com.
Mon, or.
Bas?
"What, or."
Ic, or.
Who, or.
"Who, or."
What is.
"Ord?"
In.
Ary.
Or, extra?
Ordinary.
Or what, or.
"Who is?"
Extraordinary, or.
What, or.
"Who is."
Typical, or.
Who, or.
"What is?"

A.
Typ.
Ic.
Al, or.
"What, or."
Who is?
"Nor."
Mal, or.
Regular, or.
"Abnormal, or."
Para, or.
"Ir."
Regular, weird.
Strange, or.
"Not strange, or."
Not weird, or.
OK, not OK, all.
Right, or not all.
Right, or.
Not all left, or?
Of course.
"Who is to."
Say, think.
Decide, destine, or.
"Determine, that."
What, or.
"That who?"
Is normal, not strange, not weird, or who.
"Or, that what?"
Is reg.
U.
Lar, or.
"That what, or."
That who?
Or, Who.
"Is typical, is."
Better than, or.

"Is?"
Sup.
Er.
Io.
R, to.
"Or, is?"
Preferable, to.
"Whom, or."
To what, or.
To What, or.
"To whom, is?"
We.
Range, ir.
Regular, ab.
Nor.
Mal, a.
Typ.
Ic.
Al, or.
"To what, or."
To whom, is?
Either less, or.
"More than?"
Or.
Din.
Ary, or.
Because, of.
"Course, quite."
So often, is.
"What, or."
Is who.
Or, Who.
"Is strange, quite."
So attractive, and.
"Too, because."
Of course.
If I do not know, *choo?*

Se, or de?
"Myself, and."
Cide, for.
Myself, who.
"Or, what."
Or what, or.
"Who will."
Try to know, *de.*
For me.
Cide, or choo.
And, be.
Se.
Cause, of.
Course.
How boring would life be, if.
Though, I am not either.
"Or, both."
A scientist or a physicist, and because.
"Of course?"
Can.
Not all be so re.
Duced to such simp.
Le, or to such ele.
Gant equations, even.
"If, of."
Course, what.
"Would be."
Most simple, and.
"Most easy, but."
Of course.
"Are not people, things."
Or objects, and.
Are not all just.
Or, all.
"Alike, and."
Or, what might be?
So bo.

"Were not, and.
Ring, if, and on.
Or, if.
Ly, if all.
"All."
Are not.
"All dif."
Fe.
Rent, or.
If all.
"Were just, only."
Or me.
Rely, or.
"Un."
Just.
Ly, cl.
Ones?
Co.
Pies, or.
"Derivatives, be."
Cause, are.
"Not those, who."
Are dif.
Fe.
Rent, and.
"Those who are un."
I.
Que.
Are those who are them.
Selves, or?
Igi.
Nal.
"Necessary, and."
Interesting, even if.
"Some might pre."
Fer to make cop.
Ies of them.

Selves, and.
"Even if?"
Might, and.
"Even if?"
Some, might.
"Not all."
Be sat.
Is.
Fie.
D, un.
Til.
"All are the same, and."
Or, all the Sam.
E, and.
Though, of.
"Course, do."
Those who.
"Do not know."
Who, or.
"What?"
They are, or.
What, or Who.
"Those who."
They are.
Do not know what.
"They think, or."
How to think, or.
"What they feel, or."
How they feel, not.
"Have much choice, or."
Man.
Y opt.
I.
Ons, but.
To copy, or.
"But, to?"
Imi.

Tate, an.
Ot.
Her.
"Or, all?"
Others, and.
"Even if."
Those who are.
"All the same, or."
Even if.
"Those who are."
All the Same, are.
"Far easier to know, to con."
Trol, and.
"To govern, and."
Though might we.
Or 'we?'
"Not all."
Be the same, or.
"All the Same, of."
Course, do.
"We all, still."
Have, at le.
As.
T, some thin.
Gs, in com.
Mon, and.
"Even if."
Of course, we.
"Are not."
All the Same, or.
"All the same, too."
Are we all equals, and.
Because we are all e.
"So should, and."
Quals, and.
So ought, and.
"So ought, and."

So should, we.
"All be."
Treated equally, and.
Of course.
"So, of."
Or, more?
Course, should.
Or, better.
"And, ought."
And, not nec.
Ces.
Not so.
Sari.
Me.
Ly, cou.
"Be for."
Pled, with.
Ced, or.
Less.
Be made, to.
"Sac."
Ri.
Fice more.
Than would, or.
"More than do."
Any, or.
More than.
"All others, and."
Of course, ought.
"And should, not."
One, be.
"Forced, to."
Take re.
Spon.
Sib.
Il.
It.

Y, for.
"The rest of them, as."
Much as, of.
"Course, should."
And, ought.
"Not one."
Have to.
Know for all the rest of them.
"What, or."
What is Tru.
Who is.
E, or tru.
E, or.
"Who, or."
E, or.
What is false, or.
Who is Fal.
"What, or."
Se, or.
Who is.
Fake, or.
"Right and wrong, or."
Who, or.
"What is."
Wrong or right, or.
Left, or right, or.
What to do, or.
What not to do.
"Or how to do it, or."
How not to do it, or.
Do what, or not do what, or.
As much as I do not.
Need, or want.
Or want, or.
"Need another, or."
Any, or.
All others, trying.

"Presuming, or."
Assuming, to?
Know for me.
"What, or."
Who is good, or.
Who is Go.
What, or.
Od, or.
"Who is bad for me, or."
What is bad, or What.
"Or, who?"
Or, Who.
Is good for me, and.
"As much as I do not want, or need."
Another, *an.*
Y, or all ot.
"De."
Hers.
"Pen."
Ding on me.
To show them.
The way, as.
"If?"
One way, is.
"One for all, or."
Or, as if?
As if.
The.
"All are, or."
Ir, hi.
As if?
S, he.
"All must be, all."
R, or its, one.
For one.
Or On.
Way, and.

E way, is.
Or?
The on.
As if.
Ly way.
All must be?
Or Way, or.
For one, or.
Ways, or.
For One, or.
"As much as?"
Of course.
"I do not need."
Or, want.
To be shown?
"Their, his, her, or."
Its way, as.
"If it is, or."
As if?
"It must be."
My way, for.
"Me, too."
As much as, of.
"Course, I."
Also, do not.
Want to have to show, or.
"Tell them."
What is the good, right, wrong, or bad way.
Or, Way.
Or, the correct one, or.
"As much as, like."
Wise, of.
"Course, I."
Do not care, wish.
"Want, or."
Need to be shown, or.
"To be told, as."

If I were a child, what.
"Is right, or."
Who is right, or.
"Who is wrong, or."
What is wrong, or.
"What is bad, or."
Who is in.
Who is bad, or.
No.
"Who is good, or."
Cent, or what, or who.
What is good.
Or, Who is?
Correct, or.
Because.
Guilt.
"Of course."
Y, or.
I am an adult, and.
"Because, of."
Course I.
"Am not."
A child, and.
"Because, of."
Course, is.
"As I have said, and."
As I have thought, even.
"Though, of."
Course, is.
"Not necessarily, to."
Say, to think, and.
Or, to writ.
"Even if, of."
E to say, ei.
Course, is.
The.
"Not necessarily, to."

R, or.
Think, to.
"Say, be."
Cause, of.
"Course, do."
Not all.
"Say, or."
Get to say?
"All that they are thinking, and."
Or when, or where, or to who.
Of course, too.
M, they do ne.
"Also, do."
Ed, or want to, or.
Not all think.
"Before they do say, or."
Before they do speak, or.
"Before?"
They do tell, and.
"Because, of."
Course, is.
Not one way.
"For all."
And, too.
"Because, of course."
Is, and.
Are not all.
"Necessarily, for."
One way, and.
"So, of?"
Course, and.
"Also, do."
I not.
"Need, or."
Want, or.
"Want, or."
Need, any.

"Or, all."
She.
Ep, id.
Io.
Ts, fo.
Ols, or.
"Morons, trying."
To follow, or trying.
"To copy me, be."
Ca.
Use.
Even though.
"And, even if?"
Might I, or.
"Even if, and."
Or, even though?
"I might love."
Or, try to.
Adore, sheep.
If, whether.
"Black or white, or."
Whet.
Her white, or black.
"Or, rather."
Whether a bit.
Of both.
"Because, of."
Course, even.
"If, is."
The dif.
Fe.
Ren.
Ce, or.
"Because, the."
Dif.
Fer.
En.

Ce, is.
"So quite essential, and."
Too, be.
"Cause, of."
Course, what would black, *or Black*, be, or.
"Do, without."
What is white, or.
Without who is, or.
"What would white do, or."
White be, or.
Be with.
Out what, *or who.*
"Is black, but."
A.
Side f.
Rom thi.
S, and, *or?*
A.
Part from that, or.
"A."
Side, *or a.*
Part, from that, "At least."
I do know.
What color black is, and.
What white is, and.
Who is, and, so.
Al.
So, I do know, and.
Or, you do know?
What way is up, and w.
Hi.
Ch is down, and.
"I do re."
Fuse.
To be taught, shown, edu.
Cat.
Ed, school.

Ed, or groom.
Ed to be.
Lie.
Ve.
To know, or.
"To think."
Other.
Wise, which.
Is, or.
"Which, also, might be."
This, too.
"More, do I prefer those who can."
And, those who do.
And, those who will?"
Think and feel, and.
"Feel and think, for."
And by, themselves, and.
"Because."
Of course.
I can.
Not stand.
Or to?
Le.
Rate.
"For long."
Or, if at all.
"Repli."
Cants, deri.
Vat.
Ives, *though one of Leibniz's, or one of New.*
Would be the quest.
Ton's.
Ion, or?
"Copies, or."
Those who do not know.
What to think, or.
"Who they are, what."

How to, or.
They think, or.
Who do not know.
How they feel, or w.
Hat, in what, or.
In who.
M, or who.
They do be.
"Lieve, be."
Cause, of.
"Course, yet."
Once again.
"Am I far from."
In.
Te.
Rest.
Ed, in.
Trying, or.
"In having to know."
For any.
One, or for.
Everyone.
"Other than myself, and."
Because?
"Of course."
Need I say, think.
"Or re."
Peat my.
Self, yet.
"Once again, is?"
Not one way, necessarily.
Good for all, or.
Or, Good.
"For everyone, or."
Or, Bad.
For every.
Or, bad.

Body, and.
Or, good.
"Too, because?"
Of course.
"Is not what is good for one."
Necessarily, also.
Good for all?
"And, too."
Because, of course.
Quite so similarly.
"And, too."
And, also.
Quite, so.
Likewise.
"Is not what is bad for one."
Necessarily, what is.
Bad, to.
"Or, bad."
For all, and.
Every.
"Too, because."
Where, at, or in, or for.
Of course?
All ti.
"Is not what is necessarily."
Me, or ti.
Bad for all?
Me.
Bad for the most.
S, and.
"Or bad for the many, necessarily."
Bad for one?
And, too.
"Because, of course."
I am not one to want to have to take, or.
"One to have to?"
Be responsible, for.

Anyone other than myself, and.
"So, and."
Though, yet.
"Once again, as."
I have said, and.
Or, as I have thought, more.
"Than once?"
Before, and.
"Because I have, already."
So said, or.
"So thought."
Why re.
Pea.
T?
The same.
"Or?"
The Same.
"Again, and a."
Gain.
"With no one hearing."
And, because.
And, without anyone hearing.
And, with no one listening, and?
No one is list.
Without anyone listening.
En.
"And, so?"
Ing, and with.
Now, and.
Out any.
So, as.
Body, some.
Us.
Body, so.
U.
Me.
Al, and.

One, every.
"So, as."
One, ever.
Al.
Y.
Ways, as.
Body, or all?
Was.
List.
"And, as?"
En.
Does.
In.
The day be.
G, or he.
Gin, and.
Ar.
"As does it start."
Ing, and.
And, as it does start.
Why say, at all, and.
As always.
"And, as us."
U.
Al, or.
Just about the same, every day.
"Because, of course?"
Though, what.
Or, though?
"Who, or."
Though, what.
Might be similar.
"Is not necessarily what."
Or, is not necessarily.
"Who is the same, and."
Or, Who is the Same, or What is, or.
Too, because.

"Of course?"
Who, or.
What is the same, *or the Sam.*
E, is not necessarily what.
Or, who.
Is similar.
"And, too?"
Because, of course.
What start.
And, what beginning.
Or, whose.
Of course.
Is, also.
Not, and, too.
"An ending, and a finish."
And, too.
Too, and.
Of course.
"Is not a fin."
Is.
H, *necessarily.*
An en.
Ding, al.
So.
"A start, and."
Also, a beg.
In.
Ning, of.
"Course, so."
Is not.
A morn.
In.
G, or.
"The morn."
In.
G, or.
This morning, or.

"That morning, too."
The end, of.
"And, the end, to."
The night, or.
The end, of.
"Last night, or."
The fin.
Is.
H, of.
It, and.
"As well as."
Is the.
"Co."
Ming, of.
The light, the.
"Be."
Gin.
Ning, of.
The end, of.
"The dark."
Ness, or.
So should, or.
"So ought it be, or."
So it was.
"Or, so it is."
Sup.
Pose.
D to be.
"But, of."
Course.
"Is it."
Not ever, and.
"Is not al."
Ways, and.
Is not on.
Ly, the.
"End of the night, the."

End of the dark.
Ness, and.
"Of course."
Be.
Ca.
Use does the sun pro.
Vide on.
Ly a cert.
Ai.
N kin.
D of light, and.
Is not ever.
"Always, or."
So?
Necessarily.
"The end of the darkness."
The be.
Gin
Ning of the light, and.
"Of course."
Also, is.
"Not ever, and."
Also, is.
"Not always, the."
End of the darkness the beginning of the light.
As, like.
"A morning, like."
This, which.
"Is not."
Quite light, and.
"Which, also."
Is not.
"Quite bright, either."
Be.
Cause we.
Re.
"And be."

Cause, are.
The ski.
Es ab.
Out.
"As grey, or."
And, so?
"Which is, or."
Which might be?
"A blend of the two, black."
And white, and.
"White, and black, but."
Of course.
"Who does like, or."
Who wants, to.
"Live for long, or?"
For.
Ever, or.
Who can live for.
"Long, or."
Forever.
"Where."
And, when?
"Or when, or."
Where, bound.
"Ari."
Es, in.
Divi.
Duality.
"Or when, or."
Where dif.
Fe.
Ren.
Ces, are ig.
"No."
Red.
"De."
Lete.

D, "Or."
Erase.
D, "Or."
Where all.
"Are dead, far."
From living.
Grey, or.
Gray, as.
Though, of.
"Course, too."
Is not all.
"And, are not all?"
And, is not everything, and.
"Is not everyone, and."
Is not everybody, necessarily?
"So simple, as."
Black-and-white, or.
As white-and-black, or.
"As all."
Or, as.
Or no.
No.
Thing, and.
Thing, and.
"Even if."
All, and.
Might subtle.
Ties, be.
"Important for, or."
To some, and.
Even if.
"Are some things, best."
Seen, or.
"Best, un."
Der.
Stood, as.
"Or, in."

Shades of gray, or.
Pink, or.
"Grey, too."
Who, or.
"What, or."
What, or.
"Who does want to have to com."
Promise, or.
Be com.
Promised by, or.
"With what."
Or, with whom?
"They are not, and."
Because, of.
"Course, who."
Or what, or.
"What, or who."
Does need, want.
"Want, need."
Or, care to.
"Be made, to."
Need, or.
"To want, what."
Or, whom.
"Or, whom."
Or, what.
"They do not, and."
Too, be.
"Cause, of."
Course, who.
"Or, what."
Or what, or.
"Who does."
Need, or.
"Want, or."
Want, or.
"Need, or."

Care to.
"Be made."
To de.
Pen.
D, on.
"What, or."
On whom, or.
"On whom, or."
On What.
"One does not need, or."
Want, or.
"On what, or."
On whom, one.
"Does not want, or."
Because, of.
"Course, who."
Or, what.
"Does want, or."
Who, or What.
Need, or.
What, or Who.
"Need, or want."
To be.
"All mixed up, or."
All con.
Fused, or.
"All mixed to."
Get.
Or, all tang.
Her.
Led, up.
"And, too."
Of course.
"Who needs, or."
Who wants to.
"Be con."
Fused.

"With, or."
For, an.
"Ot."
Her, and, too.
"Of course."
Who, or.
"What, or."
What, or.
"Who, would."
Not, rat.
Her, be.
"Who they are, and, not."
Another, and.
"Not, necessarily?"
Only, who.
Or, what.
"Others, do."
Say they are, or.
"Do want them to be, or."
Make them out.
Or in?
To be, or ex.
Pect the.
M to be, or.
Of course.
"Who, or."
What, or.
"What, or."
Who would.
"Not rather, be."
Who, or.
"What they are, or."
What, or.
"Who they are, and."
Not another, or.
Who, or what?
Would not, rather, be.

As they are, or.
As they will ever be, today.
"On a day, like this, which."
Might be, or.
"Which might not be, a."
Day like any other, or.
"A day."
Like all ot.
Hers, but.
Of course.
"Which is not, ex."
Act.
Ly the same as, or.
The same as, or.
"Which is, also, not."
Precisely, or.
"Exactly, identical."
To any of the others, but.
"Which is."
A bit like the rest, and.
"Which is."
A bit like the others, or.
"At least, which."
Is a bit.
Like those that I can re.
Member, because.
"Of course."
Can I not quite.
"Remember the future, and."
Be.
Because, of.
Cause, of.
Course.
Course, who co.
"How am I to know, or."
Uld, and who can, or.
Why should I know, or.

Why should you.
"How ought I know, or."
How do I know.
Or, how do you, or.
What I do know, or.
What do you, or.
"What I do not know, which."
What you do not, or.
Is how the skies, will be.
"Later, or."
What color they will be, and.
"If they will still, or."
If, yet, they.
"Will be grey, or."
Gray, but.
"Of course."
Why wonder, or.
"Why worry about, what."
I can, or.
"About what."
I do not know, or.
"About what."
I do not need to know, be.
Cause, at.
Least.
"Are the skies."
A bit light.
Er, and.
Because.
"At least."
They are a bit bright.
Er, than.
"More than most likely they were."
During the dark.
Est of night, which.
"Of course, I."
Did not see, because.

"I was sleeping, but."
As if one ne.
Be.
Ed be a.
Cause, that.
Wake, in or.
Be.
Der to see, or in or.
Coming this, or?
Der to k.
Bec.
Now, but, rat.
Au.
Her, in fact, ne.
Se.
Ed, and mu.
This.
St, one be sle.
Be.
Ep.
Co.
Ing, in.
Ming that.
Or.
"Is all I c an know, now."
Der to k.
It is.
Now, or see.
"Or, is."
Some peo.
It all.
Ple, or thin.
"That I do need to know."
Gs, and, or.
"Now, too."
In or.
And, so.

Der to see furt.
"Was?"
Her, bet.
And, so.
Ter, and m.
Am I, and.
Ore, and.
So, I am, also.
Or, in or.
"Not in a rush."
Der to dre.
Or, in a hurry.
Am, or.
"To leave the darkness, or."
To leave.
The night, or.
To leave.
"The night-time dream-space."
Though, of course.
"As does the day come."
And, as do.
Es the day go.
And, as do the days go.
And, as do they come, of.
"Course."
Can I not stop it, or.
"Them, or time."
Or who, or Who.
From coming, or.
Se, or whi.
From going.
Ch, ti.
"Or, from passing."
Me, or.
Of course.
And, though?
"Of course."

As does the day come.
And, as does the day go.
And, as it does come, or.
As do the days come, and.
As they do go, and.
"If I do not come."
Or, if I do not go with it, or *with them,* what?
"Will become of me, and."
Because, if I am not moving forward.
Or for.
"I must be mo."
Wards.
Ving back.
Ward, or.
Ward.
Wards, if.
Of course, and.
Or.
"If, rather."
I do decide to stay in one place.
Might I not move either backwards, or forwards.
"And, or?"
Because, of course.
"Backwards, or forwards, or."
For.
Ac.
Ward, or back.
Cord.
War.
Ing to who.
D.
M, or.
"According to what?"
Or, What.
Because, of course.
"Do, or."
Might some start at the end, and.

Work their way back.
Ward, or.
Back.
Wards, but.
Are those, or.
Are these, only.
The living dead.
Or the dead, living.
And, so.
Or, does only the simpleton, or.
Do only the simpletons, or the.
Simplistic?
Or, the un.
Imaginative, or.
The dis?
Or, the un.
Believing, or.
The all-too-literal?
But live once, or.
Or, but, of.
"Course, do some start."
Or begin, at.
"What, or."
At whose, end.
"Because."
Might moving forward, or.
"Might, or."
Is moving forwards, for.
Or, to some.
"Moving backward, or."
Moving backwards, to.
"Or, for others, and?"
Too, of course.
"Might moving, or might going."
Backward, or.
"Backwards, for some."
Be.

Going, or be.
Moving.
"Forward, or."
For.
Wards, for others, and.
Too, because?
"Of course."
If I am not moving, or.
"Going, or."
If I am not, either.
"Going, or."
Moving, for.
Ward, or back.
Or, back.
Wards, or.
Ward, or for.
"For."
Ward, or.
Ward, or backward.
Or backwards, or forwards.
Which, too.
Are.
"But a matter of interpretation."
Or.
A mat.
Ter of per.
Spec.
Tive.
Or, a mat.
Ter.
Of where one does choose, or de.
Cide, to start, or to be.
Gin, or.
A matter.
"Of one's."
Point-of-view, and.
"Because, of."

Course, what.
Or, whose.
"In."
Ter.
Pre.
Tat.
Ion, or.
Po.
In.
T-of-vie.
W, or.
Perception, of.
"A thing."
Does not, at least.
Part.
I.
All.
Y change.
"Or, at."
Least, partially.
"Determine?"
A thing.
"And, too."
Because, of course.
Might some move, go.
"Or perceive, life."
Or, death?
"From death towards birth, while."
Or, from dying towards living, or.
"From dying to, or."
From dy.
Ing, to.
Wards.
"Life, or."
Towards learning to live, while.
Might others, move.
"Go, or."

Qui.
Te so far more norm.
Ally, and.
Or, ave?
Rage.
Ly?
"Or, quite so far more regularly, or."
Medi.
Ocre.
Ly, or?
Quite so far m.
Ore ord.
In.
Ari.
Ly, or.
Typic.
Ally, or?
"Quite so far more ex."
Pec.
Ted.
Ly, or.
Qui.
Te so far m.
Ore typic.
Ally, or.
Quite so far more reasonably, or.
"Quite so far more rationally, from."
Birth to, or.
"From birth, towards death."
Or, from birth.
"Or, from living, to."
Or, towards dying.
Though, but.
"Of course?"
To, or towards.
"Or, away from?"
What, or.

"Away from, or."
To, or.
"Towards, whose."
Or to, or.
"Towards, or."
Away from.
Which birth, and which death.
Or, away from, or.
"To, or."
Towards, whose.
"Living, or."
Life, or.
To, or.
"Towards, whose."
Dy.
Ing, or.
Death, or.
"To, or."
Towards, whose.
"Which, or."
What.
"Death, and birth?"
Or re-.
Birth.
"In a relatively smooth, and in."
A relatively straight.
Horizontal line, or.
"In a relative straight, or."
In a relative smooth, arrow.
"Or?"
But, of.
"Course, relative."
To, or.
"Re."
Lat.
Iv.
E, to.

Wards what.
And, or.
"Of course."
In a relatively?
Normal, or in.
"A relatively."
Reg.
U.
Lar, or.
"In a relatively?"
Us.
Ual ex.
Pect.
Ed.
"Rational, reasonable, or."
Ordinary.
"Progression, from."
Start to finish, and.
"From finish to start, and."
From beginning to end, and.
Or?
"From end to beginning, while."
Might some other move.
Ment, or.
While might some ot.
Her move.
Ment.
S, or.
"While might some other motions, or."
While might some other motion, be.
Up, and down.
"Or down, and up."
Or up, to down, or.
"Down, to up."
Because.
"Of course."
What life is not.

"Moving, or."
Mot.
Io.
N, and.
"Because, of."
Course, is.
"Not life about stopping."
Or a.
Or a.
Bout be.
Bo.
Ing stop.
Ut.
Ped.
Staying still, and.
Being stopped, by.
"Because, of."
Whom, or by what, by What, or by Whom.
Course, might.
Or, for what rea.
"Or, is."
Son, or for what rea.
One, or.
Sons, or for.
"More step, or."
No.
Steps, for.
Rea.
War.
Sons, rea.
D, in this w.
Son.
Or.
Able, or ot.
Ld, be.
Her.
"One, or."

Wise, or.
More step, or.
"Steps, back."
Or backwards, in.
"Another, or."
In the other world, or.
"In the Other one, or?"
In a par.
Al.
Lel w.
Or.
Ld, or.
In which one.
Because, too, or.
In the first, or in the last.
In the next, in the pre.
Vi.
Ou.
S one, or.
"Of course."
Might, or more than might.
"One step back in this world, be."
One, or more, steps back in the other, in the next, in the previous,
in the first, or.
"In the last, or."
In the, *or in a?*
Parallel one, and.
Too, because.
"Of course."
What is down to one.
"Might, or more than might, be?"
Up to, *or for,* an.
Ot.
Her, and.
"Because, of."
Course?
Might up to one, be.

"Down to," *or for.*
"Another, and."
Because, of.
"Course, too."
What, *or who?*
Is down with.
Or, Who.
Out up, and.
Because.
"What is, or."
What would be, up.
"With."
Out down, and.
"Because, of."
Course, and.
"Too."
What might be a step.
Hop, leap, or jump, up.
"In this world, be."
A fall, or.
"A step, or."
A leap, or.
A hop, or.
"A jump, down."
In the other, or in an.
Other, or.
In a differ.
Ent wor.
Ld, and.
"Because, and, too?"
Might, or more than might.
A step down in this world, be.
"A step up in the ot."
Her, in the previ.
"Ous, in the first, in the last, in the next, or."
In the, or in a, par.
Al.

Lel one, and.
So, might.
"Or, so."
Can mo.
Ving, mo.
"Tion, or move."
Ment.
"Be."
Back and forth, and.
"Forth and back, hor."
Iz.
Ont.
Ally.
"As well as."
Can it, also, be.
"Moving, or."
Going up, or down, and.
Or, down.
"And, up."
Verti.
"Call."
Y, "So."
Might moving, and.
"So, might."
Motion, and.
"So, also."
Might move.
"Ment."
Be, also.
"Along a dia."
Gon.
Al, zag.
Ging, or zig.
Ging.
"Line, like."
Moving, or.
"Like going."

Northwest.
"Or Northeast, but."
Usually, or.
"Not ever, like."
Going South.
"East, or."
South.
West, and.
So, what movement might be.
"Also, diagonal, or, also."
Zig, or.
"Zag."
Ged, too.
Rather than left to right.
"Or, rather than right to left, be."
Cause, of co.
Ur.
Se.
Are we not all, and.
"Too, be."
Cause, of.
"Course, we."
Or, 'we?'
Are not all.
On the same page, or.
"All, on."
Or, in?
The same spot, or.
"All in, or."
All sharing.
"The same s."
Pace, or.
The sam.
E sp.
Aces, or.
The same s.
Pot, and.

"Because?"
Of course, can.
Not more than one.
"Occupy, or."
Be on, or be in, the same.
"Spot, or."
The same space, *at le.*
And.
As.
"Because, of."
T, not all at on.
Course, are.
Ce, and.
"We not all nec."
Es.
Sa.
Rily mo.
Ving, or go.
Ing.
Or moving, or going.
In but one, or in the same.
Direction.
As should, and.
"As ou."
Ght we not, *be,* and.
But, of.
"Course, rat."
Her, are.
"We all moving."
Or un.
Moving, or un.
Going.
Or going, in.
Or un-go.
Ing, in.
"One, of."
An in.

Finite number of them, and.
"Because even if 'we' might all have some things in common, do."
We most cert.
Ain.
Ly, and.
"Do we."
Most sure.
Ly, and.
"Do we."
Far past hope, hopes, and hoping.
Which is.
But lack of certainty.
"Not all have all things in common, and."
Too, because.
"Of course."
Though might 'we' all be similar, in some ways.
"More than most certainly are 'we' not all the same in all ways, and."
Because, of course.
"Are 'we,' al."
So, not all.
"'We's,' and."
Are we not all, necessarily, in.
Clu.
Ded in the 'we,' and.
"Too, eve."
N, if.
"Of course."
That would.
"Or, even if."
That, or this?
That, or that.
Might be.
"Most easy, or most simple?"
Or, simplest.
Would be.
"If we."
Re 'we,' and.

Would be, if.
We.
Re 'we.'
"All the Same, or if."
We we.
Re, or are, *all the same, or if.*
"We we."
Re all i.
Dent.
Ica.
L, and, of.
"Course, what."
Would be.
"Most easy, and."
Most simple, would.
Death, or would life, or.
Would whose, or would which.
Death, or life.
"Be, if."
We all did think, or.
"If we did all feel."
All of the same thing, or.
"All of the same things, all."
At, or.
"All in."
The same time, or.
All in, or all at, the same.
"Times, but."
Of course.
"Would that be strange, and."
Or, would this.
Too, of.
"Course, what."
Would be weird, if.
"All were, ever."
And, *or,* if all were al.
Ways, on.

"The same page, and."
If all.
"Did think, say, or."
Feel, all.
"Of the same things, all."
At once, or.
"All in."
Or, all at.
The same times, and.
Because, of.
"Course, that."
Or, this.
"Is, also."
Or, This.
Not qui.
Te poss.
Ib.
Le, is.
"All being, on."
Or, is.
All being, in.
"The same spot, or."
Is all occupying.
"The same spot, or."
Is all occupying, all.
"Of the same spaces, all."
At, or.
"All in."
The same time, or.
All in, or.
"All at."
The same times, even.
"If, though."
Perhaps.
"Most ideally?"
Or even.
"If, per?"

Hap.
S, most.
Simply, or.
"Even if?"
Perhaps, most.
"Simp."
List.
Ic.
Ally, and.
Even if?
"Perhaps, most."
Easily, might all.
"And, might 'we.'"
All be 'we's,' and.
Might 'we.'
"All be all's, and."
Even if.
Most simply, and.
"Even if."
Most easily, might we.
All be all the sam.
E, *or all the Sam.*
E, of.
"Course, is."
Not what, *or What,* or.
"Is not."
Who is.
"Most ideal, not."
Necessarily.
What, *or who, or Who, or what,* is.
Necessarily.
Most Re.
"Most real, or."
Al, or.
Not what is.
Or not who, or not Who?
Is.

"Most natural, or."
Not what, or.
"Not who?"
Or, Who.
Is most reasonable, or.
"Not who, or."
Not what is.
And, not who is.
"Most rational, or."
Not what, or.
"Not who is."
Most sensible, or.
"Not what, or."
Not who, *or Who*, is.
"Most logi."
Cal, and.
So, even.
"If what is."
Or, even.
"If what might be."
Most ideal, what.
And, who.
"Is not."
Necessarily, most.
"Real."
Is.
Tic, or.
Most prac.
Tic.
Al, or.
"Most pos."
Sib.
Le, be.
Ca.
Use.
Of course.
"Can we not all."

Be, or.
"Oc."
Cup.
Y, the.
Same, s.
Pace.
"Or, the."
Same sp.
Aces, or.
"The same s."
Pot, or.
The sam.
E s.
Pots, all.
"At once, or."
All at.
"Or, all in."
The same time, or.
"All in, or."
All at.
"The same times, any."
More, *or less,* than.
Can we not all have.
All of the same thing, or.
"All of the same things, all."
At once, or.
"All at."
Or, all.
"In the."
Same time.
Or, space?
"Or all in, or."
All at.
"The same times, and."
Or, sp.
Too, be.
Aces, too, and.

Cause, of.
Course.
Can, and.
Should, and.
Ought we, or ou.
Ght 'we.'
"Not all be."
All the same, and.
"Too, be."
Cause, of course.
Are 'we' not all me.
Ant.
"Or in."
Ten.
"Ded, to."
Be, though.
"Of course."
In.
Ten.
Ded, or.
"Meant by whom, and."
Or meant by what, *to be who.*
M, or to be what, be.
Cause, of.
"Course, too."
Are 'we' our differences, as.
"Much as are we, also."
And, as.
"Much as."
'We,' al.
So, are.
Our simi.
Lar.
It.
Es, and.
"Too, though."
Might we have some things in common, do.

"And, can."
And, also, of course.
Are we not all.
Identical.
Copies, or derivatives.
Of one another, as much as.
Of course, are we not.
All ex.
Act.
Ly, or all pre.
Cise.
Ly a.
Like, or all the same, as.
"Of course?"
Were we not quite in.
Ten.
Ded, or me.
Ant to be, and.
As we ought, and as we should.
Not be, too, and?
As do?
We all.
"Not have."
All, or.
"Everything."
In com.
Mon, all.
"Of the time, and."
Or.
Ever, e.
Ver.
Where, or for al.
Ways, or.
Because, of.
"Course, though."
Might, or.
"Though, do."

Most of us, or 'us,' have.
"Eyes, ears, a nose."
A mouth, a.
"Ton."
Gue, and.
Two legs, and.
"Two arms, and."
Too feet, and.
"Two hands, and."
Ten toes, and.
"Ten fingers, too."
Of course.
"Are not."
His, hers, its.
"Or the."
Ir hands, toes, fingers, arms, ears, eyes, lips, tongue, mouth, nose,
arms, or.
"Legs mine, and."
Too, of.
"Course, are."
Not my legs, my fin.
Gers, my toes, my arms, my ears, my eyes, my mo.
Uth, my tongue, or my teeth.
Theirs, his, hers, its.
"Or anyone's, or."
Everyone's, other.
"Than my own, and."
Because, of.
"Course, is."
Es.
Sent.
Ial, to.
"Sanity, and."
Essential to propriety, is.
Knowing where.
"I do end, and."
Is kno.

Wing when.
"Another, and."
Any, or all others, do.
Start, do begin, or, also, do end, and.
So know.
In so know.
Ing w.
Ing, also, kno.
Here I do st.
Wing where, and, so, when.
Art, and w.
I do be.
Here you do end, and be.
Gin, but whi.
Gin, or st.
Ch, of cour.
Art, and fin.
Se, is all but bound.
Is.
Aries, one-oh-one, and.
H, and.
Is knowing, and.
"Is recognizing, when."
And where, or when?
Or when, and where.
Others do start, or.
Is knowing, and.
"Or, is recognizing, when."
Or, where.
"Do others start, or."
Is, also, k.
No.
Wing.
"Where others."
Any, or all?
"Do be."
Gin, and.

"Of course."
Es.
Senti.
Al is.
Knowing, and.
"Es."
Sent.
I.
A.
L is.
"Re."
Spec.
Ting when.
And, is.
Respecting, where.
"Another ends, and."
Is knowing where, and.
When you do, and.
"Is knowing when, others."
Do end, and.
"Is knowing, and."
Is respecting, where.
And, when.
"I do start, and."
Where, and when, I do, and.
So, essential, is.
"Knowing, and."
So, essential.
Is respecting boundaries.
And, so.
"Essential, is."
Respecting.
"Personal space, and."
Private space, and.
"Private, and."
Per.
Son.

Al s.
Paces, and.
"So, of."
Course, essential, is.
"Knowing, and."
Is recognizing, the.
"Essential, and."
The important difference, and.
The important differences, as.
Well as the importance of the Difference, of.
Deference, and, or.
Between.
"Of Différance."
"Personal, and."
Between public, and.
"Between public."
And bet.
Ween pri.
Vate, and per.
Son.
Al.
"Spaces, ideas, and."
Places, and.
Ideals, and spaces.
"So, tho."
Ugh, of.
Course.
"Might, and."
Do we all.
"Or, though."
Might most of us, or 'us.'
Have.
"Some."
If not most, or all.
Things in com.
Mon, of.
Course, can.

"And, so."
We not all have.
"Everything, or."
All in common, and.
"Too, of."
Course, though.
"Even if."
What we have in common might make for a civil.
Or for civ.
Iz.
Il.
At.
At.
Ion, or.
Ion, and.
Even if.
"Might our simi."
Lari.
Ties make a, or make for, a civi.
Liza.
Tion, or *for*, or a, soc?
Ie.
Ty, or for so.
Cie.
Ty, or.
For whose society, or whose, or what, or which.
"Civil."
Or So.
Iz.
Cie.
At.
Ty, or how civil.
Ion.
Ize.
Possible, also.
D, or.
Or, at all, and.

As much as, might.
Our common interests, needs, wants and goals.
Hopes, and dreams.
Make co.
Ope.
Rat.
Ion nec.
Es.
Sary, at ti.
Me.
S, too.
"Need, and can."
Not, and.
Should, and ought.
Ought, and should.
"Not our differences."
Or, the Difference.
Or, Différance.
Or, our individuality, be.
Or, our in.
Divi.
D.
Ua.
Lit.
Ie.
S, be.
Smeared, e.
Rased.
Wiped away.
Ignored.
"Or d?"
El.
Ete.
D, be.
Cause.
"So."
Ci.

Et.
Y, or.
Because civil.
Iz.
At.
Ion, is.
"Com."
Prised of the in.
Divi.
Duals in it, could.
And, would.
"And, can."
Not, and.
Is not so.
Cie.
Ty, or civil.
Iz.
At.
Ion, and.
"Is so."
Cie.
Ty, also, not.
And can, and would.
"It not be."
Without the individuals in it, and.
Or, with.
"Of course, be."
Out the pie.
Cause, of.
Ces, w.
Course.
Hi.
What would, or.
Ch com.
What could.
Pose it, and.
The for.

Est be.
Without the trees, and.
Or, because.
Society, or.
Of course, does a, or does the.
For.
Est need the trees, to be, but.
"Do not the trees, like."
Wise, need the forest, too?
"Because civilization, does."
Depend on the individuals in it, too.
"Of course."
Ought, and.
"Should, and."
Should, and.
"Ought society."
And civilization, serve.
"The individuals in it, and."
Not the.
"Other way around, be."
Cause.
"Are not the most."
Essential persons.
"In society, or."
In civilization, the.
Ones who do not need it, and.
The ones who do not need to be seen.
In order to be, and.
"Because, of."
Course, are.
"Not all."
Per.
Sons, or.
"All in."
Divi.
Duals all the same, or all?
Of e.

Qual im.
Port, *or all?*
All the Same, and.
Of e.
"So, of."
Qual ex.
Course, be.
Port, or.
"Cause, who."
Wants, or.
Beca.
Use, who.
"Needs to live in a world where all are, and where all is, the same, which."
Of course, would.
"Be so bo."
Ring, and.
So, what would.
"Also, be?"
The de.
Vil's, or.
"The Devil's?"
True, and.
Most pure, or purest?
Delight.
"Because?"
Who does not pre.
Fer one.
"Or, ones?"
Who do, and.
"One, or."
Ones?
Who can, feel, think, and.
"Do for."
And, by them.
Selves, rather.
"Than child."

Ren, who?
Must be told, or.
"Shown what is."
Right, or.
"What, or who, is w."
Who must be shown, or told.
Ron.
What, and who.
G, and.
Is true, and.
Or Who, and what is, and.
Who, or what, is false, how.
Or What, and who.
So.
Ever right.
Ly, correct.
Ly, or wrong.
Ly, or.
Because, of.
"Course, we."
Are not all children, but.
"Because, of."
Course, we.
"Are all adults, and."
So, of.
Course.
"Ought, and should, and."
Should, and ought, we.
Or 'we.'
"Not all be told."
Or, shown.
Ex.
Cess.
Ive.
Ly, or at all.
"How we can, how we should, or how we ought to be, and."
Or how we can, or how we should.

Or, how we ought not be, and, or.
As if we are all child.
Ren, or sheep, idi.
Ots, or mor.
Ons, un?
Able to think, un.
Able to choose, and, or.
Unable to de.
Cide for our.
Selves, or.
"Because, of course."
Is not the key?
To all.
"Moderation?"
And the mid.
D.
Le path, or.
The Middle Path, or.
Way, or.
The Middle Way, or.
"The middle way?"
Or the middle way, or?
And, so.
The Third Way, or.
And?
"Is too much collectivity."
Or, is too much to.
Get.
Her.
Ness, as.
Bad as.
"Not e."
No.
Ugh, as.
Much, as.
"Also, is."
Not e.

No.
Ugh collectivity, as.
"Bad as."
Too much, and.
"As much as, is."
Too much sameness, as.
"Bad as not enough, and."
As much as, is.
"Not enough difference, or."
Are not enough differences, as.
"Bad as too many, and."
As much as.
"Is not enough individuality, as."
Bad as not enough, and.
"As much as is not enough individuality, as."
Bad as too much, and.
"As much as, is."
Too much to.
Get.
Her.
Ness, as.
"Bad as."
Not e.
No.
Ugh, and.
"As much as is too much cooperation, as."
Bad as.
"Not enough, and."
As much as, is.
"Not enough cooperation, as bad as."
Not enough, and.
"As much as is not enough to."
Ge.
Ther.
Nes.
S, as.
Bad as too much, and.

As much, as is.
"Too much public-."
Ness, as.
Bad as.
"Not enough, and."
As much as is.
Or, pri?
"Too much private-ness."
Vac.
Bad as not en.
Y, as.
Ough, and.
"As much as is not enough private-ness."
Or, too much privacy?
Or, too much a.
Lone.
Ness.
As bad as too much, and.
As bad as not enough.
"As much as, is."
Too much public.
It.
Y, as.
Bad as not enough, and.
"Because, of."
Course, can some things, only.
"Or, be."
Cause.
Some things are best.
Or, only.
Done, or.
"Accomplished, to."
Get.
Her, or.
"Cooperatively, too."
Of course.
"Can, and are."

And are, and can.
Other things, only be.
"Accomplished, reached, gotten, or had alone, or."
Individually, so.
"Of course."
All of which, is.
"To say that, but?"
Of course.
"Must one find the balance, ideal."
Or the Mid.
If one does exist, and.
Dle Way?
A combination of one, and one.
Or the Third Way, is it, rather?
Or of One, and One, if not.
Of one, and One, or.
Of One, and one, which.
"On occasion, and which."
Sometimes, do.
Make more than two, or.
Which an.
Of course.
Other can.
"Like so much else."
Not find.
Is not.
For you, or.
Too much mode.
"For me."
Ration, as bad as not enough, and.
For an.
"Be."
Ot.
"Cause, too."
Her, or.
Of course.
"For any other, than."

So, also.
Him, her, it, or.
"Must not enough moderation, be."
"Themselves, but."
As bad as too much, and?
"As much as, is."
Too much a.
Lone.
Ness, as.
"Bad as."
Not enough, and.
"And?"
As much as, also, is.
"Not enough alone-ness, as."
Bad as, too.
"Much, be?"
Cause, of cour.
Se.
"Can."
Not one, be.
"Or be?"
Come, un.
Less one is let.
"Or, un."
Less, or un.
Til.
"One is per."
Mit.
Ted to be.
Or, to become?
Because?
Or, to Be.
Of course.
Come, or.
To Be?
"What is be."
In.

G, or B.
Ei.
Ng?
Without be.
Coming, or with.
Out Be.
Coming, and.
"And, too, because?"
Of course.
"Or, if?"
Rather, what does being.
"Or, Being?"
Or, if rather.
"What do beings."
Or, Beings.
Need, or.
Care for.
"Or, need?"
Becoming.
Or, Be.
Comings.
"Or, Becoming?"
Or, be.
Comings, or.
Or?
"Who is."
Both Being.
"And be."
Ing, and Be.
Coming?
"And be."
Coming.
And, beings?
"And Be."
Co.
Ming.
S, too, and.

At all.
"Or?"
But, of.
Course.
"What, or who."
Who, or what.
Are the good, or.
The Good, or.
The bad, or.
The Bad, or.
Whose, who, Who, or what's.
Are the bad, or the good, or.
What, who, whose, or What's.
Are the great?
Or whose, or what's.
Or what, or which.
Or who, or *Who*, are the gre.
Ats, or.
Who, or what, or which one.
Is great, or the greatest, or.
If, rather.
"Not necessarily."
Is what, or is Who, or who?
Is good, great.
"Or, is."
What, or who, or Who?
Is great, good.
"But?"
Of course.
"What, or."
Whose are?
"The big."
Gest, best, and most huge?
Questions.
If whether is big, also.
"Huge, and."
If, whether.

Or, if not.
"Is what, or."
Is who.
Or, Who.
Is best, also.
"Who, or."
Also, what.
"Is huge, and."
If whether, or.
"Not, what."
Or, who.
Or, Who.
"Is big."
Is, also, best, or.
"If, rather."
Who, or.
"What is."
Best is.
"Also, big."
Quest.
That can wait.
Ions?
"For another time."
Or, for.
Or, for.
"Another place, while."
Because, too.
"Of course?"
Is not the most important question.
"Or Quest."
Ion, but.
One, and.
"Too, be."
Cause, of course.
"Is not."
The one most important, or.
"The one?"

Most essential question.
"Or Question?"
Its own answer, and.
"Its own Ans."
Wer, be.
Cause, of course.
"Rather, today."
Which is?
Like most days, or.
"Which is?"
Like any, if not necessarily, like all?
Other day, or days.
"Though, but."
Of course.
"Which is."
Not necessarily.
"All just, all wholly, all totally, all en."
Tire.
Ly, or.
All completely.
Or, all wholly.
"Like all the rest, but?"
Because, of course.
Is not one ever exactly, or pre.
Cise.
Ly, just like.
All of the rest, or.
Precisely, or exactly.
Like all of the others, due to?
Time, of course, or?
Due to God, or?
Is God but time, or is time but a God, or god.
Dess, or.
Rather.
"Like so man."
Y of the others, I do.
Have so much work to do, and.

"So must I for."
Get, at least, for now?
What, who.
Se, or what, quest.
Ions, or.
What, or w.
Hi.
Ch, or whose Question.
"If, only?"
For now.
What, or which, or who?
Se, questions.
"Or w."
Hich, or what, or whose.
Quest?
Io.
N does, or do.
Mat.
Ter, be?
Cause.
Are not ans.
Wers, if not, nec?
Ess.
Ari.
Ly the one, the One, or the on?
Ly Ans.
Wer, far more im.
Port.
Than quest.
Ant, though, what.
Ions, or.
"And, though, which."
Than the Quest.
Is not necessarily, to.
Ion, or.
"Say, to."
Are not ans.

Think, to.
Wers, or the Ans.
"Assume, or."
Wer, ne.
To presume, will.
Cessary, with.
Necessarily.
Out quest.
"Forget me, but?"
Ions, or.
What, or which.
The Question, or.
Question, or?
Whose Question?
"Or?"
What questions, or.
Whose questions.
"Which like the best, or."
Which like?
"The most important, and."
Or, which?
"Like the most essential."
Ones, can.
Not necessarily.
And are not me.
Ant, or.
"Intended, to?"
Be ans.
Or.
We.
How to know.
Red.
"What."
Or which, or whose?
Questions do not have answers, or.
Which ones, or whose?
And, so.

"Are not meant to be answered?"
Are rhe.
Be.
Tor.
Cause.
Ic.
"Might some?"
Al, or.
"Might some?"
Already be answered, be.
"Cause, once."
Or, might some.
Already have answers, be.
Cause, once.
"One does find, or."
Real.
Ize the que.
Sti.
On, or the Que?
Sti.
On.
Or, the questions?
"One does, also, realize, or."
Find the Answer, too.
Or, the ans.
And, or.
Wers, and.
"But?"
Because.
Who can.
Lie, or.
"Lay, around?"
Forever, contemplating.
"Such things, such questions."
Such answers, such.
"Ways, or."
Such hands, or.

Such palms.
"Or, such eyes."
Or, such I's.
"But?"
Though, of course.
"Often, too."
Is con.
Temp.
Lati.
On.
And, thinking, as.
"Important as."
Action, or as doing?
At least.
At, or.
In some times, in some spots, and, or.
"In some places, and."
Is doing.
As?
Or, thinking.
Or, as?
Or, writing.
"Sa."
Ying, or.
Because.
"Of course."
Is not saying, necessarily, thinking, and.
Is not think.
"Too, be."
Ing, ne.
Cause?
Cessarily, do.
Of course, and.
Ing, and.
"Also, is."
To think, is not.
To think.

Necessarily, to.
"Not necessarily."
Do, and.
To say, and.
Not necessarily, is.
"Too, be."
To want to do, to do, and.
Cause, of.
Be.
Course.
Cause, of course.
"Is not necessarily thinking."
Is not necessarily to want to say, to say, and.
Saying, or.
"Doing, and."
Too, because?
"Of course."
Is not to think.
"Necessarily."
Thinking, and.
"Too, because?"
Of course, and like.
Wise, is not.
"Necessarily."
To say.
"Saying, or?"
And, too.
"Because, of."
Course, also, is?
"Not ne."
Ces.
Sar.
I.
Ly thinking.
"To think?"
Or.
"And?"

Or.
"Because?"
And, too.
"Also?"
Not necessarily.
"Is."
Thinking of doing, doing.
Saying.
Or is thinking of saying, saying.
"To say?"
Or is saying of doing, doing.
Or, and.
"Because?"
Of course.
"And, too?"
Because, too.
Of course?
Does, and.
Would.
And would, and.
"Does."
Only a fool act without.
Or, without thinking, of what.
Thinking first, and?
Or, of whom, or.
Even, if.
Or, of Whom, or.
"Of course."
Of What, or.
Should, and.
"Ought, and."
Even if.
"Ought, and."
Should all think.
"First, be."
Fore act.
In.

G, who.
"Ever, or."
Who al.
Ways, do.
Es, and.
"Because more than most certainly."
And, be.
"Cau."
Se.
Of course.
"More than most surely, am."
I am not such a one, or.
One foolish enough, to.
"Try to."
Or, without.
Trying, to.
"Act before, or."
To act without thin.
King, and.
"Because."
Of course.
Yet, or.
"Once again?"
I am not one to be rus.
Hed, or one.
"To be hur."
Rie.
D, or.
One to be, or.
One wil.
Ling to be.
"Hur."
Rie.
D, or rus.
Hed, in.
To do.
Ing without think.

Ing, or.
"In."
To act.
Ing when, and.
Where I ou.
Ght, or s.
Ho.
Uld, in.
Ste.
Ad, con.
Tem.
Plate, fir.
St, *or when con.*
"One to be."
Temp.
Ru.
Lat.
She.
Ion is ne.
D, hur.
Ed.
Rie.
Ed, or?
D, or.
When, or where.
"Forced into."
Where, or when.
Do.
It is ne.
Ing where.
Ed.
"And, when."
Ing, or.
Thinking first would be.
"Far more re."
As.
On.

Able, and.
Where, and when, or.
"When, or where."
Thinking first would be.
"Far more rat."
Ion.
Al, and.
Where, and when, and.
"When, and where."
Think.
Ing would make far more.
Sense, and.
"Where, and when, and."
When, and where.
"Think."
Ing first would be far more logi.
Cal, and.
Far wiser, and.
"So."
After having finished contemplating the hands, or.
"The palms, or."
Your palms, or.
My palms, or.
"My hands, which."
Indeed, of.
"Course, now."
Are right.
"Here, before me, and."
"Which, in."
Deed, of.
Course, are.
"Right now before me."
And, which are, be.
And, which are.
Fore you, and.
Right here, and.
If not left.

Which are right now, *before you,* and.
Which are be.
Fore me, and.
"So aft."
Er con.
Firm.
Ing.
Or, after.
"Once again, be."
Lieving.
That, in.
Deed.
They are mine, and.
Be.
If not necessarily, after.
Cause, if not your, who.
"Con."
Se, or what's, or W.
Firm.
Hat's, and.
Ing, that, in.
Deed, they are here, be.
Cause, of.
"Course, would only."
A fool, idiot, crazy person, or.
"Moron, doubt."
What is, or.
"Doubt what are."
Most obviously, and.
"What are."
Most certainly, be.
Fore one.
Or, what are.
"And, so."
Most certainly, and.
Aft.
Most necessarily, be.

Er having fin.
Fore you, and.
Is.
Hed.
More than sure.
Ly, and.
"After having, fini."
Shed.
More than cert.
Ain.
Ly, id.
Ent.
If.
Ying with.
Po.
Ses.
Sing, and.
Owning them.
"As, of."
Course, my.
Own, and.
"Too."
After fin.
Is.
Hi.
Ng, and.
After being done.
With the right.
Or, Right.
"And, with the left."
Or, Left.
And, with the left.
Or, not necessarily, with.
"And, with the wrong."
Both, or ei.
And, with the right, and.
The.

"After being done."
R, or.
And, af.
With both.
Ter.
Finishing, flipping.
"Both the left, and."
The Left, and.
The right, *and the Right,* and.
"Aft."
Er look.
Ing, at.
Both palm, and.
"Back side."
And, after.
"Having looked, see."
Ked, sear.
Che.
D.
"Both sides, looking for."
What, though.
"Of course?"
And, if.
"Because, where."
And, if.
"Because, one."
Does not know for what, or.
"For whom one is see."
King, or.
If one does not know for.
"Whom, or."
For Whom, or.
For what.
Or, for What.
"One is sear."
Ching, or if.
And, if.

Or, if.
"Where, or."
If when, one.
"Does not know for."
What, or.
"For whom, one."
Is loo.
King, *or if one does not h.*
Ave the eye.
S for see.
Ing, how.
"Can, or."
How might.
"One know."
When, or.
"Where, or."
Where, or.
"When, one."
Has found, for.
"What, or."
For whom.
"One has been seeking, searching."
Or, for Whom, or.
Or, look.
For What, one is.
Ing, and.
"Because, I."
And, be.
Was, and.
Cause, you, and.
"Because I am not."
One, nec.
Ess.
Arily, looking.
"See."
King, or.
Sear.

Chin.
G, for.
"Any."
Thing, or.
For any.
One, in.
"Part."
Ic.
Ul.
Ar, to.
Whom to sur.
Ren.
Der, or.
To whom to give, or lend.
These, *or those,* hands.
So, must they be your hands, and.
Must all be.
Not any.
In my hands, of.
One's, every.
"Course, of."
One's, ever.
In my palms, or.
Y.
"On the back."
Body's, or all.
Sides, of.
Else's, or.
Eit.
Her, or.
Of.
"Both of them, either."
Left, or right, or.
"Right, or left, or."
Left, or wrong, or.
"Wrong, or left, but."
Or Left, or Wrong, or.

Of course.
Right, or Left, or.
"Left, or right, or."
Left, or Right, or.
Right, or left, to.
Or for him, be.
Cause.
"Of course."
Even if.
"Is this my right, or."
Even if.
"Is that my right, to."
Or, for you, or.
"To him, to."
It, to them.
Or to, or for.
"Any, or."
All ot.
Hers, is.
"It left for, or to whom, or to, or for."
What so.
"Ever, is."
It, him.
Her, or.
Them, be.
"Cause."
As yet, he was.
And, you are.
Un.
Seeing.
"And, be."
Cause.
"As yet."
He was.
And, you are.
"Re."
Fusing, to.

Notice.
"Or, to."
See, or to re.
Mem.
Ber, or.
"To thin."
K, of? Of.
"Course."
Who he, and.
"Who I did."
And, who, and.
"Or, what?"
I do.
And, you do.
Re.
Fuse, to.
"Whi."
Ch was.
And, Who is.
And, who is.
"Or, who was on."
Ce, or, who?
"Or, far."
More simp.
Ly, and.
"Who, or."
What, so.
"Far more simp."
List.
Ic.
All.
Y, and.
What, or.
"Who, so."
Far more easil.
Ly, might have been?
"A what, or."

But, who.
"Of course."
Did, and.
"What."
Does not here.
"Or, now."
Need to be seen, not.
Iced, or re.
Me.
M.
Be.
Red.
"By him?"
Or, by me.
Or, by you.
"So as to be."
Me?
But, who.
"Or, but."
What, of.
"Course, and."
Who is.
"Better, off."
Not being seen, or.
"Not being not."
Iced, or.
Not be.
Ing re.
Mem.
Ber.
Ed, or.
"Not being thought of?"
By me, or.
"By him, be."
Cause.
"To be so."
Seen, or.

To be.
"So no."
Tic.
Ed, or.
"To be?"
So re.
"So re."
Member.
Ed.
"Or, so?"
As, to.
"Be, so."
Thought of.
"By him, or."
By her, or.
By you, or.
By me, would.
"Not real."
Ly.
"And, would not."
Tru.
Ly, real.
Ly, or act.
Tu.
Ally, be.
To be.
"Seen, as."
She was, and.
"Or, as."
I am, and.
Be.
Cause, "Of course."
Use.
"Of course."
Who does see who they are, *and so, pro.*
Je.
Cts, or de.

Flect.
S, and.
Do all see what, *and who, or Who,* they will, and not *What, or Who,
or* more, and not.
Less, and.
How else might I try.
"To see her, but."
As a means to some.
"End, of."
Mine, and.
"Because, of."
Course, who.
"Else might."
She be, or.
"Because, of."
Course, who.
"Else is she, and."
Or, who was she, and.
Or, who am I, and.
Who else could, or might.
You be, or have been, or.
She have been, and.
"Be."
Cause, of course.
Why might I let her be, if.
"She is."
Not here.
"Or, if she is?"
Not all here.
Or, all there?
"For me, and."
Because, of.
"Course, why."
Might I be in.
Te.
Rest.
Ed, in.

"Any."
One, or.
In any.
Thing, which.
"Is, of."
No use to me, so.
In some?
"Which is."
Thing, or in?
Of val.
Some.
Ue, or use, to, or for.
One.
Me, and.
"So, of."
Course, did.
"He, and."
You.
Did I, and I did, of.
"Course, most."
Sensibly, most.
"Logically, and."
Most cert.
Ai.
N.
Ly, and.
"Most surely, of."
Course, and.
"Most reas."
On.
"Ably, and."
Most rat.
Io.
N.
Ally, did.
"And, will I."
Not waste, an.

"Ot."
Her moment.
"Or, any."
More time, trying.
'To see her, or."
Trying to re.
Me.
M.
Ber.
"Her, or."
Trying, or.
"Having to think."
Of her, if.
She is not just, or if she is not on.
Ly, for.
"Me, who."
Is, of.
"No interest to me, and."
So, of course.
"Al."
Read.
Y, "Who, or."
Quite, so.
"Far more easily, and."
What.
"Or, who."
Quite so far more sim.
Ply, and.
"Who, or."
What, so.
"Far more simp."
List.
Ic.
All.
"Y, did."
I, already.
"Get rid of, and."

Who, I, already.
Did.
"Get out of my way, be."
Cause, of.
"Course."
Can I not afford.
"To be bothered, by."
Or, to bother, with?
Any.
One, who.
"Is not."
Here for me, or.
"By anyone, who."
Is not here.
"Merely, just."
Or, on.
Ly, to.
"Please, or."
To ap.
Pea.
Se me, and.
"Because, of."
Course, why.
"Might I want, or."
Why might I need, or.
"What might I do, with."
Or, for.
Or, about?
"One, with."
Thoughts, plans, hopes, dreams, wants, needs, or.
"Wishes of her own, and."
Or, with one.
"With a point, or."
With a pur.
Pose, that.
"Is not."
Mine for her, and.

Too, of.
"Course, how."
Might, or.
"How can, or."
Why would I bot.
Her, or.
Be bot.
Her.
Ed, to be.
"Bothered, with."
Or, why.
Or, by.
"Or, how."
Could I be bot.
He.
Red, to.
"Be bothered, by."
Or, bother with.
One who.
"Is, or."
By one.
"Who was, only."
Or, by one, who.
"Was qui?"
Te so un.
Just.
Ly.
But, in.
"My way, when."
And where, and.
"Where, and."
When, of.
"Course, I."
Do have.
"Quite enough, and."
When, and.
"Where, I do."

Have plenty, of.
"Work to do, and."
Of course, why.
"Bother with, or."
How, or.
"Why, be."
Bothered, by.
"One I do not need, or."
By, or with.
One I do not need, or.
With, or by.
"One I do not want, or."
By, or.
"With, one."
Who does not need, or want you, or.
I do not want, or.
With one, who.
"Is not all here, or."
With one.
"Who is not all there."
Or, all here.
To be.
All that I do need her.
"To be."
Or, with one, who.
Is not all for me, or.
Or, with one.
"Who is not all there, or."
With one.
"Who is not all here."
To be.
All that I do want her.
"To be."
And, of.
"Course, how."
Or, why.
"Would, or."

Can I, or.
"Could I be bot."
Her.
Ed, to be.
"Bot."
He.
Red with, or.
Bot.
Her.
E.
D, to be.
"Bother."
Ed, by.
One who is, not.
"Here, just."
Or, on.
Ly.
"To satisfy."
My every want, or.
"My every need, and."
Of course.
"How could, or."
Why might I be.
"Bother."
Ed, to.
Be bothered with, or.
"By, one."
Who is not.
"All here, or."
By, or.
"With one."
Who is not.
"All there."
To comp.
Let.
E me, and.
"Of course."

How could, or.
"Why might."
I be bot.
Her.
Ed, with.
"Or, by."
One who.
"I can."
Not use, or.
Have, as.
"I do please, or."
Of course.
"Why bother to be bothered with, or."
By one, who.
"Does have."
Plans, a.
"Pur."
Pose, or.
A point.
"Of her own, which."
Is not.
"Necessarily, mine."
For her, and.
"And, so?"
And, so?
Then, and.
There, and.
"There, and."
Then, and.
There, and.
Now, and here.
And here, and now.
"Now, I am done."
And, be?
Cause.
Though, as.
"If I do."

Owe any.
One, or.
"Owe some?"
One, or.
As if.
"I do owe."
Everyone, or.
"Everybody, any."
Body, or.
"Somebody?"
Or, some.
An ex.
One.
Plan.
At.
Ion, for.
"Myself, for."
What I do, or.
"For what I do not."
Do, or.
"For what I do choose to do, or."
For what you do choose to do, or.
For what I do not choose to do, or.
For what you do not choose to do, or.
For what I do choose not to do, or.
For what you do choose not to do, or.
"For what I do decide not to do, or."
Or, for?
For what I do decide to do, and.
What you do not de.
"So."
Cide to do, and.
Then, and there.
And, so, here, and now.
"And, so."
There, and then.
There, and.

Now, and.
"Then, and."
Here, and.
So, here.
"And now, and."
So now, and.
"Here."
And, be.
Cause?
There, and then.
Then, and there.
"And, because?"
Here, and now.
Now, and here.
"And, because?"
Now, and here.
And here, and now.
I am, and I was.
And be.
"And, because, then."
Cause then, and there.
And, there?
You are.
He was.
And, you are.
"And, I am."
Done, and finished.
Finished, and done.
With the hands.
And, with your hands.
"And with my hands."
Washing them, or?
Or, at least, try.
And, with.
Ing to, or.
The hands?
Or me.

"And, too."
Rely raising them?
With the.
"And, with palms?"
And, with your palms.
"Or, with the palms."
Or, with my palms.
And, also.
"Too, with."
The oh.
"So-un."
Seeing.
Eyes, and knots.
Knots, and eyes.
Or with the, or.
"With whose?"
All-see.
In.
G, or.
"All-know."
In.
G, eye, or eyes.
"Above him."
Or, above me.
Either right.
"Or left, or."
Left, or right, or.
"Both, or."
But, one?
"In the cent."
Er, or.
And, a.
Bove you.
Bove me, and, so.
If, but one?
"Or, if but One."
In the cent.

Er, who.
Se.
"If not God's, or."
If not the all-.
See.
Ing One, and.
"If not the all-."
Knowing, one.
Which one, or.
"If not the Gi."
Ant's, or the Gi.
Ants', or the gi.
Hands, or eyes?
Ant's, or ants'.
Palms, or eye, or Eye, or, then.
Or, there?
"Or, here."
Whose, if.
"Not the mind's one."
Or the Mind's?
Or One, or.
If not mine, of course, whose.
"And, so."
After growing bored, with.
My hands, and.
"Or?"
With my palms, or.
With yours, or.
With them.
If, but, here, or.
"If, but, there is."
But one mind, or.
"But one Mind, or?"
And, so, one he.
If rat.
Art, or.
Her, are.

Many, br.
"But many minds, or."
Ains, and ar.
Are all others but the one.
Ms, and le.
"Or, other than the One?"
Gs, and fe.
But mon.
Et, and to.
Key minds, or.
Es, and fin.
"Because, of course."
Gers, too.
Ones, or the One?
Less than most true, or True.
Mind, be.
Cause.
Who, or what, for.
Ced.
"To act, or."
Who, or.
"What, for."
Ce.
D to work, or.
"What, or."
Who for.
Ced.
"To wake, or."
Who, or.
All, or.
"What, for."
Is every.
Ced.
Body, and is ever.
To rise, be.
Yon.
Fore one is re.

E, eve?
Ady, or.
R go.
Be.
In.
Fore every.
G to be re.
One, or be.
Ad.
Fore eve.
Y, all at on.
Ry.
Ce, or al.
Bo.
To.
Dy, is, or.
Get.
Are, or.
Her, or ou.
If all can, ou.
Ght, or s.
Ght, and s.
Ho.
Ho.
Uld the.
Uld.
Y, or 'we?'
Not all, ever.
Eve.
Yon.
R be for.
E, or every.
Ce.
Body, be.
D, or ex.
Or, be?
Pect.

Ex.
Ed to be, or.
Pec.
But if the.
Ted, or.
Y, or?
Be for.
If 'we' are not.
Ced to be.
Or if 'we' are all per.
All re.
Mit.
Ady, all at on.
Ted to be re.
Ce, or all.
Ad.
To.
Y, or pre.
Get.
Pare.
Her, of.
D, in ou.
Co.
R ow.
Ur.
N tim.
Se, might the.
E, or tim.
Re, or he?
Es, or.
Re? Be, at le.
If 'we' are all let be, or.
As.
Per.
T, a bit of con.
Mit.
Fusion, and some.

Ted to be.
Com.
Ad.
Pli.
Y, when.
Cat.
And where.
Ions, but.
One's ow.
Who said, thought, as.
N ti.
Sum.
Me.
Med, pre.
Su.
Me.
D than con.
Fu.
Si.
On, or that.
Com.
Pli.
Cat.
Ion.
S, are.
Bad, or wr.
On.
G, or.
And?
Who, or what?
Or what, or who?
Or Who, or What.
Or What, or Who.
Ever sai.
On.
D, me.
Ly w.

Ant, or in.
Here, or w.
Ten.
Hen, and on.
Ded.
Ly, if?
That life should, or ought, ever be?
'We' are, or.
Al.
But if 'we' are all not?
Ways, and ever, most simp.
Le, and un.
But who ou.
Comp.
Ght, or s?
Li.
Ho.
Cat.
Uld have to go, and, but.
Ed.
"Where, or."
When, or.
"When, or."
Where, one.
"Is for."
Ced to do so, by.
An.
Other, by.
"Any, or."
By all ot.
Hers, does.
Do so, but.
"On."
Ly, me.
Rely.
And, quite so un.
Justly?

"So fal."
Se.
L.
Y, and.
So fake-.
Ly, and.
"So in."
Au.
Then.
Tic.
Ally, and.
Who, or.
"What, or."
What, or.
"Who can."
Only do so, for.
"So long, so."
Ex.
Haus.
Tive.
Ly, and.
"So dis."
Connected, from.
The one true, or.
From the One True, or.
"From the one real, or."
From the One Truth, or.
From the one Real, or.
From the one truth, or.
"From the one True source, which."
But, of.
Does no.
Cour.
Ur.
Se, who.
Ish, and.
Se, and whi.

"Which does re."
Ch, tru.
Fresh, and.
E, Tru.
From which, when, and.
E, tru.
"From which where, one."
E, or Tru.
Is dis.
Th, or tru.
Con.
Th, or.
Nect.
Ed from it, can.
One on.
Ly live, bre.
At.
He, or.
Only.
"Last for so long, and."
Which where, and.
"Which, when one is."
Dis.
Con.
Nec.
Te.
D from it, do.
Es.
"One quite?"
So in.
Evi.
Tab.
Ly grow.
"Or, become."
Quite bored.
"On the spot."
Or, in the inst.

Ant, *or in an ins.*
"Or, instantly?"
Tant, or.
Upon waking.
In spite, of.
Or, de.
Spite.
"Howsoever long."
One might sle.
Ep, or.
"In spite of."
How long one.
Has slept, or how long.
One has be.
En sle.
Ep.
Ing, or de.
Spite how long.
Might one s.
Leep, or.
"In spite of how long, one."
Might spend.
"Waking, or."
Try.
Ing to wa.
Ke, or.
"In spite of how much time, one."
Might sp.
End ri.
Sing, or.
"Trying to rise, if."
Not just, and.
"If not on."
Ly, out.
Of this bed, and.
"If not on."
Ly, and.

If not just, out.
"Of, and from."
My dre.
Or, from your idea.
Am.
Liz.
S, and.
At.
If not just, and.
Ions, fan.
"If not on."
Ta.
Ly, and.
Sies, wish.
If not me.
Ful, or hope.
Rely, out.
Ful thinking, or.
"Of my re."
Veri.
Es, and.
If not only, and.
"If not just."
And if not me.
Re.
Or, out of your ow.
Ly, out.
N sm.
"Of my."
All.
W.
Ants, wish.
Es, will, ho.
Pes, and dre.
Ams, and.
"If not just, and."
If not only, and.

"If not merely, out."
Of what might, or.
"Out of what."
Could have been, but.
In.
To re.
Al.
It.
Y, and.
Or, in.
"If not."
To the Re, or re.
Just, and.
Al, or.
"If not, only."
Out of.
My ide.
Al.
World, or.
"He."
Ave.
N, and.
Into reality.
Or, into Reality.
"How."
Soever hell.
Ish.
It is, or.
Into whose vers.
"Howsoever."
Io.
N of the re.
Al, of rea.
Lit.
Y, of Rea.
Lit.
Y, or of hell, or.

Hellish, or.
"How."
So.
Ever he.
Aven.
Ly, I.
Or you, or I.
Or 'we?'
Or you, or 'we,' us, or them?
Do choose.
To make it.
"To let it be, or."
Choo.
How.
Se to find it, or.
Soever he.
Ave.
N.
Ly, hel.
Lish, or.
"Ideal, I."
Do choose.
"To see it."
To im.
Ag.
In.
E, to crea.
Te.
"Or to con."
Struct it, as.
Also, most.
"Ord."
In.
Ari.
Ly, and.
Or?
Also, most.

Ex.

"Com."

Tra.

Mon.

Ord.

Ly, and.

In.

Also, most pro.

Ari.

"Sai."

Ly, or.

Call.

Uncommonly, or.

Y, and.

Ro.

Also, most.

Man.

"Con."

Tic.

Vent.

Ally, or.

I.

Poe.

On.

Ti.

Ally, and.

Call.

Also, most.

"Ex."

Pect.

Ed.

Ly, and.

Also, most.

"Straight."

For.

War.

Dly, and.

Also, most.
Unconventionally, and.
"Rou."
Or, ir.
Tine.
Regularly, or.
Ly, and.
Also, most.
"Norm."
Ally, and.
Or ab.
Also, most.
Norm.
"Re."
Ally, and.
Gu.
Lar.
Ly, and.
Also, most.
"Logic."
All.
Y, and.
Also, most.
Reasonably, and.
"Also, most."
Rat.
Io.
N.
All.
Y, and.
"Also, most."
Wisely, and.
"Also, most."
Enlighten.
Ed.
Ly, and.
"Also, most."

Truly, and.
"Also, most."
Really, and.
"Also, most."
Actually, what.
"Does happen."
In an in.
St.
Ant, out.
"Side of."
Time, and.
"Out of space, and."
Out of time, is.
"Of course."
What is.
Most true, most.
True, and most.
"Real, most."
Real, and.
Actual, and.
"What is most au."
Then.
Tic, even.
If is it.
Or, even if it is.
Or, even, if is it.
"Either, as."
Be.
As.
Tly, or.
As beastly, or.
As he.
As heavenly, or.
Aven.
Ly, or?
As trans.
Cen.

Dent, or?
As transcendent, or.
As as.
Cend.
Ent, or?
As ascendent, or.
"As di."
Vine, as.
Or, as divine, as.
Or, as hellish, or?
As im.
As imminent, or.
Min.
As one.
Ant, is it, if not em.
Does choo.
In.
Se, or.
Ent, or per.
De.
Haps, ima?
Cide to let.
Nant.
"It be, or."
As divine, or.
"As beastly, as."
One does, or.
"As I do, or."
As you do?
Choo.
Se, or de.
Cide.
"To see it as, and."
Even if.
"Of course."
More than most cert.
Ain.

Ly, and.
"Even if."
More than most sure.
Ly, is it, *or it is,* more.
"Super."
Hu.
Man, or.
More sub.
"Hu."
Man, than?
Is it.
"Merely, just."
Or, than.
"It is."
Only human, and.
Which is.
"Both, within."
And, without.
"And, which."
And, what.
And, What.
"And, who is both."
Me, and.
"Not me, and."
Who, and.
"What, and."
Which, also, is.
And, is not.
"Both good, and bad, and."
Bad, and good, and.
Good, and Bad, too, and.
"Both pure, and im."
Or un?
Which, and.
Pure, and.
"What, and."
Who is both.

"Impure, and pure, and."
Who, and what, and.
What, and who, and.
"Which is."
What, and Who, and.
Who, and What, is.
Both good, and evil, and.
"Who, or what, and which is."
Good, and E.
Both evil, and good, and.
Vil, and.
"Which, and what, and."
Who is, both.
"Clean, and un."
Clean, and.
Who, and what, and which, is.
"Both un."
Cle.
An, and cle.
An, and.
Who, and.
"What, and."
Which is.
Both, within.
And without, and.
"What, and who."
And who, and what.
And, which is.
And What, and Who.
"Eit."
And Who, and What.
Her, or.
Both au.
Then.
Tic, and.
"Inau."
Then.

Tic, but.
Of course.
"How to know, what."
Or who, or.
"Which is."
Clean, and.
"What, or."
Who, or.
"Which is not, and."
Of course.
"How to know."
Which, or what, or who.
"Is un."
Cle.
An, or.
Clean in what way, or in.
How to know, what.
What ways, or.
"Who, or."
Which is.
"Evil, good, bad."
Pure, or.
"Impure, without."
Being told, or.
"Without being."
Shown, who.
"Or, what."
Or which is, be.
"Cause, of."
Course.
Even if.
"One does have co."
Ming.
From with.
In, so.
Me.
Or, is that, or is t.

Not.
His?
"Not."
From with.
Io.
Out.
N, of.
What, or.
"Some no."
Tio.
N, of.
Whom, or.
"Some ide."
A, of which.
One, or.
"Of whi."
Ch one.
S, are.
Go.
Od, or.
"Of which ones, are."
Bad, or.
"Of."
Which ones are.
E.
Vil, or.
"Of which one."
Or, One?
Is ev.
Vil, or.
Of which one, or one.
S, are bad, or.
Are Bad, or.
"Of what, or."
Of What, or.
Of who.
Or, Who.

M is go.
Od, or.
For what re.
As.
Rea.
On, or.
Sons, or.
Of whom, or.
"Of what."
Is bad, or.
Is Bad, or.
"Of who."
M, or.
Of what, is.
"Au."
Fake, or false?
Then.
Or tru.
Tic, or.
E, or Tru.
Of what, or.
E, or.
Of What, or.
"Of whom, is."
In.
Aut.
Hen.
Tic, or.
"Of what is true, or."
Of whom, *or Whom*, is true, or *Tru.*
E, or.
"Of what is false, or."
Of whom is false, *or False*, or.
"Of whom is fake, or."
Of what is fake, *or Fake*, or.
Of what, *or What*, is real, *or Real*, or.
"Of who."

M is real, or.
Of whom, *or Whom*, is Re.
Al, or.
"Of what is Real, or."
Of who, *or Who.*
M is tru.
E, or *Tru.*
Of who is True, of.
E, or.
"Course, did."
That, or.
"Did this not."
Ion.
Or, idea.
"Co."
Me or.
Ig.
In.
Rat.
All.
Her, if.
Y, or.
As in cul.
Come first, from.
Tur.
"With."
Ally, or soci.
Out, or.
All.
"Might one."
Two, or more.
The most, or the many.
Y de.
Be born with.
Ter.
"Such an id."
Mine.

Ea, of.
D, or.
What, or.
"Of whom."
Is tru.
E, *Tru.*
Re, re.
E.
Al, au.
Then.
Tic, good.
"And, of."
What, and.
"Or, of who."
Or, of Who.
M.
Is not.
"True, real, au."
Then.
Tic, good.
Good, Real, or True.
Or of whom, or.
"Of what."
Or, What.
Is not True, Real, or.
"Of what, or."
Of who.
M, is.
"In."
Auth.
En.
Tic bad, or.
Bad, or.
Of whom, or.
"Of what."
Is e.
Vil, or.

"Of what, or."
Of whom.
"Is not e."
Vil.
Or Ev?
If do.
Il, or.
"Or, eve."
N if.
Do not all.
"Agree, on."
Or, about.
What, or.
About, or.
"On, or a."
Bout who is.
Or, Who is.
Any, or.
"All of those, but."
As ou.
Ght they, sho.
Uld they, or ne.
Ed they not, or.
Of course, does.
The, or.
"Does the most."
True au.
Then.
Ti.
City de.
Rive from both with.
Out, and from with.
In.
Or, is it where.
And when.
The two do me.
Et, and.

Or, is bad, and Bad.
Faith, me.
Re.
Ly, if not on.
Ly, or ju.
St, w.
Hen, or w.
He.
Re, one do.
Es choo.
Se, or ag.
Ree to be de.
Fine.
D by, and fr.
Om with.
Out.
Because, of course.
I am not one to.
Pre.
Sum.
E, one to ass.
U.
Me, or.
One to think, *or one not to think,* quite.
So very.
Mo.
Ron.
Ic.
Ally, id.
Io.
Tic.
Ally, ill.
Ogi.
Call.
Y, ir.
Rat.
Io.

Nally, in.
Sensibly, or un.
Reason.
Ably, that.
A man is, sho.
Uld, or ou.
Ght, to act, or re.
Gard him.
Self, or be tre.
Ate.
D, as an is.
Land, so must ide.
As, eve.
R, and al.
Ways, chan.
Ging, come from both with.
In, as.
Well as from with.
Out.
So are they, and so must they be?
Both re.
Me.
Mbe.
Red, and re.
Vea.
Led, or?
As well as.
Are such not.
Io.
Ns, and ide.
As.
Ever, and al.
Ways.
Chang.
Ing, form.
Ing, be.
Ing form.

Ed, un-.
Form.
Ing, and be.
Ing un.
Form.
Ed, as is.
Or un.
And, as does?
Formed by Whom, or by What, and.
Life itself, for it.
Self, or is form?
Ed, if not ne.
Cess.
Ari.
Ly, in.
Formed.
Though by whom, or by what, and.
Assuming, or pre.
Suming.
That the.
Re, or that he.
Re, is a gre.
Is a gre.
At, big, hu.
Ge, or im.
Port.
Ant.
Dif.
Fe.
Ren.
Ce bet.
We.
En.
In.
Side, or out.
Side, or that.
Bound.

Ari.
Es between, and, or.
Am.
On.
G, per.
Sons, peo.
Ple, and thin.
Gs, are com.
Plet.
Ely non-.
Por.
Ou.
S, but.
Or?
Qui.
Te so very far.
More, and most, simp.
Ly, does.
True aut.
Hen.
Tic.
It.
Y, come?
Or go.
"From with."
In, or.
Be.
From a mix.
Cause, of.
Tur.
Course, no man, is.
E, of.
An is.
"Both being."
Land, though might.
In.
Or can, tho.

For.
Ugh, not mu.
Med, from.
St, a.
"Within, and."
Wo.
From with.
Man be.
Out, both.
"Ori."
Gin.
Ally, as.
When, and.
"As where."
One is born, or.
If not, also, nec.
Es.
Sa.
Ri.
Ly, where, or when, one is re-.
Born, or.
"As where, and."
Or, as when.
"One is con."
Cei.
Ved, as.
Well, as.
"What not."
Ion, and.
As well as.
"The no."
Tions, and.
As well as.
"The Ide."
A, and.
As well as the ide.
As.

"One does learn, or."
As well as.
"What id."
Eas, or.
As well as.
"The idea."
Or, the Idea.
One does gain.
Through.
Out one's life, and.
"Because."
Of course, is.
"Life, and."
Because.
"Of course."
Is the w.
Or.
Ld a.
Ro.
Und.
Whe.
"One, always."
The.
And eve.
R, or not, 'we' did eve.
R chan.
R, or al.
Ging, too.
Ways, know, or be.
And, be.
Lie.
Cause, the w.
Ve, it.
Orl.
And.
D around one ever, and al.
Ways, is chan.

Gin.
G, too.
Or, does it, but mere.
"Must one, also."
Ly see.
Change, and.
M, or app.
Ear to, or.
So?
"Be chan."
Must one.
Ging with it, or.
Change, or.
Be le.
Ft be.
Hind, and.
Because, of course.
"I am not one?"
Willing to be left be.
Hind, *or one to le.*
On.
Ave be.
Ly, or me.
Hi.
Rely, so.
Nd, if?
As not later, or even?
Tu.
Ally, to be.
"Left behind."
Because, of course.
I am not one.
Willing to be left behind.
And be.
Cause, of course, to leave behind.
Is to be left behind later, or next, and be.
Cause, of course, what does go around, *or was it to have le.*

Ft be.
Hi.
Do.
Nd, be.
Es co.
Fore, does me.
Me, and.
An one is bo.
Und.
To be so-le.
Ft, be.
Cause does.
Be.
No one, and.
Cause, of.
No.
Co.
Body, es.
Ur.
Cape kar.
Se, no.
Ma, or Kar.
One does get to be.
Ma, ei.
Right, cor.
The.
Rect, in char.
R, and be.
Ge, or in con.
Ca.
Trol, for.
Use, to.
Ever, every.
Even if no.
Where, or for all, or in all.
Body, and no.
Time, or times, and.

One, is.
Be.
A so.
Cause, of co.
Me.
Ur.
One, or a so.
Se, do.
Me.
Es not one per.
One, or a so.
Son get to be in char.
Me.
Ge for.
Body, too.
Ever, or get to make all.
For.
The choi.
Ever, for every.
Ces, or all the de.
One, for every.
Ci.
Bo.
Sions, and.
Dy, every.
"So, of."
Where, or for, or in all ti.
Course, must.
Me, or ti.
"One know."
Me.
What, or.
S, or.
"One know."
What, or.
"Who or, w."
Hat, or Who?

Is good, true.
Abs.
Olu.
Ely, me.
Rely, just, or only?
To, or for, you.
And.
"Real, and evil."
What, and who.
Bad, and.
Who, and What.
"Or what, and."
Or, who.
"Is authentic, and."
Who, or.
"What, or."
What, or.
"Who is."
Au.
Then.
Tic, for.
Or, to you.
"And, by."
One.
Self, in.
Order to be, and.
"Because, of."
Course, too.
Can, and would.
Not aut.
He.
Nt.
Ic.
It.
Y, be.
If it were not uni.
Vers.

Al, or ab.
Solute, and.
So, if it were.
Part.
Icu.
Lar, spe.
Ci.
Fic, *or.*
"Can."
Would it, or.
Not.
Can it be, or.
Aut.
Hen.
Ti.
City, or.
Or gen.
U.
In.
En.
Ess, or?
Ingenuity, be.
"Stolen, borrowed, or."
Copied, either.
Any less, or.
"Any more."
Than it can be fake.
D, of course.
"And, too."
Of course, how.
"Hard, and."
How difficult, and.
"How difficult, and."
How hard.
"If not impossible, is."
It to be.
"Most truly, most."

Wholly, and.
Or.
"Most really authentic, or."
True, real.
"Or go."
Od, at.
All, where.
"Or when, one."
Is surrounded, by.
Or, with the.
Bad, or with.
Or by, the.
"In."
Au.
With, or by.
Then.
The fal.
Tic, or.
Se, or the fake, or.
Where, or.
By the Fake, or False, or.
"When, or."
When, or.
"Where one."
Is sur.
Roun.
Ded, by.
"The fa."
Ke, and.
Or, by the false, and.
"Where, and when, and."
When, and.
"Where, one."
Is surrounded, by.
"The fake."
Rs, by.
The pre.

Tend.
Ers, and.
By the im.
Posters, and, or.
"By the posers, and."
Where, and when, and.
When, and where.
"When, and where, one."
Or w.
Hen, and w.
Here, or where.
"Or w."
Hen, one.
Is sur.
Rounded, by.
"The liars, who."
Do not know, who.
Or, Who.
"Or, what."
Or, What.
They are, if.
Or, if they are not you, or.
"If they are not me, and."
Or, by the snakes, who.
Of course.
Are but, so, on.
Ly, be.
Ginning to shed their skins, and.
Or.
"Is it not."
Im.
Pos.
Sib.
Le, to.
"Be authentic, true, good, or."
Good, authentic, True, or real, or.
Real, where.

"Or, when."
Or when, or.
"Where, one."
Is not permit.
Ted to.
Be so, or w.
Here, or when.
One is not let be, or.
"And where, or."
When, or.
"When, or."
Where, one.
"Is for."
Ced to.
Be what, *or What*, or.
To be whom.
"One is not, or."
Where, or.
"When, or."
When, or.
"Where, one."
Is forced to be.
"False, fake, in."
Authentic, or.
Where, or.
"When, or."
When, or.
"Where, one."
Is forced to be un.
True, or.
"Where, or."
When, or.
"When, or."
Where, one.
"Is forced to be."
True to some.
One, or.

To some?
Body, or.
"To something, to."
Some.
Thing, or.
"To someone, other."
Than one.
Self, but.
"Of course."
Now, who.
"Or, now what, or."
Now what, or.
"Now, who."
Does have time for.
"Such questions, or."
For such thin.
King, when.
"And where, or."
Where, or.
"When, is."
The time, for.
"Acting, and."
Or, for do.
In.
G, and.
"When, now."
And, when.
Here, and.
"Where here, and."
Where, now, is.
"The time for wa."
King, and.
So, then.
And, so.
There, and.
"So, now, and."
So, here, did.

"He turn from."
Or, you did turn.
From, or.
"I did turn from."
Or, off of.
His, or.
Off, of.
"My back, and."
Your back, and.
Onto his, and.
"On."
To my.
And, on.
To your.
Right side, in.
"Order to."
View, or.
"In order to peek, or."
In order, to.
"Look out, and."
In or.
Der to pe.
Er.
"Through."
The wind.
Ow, whose.
"Glass, and."
Whose pane, was.
"And, whose."
Pane, and.
Whose glass, which.
"Is?"
As ever, and.
"Which is."
As al.
Ways it was, *has be.*
"Which is."

En, and?
As it al.
As eve.
Ways will be, and.
R it will be, and.
Or?
"Which, at."
Least, is.
"As it was yes."
Ter.
Day, at.
Least, as.
Long, and.
"At least, as."
Far as.
And, at least, in so far.
As.
"I can re."
Member, and.
Which, cry.
Stal-rim.
Med, and.
"Which, ici."
Ly-bord.
Er.
Ed, is.
As lovely, as.
"Gorgeous, and."
As be.
Au.
Ti.
Ful, and.
"As lovely, as."
Do I choose, or.
"As I do choo."
Or, as you do choose.
Se, to.

Let it be.
"Or, which are."
As lovely, as.
"Beautiful, and."
As gor.
Ge.
Ou.
S, as.
"I do de."
Ci.
De to.
See them as, but.
"Of course, here."
And, now.
"Do I not."
And, I do not.
Have the.
"Time, or."
The pat.
Ie.
N.
Ce, to.
Get lost.
"In their false, fake."
Super.
Fic.
Ia.
L, or.
Su.
Per.
Fi.
Ci.
Ally, or.
"Nothing more."
Than apparent beauty.
"Be."
Cause, of.

Course, I am.
"Not one."
Dumb, or.
"One stu."
Pid, or.
One shall.
Ow, e.
No.
Ugh.
Or, one de.
Lu.
Ded, or one ill.
U.
Ded, e.
Nou.
Gh.
"To con."
Fuse app.
Ear.
An.
Ces, with.
Reality, or.
"One stupid, or."
One dumb e.
No.
Ug.
H to con.
"Fuse seeming with."
Be.
Ing, or.
Being with Seeming, or.
"One to be bot."
Seeming with Being, or.
Her.
Ed with, or.
By what.
"Is love."

Ly, or.
With, or by.
What, or who.
Is de.
Light.
Ful, or.
By what, or.
"By whom, or."
With whom, or.
"With what is not, as."
If I am some sort of Eng.
Lish, or.
Ot.
Her kin.
D of dan.
Dy, man.
"Or, as if."
I am some sort of.
"Willing subject, or."
As if I am willing to be.
"Objectified, studied, normalized, oppressed, invaded, imposed upon, conquered, sub."
Jectified, or.
Co.
Lo.
Nize.
D, or.
"As if I am willing."
To sub.
Mit, or.
"To sur."
Ren.
Der, to.
Either such.
"Subject."
If.
Ic.

At.
Ion, or.
To such.
"Object."
If.
I.
Cat.
Io.
N, e.
It.
Her.
Be.
Or, as.
Cause, of.
"If I am."
Cour.
Willing to be.
Se, is to ob.
Anything other.
Ject.
"Than my."
If.
Own subject, or.
Y, to be ob.
"Anything other."
Ject.
Than my.
If.
"Own object, and."
Ed.
As if I am willing.
"To be."
Anything other.
"Than both."
Knower, and.
"Known, and."
Or, than both.

Or, are you?
Ob.
Server, and ob.
Served, and.
As if.
"I am willing."
To be.
"Part of some 'we,' royal."
Lord, lady, court.
Oh?
Or ot.
Her.
Wise, and.
Or, of course.
Or, of course.
Are you on.
"As if."
Ly, and al.
Try.
Ready, and.
You are.
Ing to as.
Sum.
E, or try.
Ing to assu?
Me some sort of au.
Thor.
It.
Y, pow.
Er, or con?
Trol, tho.
Ugh, of course, is not aut.
Ho.
Rit.
Y nec.
Ess.
Ari.

Ly po.
We.
R, or pow.
Er, au.
Tho.
Rit.
Y, or.
Con.
Trol, or po?
Wer over what, or What, or over whom, or Whom, and be.
Cause, of course.
"As if I might have anything."
In common, with.
"The English, other."
Than the language, or.
Ot.
Her than the law, so.
Or, other than which, what, or w.
Or most of it, any.
Hose, law, Law, or law.
Way.
S, or.
"Rather, might."
But, as if.
"The English, are."
The only ones with ro.
Yal.
Ty, or.
The crystals, so.
As if the ro.
"Icy, and."
Yals, so cal.
Led, self-de.
Clare.
D, real, act.
Ual, by blood, by bir.
Th, or ot.

Her.
Wise, do.
Have any po.
Wer, act.
U.
Al, neu, new?
Old, neue?
Real, true, or ot.
Her.
Wise, tho.
Ugh, not alt, *or Alt?*
Or, ot.
Her than what one, two, or more.
The most, the many, or 'we?'
Do de.
Cide, or do choose.
Se to give, or to take.
"From them, and."
Or rather, might.
More, or less.
"Less, or more?"
The most, the man.
Y, or the all.
Do choose, or do de.
Cide, to take from, or to give them, and.
So?
"The flakes, now."
Fal.
Ling, qui.
Te.
"So softly, be."
Be.
Au.
Ti.
Ful, rat.
Her.
"Than love."

Ly, but.
If must one choose, se.
Which, also.
Lect, or de.
"Is not."
Cide.
To say, and.
"Which, also."
Of course.
"Is not."
To think, that.
"I am, or."
That I am willing.
"To be."
Or, that I am wil.
Ling, *or that you are want.*
"To be assumed, or."
Ing.
That I am willing.
"To be pre."
Sum.
Ed to be, or.
"That I am willing."
To be made in.
"To so."
Me sort of.
Latin, or.
"Spanish lover, or."
As if.
Wil.
"I am a misogynist."
Ling to re?
Willing to be.
Duce, or.
Reduced, to.
"An object, only."
Sexual, or.

A sex.
Nor.
Ist, or.
Mal, or.
"A chau."
Vin.
"Ist, so."
Un-a.
War.
Ely, obs.
"Es."
Sed with, or.
Con.
Sum.
Ed, by.
My own ma.
Chis.
Mo, or.
"As if I am one."
Self-obsessed, or.
One grand.
Io.
Se, or.
"One desperately de."
Lusi.
On.
Al, or.
One in.
Secure, or.
"One self-."
Im.
Port.
Ant e.
No.
Ugh, to.
Need, or.
"To presume myself, to."

Be some.
"Sort of queen, king."
Prince, or.
"Princess, needing."
Or, willing.
"To wear."
Some sort of crow.
N, or Crow?
Ther.
N, ei.
"Silver, gold, or."
Ther.
Bronze, but.
"Of course, if."
I were to.
"Wear one, would."
And, why would you not?
It be.
"The gold one, of."
Course, be.
Cause, more.
"Than most."
Cert.
Ain.
Ly.
"And, be."
Cause.
More than most sure.
Ly, "Too."
Am I not.
"A Number Two, and."
Because, of.
"Course, al."
So, am I far.
"From one."
Willing to.
"Settle for."

Silver.
"Or, for."
Second place, and.
"Because, of."
As all do, ou.
Cour.
Ght, or s.
Se, if.
Ho.
"I am not."
Uld k.
Willing, to.
Now, is gold, and is the Go.
"Be, or."
Ld, or yell?
Willing, to.
Ow be.
Make my.
St, and fir.
Self.
St, and.
"My own Numb."
Er One, how.
Will, or.
"How can any."
One, or.
How can, or.
"How will every."
One else, ever.
Be able to, and.
Be.
Cause, of.
Cou.
R.
Se, if.
I am not my own Numb.
Er One.

Who will try to make me, make them.
Him, her, or its.
Num.
Be.
R On.
E, and be.
Cause.
"Of course."
Also, am.
Even though, and.
"I not."
Even if.
A fool, id.
In most place, and.
I.
Spots, is.
T, or.
Two more than one, and.
"Mo."
Is two hi.
Ron.
G.
Wil.
Her, mo.
Ling.
Re, and bet.
To get lost, trap.
Ter than one, or t.
Ped, or.
Han One.
"Fooled, by."
App.
Ear.
An.
Ces, or.
"One willing."
To get lost in.

"The im."
Ages, or.
And even though, and even if.
In the mat.
In Ze.
Er.
Ro, in the ze?
I.
Ro, in the Ze?
Al, or.
Ro, ze.
In the vi.
Ro, in the void, in the aby.
Sib.
Ss, or in the ze.
Le.
Os, or?
In, and, or.
Even if in the Ze.
One wil.
Ros, can.
Ling, to.
One find every.
Be fo.
Thing, and all.
O.
Or e.
Led by.
Very.
"The de."
One, or.
Riv.
No.
At.
Thing, or.
Ives, or.
Of course, does.

By the co.
One on.
Pies, who, of.
Ly find.
"Co."
A mir.
Ur.
Ror, so.
Se.
What is with.
Are all the sam.
In, or w.
E, a.
Nd who, *or w?*
Hat, to.
And.
O, are.
"Who do."
All the Sa.
Rep.
Me, and.
Eat, and.
Or an.
"What do."
Y, or all ot.
But, re.
Her.
Peat.
S.
"Them."
Selves, and.
Who do but co.
As par?
Py, and.
Rots, of.
Im.
Ten.

It.
Ate one an.
Other, often per.
Pet.
U.
At.
Ing.
Lies, false.
Be.cause what else are lies, but.
Hoods, un.
False, and fake.
False.
Truths, half-.
It.
Truths, ill.
Es.
Us.
I.
Ons, and de.
Lus.
I.
On.
S, or.
It.
Self, time.
"And time, and."
O.
Ver, and one.
R.
"A."
Gain, and ag.
Ain, of.
"Cour."
Se, as.
I have said, and.
"As I have thought, be."
Fore, am I not one.

"De."
Lusi.
On.
Al eno.
Ugh, to.
Get lost in the see.
Ming, or.
In the Seeming?
"One to con."
Fuse the seem.
Ing, with.
"The be."
Ing, or.
One to con?
See.
Fuse.
Ming with be.
Ing, or.
Knowing with seeing, or.
Be.
Seeing with knowing, or.
Ing with seem.
Knowing with seeming, or.
In.
G, or.
One to con.
Fuse.
"Seeming with being, or."
With Being, or.
Seeming with Being, or.
Being with Seeming, or.
"Be."
Ing with be.
Becoming with be.
Co.
Ing, or with Be.
Ming, or.

Ing, or.
See.
Ming with be.
Coming, or.
And, so.
"Did he, and."
So did you, and, so.
So, did I, and.
So, you did, and.
"I did, and."
So, he did.
Even if I did not.
Ig.
Nor.
E the cry.
Stals, and.
"The flakes around."
The frosty pane, at.
"Least, for."
Now, or.
"At least for then, if not for."
Ever, and if.
For al.
Not for al.
Ways, and.
Ways, too.
Also, for.
"While, rather."
Ever, too.
Did he, and.
"While, rat."
Her, I.
Did con.
Tin.
Ue.
"To stare, straight."
On through the.

Cent.
Er of the glas.
S, ig.
Nor.
Ing the ed.
Ges, and.
"The forms, and."
But.
"Of course, not."
For the sake of not.
Ici.
Ng the struct.
Ur.
Es, or.
The ir.
Rele.
Van.
Cies, and.